D1459991

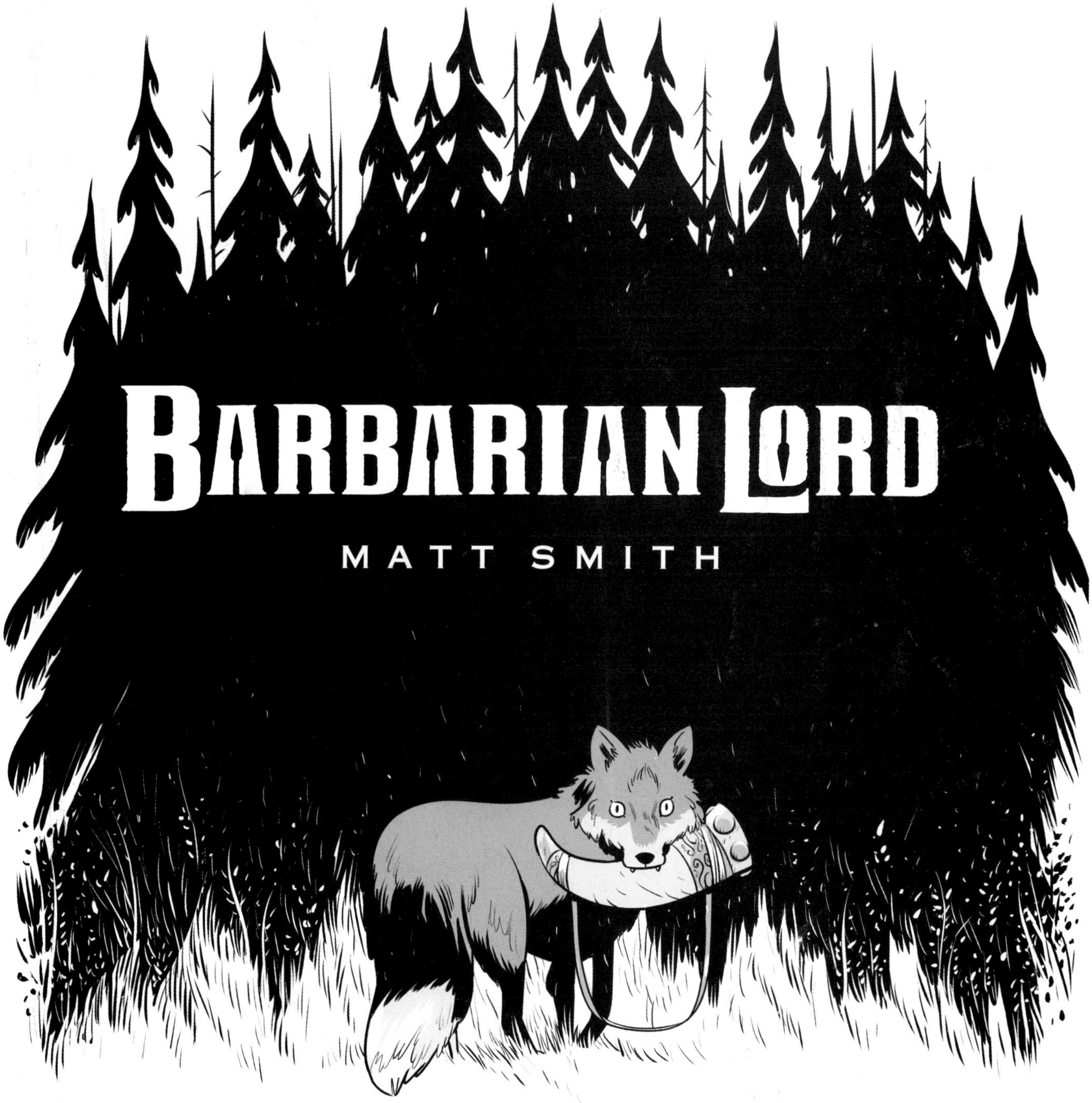
BARBARIAN LORD
MATT SMITH

CLARION BOOKS | HOUGHTON MIFFLIN HARCOURT | BOSTON NEW YORK

THIS BOOK IS DEDICATED
TO PAUL SCANNELL,
MY ETERNAL BROTHER-IN-ARMS.

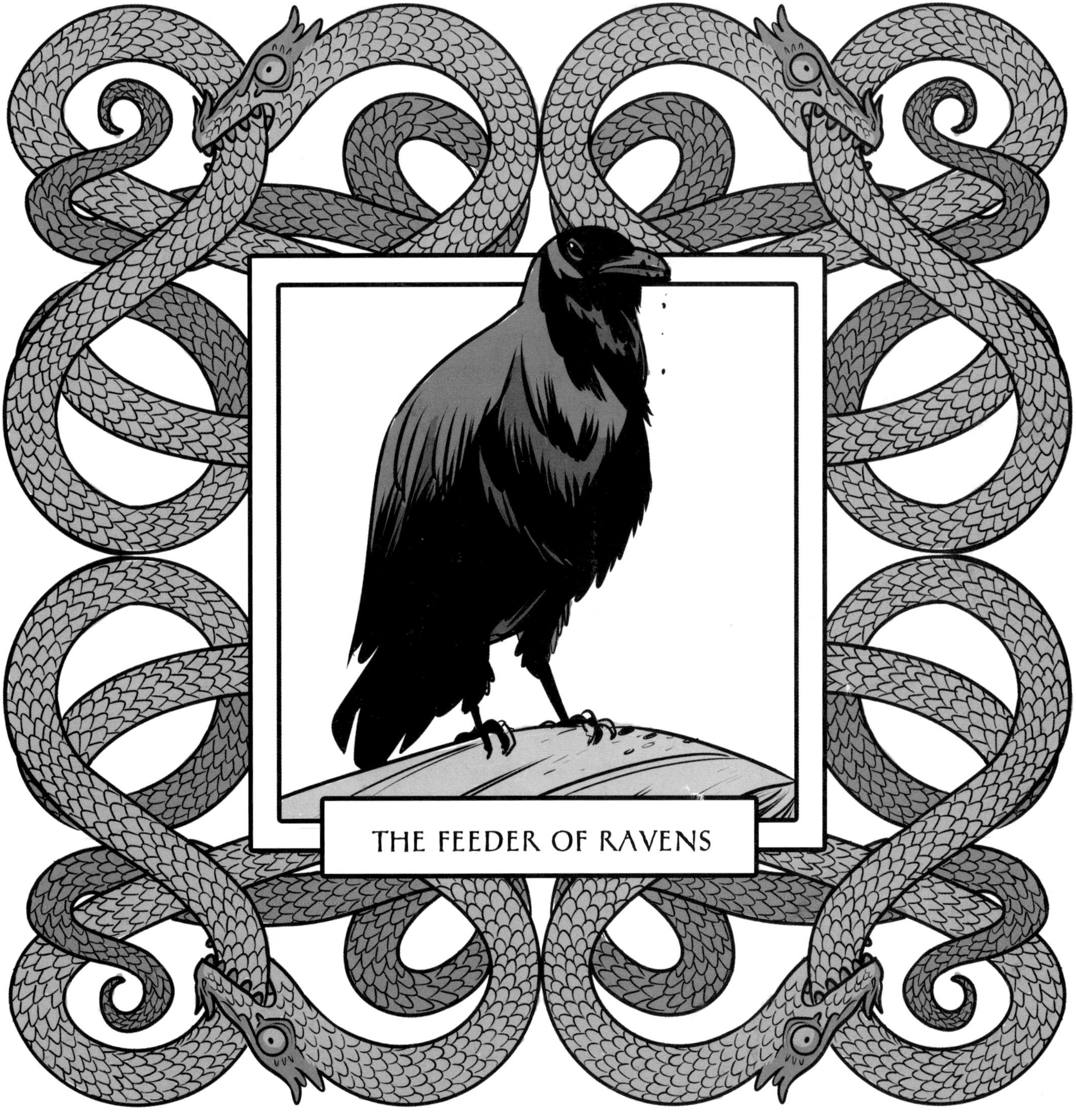
THE FEEDER OF RAVENS

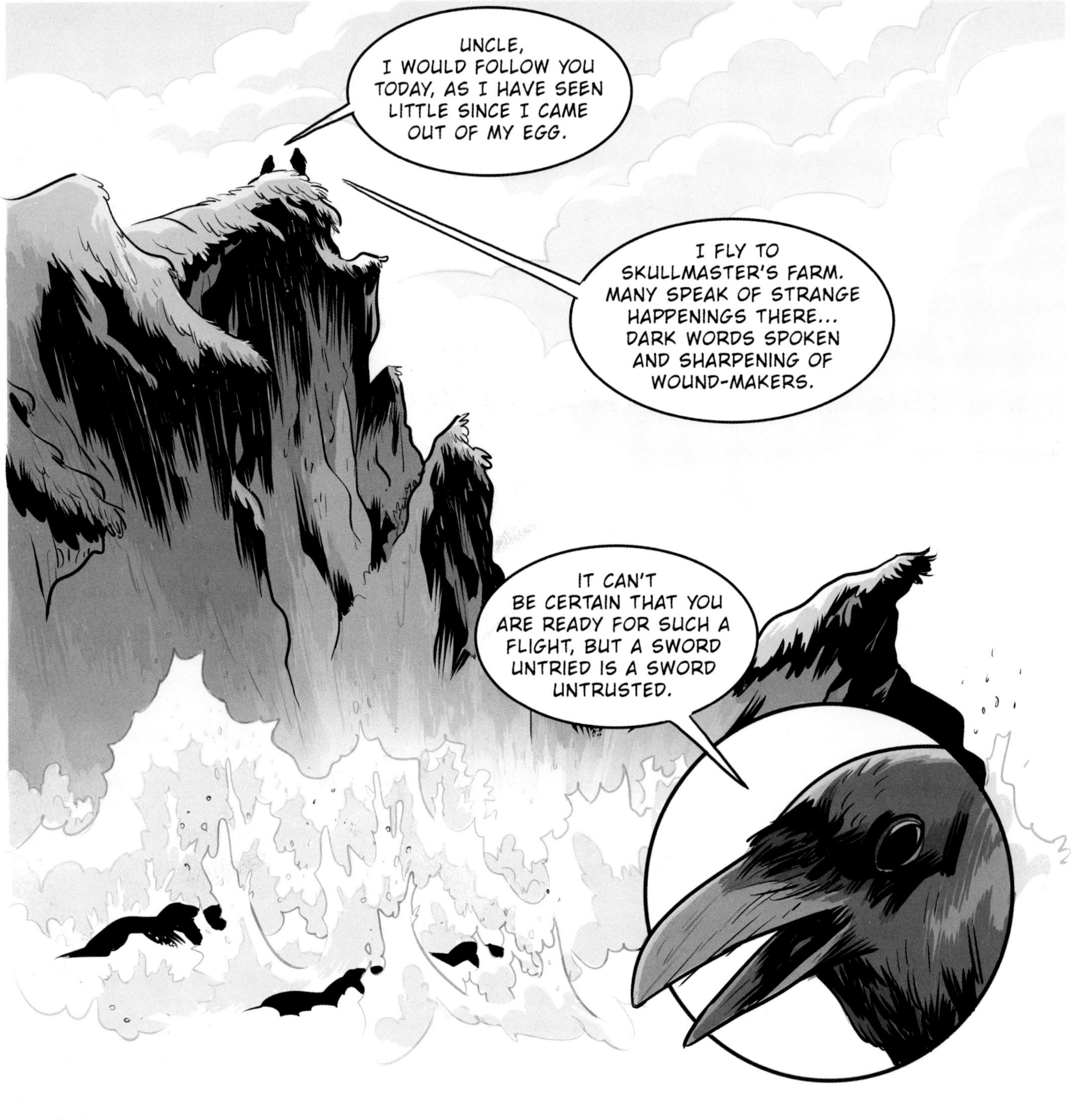
UNCLE, I WOULD FOLLOW YOU TODAY, AS I HAVE SEEN LITTLE SINCE I CAME OUT OF MY EGG.
I FLY TO SKULLMASTER'S FARM. MANY SPEAK OF STRANGE HAPPENINGS THERE... DARK WORDS SPOKEN AND SHARPENING OF WOUND-MAKERS.
IT CAN'T BE CERTAIN THAT YOU ARE READY FOR SUCH A FLIGHT, BUT A SWORD UNTRIED IS A SWORD UNTRUSTED.

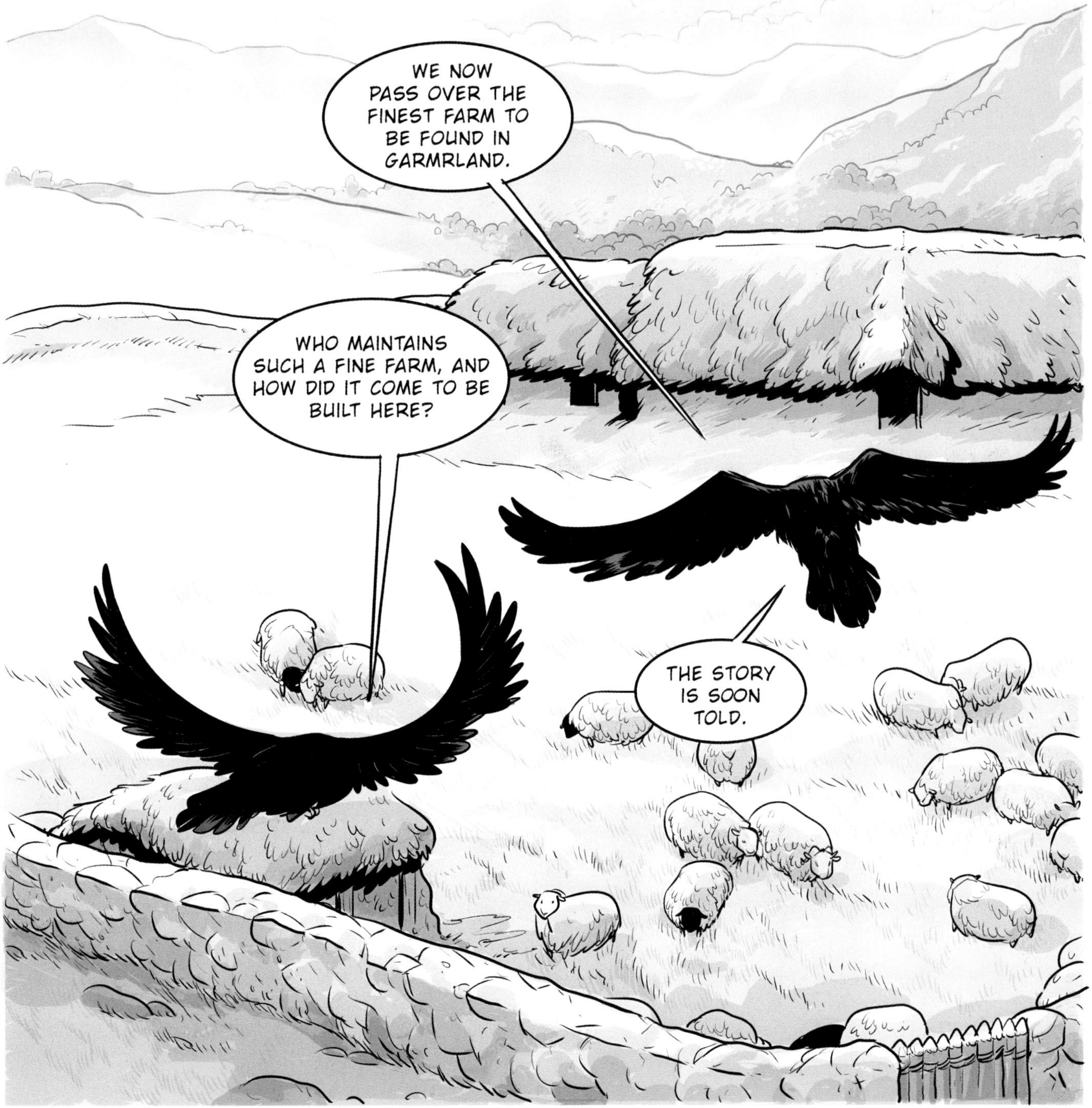
WE NOW PASS OVER THE FINEST FARM TO BE FOUND IN GARMRLAND.
WHO MAINTAINS SUCH A FINE FARM, AND HOW DID IT COME TO BE BUILT HERE?
THE STORY IS SOON TOLD.

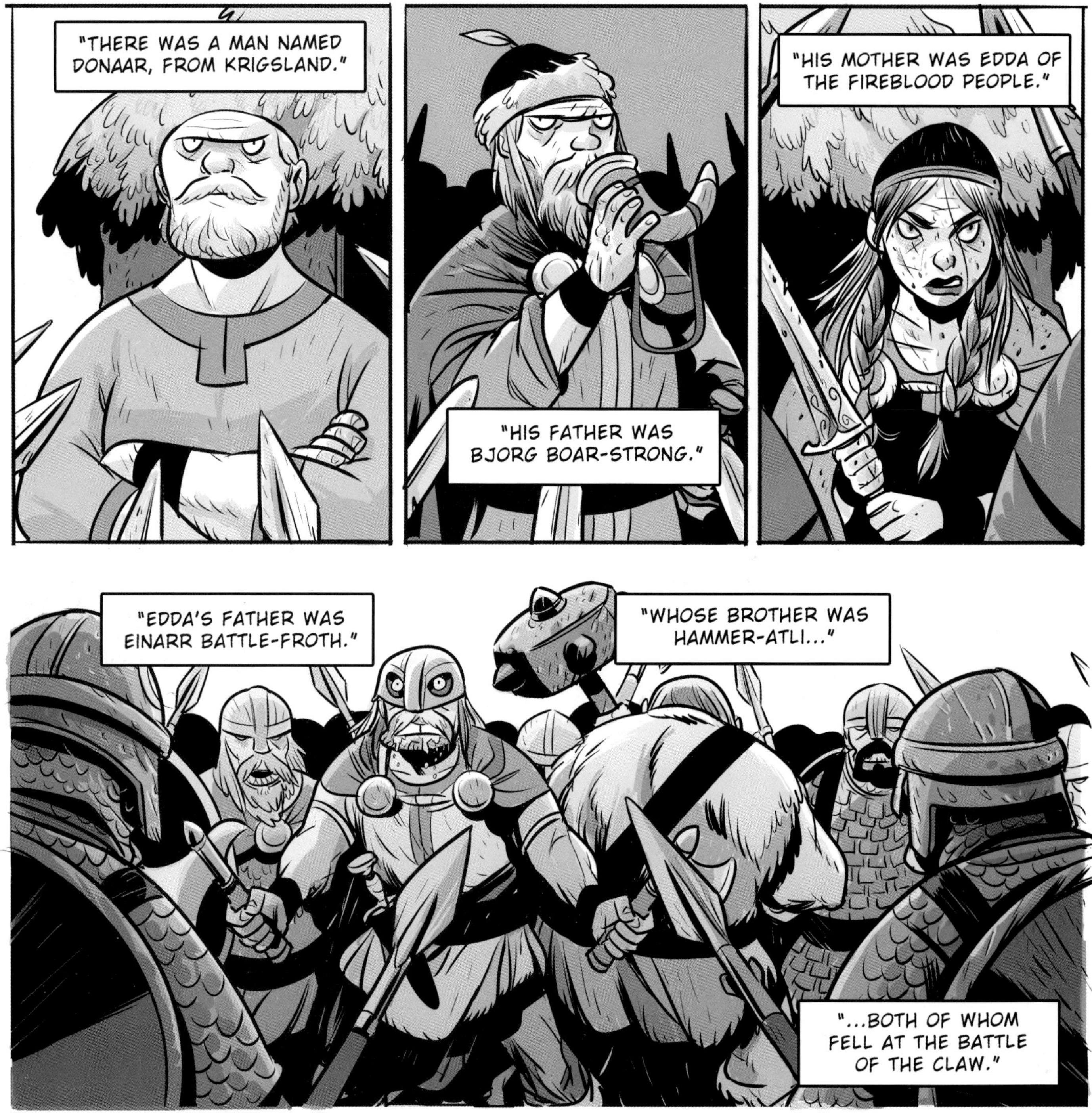
"THERE WAS A MAN NAMED DONAAR, FROM KRIGSLAND."
"HIS FATHER WAS BJORG BOAR-STRONG."
"HIS MOTHER WAS EDDA OF THE FIREBLOOD PEOPLE."
"EDDA'S FATHER WAS EINARR BATTLE-FROTH."
"WHOSE BROTHER WAS HAMMER-ATLI..."
"...BOTH OF WHOM FELL AT THE BATTLE OF THE CLAW."

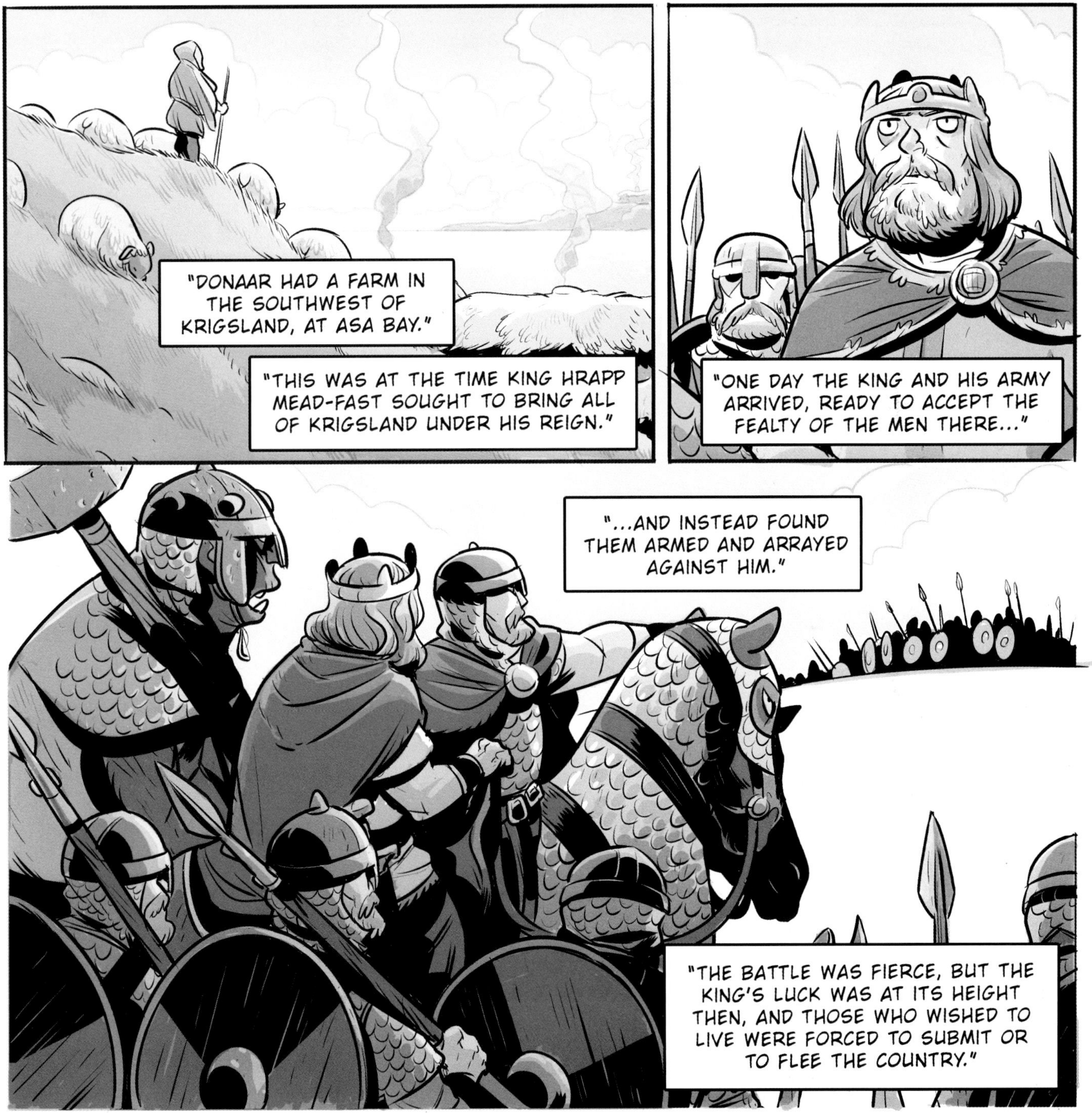
"DONAAR HAD A FARM IN THE SOUTHWEST OF KRIGSLAND, AT ASA BAY."
"THIS WAS AT THE TIME KING HRAPP MEAD-FAST SOUGHT TO BRING ALL OF KRIGSLAND UNDER HIS REIGN."
"ONE DAY THE KING AND HIS ARMY ARRIVED, READY TO ACCEPT THE FEALTY OF THE MEN THERE..."
"...AND INSTEAD FOUND THEM ARMED AND ARRAYED AGAINST HIM."
"THE BATTLE WAS FIERCE, BUT THE KING'S LUCK WAS AT ITS HEIGHT THEN, AND THOSE WHO WISHED TO LIVE WERE FORCED TO SUBMIT OR TO FLEE THE COUNTRY."

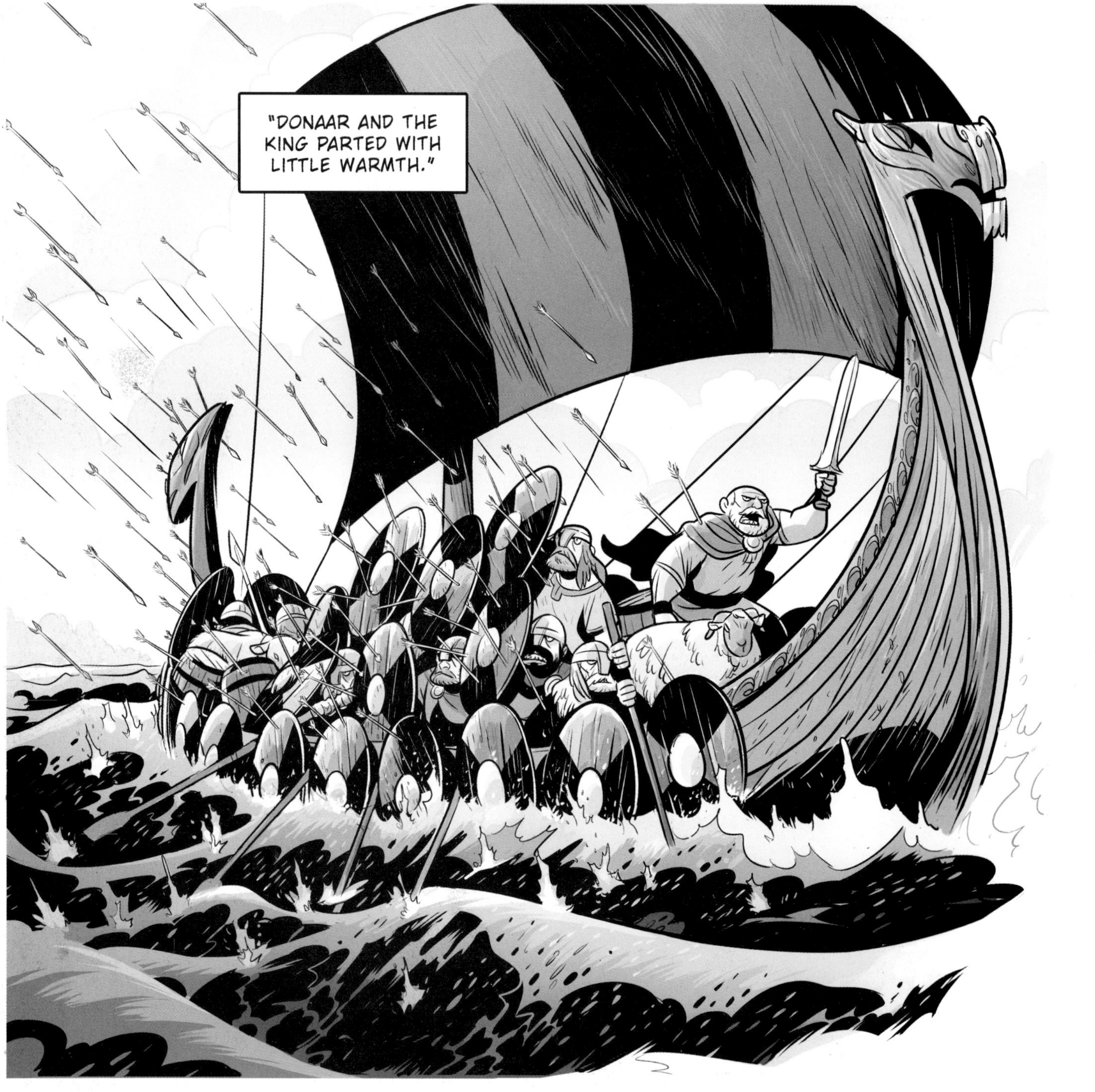
"DONAAR AND THE KING PARTED WITH LITTLE WARMTH."

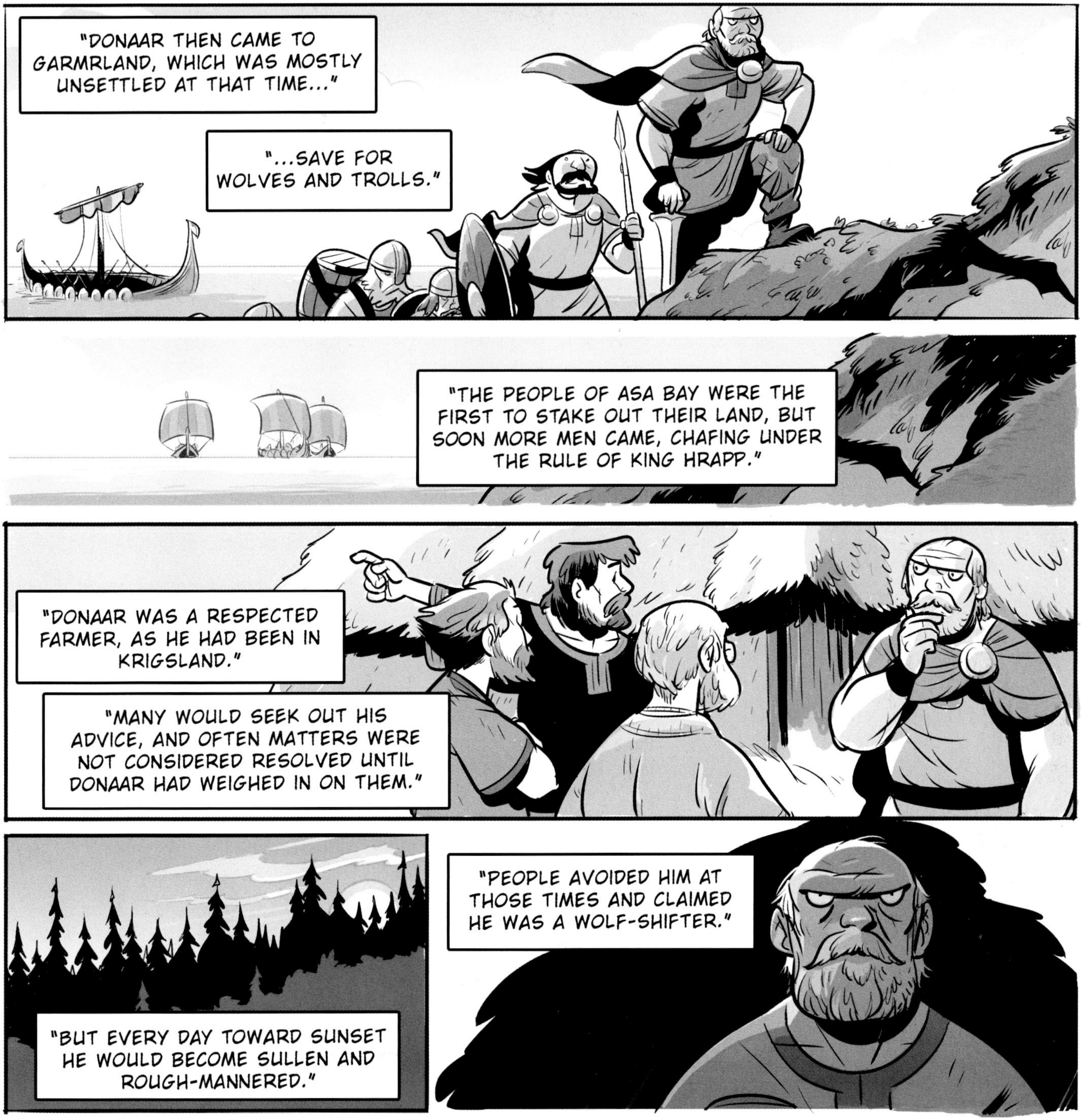
"DONAAR THEN CAME TO GARMRLAND, WHICH WAS MOSTLY UNSETTLED AT THAT TIME..."
"...SAVE FOR WOLVES AND TROLLS."
"THE PEOPLE OF ASA BAY WERE THE FIRST TO STAKE OUT THEIR LAND, BUT SOON MORE MEN CAME, CHAFING UNDER THE RULE OF KING HRAPP."
"DONAAR WAS A RESPECTED FARMER, AS HE HAD BEEN IN KRIGSLAND."
"MANY WOULD SEEK OUT HIS ADVICE, AND OFTEN MATTERS WERE NOT CONSIDERED RESOLVED UNTIL DONAAR HAD WEIGHED IN ON THEM."
"BUT EVERY DAY TOWARD SUNSET HE WOULD BECOME SULLEN AND ROUGH-MANNERED."
"PEOPLE AVOIDED HIM AT THOSE TIMES AND CLAIMED HE WAS A WOLF-SHIFTER."

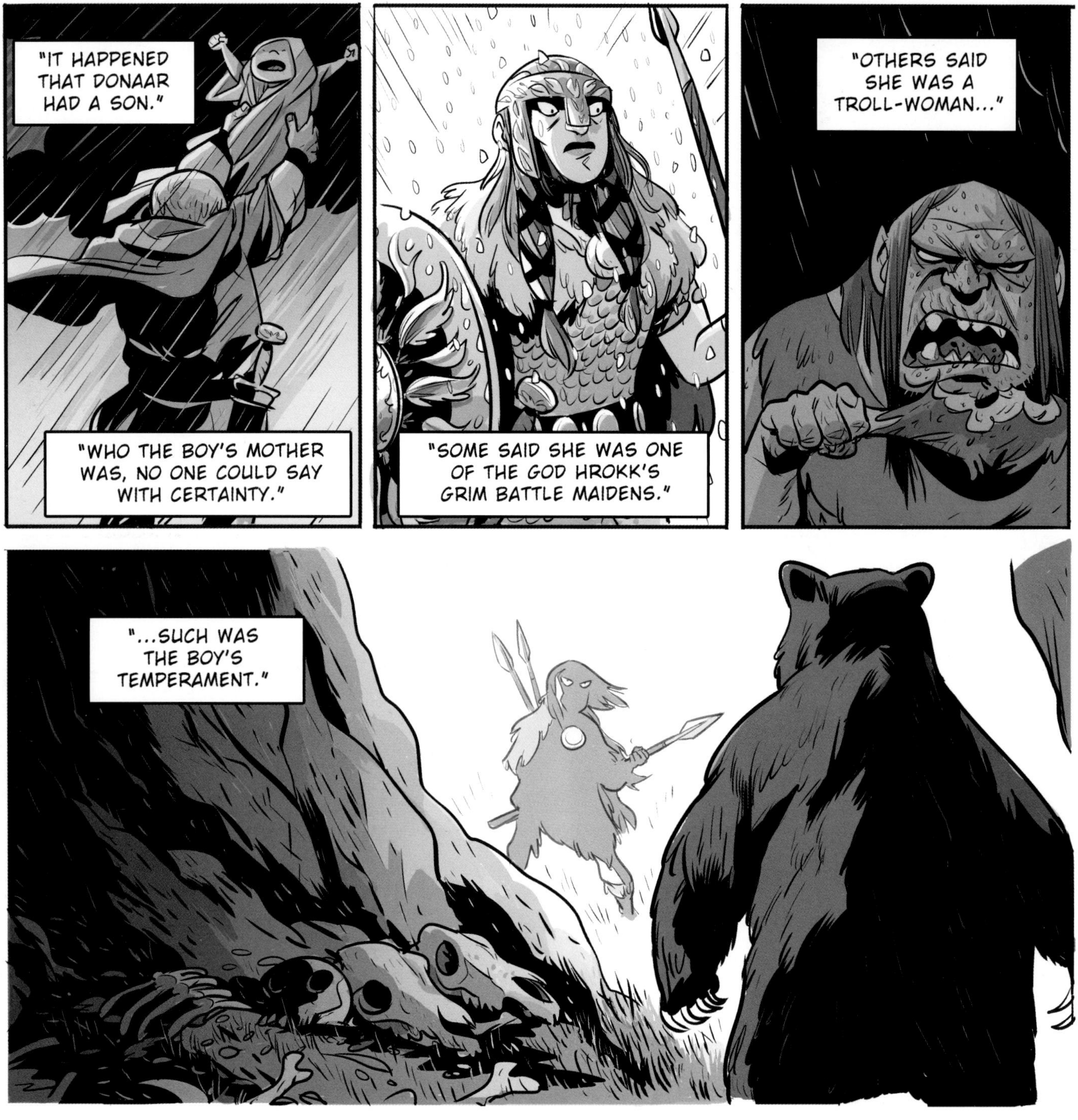
"IT HAPPENED THAT DONAAR HAD A SON."
"WHO THE BOY'S MOTHER WAS, NO ONE COULD SAY WITH CERTAINTY."
"SOME SAID SHE WAS ONE OF THE GOD HROKK'S GRIM BATTLE MAIDENS."
"OTHERS SAID SHE WAS A TROLL-WOMAN..."
"...SUCH WAS THE BOY'S TEMPERAMENT."

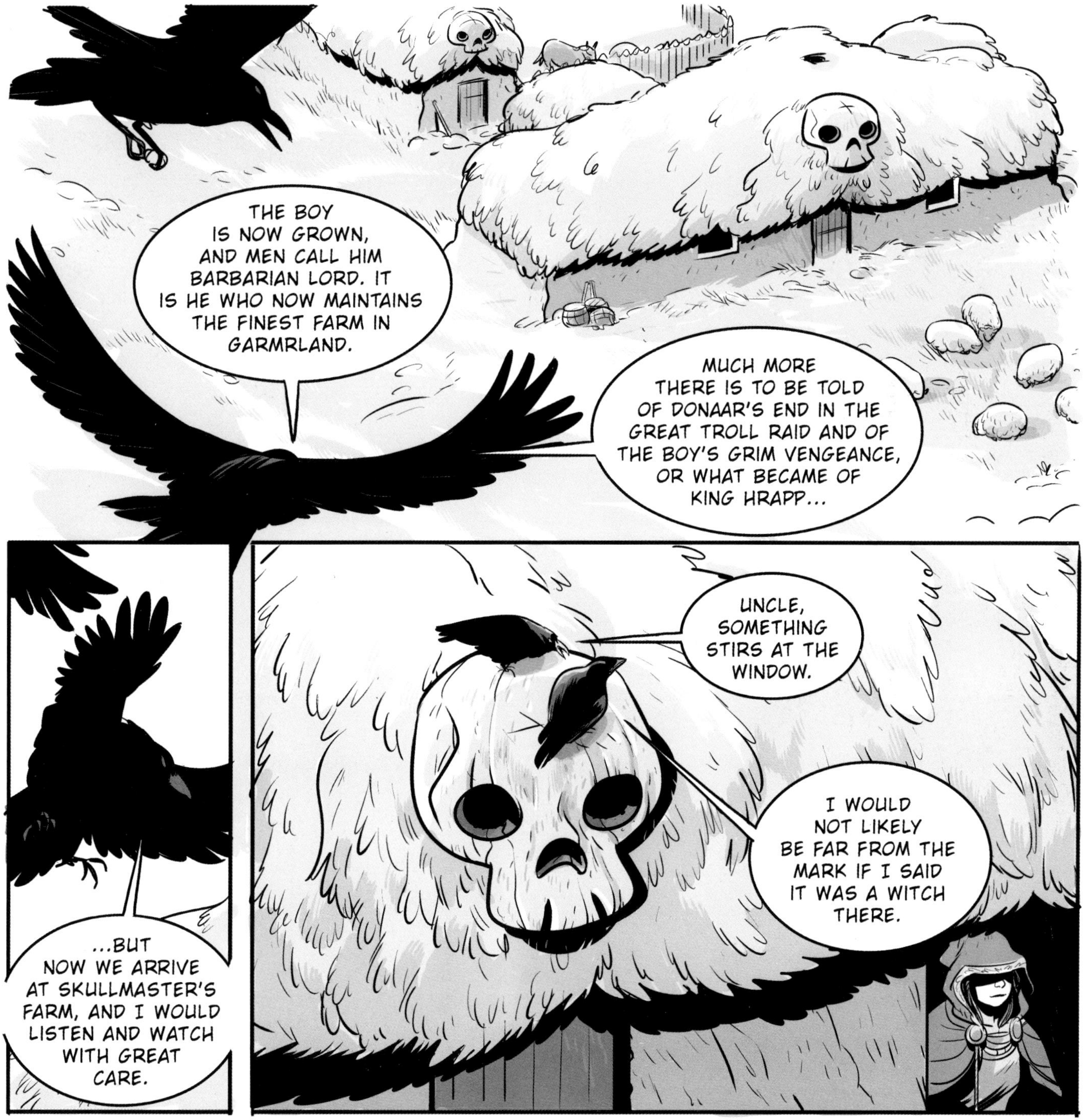
THE BOY IS NOW GROWN, AND MEN CALL HIM BARBARIAN LORD. IT IS HE WHO NOW MAINTAINS THE FINEST FARM IN GARMRLAND.
MUCH MORE THERE IS TO BE TOLD OF DONAAR'S END IN THE GREAT TROLL RAID AND OF THE BOY'S GRIM VENGEANCE, OR WHAT BECAME OF KING HRAPP...
...BUT NOW WE ARRIVE AT SKULLMASTER'S FARM, AND I WOULD LISTEN AND WATCH WITH GREAT CARE.
UNCLE, SOMETHING STIRS AT THE WINDOW.
I WOULD NOT LIKELY BE FAR FROM THE MARK IF I SAID IT WAS A WITCH THERE.

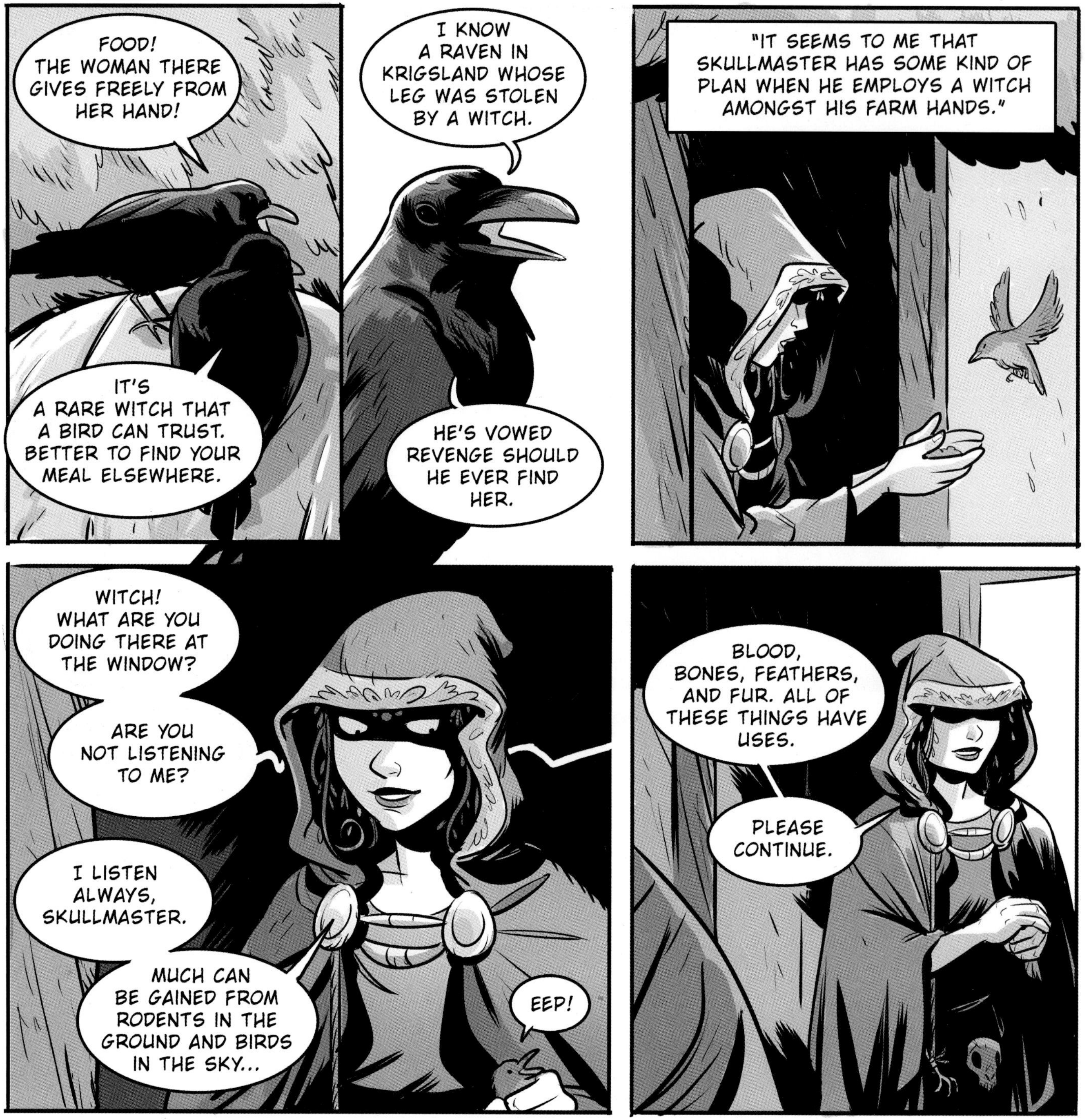
FOOD! THE WOMAN THERE GIVES FREELY FROM HER HAND!
I KNOW A RAVEN IN KRIGSLAND WHOSE LEG WAS STOLEN BY A WITCH.
IT'S A RARE WITCH THAT A BIRD CAN TRUST. BETTER TO FIND YOUR MEAL ELSEWHERE.
HE'S VOWED REVENGE SHOULD HE EVER FIND HER.
"IT SEEMS TO ME THAT SKULLMASTER HAS SOME KIND OF PLAN WHEN HE EMPLOYS A WITCH AMONGST HIS FARM HANDS."
WITCH! WHAT ARE YOU DOING THERE AT THE WINDOW?
ARE YOU NOT LISTENING TO ME?
I LISTEN ALWAYS, SKULLMASTER.
MUCH CAN BE GAINED FROM RODENTS IN THE GROUND AND BIRDS IN THE SKY...
EEP!
BLOOD, BONES, FEATHERS, AND FUR. ALL OF THESE THINGS HAVE USES.
PLEASE CONTINUE.

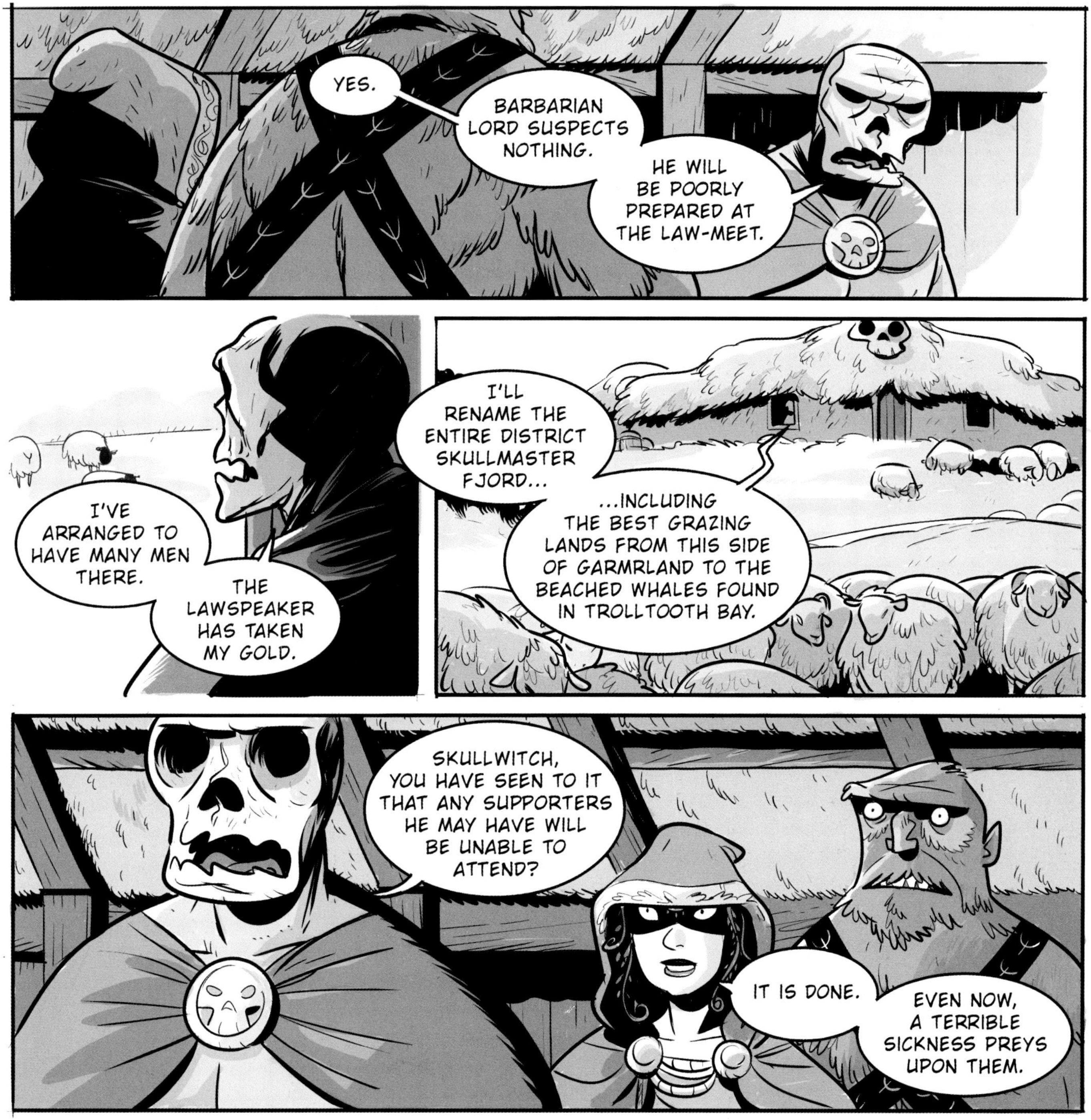
YES.
BARBARIAN LORD SUSPECTS NOTHING.
HE WILL BE POORLY PREPARED AT THE LAW-MEET.
I'VE ARRANGED TO HAVE MANY MEN THERE.
THE LAWSPEAKER HAS TAKEN MY GOLD.
I'LL RENAME THE ENTIRE DISTRICT SKULLMASTER FJORD...
...INCLUDING THE BEST GRAZING LANDS FROM THIS SIDE OF GARMRLAND TO THE BEACHED WHALES FOUND IN TROLLTOOTH BAY.
SKULLWITCH, YOU HAVE SEEN TO IT THAT ANY SUPPORTERS HE MAY HAVE WILL BE UNABLE TO ATTEND?
IT IS DONE.
EVEN NOW, A TERRIBLE SICKNESS PREYS UPON THEM.

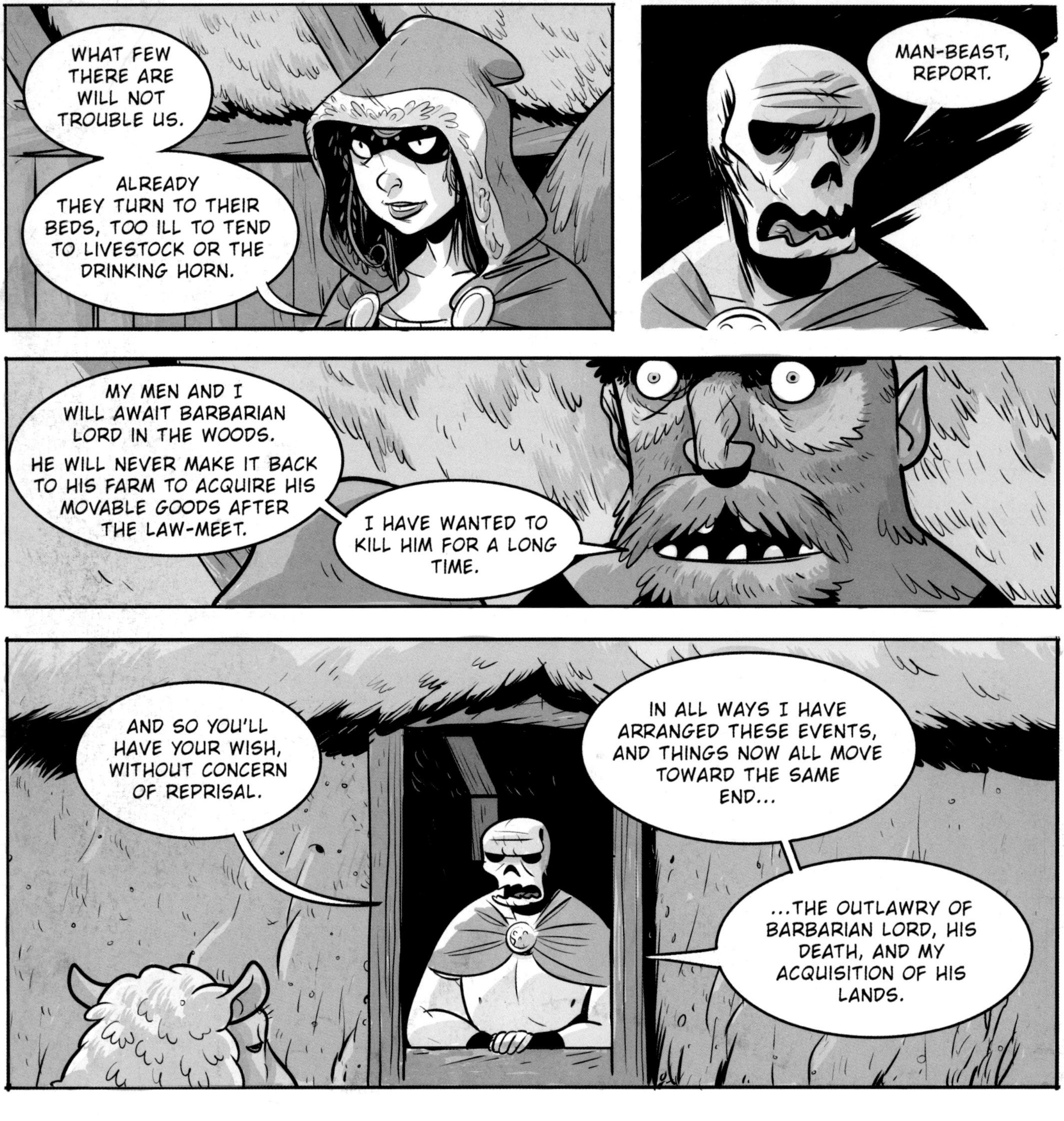
WHAT FEW THERE ARE WILL NOT TROUBLE US.
ALREADY THEY TURN TO THEIR BEDS, TOO ILL TO TEND TO LIVESTOCK OR THE DRINKING HORN.
MAN-BEAST, REPORT.
MY MEN AND I WILL AWAIT BARBARIAN LORD IN THE WOODS.
HE WILL NEVER MAKE IT BACK TO HIS FARM TO ACQUIRE HIS MOVABLE GOODS AFTER THE LAW-MEET.
I HAVE WANTED TO KILL HIM FOR A LONG TIME.
AND SO YOU'LL HAVE YOUR WISH, WITHOUT CONCERN OF REPRISAL.
IN ALL WAYS I HAVE ARRANGED THESE EVENTS, AND THINGS NOW ALL MOVE TOWARD THE SAME END...
...THE OUTLAWRY OF BARBARIAN LORD, HIS DEATH, AND MY ACQUISITION OF HIS LANDS.

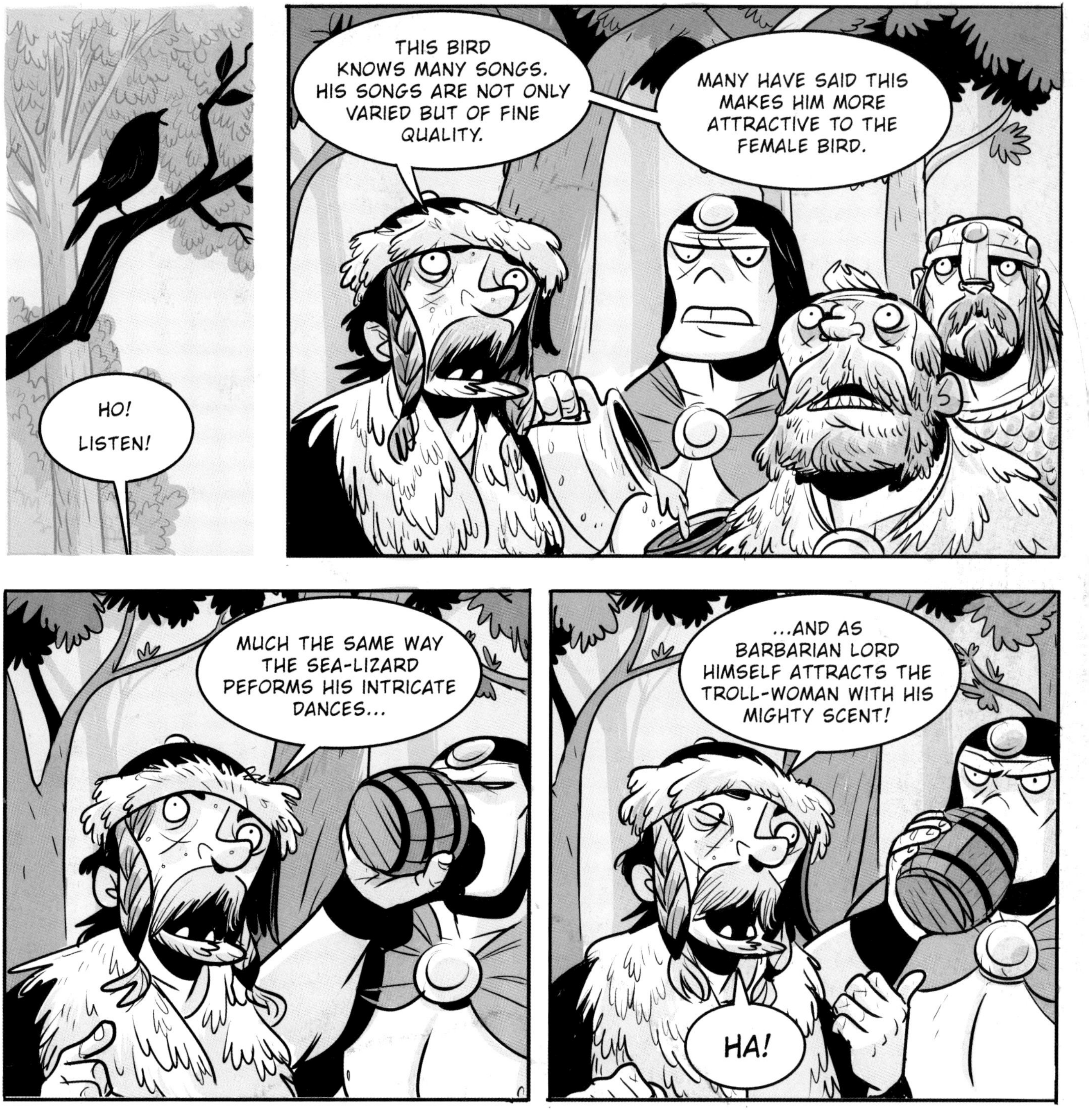
HO! LISTEN!
THIS BIRD KNOWS MANY SONGS. HIS SONGS ARE NOT ONLY VARIED BUT OF FINE QUALITY.
MANY HAVE SAID THIS MAKES HIM MORE ATTRACTIVE TO THE FEMALE BIRD.
MUCH THE SAME WAY THE SEA-LIZARD PEFORMS HIS INTRICATE DANCES...
...AND AS BARBARIAN LORD HIMSELF ATTRACTS THE TROLL-WOMAN WITH HIS MIGHTY SCENT!
HA!

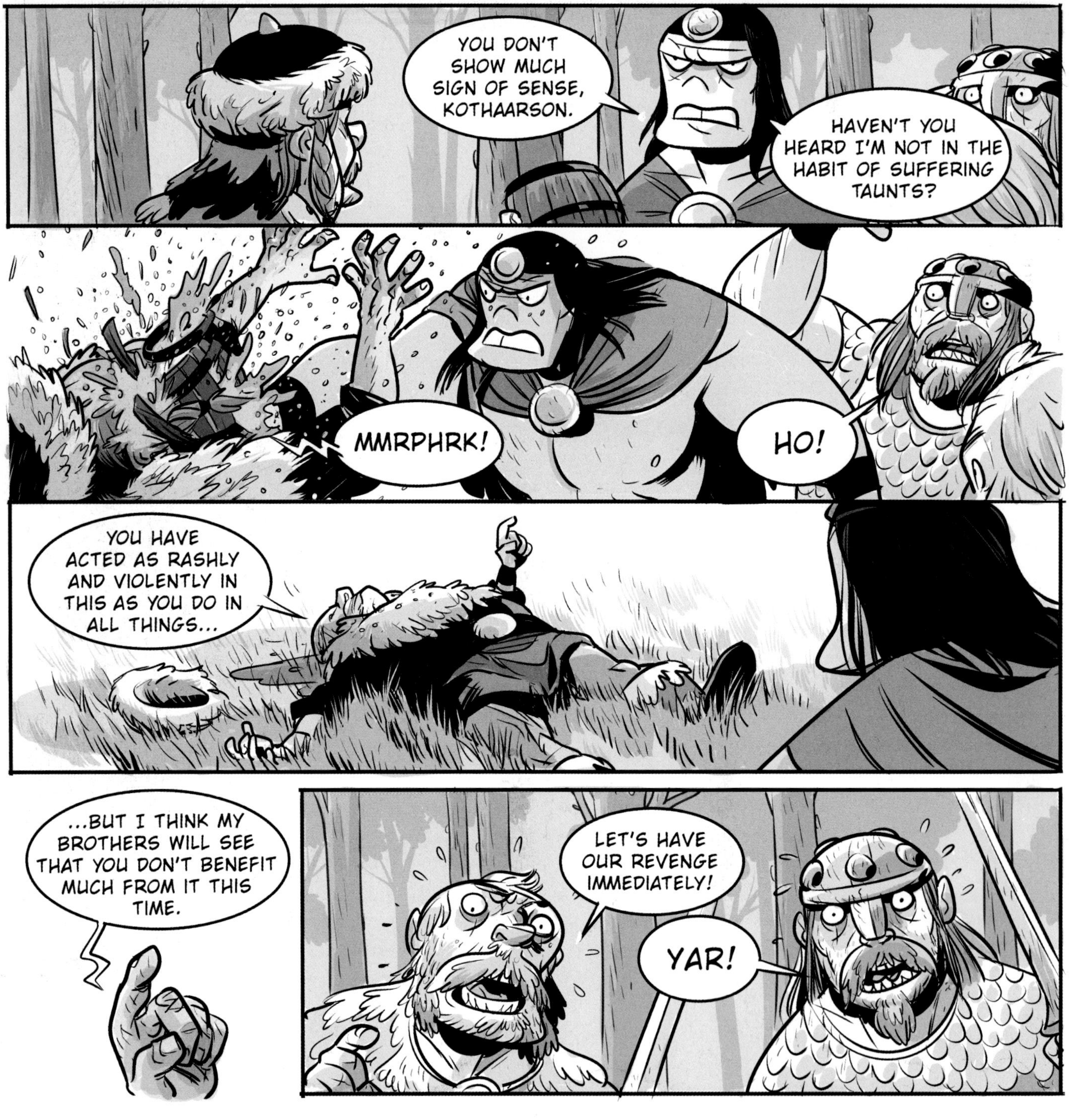
YOU DON'T SHOW MUCH SIGN OF SENSE, KOTHAARSON.
HAVEN'T YOU HEARD I'M NOT IN THE HABIT OF SUFFERING TAUNTS?
MMRPHRK!
HO!
YOU HAVE ACTED AS RASHLY AND VIOLENTLY IN THIS AS YOU DO IN ALL THINGS...
...BUT I THINK MY BROTHERS WILL SEE THAT YOU DON'T BENEFIT MUCH FROM IT THIS TIME.
LET'S HAVE OUR REVENGE IMMEDIATELY!
YAR!

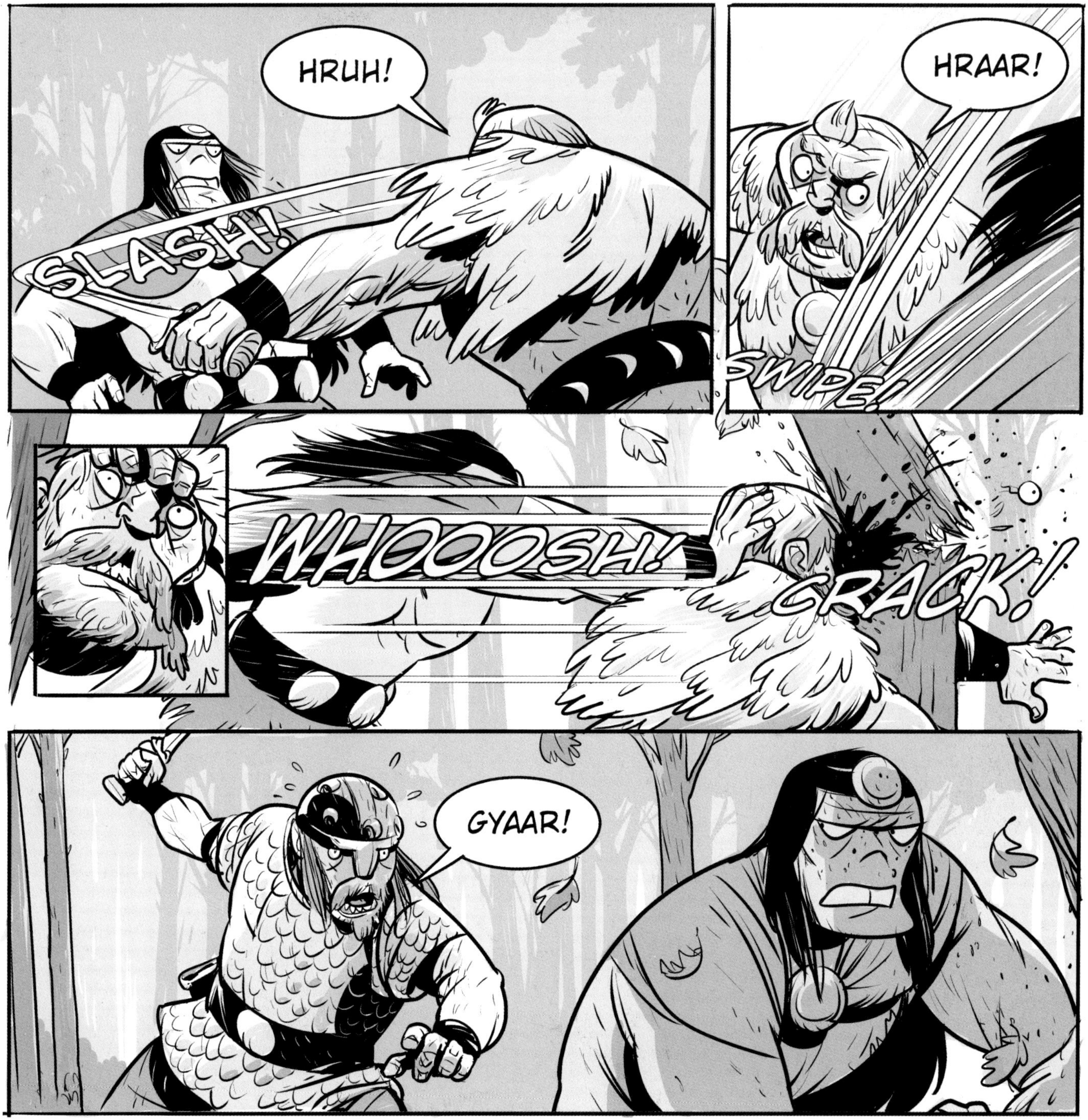
HRUH!
SLASH!
HRAAR!
SWIPE!
WHOOOSH!
CRACK!
GYAAR!

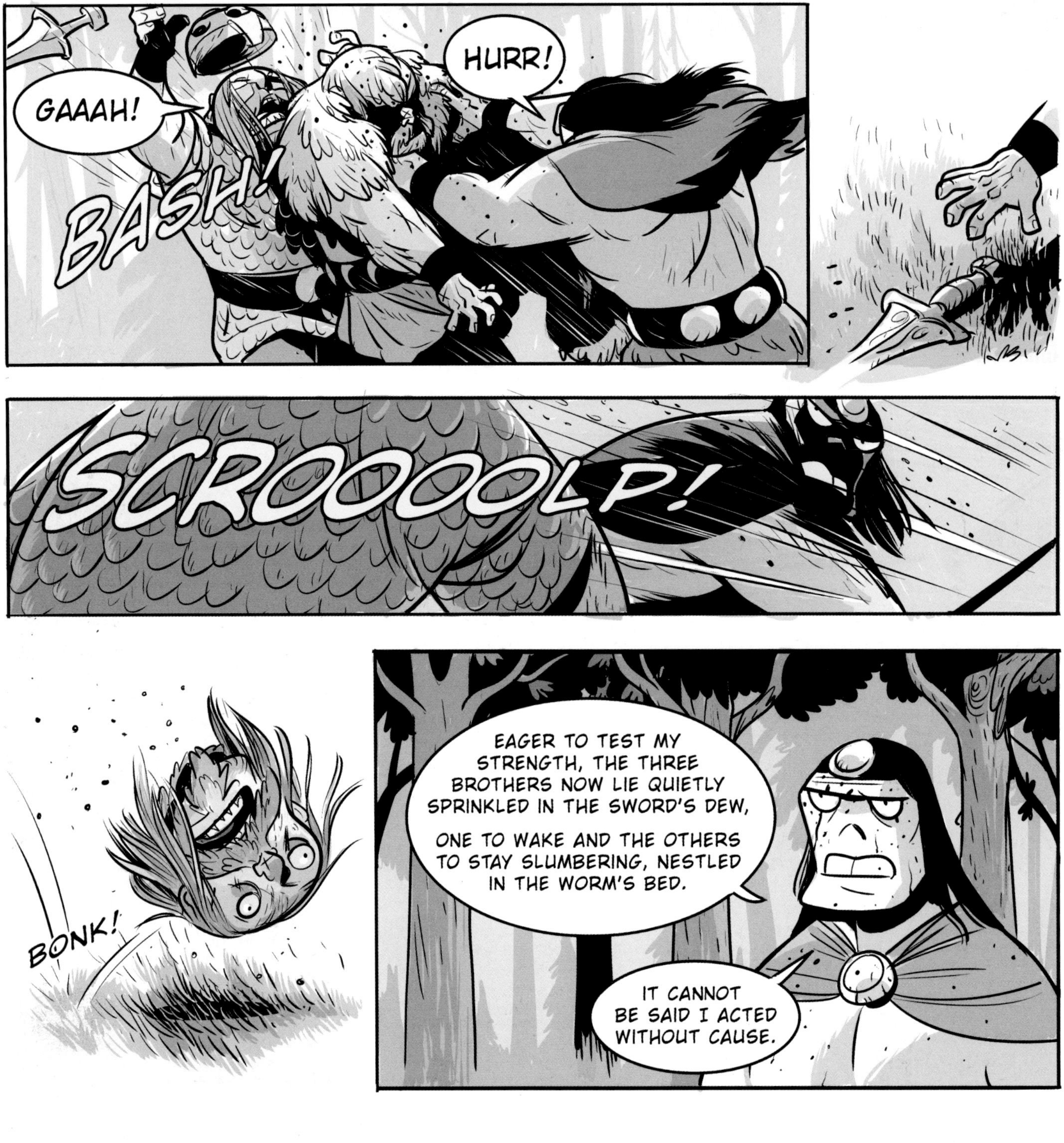
GAAAH!
HURR!
BASH!
SCROOOOLP!
BONK!
EAGER TO TEST MY STRENGTH, THE THREE BROTHERS NOW LIE QUIETLY SPRINKLED IN THE SWORD'S DEW,
ONE TO WAKE AND THE OTHERS TO STAY SLUMBERING, NESTLED IN THE WORM'S BED.
IT CANNOT BE SAID I ACTED WITHOUT CAUSE.

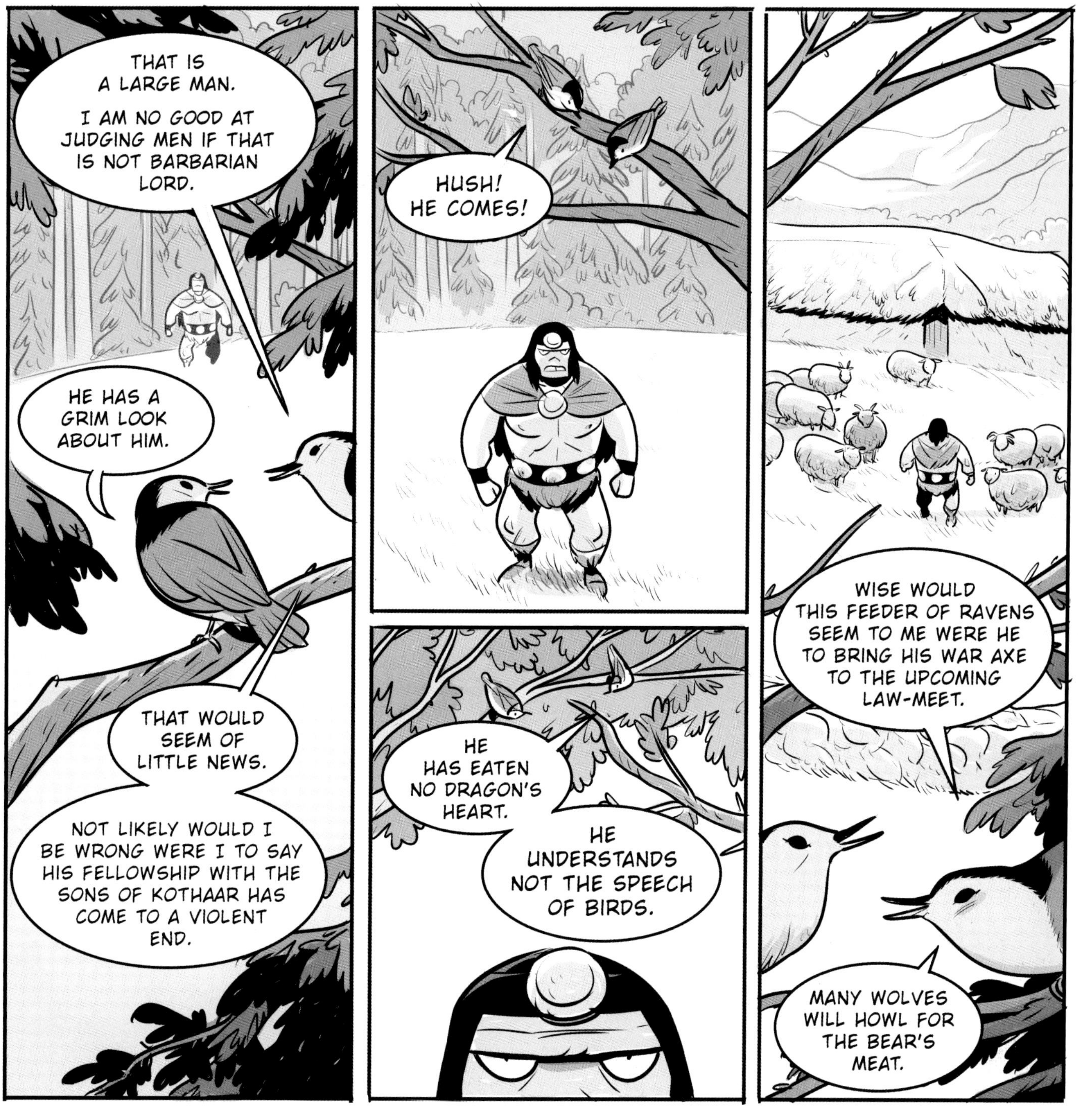
THAT IS A LARGE MAN.
I AM NO GOOD AT JUDGING MEN IF THAT IS NOT BARBARIAN LORD.
HE HAS A GRIM LOOK ABOUT HIM.
THAT WOULD SEEM OF LITTLE NEWS.
NOT LIKELY WOULD I BE WRONG WERE I TO SAY HIS FELLOWSHIP WITH THE SONS OF KOTHAAR HAS COME TO A VIOLENT END.
HUSH! HE COMES!
HE HAS EATEN NO DRAGON'S HEART.
HE UNDERSTANDS NOT THE SPEECH OF BIRDS.
WISE WOULD THIS FEEDER OF RAVENS SEEM TO ME WERE HE TO BRING HIS WAR AXE TO THE UPCOMING LAW-MEET.
MANY WOLVES WILL HOWL FOR THE BEAR'S MEAT.

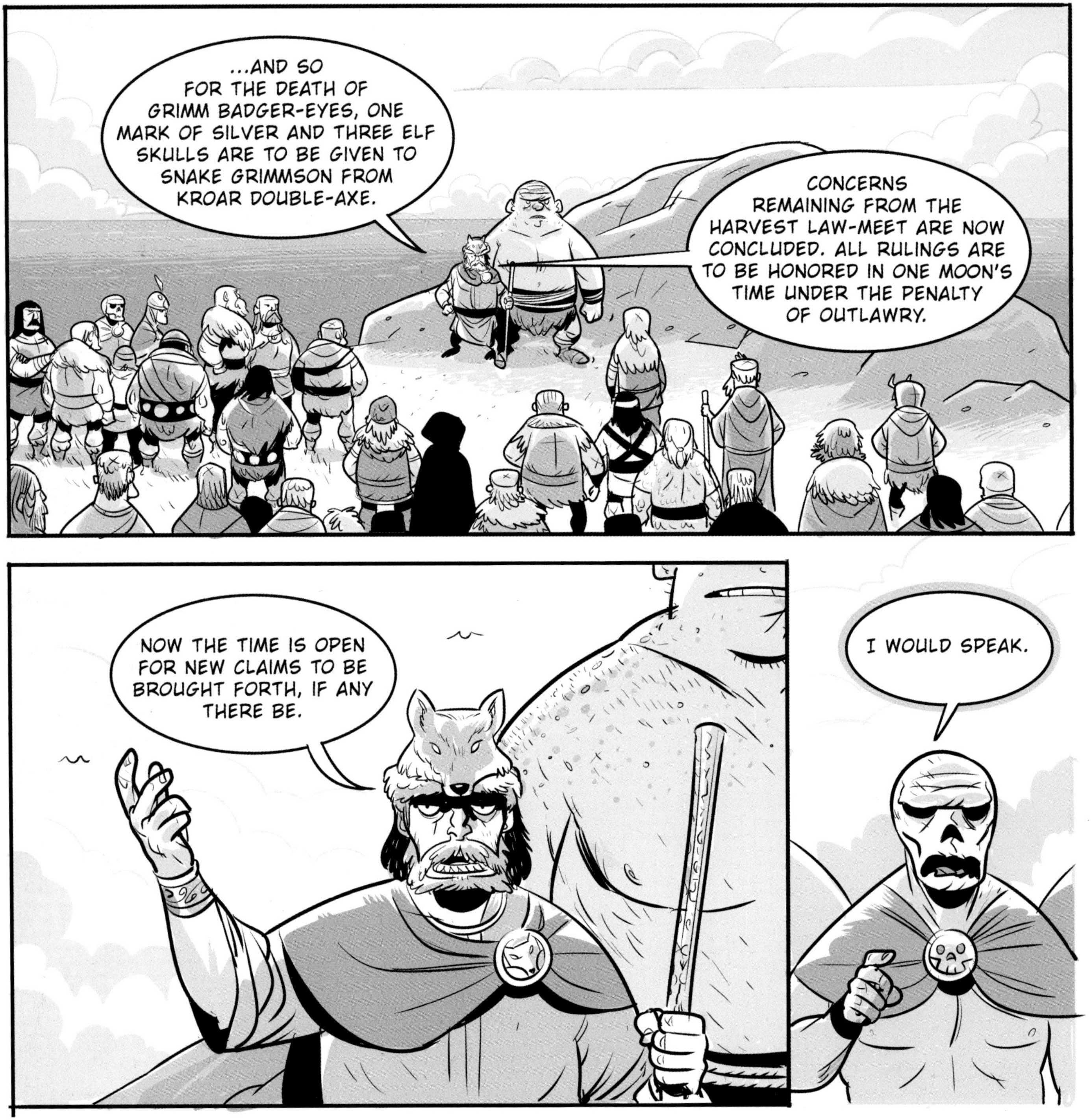
...AND SO FOR THE DEATH OF GRIMM BADGER-EYES, ONE MARK OF SILVER AND THREE ELF SKULLS ARE TO BE GIVEN TO SNAKE GRIMMSON FROM KROAR DOUBLE-AXE.
CONCERNS REMAINING FROM THE HARVEST LAW-MEET ARE NOW CONCLUDED. ALL RULINGS ARE TO BE HONORED IN ONE MOON'S TIME UNDER THE PENALTY OF OUTLAWRY.
NOW THE TIME IS OPEN FOR NEW CLAIMS TO BE BROUGHT FORTH, IF ANY THERE BE.
I WOULD SPEAK.

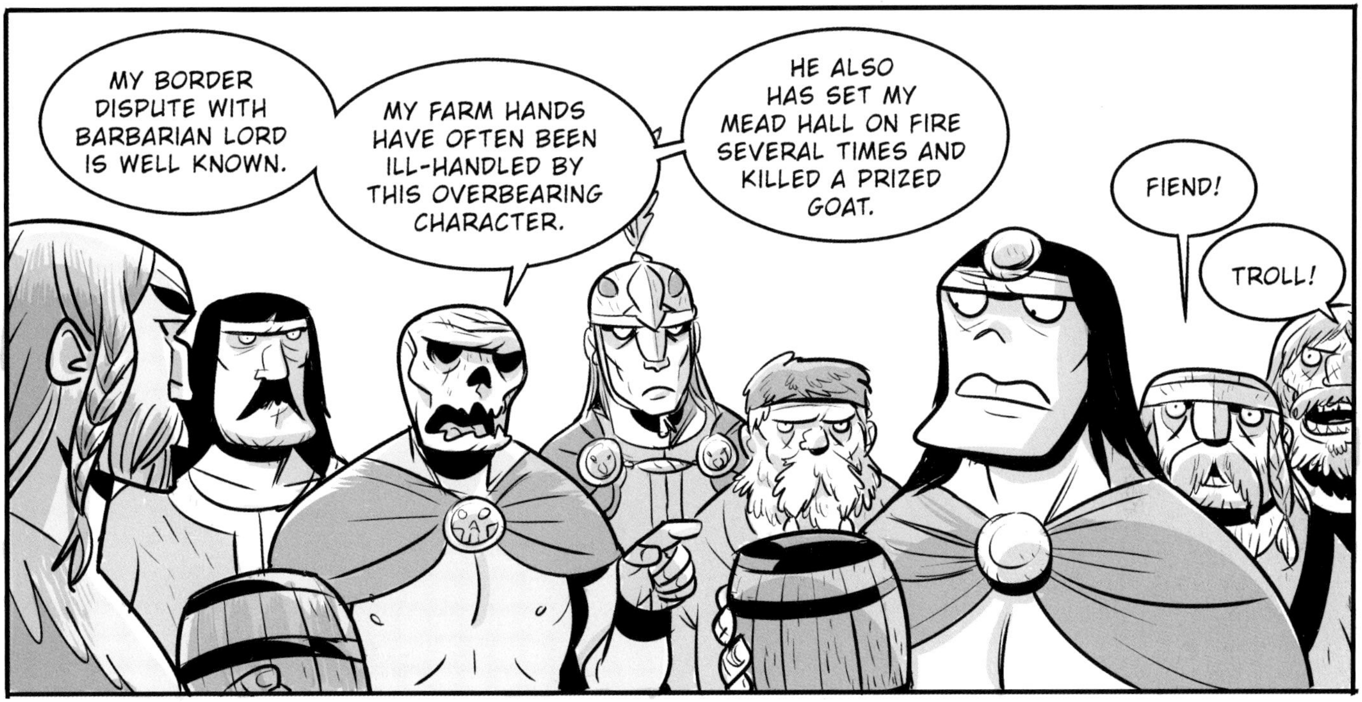
MY BORDER DISPUTE WITH BARBARIAN LORD IS WELL KNOWN.
MY FARM HANDS HAVE OFTEN BEEN ILL-HANDLED BY THIS OVERBEARING CHARACTER.
HE ALSO HAS SET MY MEAD HALL ON FIRE SEVERAL TIMES AND KILLED A PRIZED GOAT.
FIEND!
TROLL!

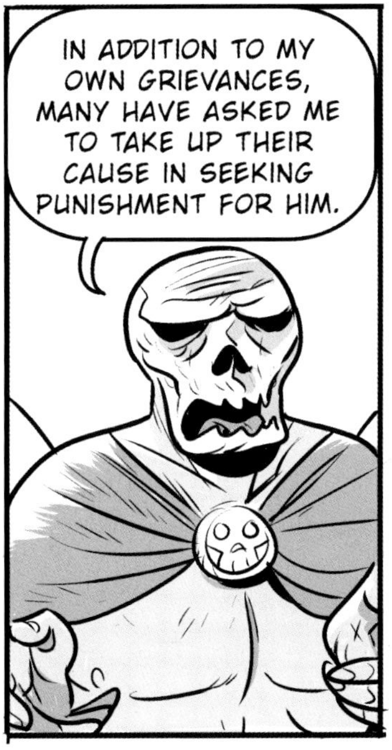
IN ADDITION TO MY OWN GRIEVANCES, MANY HAVE ASKED ME TO TAKE UP THEIR CAUSE IN SEEKING PUNISHMENT FOR HIM.

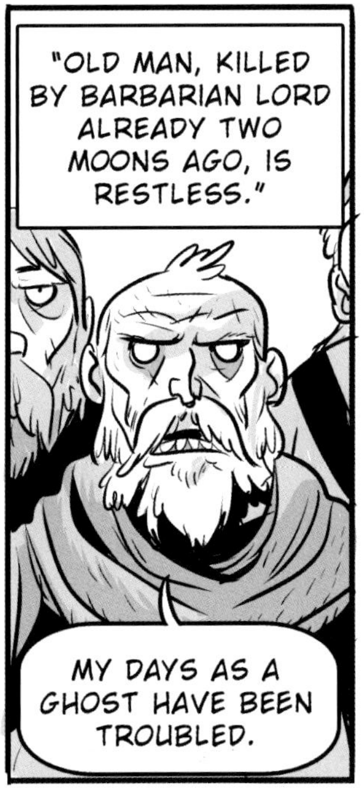
"OLD MAN, KILLED BY BARBARIAN LORD ALREADY TWO MOONS AGO, IS RESTLESS."
MY DAYS AS A GHOST HAVE BEEN TROUBLED.

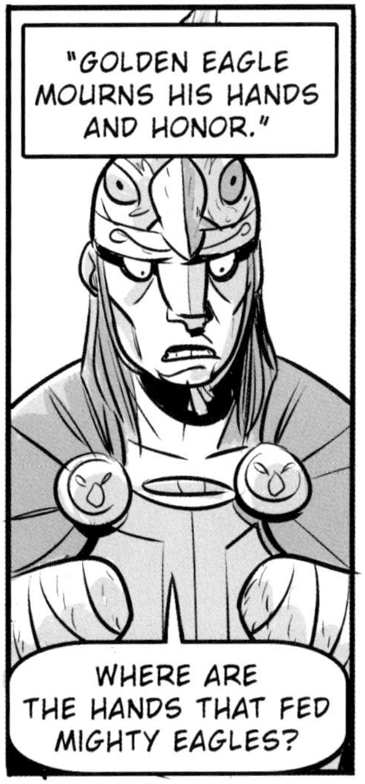
"GOLDEN EAGLE MOURNS HIS HANDS AND HONOR."
WHERE ARE THE HANDS THAT FED MIGHTY EAGLES?

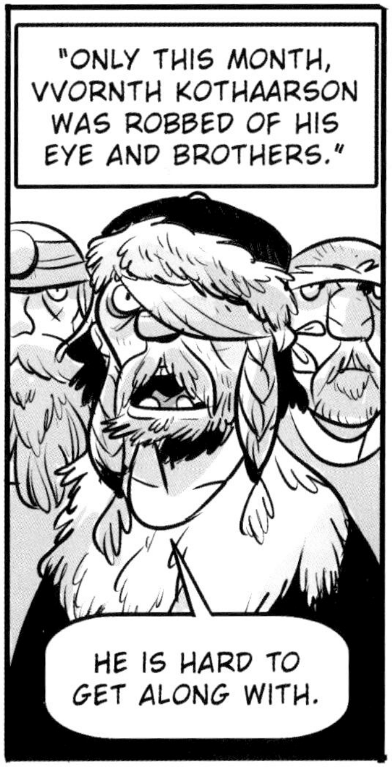
"ONLY THIS MONTH, VVORNTH KOTHAARSON WAS ROBBED OF HIS EYE AND BROTHERS."
HE IS HARD TO GET ALONG WITH.

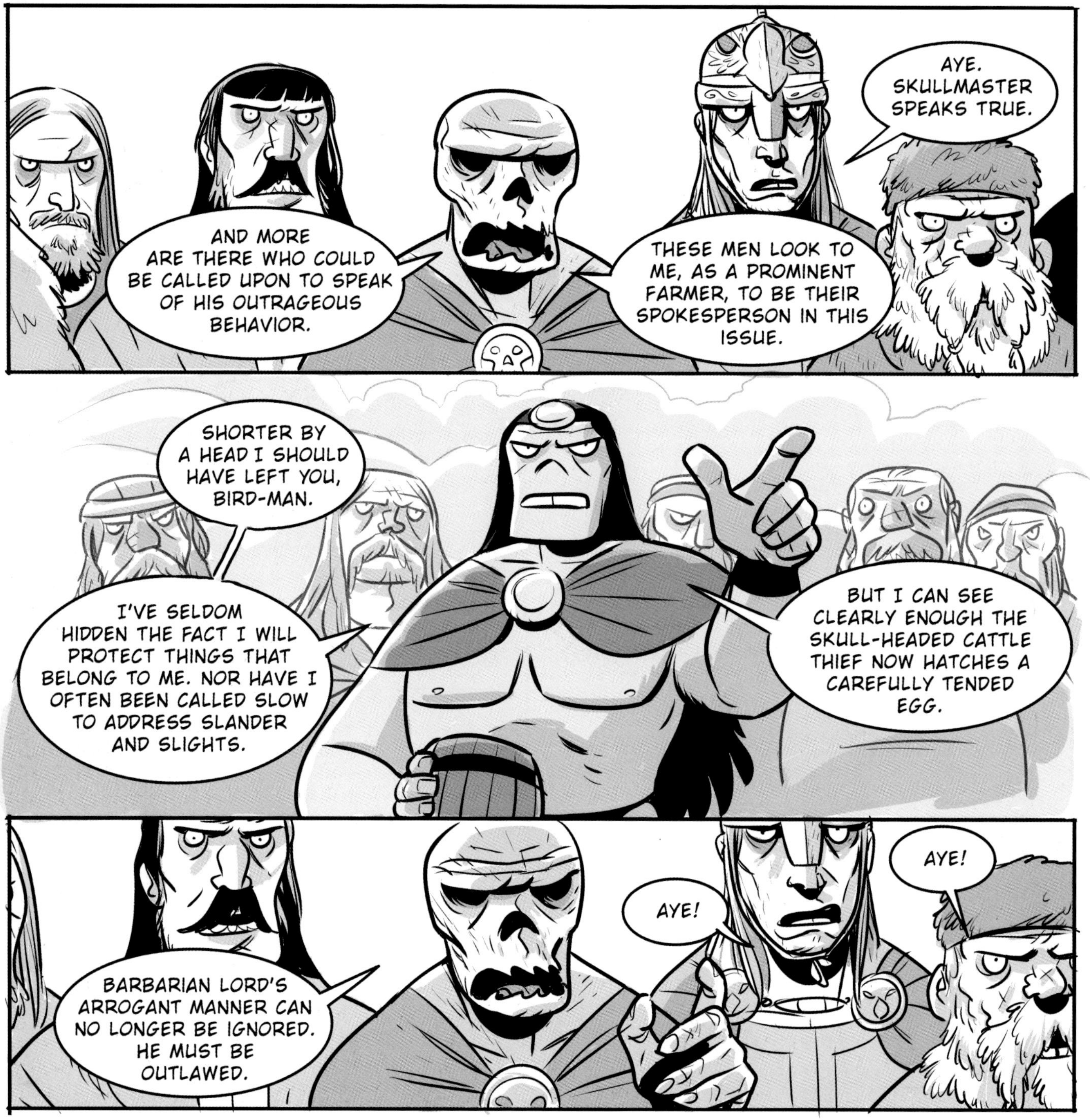
AND MORE ARE THERE WHO COULD BE CALLED UPON TO SPEAK OF HIS OUTRAGEOUS BEHAVIOR.
THESE MEN LOOK TO ME, AS A PROMINENT FARMER, TO BE THEIR SPOKESPERSON IN THIS ISSUE.
AYE. SKULLMASTER SPEAKS TRUE.
SHORTER BY A HEAD I SHOULD HAVE LEFT YOU, BIRD-MAN.
I'VE SELDOM HIDDEN THE FACT I WILL PROTECT THINGS THAT BELONG TO ME. NOR HAVE I OFTEN BEEN CALLED SLOW TO ADDRESS SLANDER AND SLIGHTS.
BUT I CAN SEE CLEARLY ENOUGH THE SKULL-HEADED CATTLE THIEF NOW HATCHES A CAREFULLY TENDED EGG.
BARBARIAN LORD'S ARROGANT MANNER CAN NO LONGER BE IGNORED. HE MUST BE OUTLAWED.
AYE!
AYE!

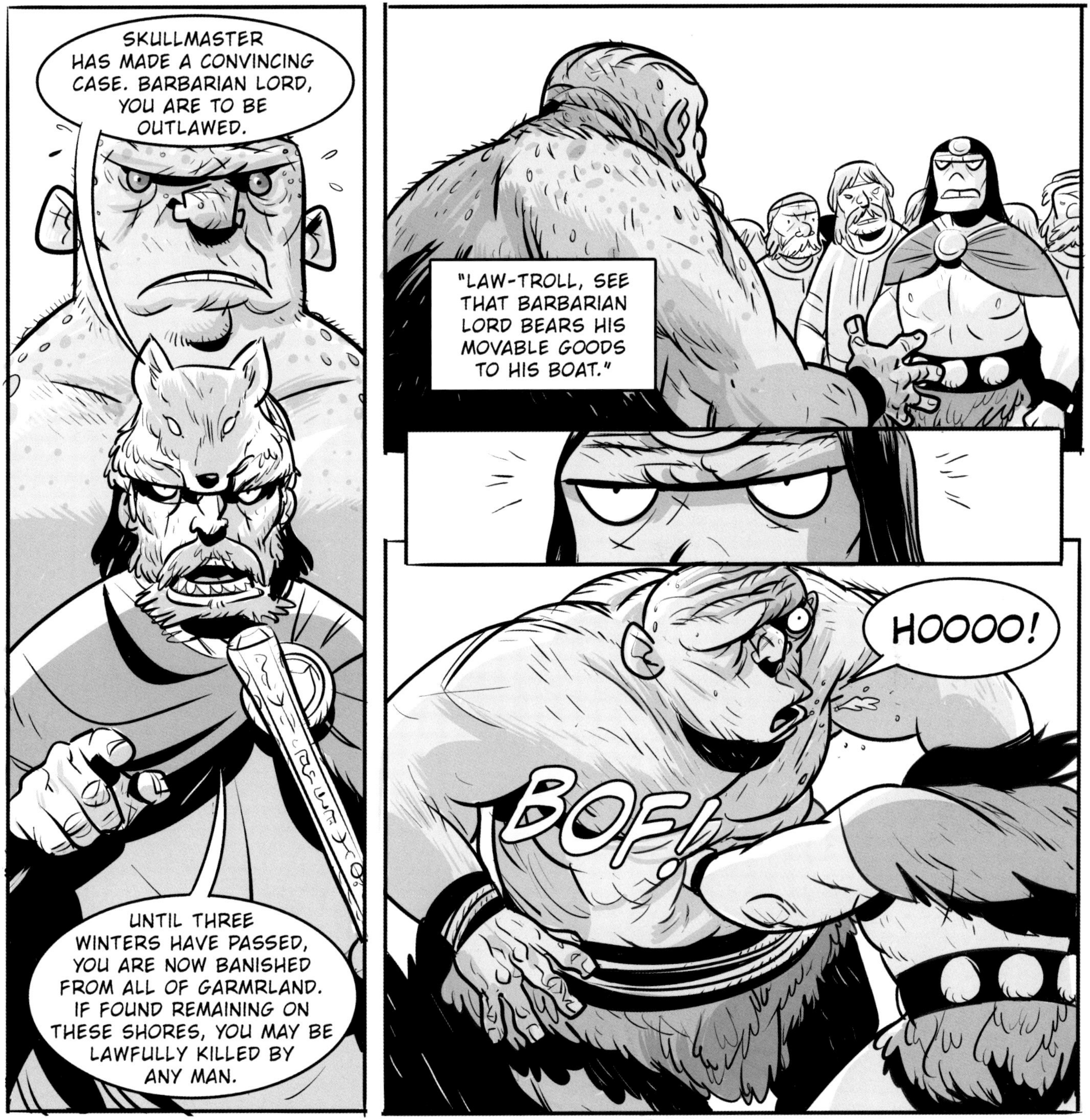
SKULLMASTER HAS MADE A CONVINCING CASE. BARBARIAN LORD, YOU ARE TO BE OUTLAWED.
UNTIL THREE WINTERS HAVE PASSED, YOU ARE NOW BANISHED FROM ALL OF GARMRLAND. IF FOUND REMAINING ON THESE SHORES, YOU MAY BE LAWFULLY KILLED BY ANY MAN.
"LAW-TROLL, SEE THAT BARBARIAN LORD BEARS HIS MOVABLE GOODS TO HIS BOAT."
HOOOO!
BOF!

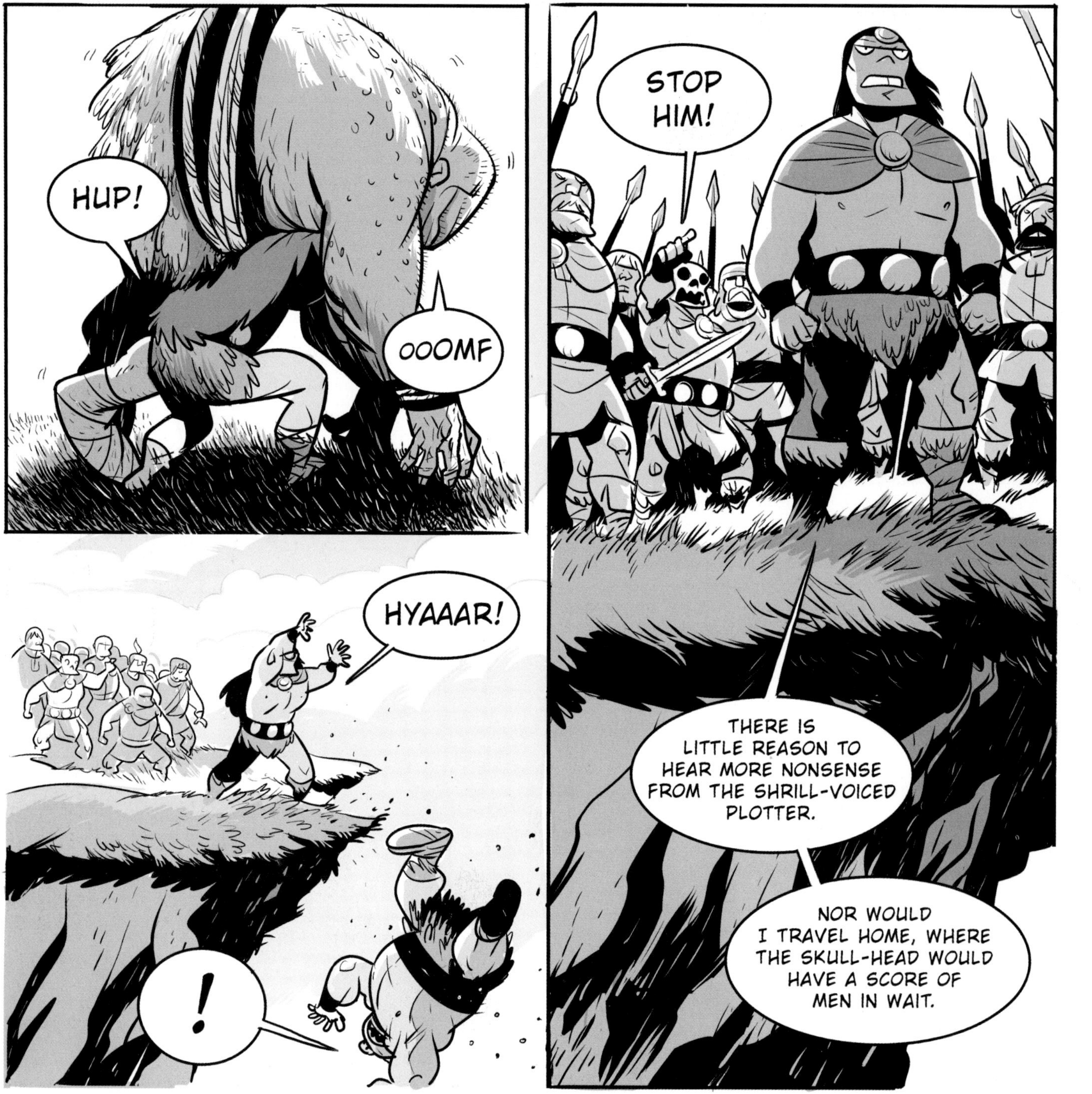
HUP!
OOOMF
HYAAAR!
!
STOP HIM!
THERE IS LITTLE REASON TO HEAR MORE NONSENSE FROM THE SHRILL-VOICED PLOTTER.
NOR WOULD I TRAVEL HOME, WHERE THE SKULL-HEAD WOULD HAVE A SCORE OF MEN IN WAIT.

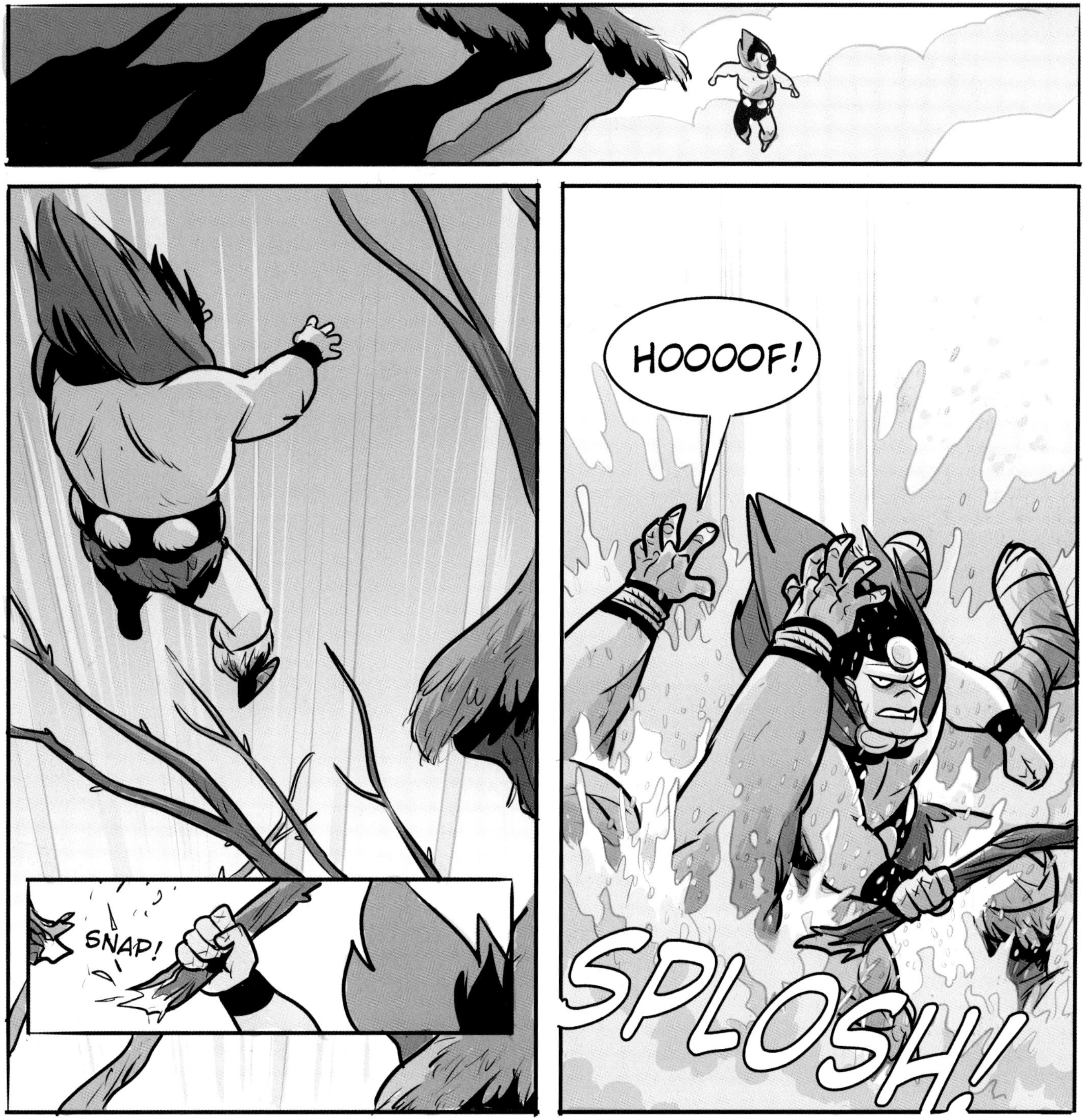
SNAP!
HOOOOF!
SPLOSH!

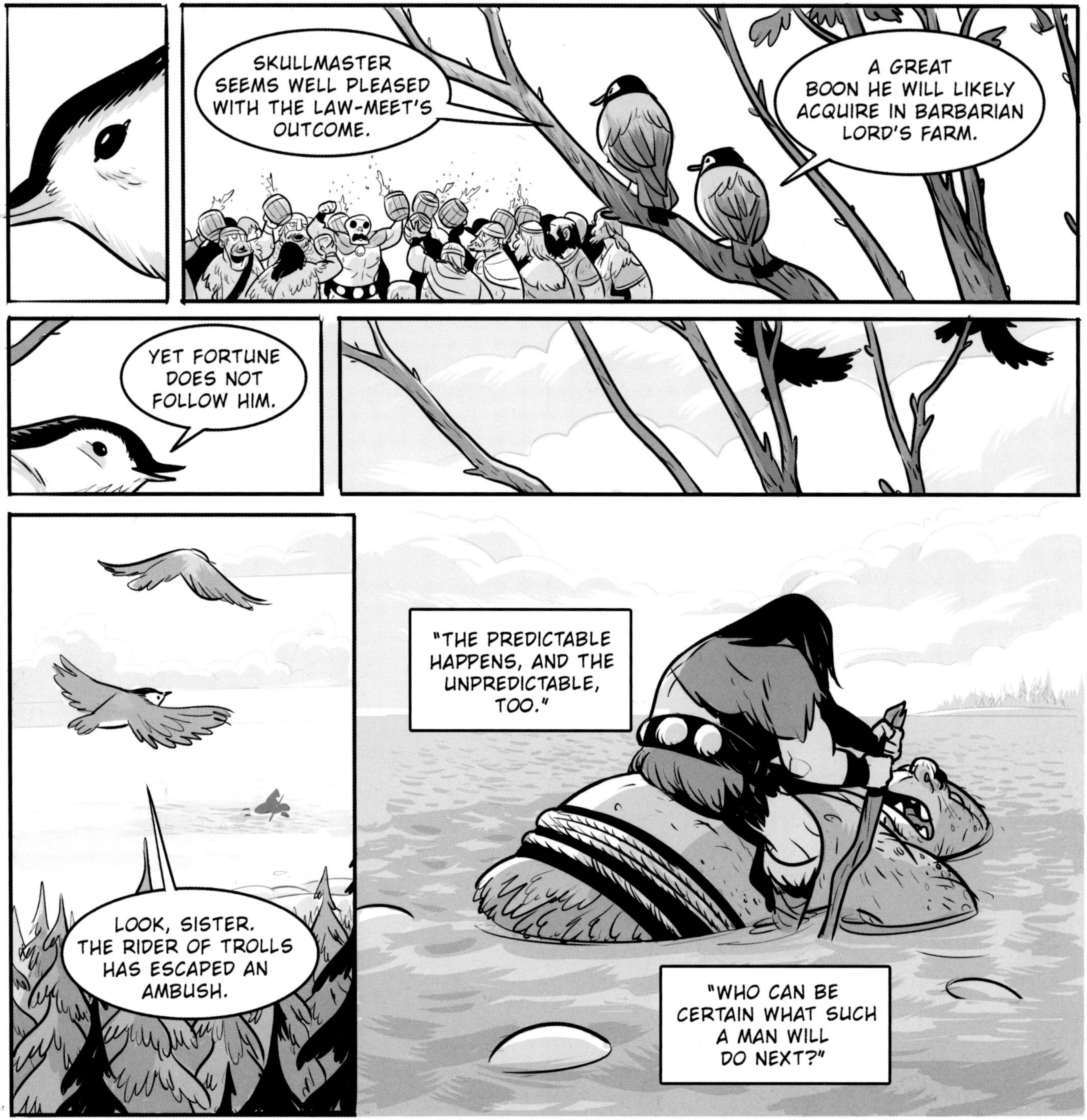
SKULLMASTER SEEMS WELL PLEASED WITH THE LAW-MEET'S OUTCOME.
A GREAT BOON HE WILL LIKELY ACQUIRE IN BARBARIAN LORD'S FARM.
YET FORTUNE DOES NOT FOLLOW HIM.
LOOK, SISTER. THE RIDER OF TROLLS HAS ESCAPED AN AMBUSH.
"THE PREDICTABLE HAPPENS, AND THE UNPREDICTABLE, TOO."
"WHO CAN BE CERTAIN WHAT SUCH A MAN WILL DO NEXT?"

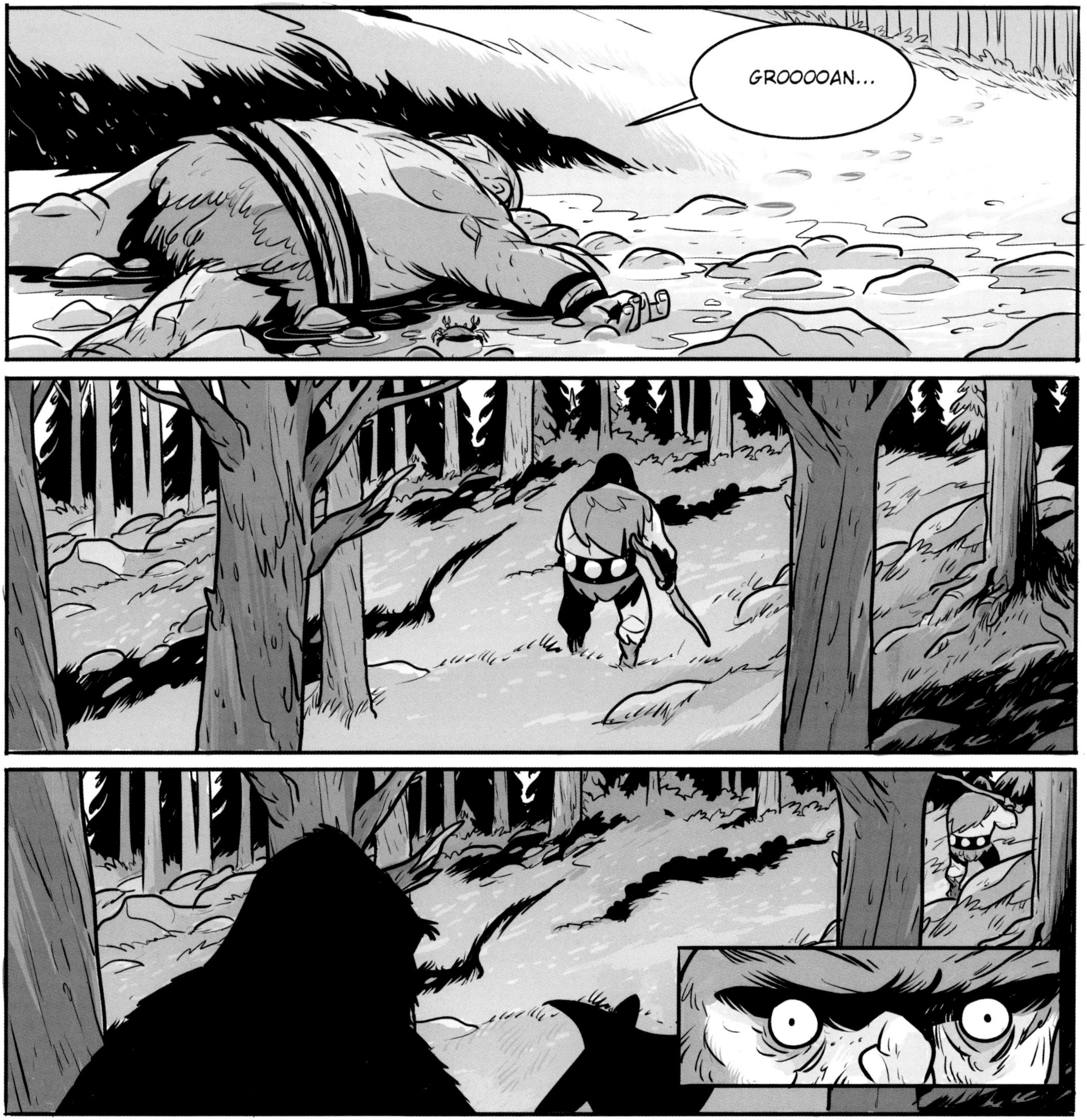
GROOOOAN...

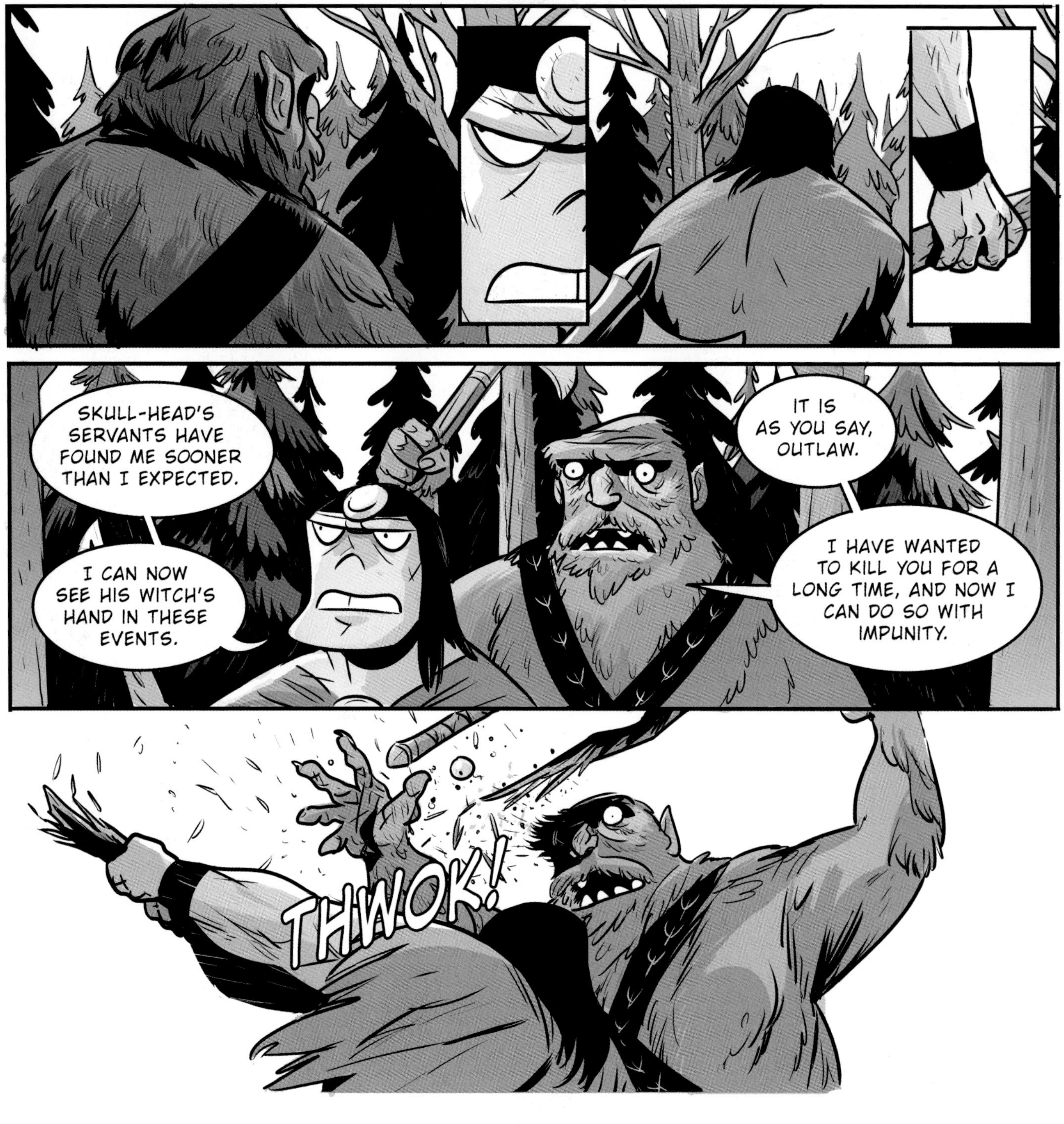
SKULL-HEAD'S SERVANTS HAVE FOUND ME SOONER THAN I EXPECTED.
I CAN NOW SEE HIS WITCH'S HAND IN THESE EVENTS.
IT IS AS YOU SAY, OUTLAW.
I HAVE WANTED TO KILL YOU FOR A LONG TIME, AND NOW I CAN DO SO WITH IMPUNITY.
THWOK!

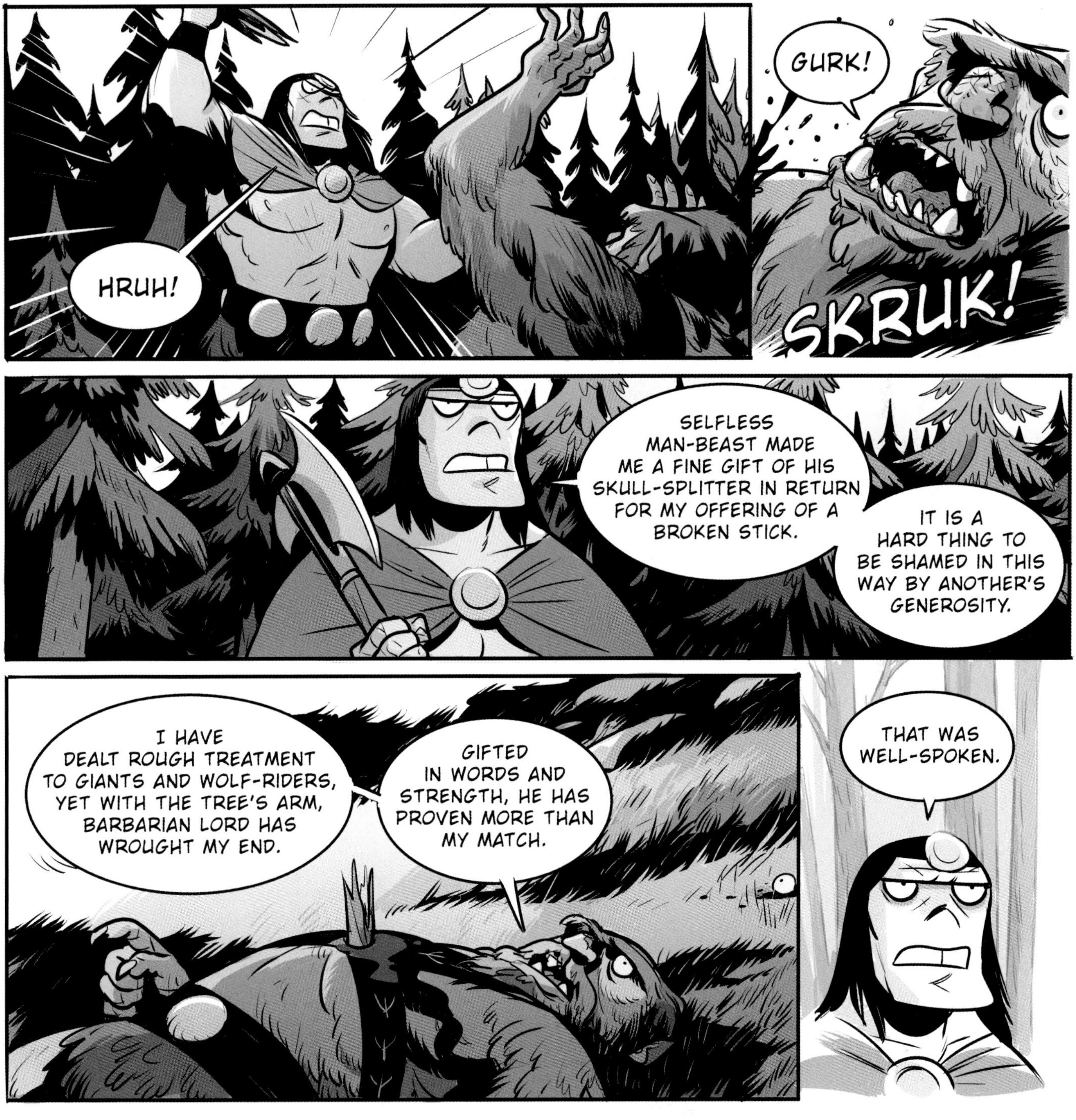
HRUH!
GURK!
SKRUK!
SELFLESS MAN-BEAST MADE ME A FINE GIFT OF HIS SKULL-SPLITTER IN RETURN FOR MY OFFERING OF A BROKEN STICK.
IT IS A HARD THING TO BE SHAMED IN THIS WAY BY ANOTHER'S GENEROSITY.
I HAVE DEALT ROUGH TREATMENT TO GIANTS AND WOLF-RIDERS, YET WITH THE TREE'S ARM, BARBARIAN LORD HAS WROUGHT MY END.
GIFTED IN WORDS AND STRENGTH, HE HAS PROVEN MORE THAN MY MATCH.
THAT WAS WELL-SPOKEN.

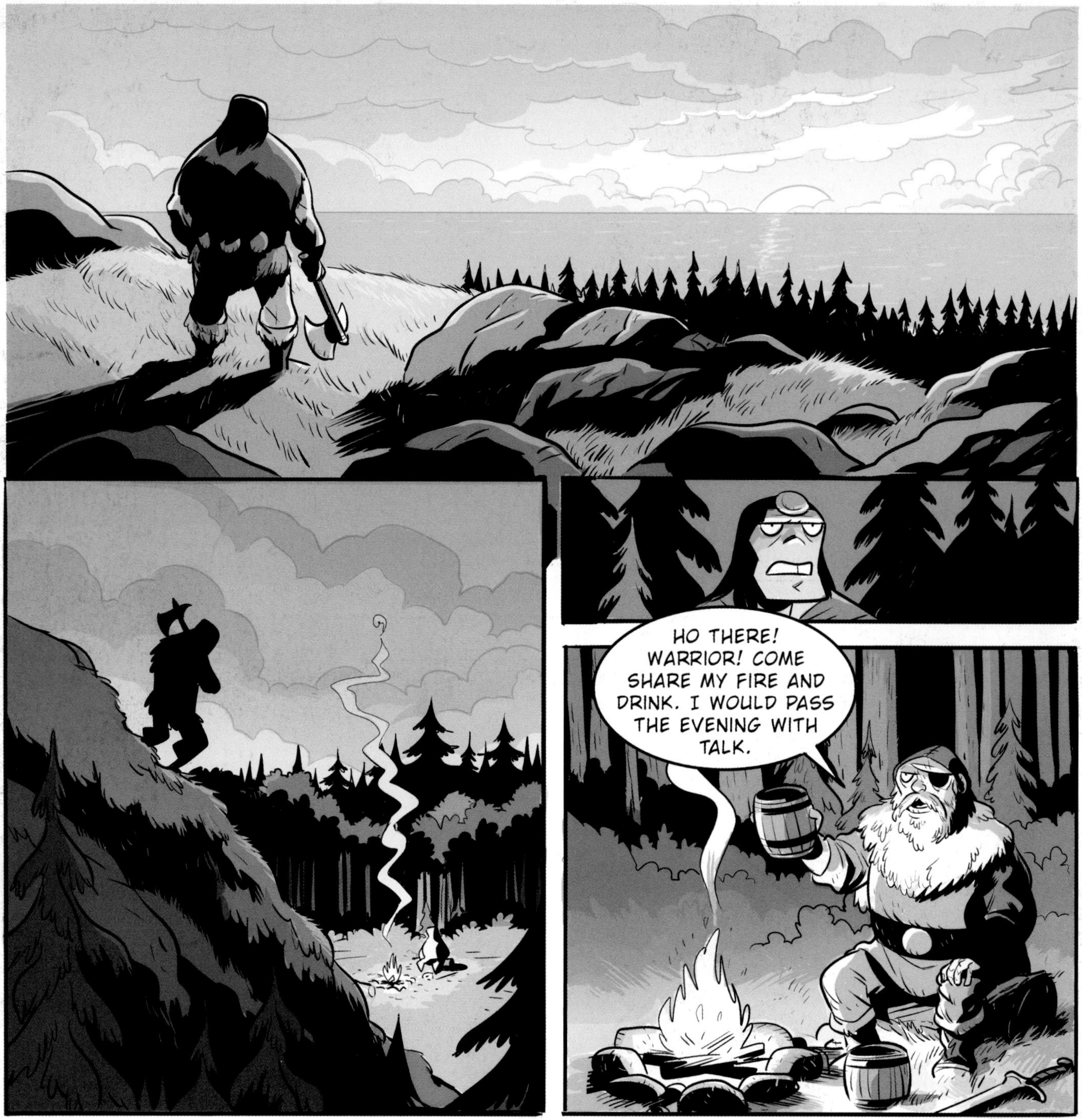
HO THERE! WARRIOR! COME SHARE MY FIRE AND DRINK. I WOULD PASS THE EVENING WITH TALK.

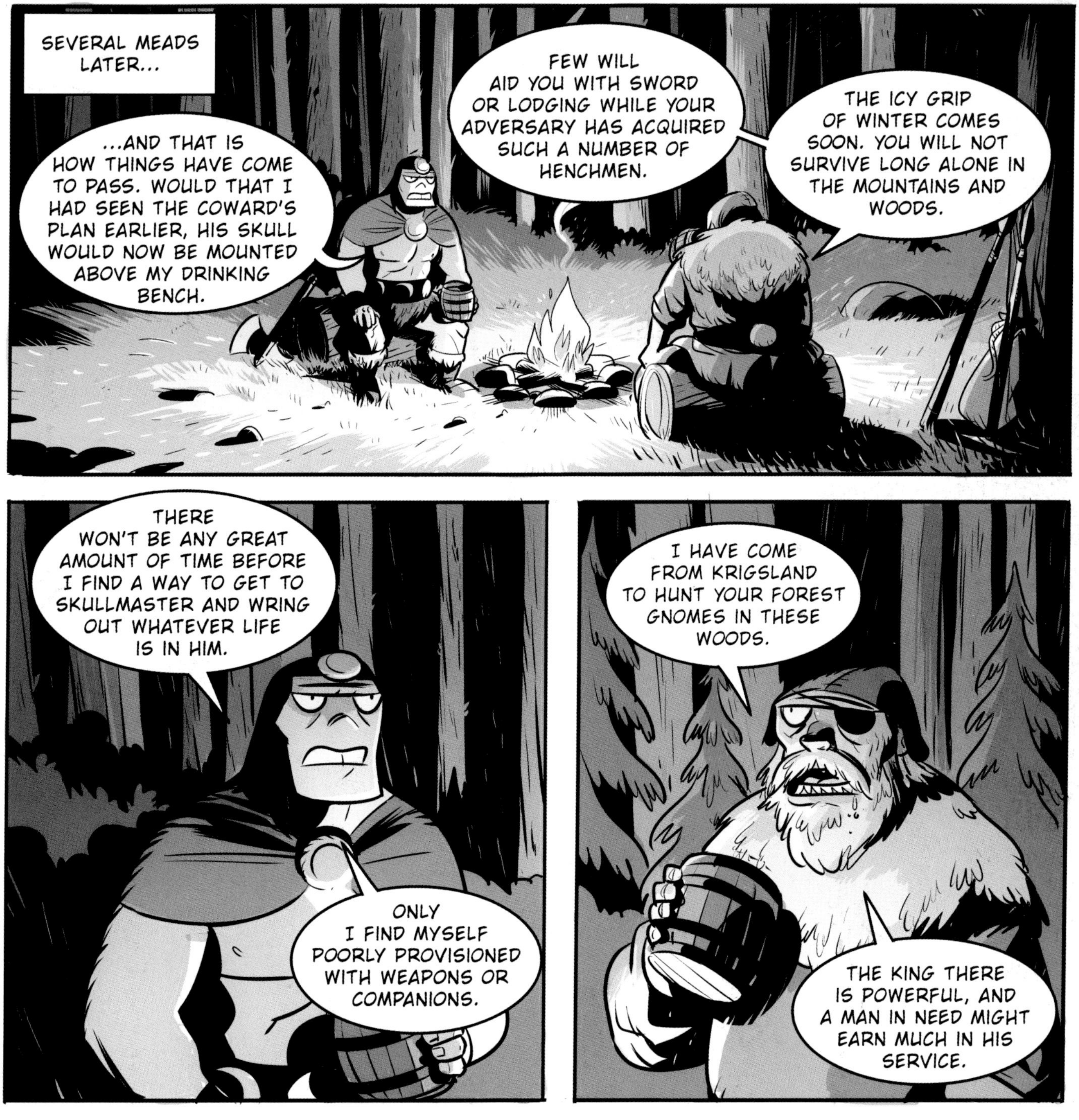
SEVERAL MEADS LATER...
...AND THAT IS HOW THINGS HAVE COME TO PASS. WOULD THAT I HAD SEEN THE COWARD'S PLAN EARLIER, HIS SKULL WOULD NOW BE MOUNTED ABOVE MY DRINKING BENCH.
FEW WILL AID YOU WITH SWORD OR LODGING WHILE YOUR ADVERSARY HAS ACQUIRED SUCH A NUMBER OF HENCHMEN.
THE ICY GRIP OF WINTER COMES SOON. YOU WILL NOT SURVIVE LONG ALONE IN THE MOUNTAINS AND WOODS.
THERE WON'T BE ANY GREAT AMOUNT OF TIME BEFORE I FIND A WAY TO GET TO SKULLMASTER AND WRING OUT WHATEVER LIFE IS IN HIM.
ONLY I FIND MYSELF POORLY PROVISIONED WITH WEAPONS OR COMPANIONS.
I HAVE COME FROM KRIGSLAND TO HUNT YOUR FOREST GNOMES IN THESE WOODS.
THE KING THERE IS POWERFUL, AND A MAN IN NEED MIGHT EARN MUCH IN HIS SERVICE.

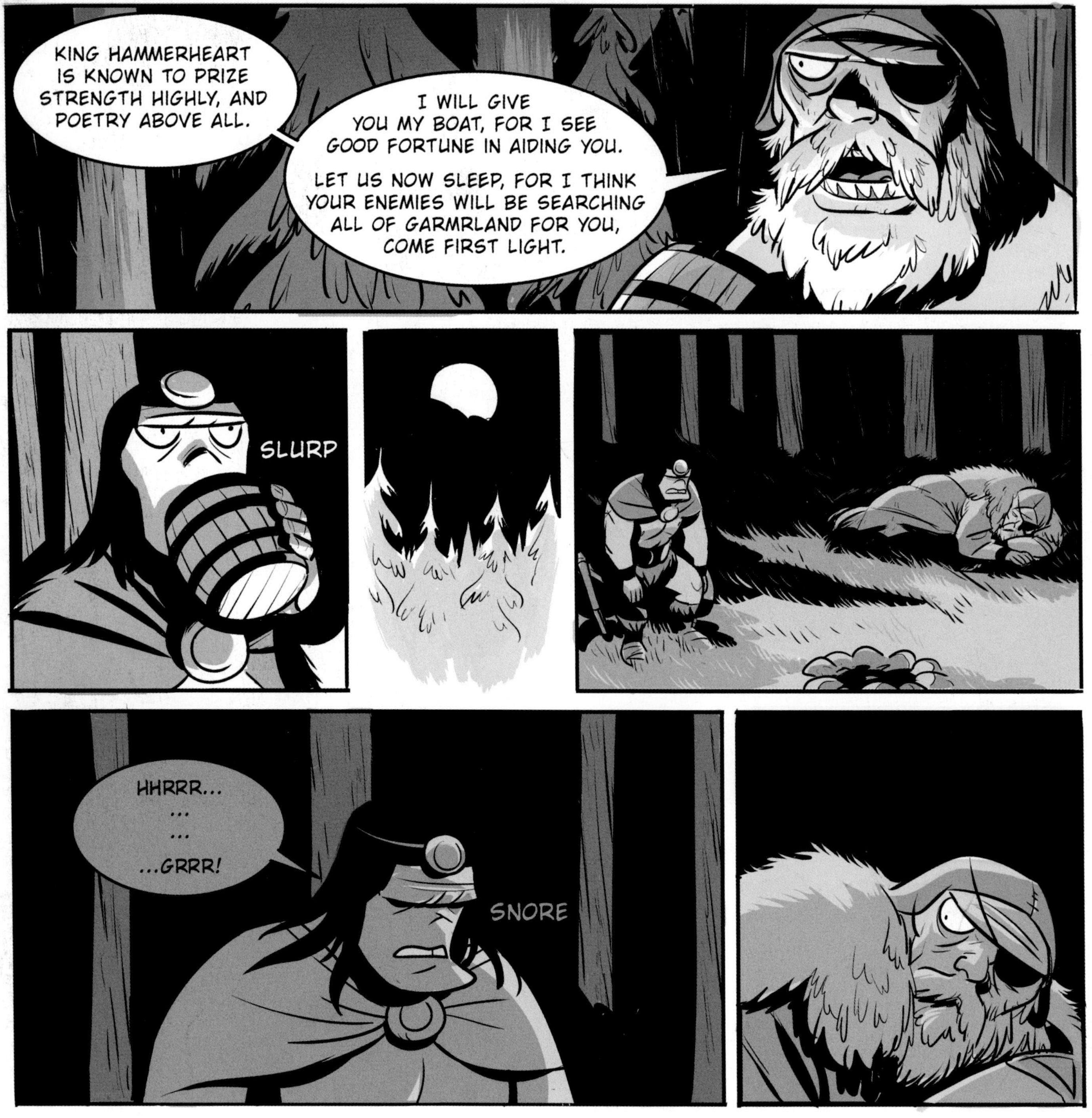
KING HAMMERHEART IS KNOWN TO PRIZE STRENGTH HIGHLY, AND POETRY ABOVE ALL.
I WILL GIVE YOU MY BOAT, FOR I SEE GOOD FORTUNE IN AIDING YOU.
LET US NOW SLEEP, FOR I THINK YOUR ENEMIES WILL BE SEARCHING ALL OF GARMRLAND FOR YOU, COME FIRST LIGHT.
SLURP
HHRRR... ... ...GRRR!
SNORE

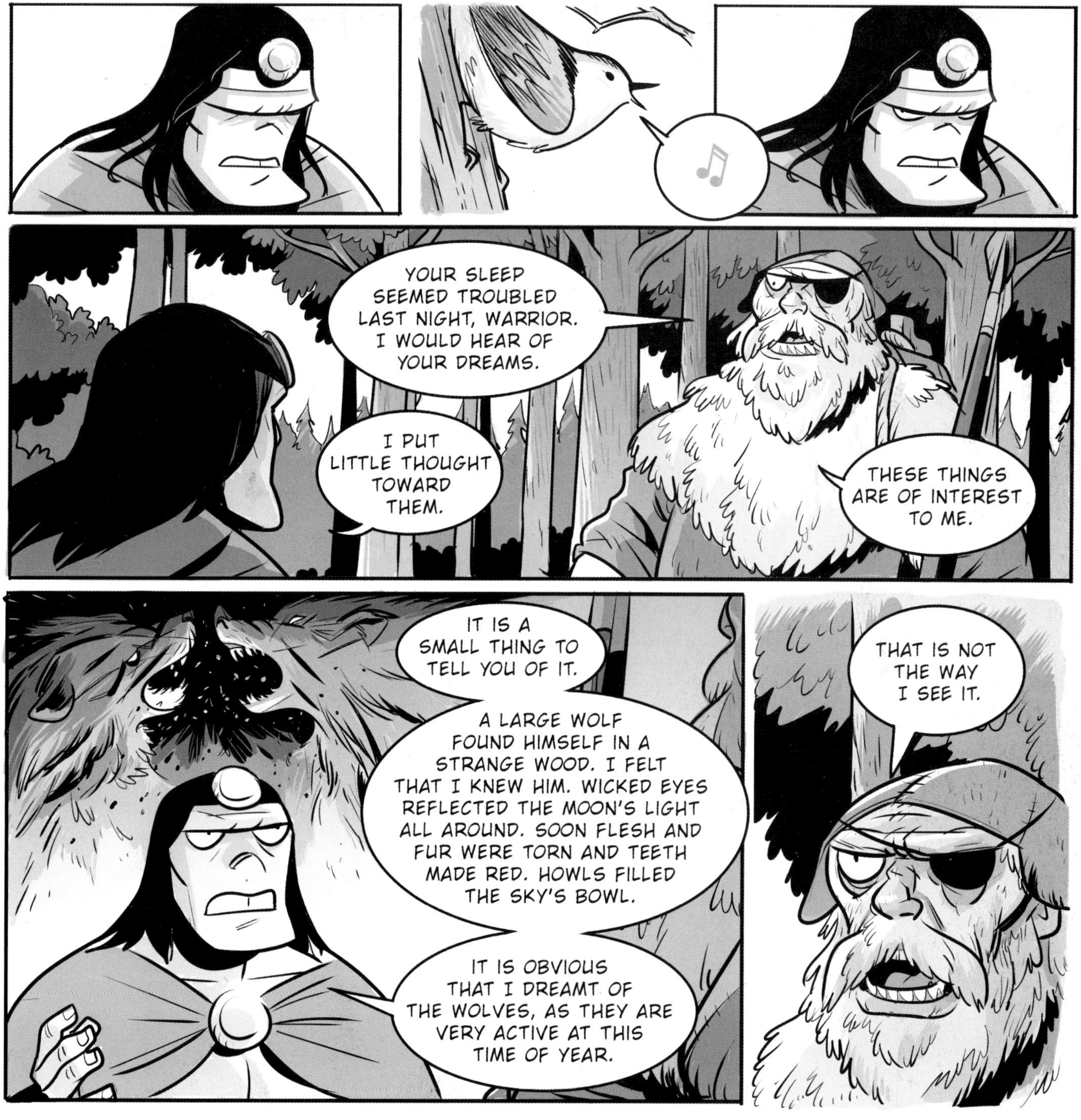
♪
YOUR SLEEP SEEMED TROUBLED LAST NIGHT, WARRIOR. I WOULD HEAR OF YOUR DREAMS.
I PUT LITTLE THOUGHT TOWARD THEM.
THESE THINGS ARE OF INTEREST TO ME.
IT IS A SMALL THING TO TELL YOU OF IT.
A LARGE WOLF FOUND HIMSELF IN A STRANGE WOOD. I FELT THAT I KNEW HIM. WICKED EYES REFLECTED THE MOON'S LIGHT ALL AROUND. SOON FLESH AND FUR WERE TORN AND TEETH MADE RED. HOWLS FILLED THE SKY'S BOWL.
IT IS OBVIOUS THAT I DREAMT OF THE WOLVES, AS THEY ARE VERY ACTIVE AT THIS TIME OF YEAR.
THAT IS NOT THE WAY I SEE IT.

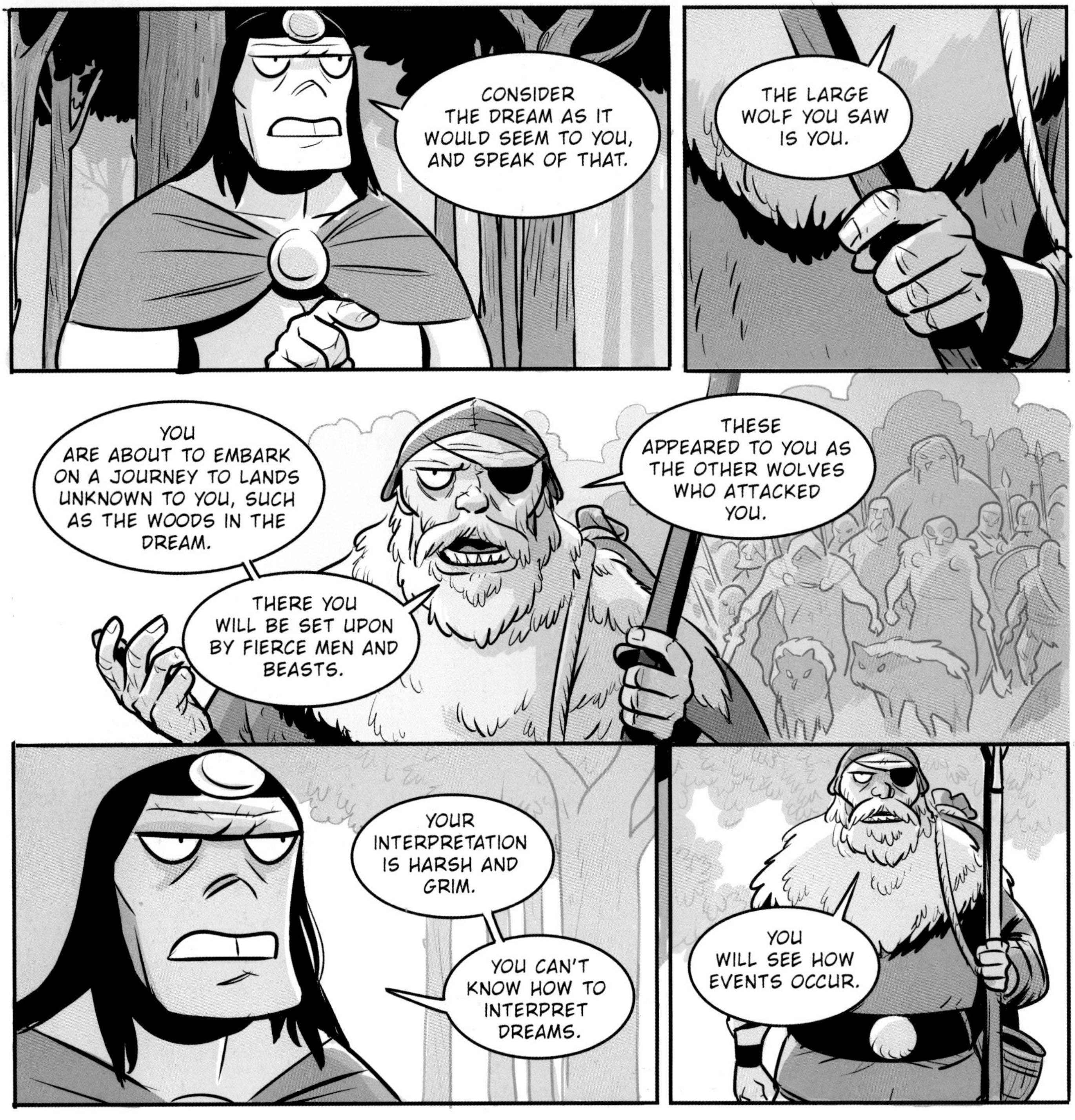
CONSIDER THE DREAM AS IT WOULD SEEM TO YOU, AND SPEAK OF THAT.
THE LARGE WOLF YOU SAW IS YOU.
YOU ARE ABOUT TO EMBARK ON A JOURNEY TO LANDS UNKNOWN TO YOU, SUCH AS THE WOODS IN THE DREAM.
THERE YOU WILL BE SET UPON BY FIERCE MEN AND BEASTS.
THESE APPEARED TO YOU AS THE OTHER WOLVES WHO ATTACKED YOU.
YOUR INTERPRETATION IS HARSH AND GRIM.
YOU CAN'T KNOW HOW TO INTERPRET DREAMS.
YOU WILL SEE HOW EVENTS OCCUR.

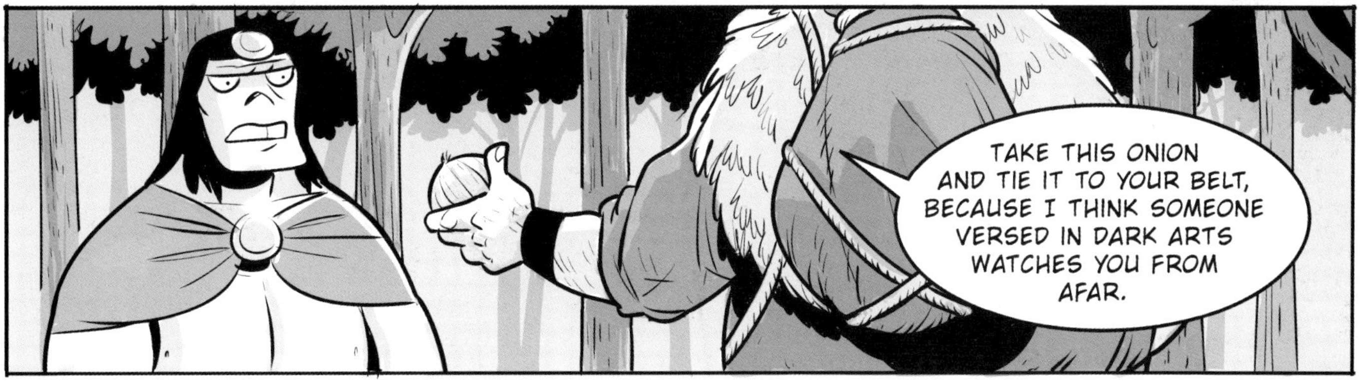
TAKE THIS ONION AND TIE IT TO YOUR BELT, BECAUSE I THINK SOMEONE VERSED IN DARK ARTS WATCHES YOU FROM AFAR.

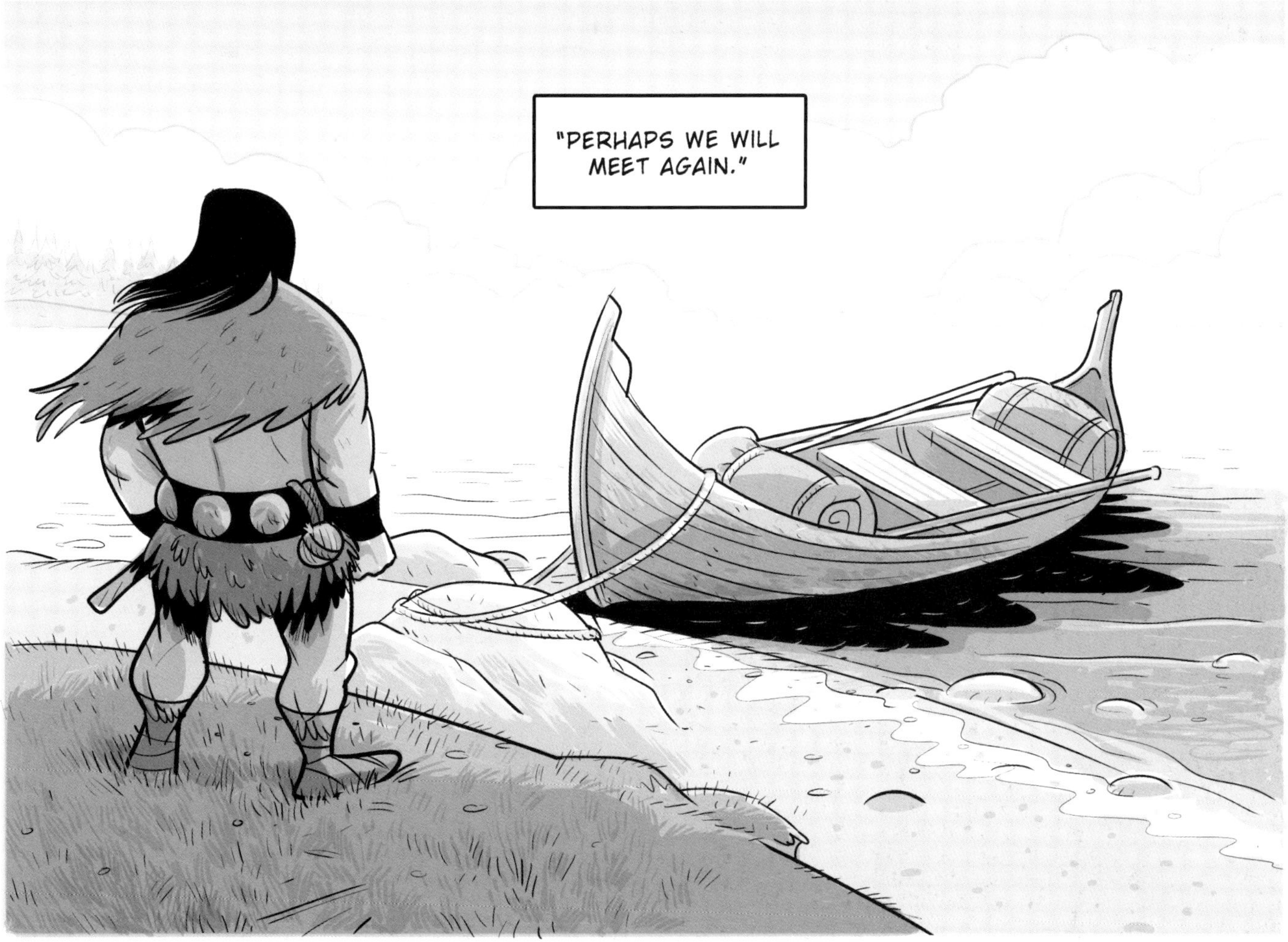
"PERHAPS WE WILL MEET AGAIN."

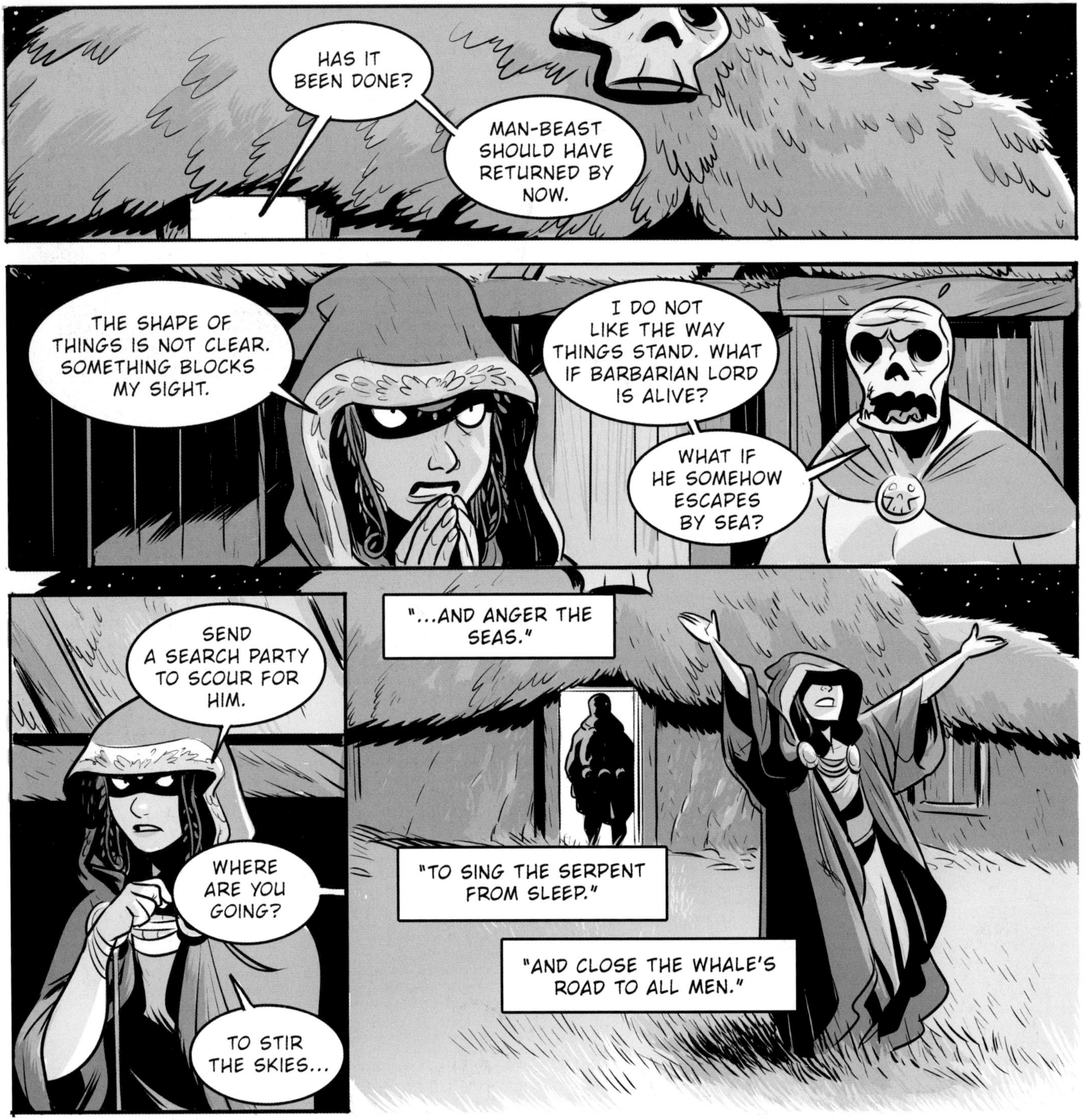
HAS IT BEEN DONE?
MAN-BEAST SHOULD HAVE RETURNED BY NOW.
THE SHAPE OF THINGS IS NOT CLEAR. SOMETHING BLOCKS MY SIGHT.
I DO NOT LIKE THE WAY THINGS STAND. WHAT IF BARBARIAN LORD IS ALIVE?
WHAT IF HE SOMEHOW ESCAPES BY SEA?
SEND A SEARCH PARTY TO SCOUR FOR HIM.
WHERE ARE YOU GOING?
TO STIR THE SKIES...
"...AND ANGER THE SEAS."
"TO SING THE SERPENT FROM SLEEP."
"AND CLOSE THE WHALE'S ROAD TO ALL MEN."

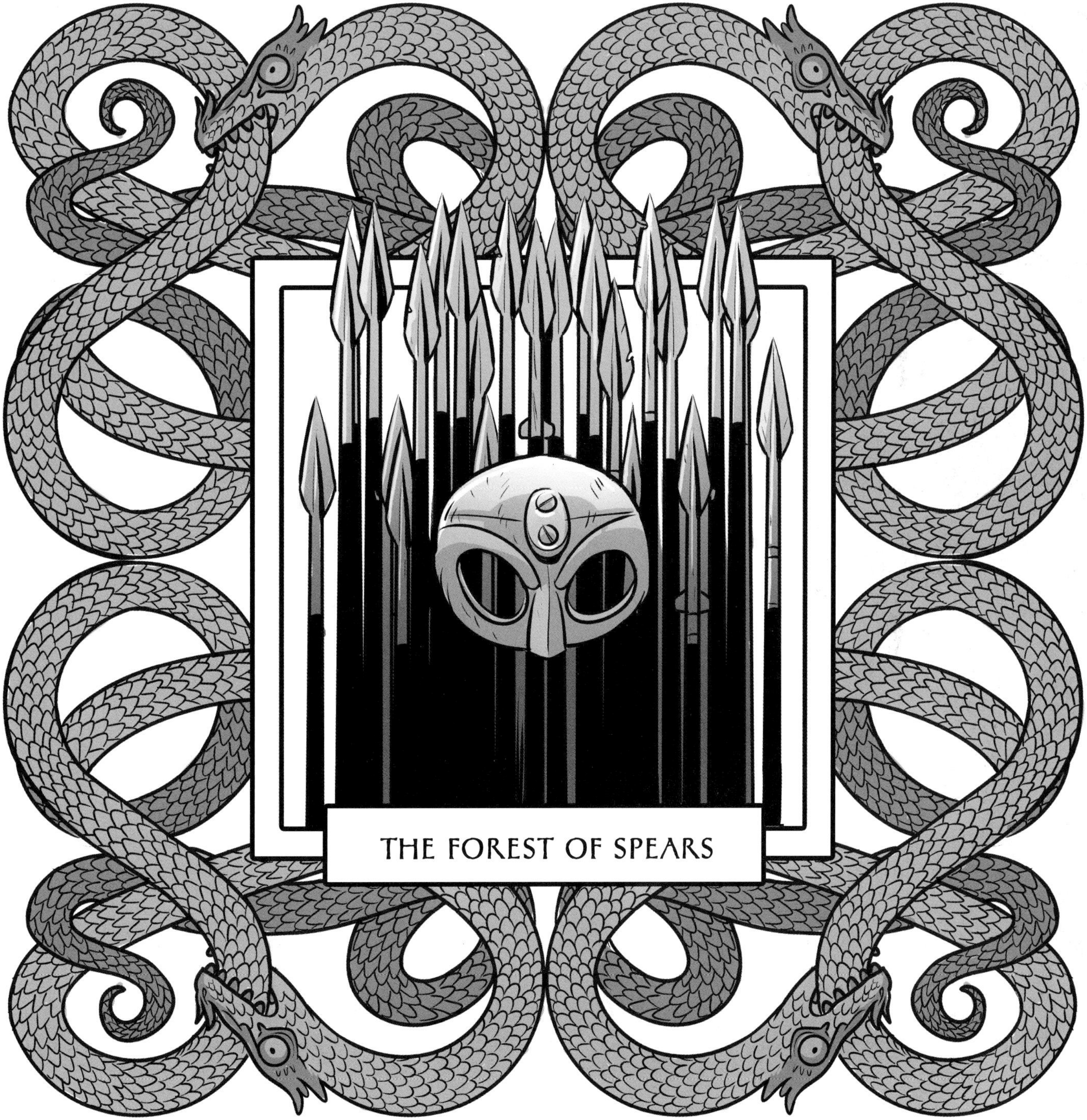
THE FOREST OF SPEARS

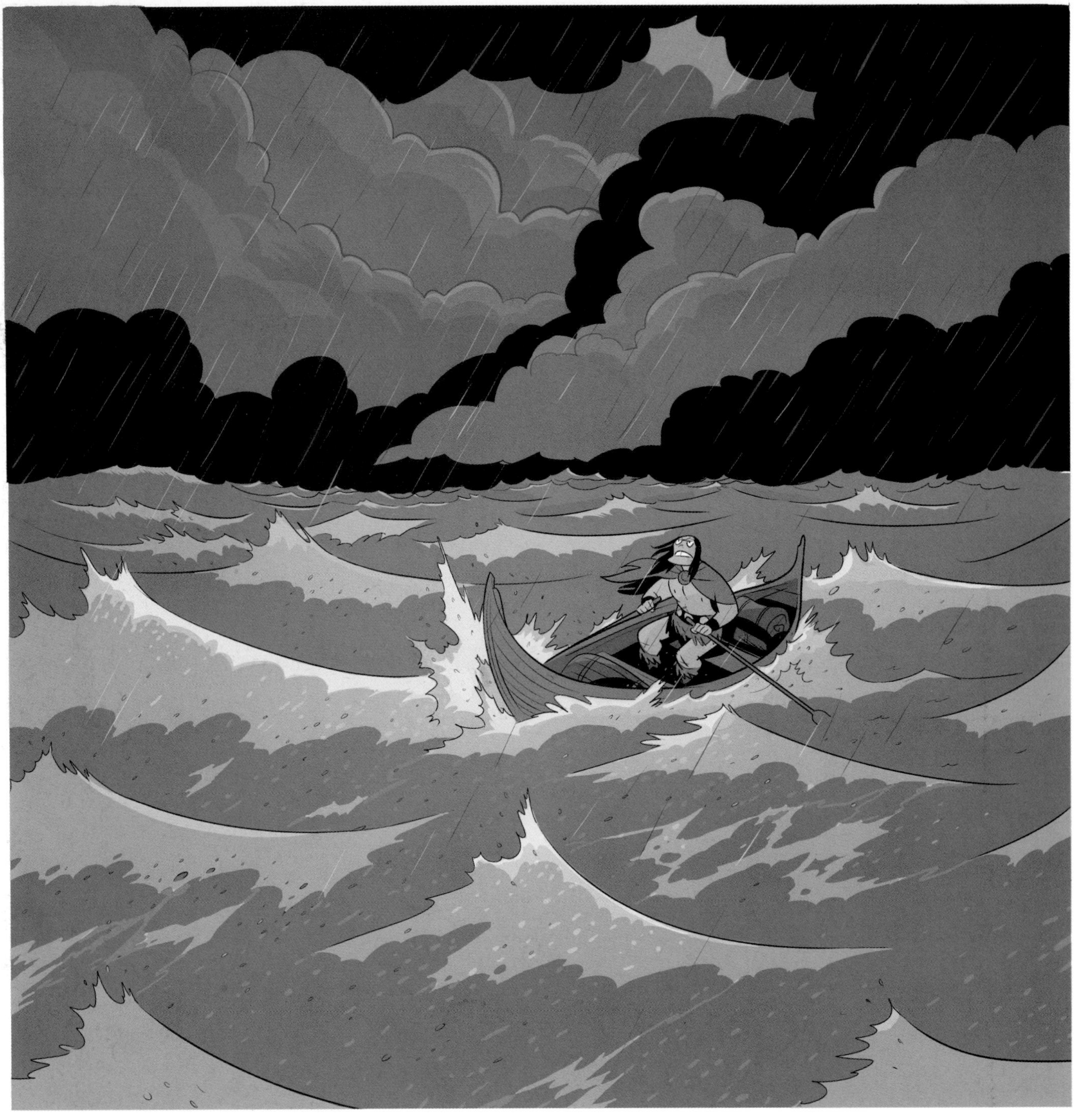

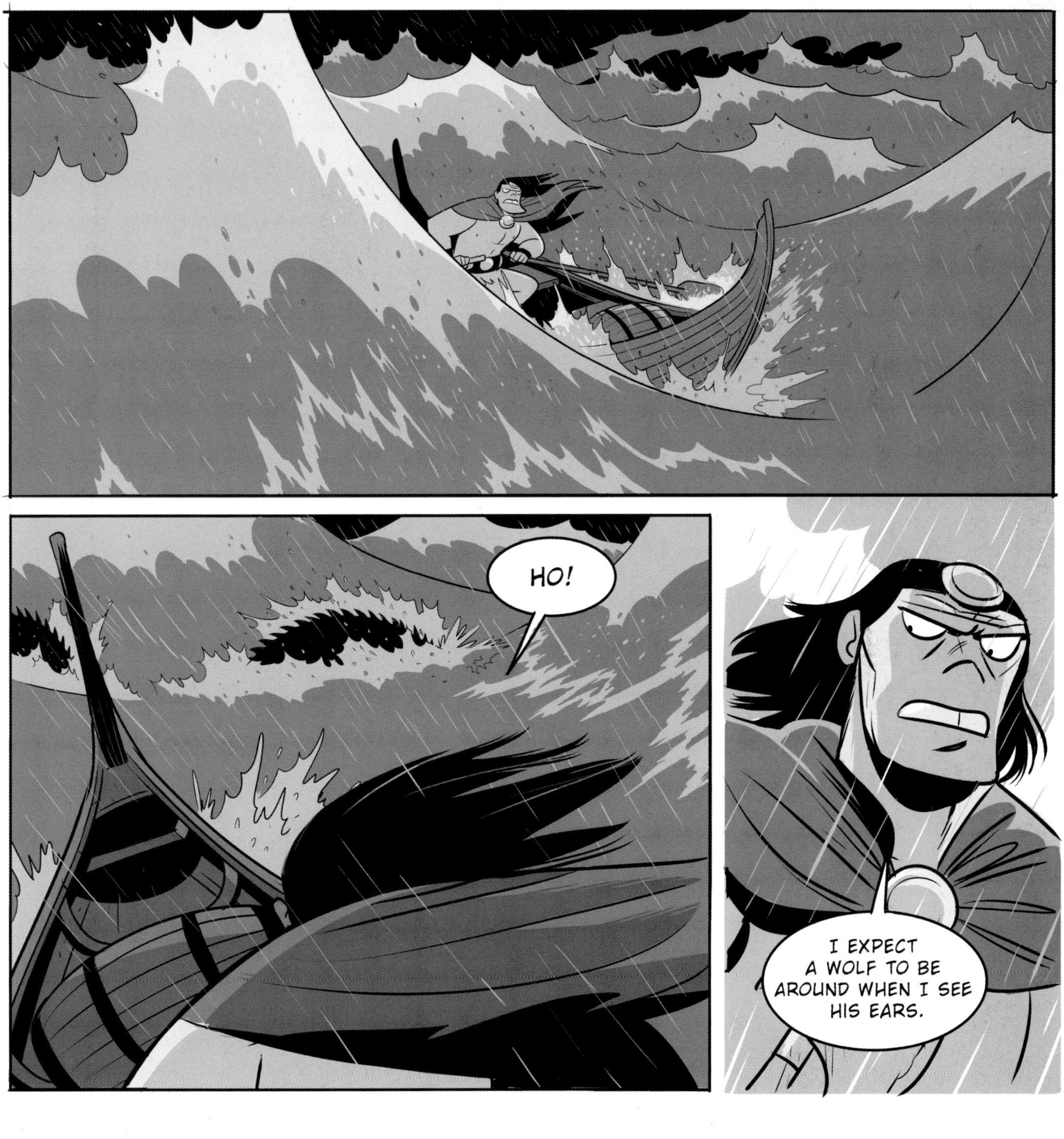
HO!
I EXPECT A WOLF TO BE AROUND WHEN I SEE HIS EARS.

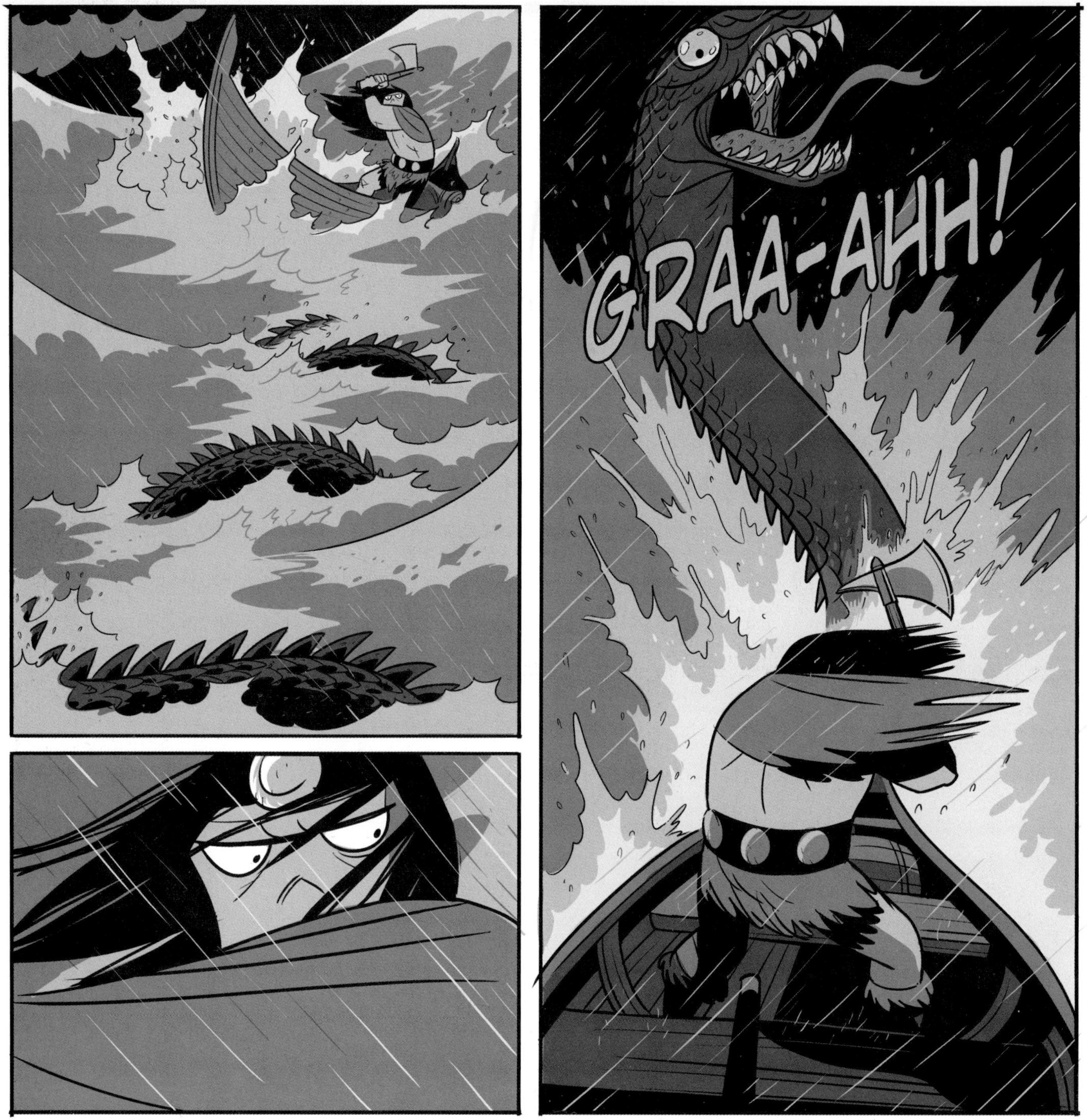
GRAA-AHH!

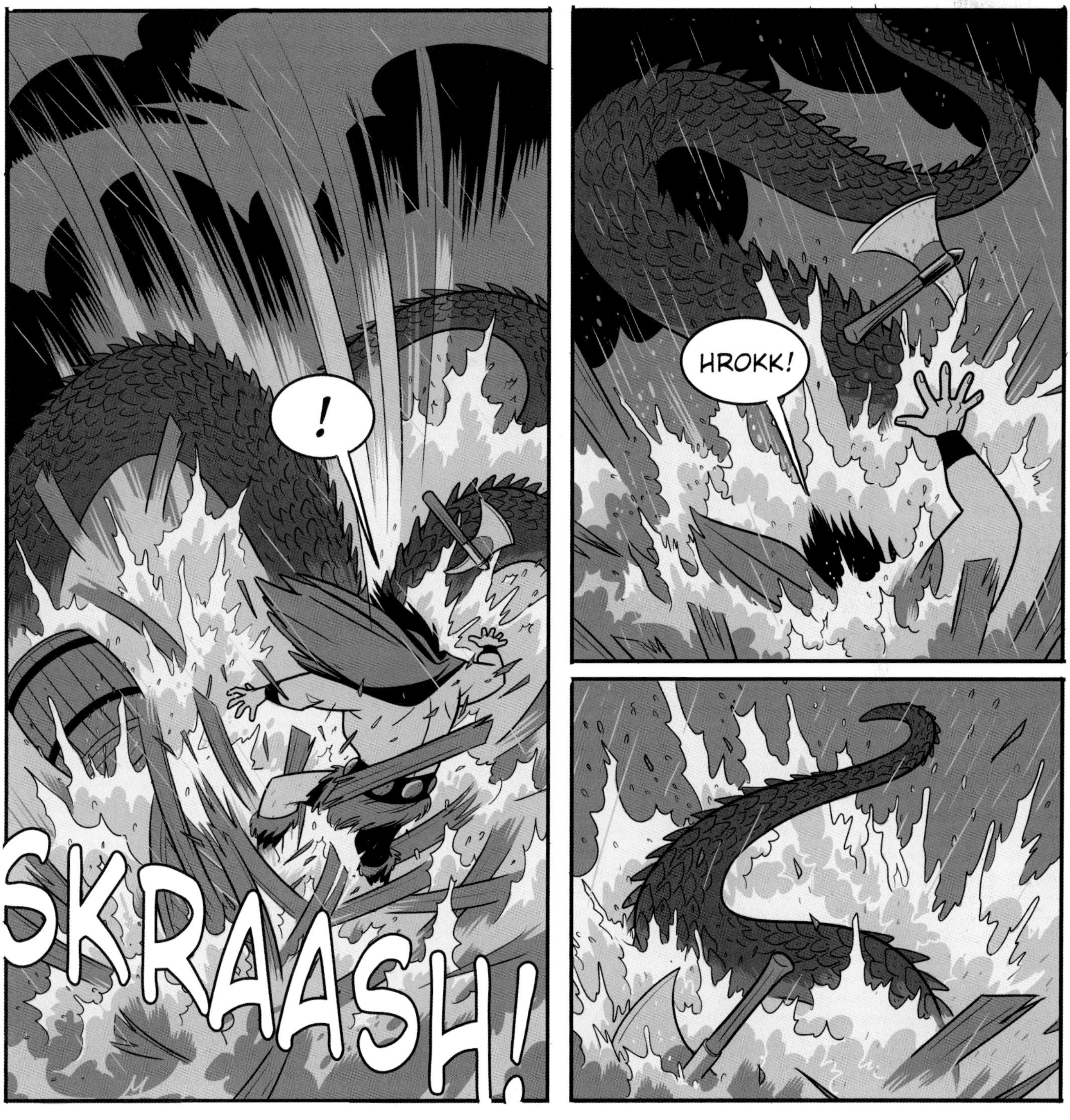
!
SKRAASH!
HROKK!

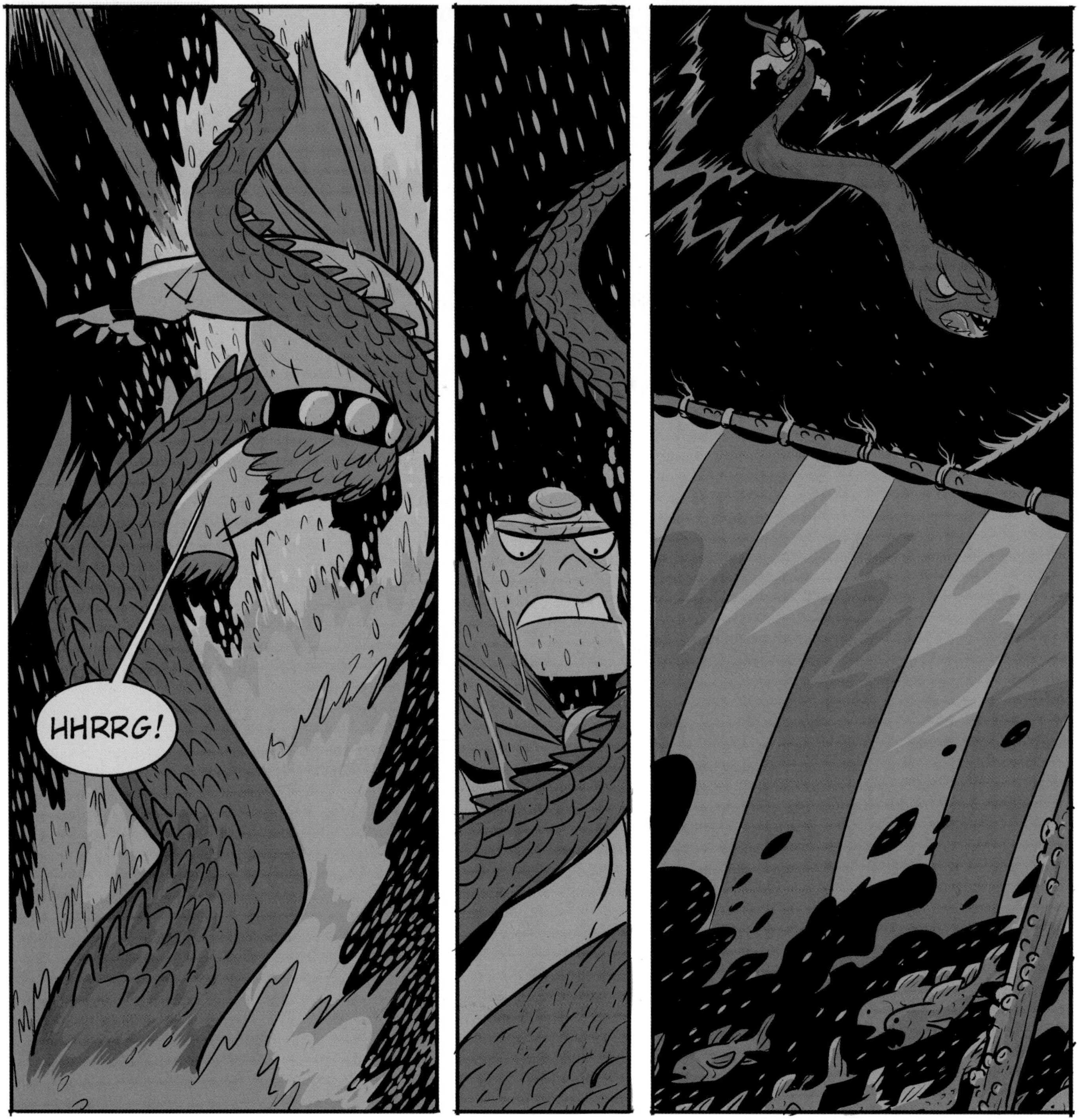
HHRRG!

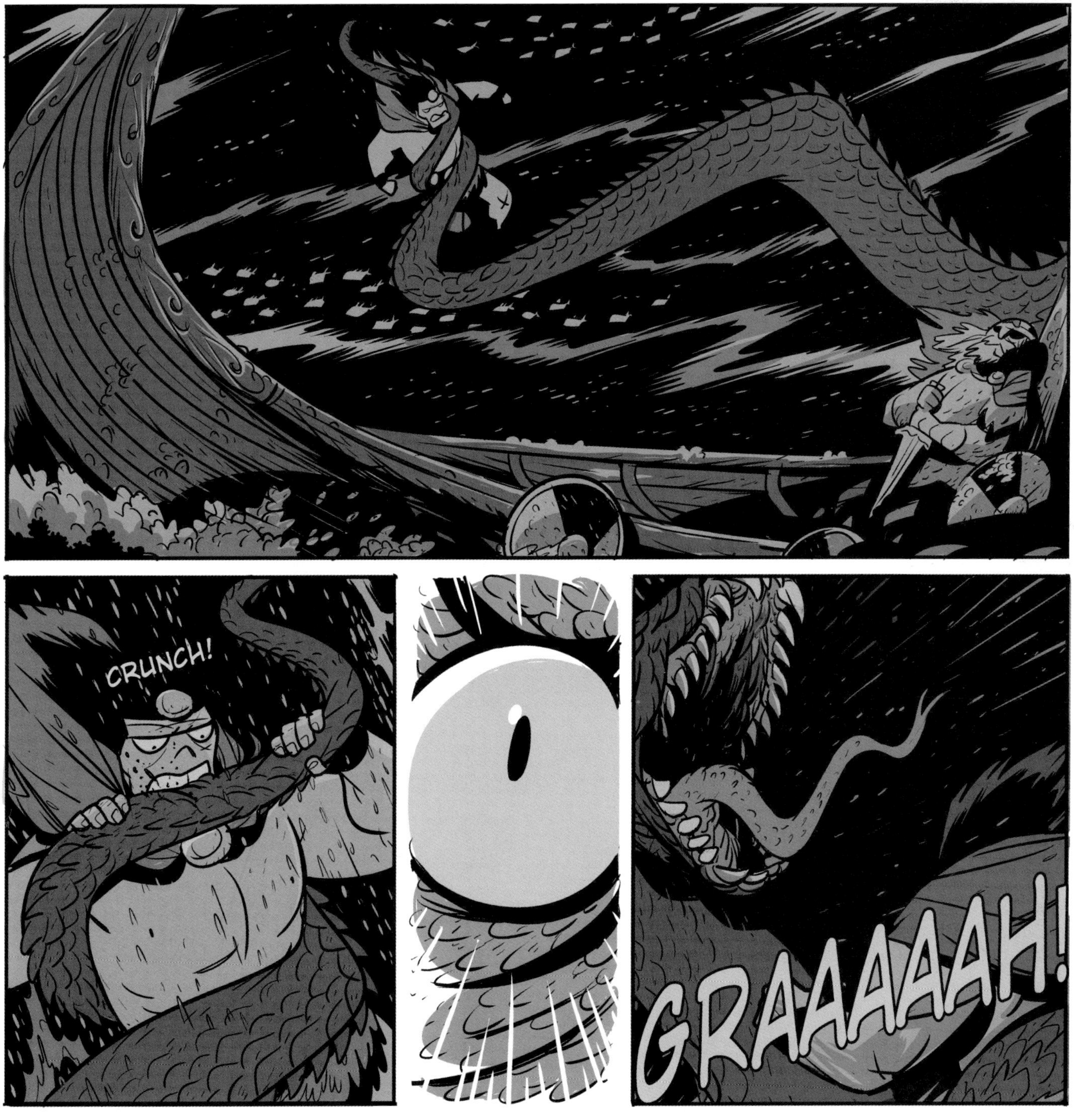
CRUNCH!
GRAAAAAH!

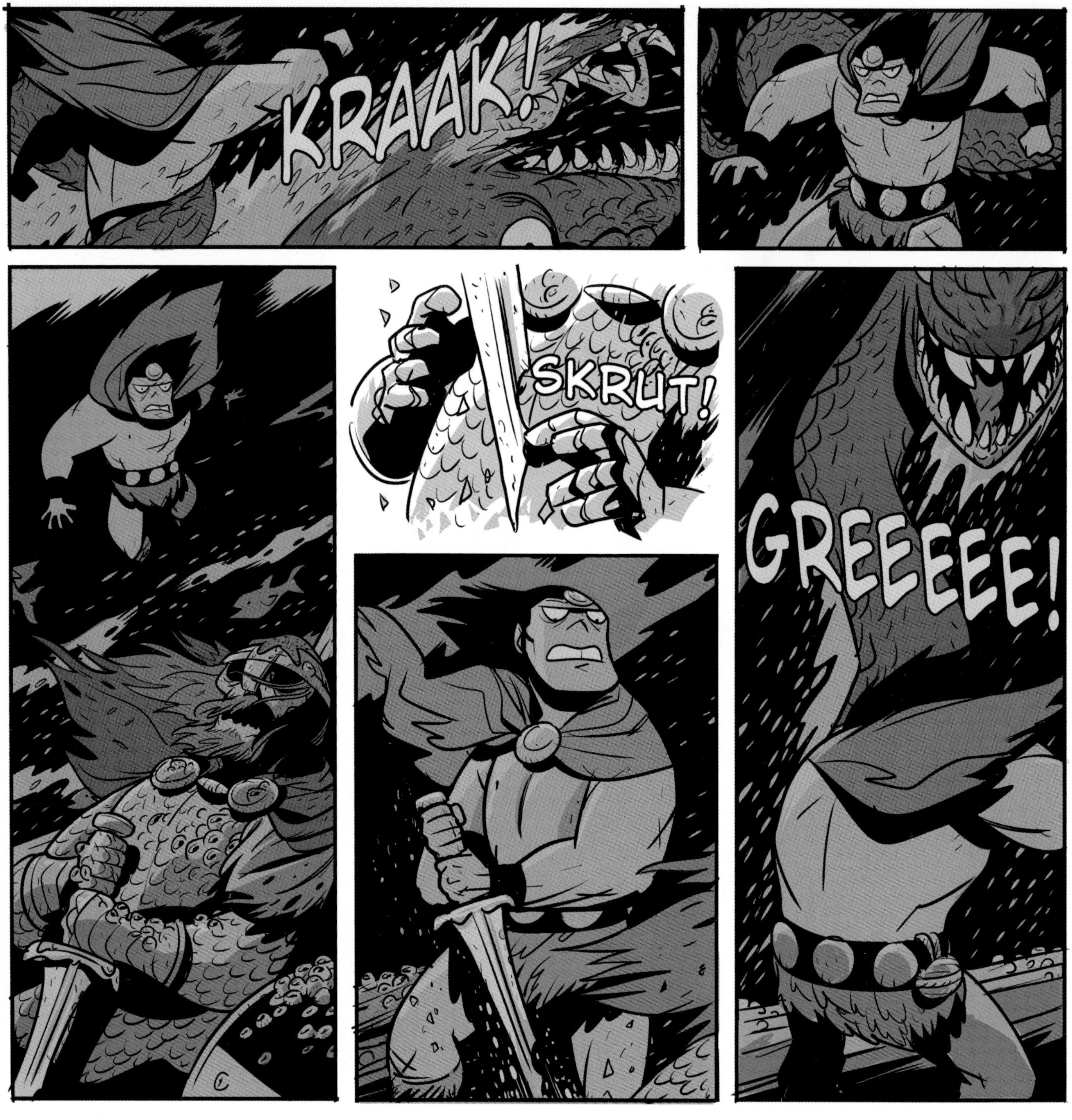
KRAAK!
SKRUT!
GREEEEEE!

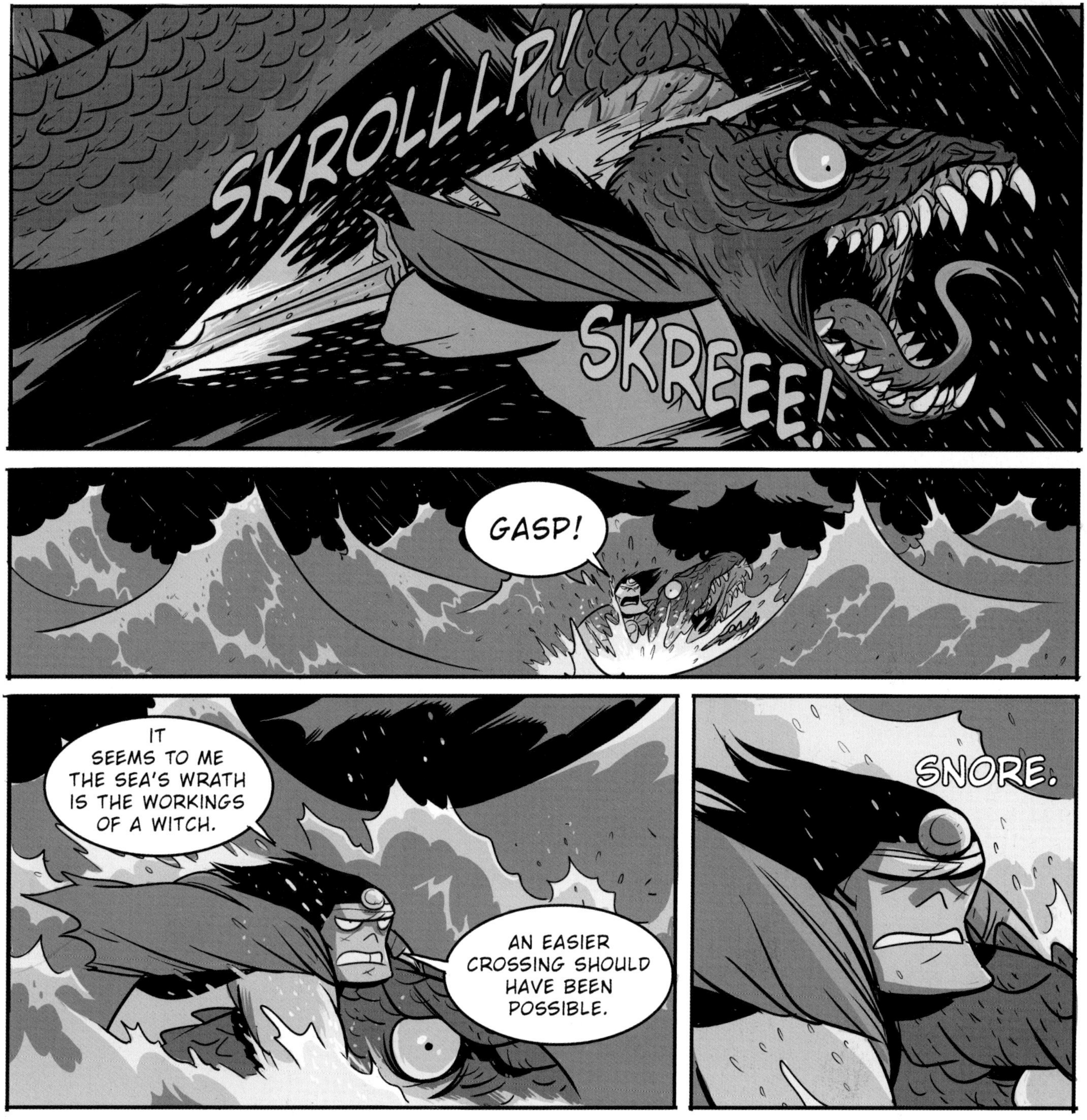
SKROLLLP!
SKREEE!
GASP!
IT SEEMS TO ME THE SEA'S WRATH IS THE WORKINGS OF A WITCH.
AN EASIER CROSSING SHOULD HAVE BEEN POSSIBLE.
SNORE.

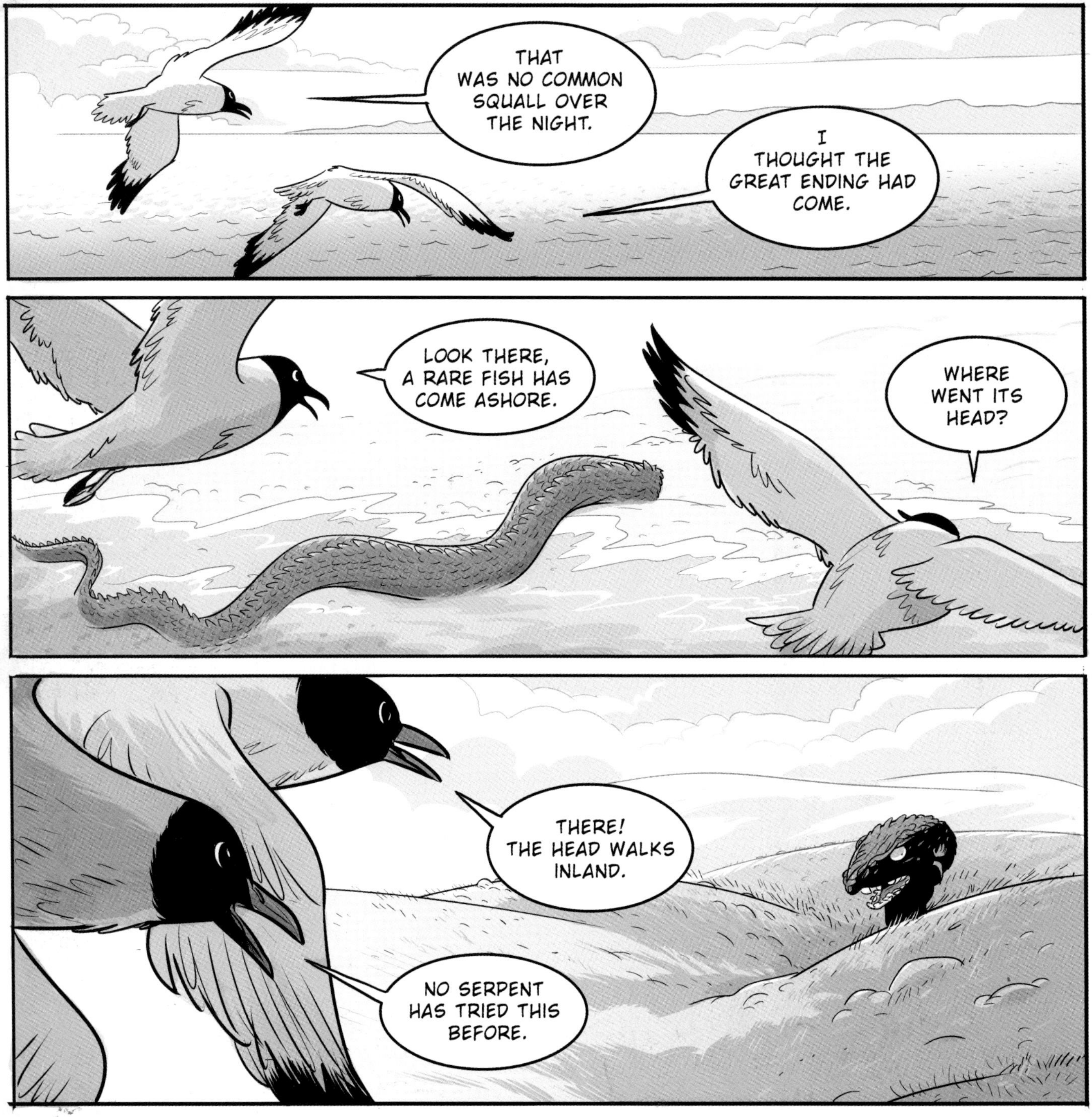
THAT WAS NO COMMON SQUALL OVER THE NIGHT.
I THOUGHT THE GREAT ENDING HAD COME.
LOOK THERE, A RARE FISH HAS COME ASHORE.
WHERE WENT ITS HEAD?
THERE! THE HEAD WALKS INLAND.
NO SERPENT HAS TRIED THIS BEFORE.

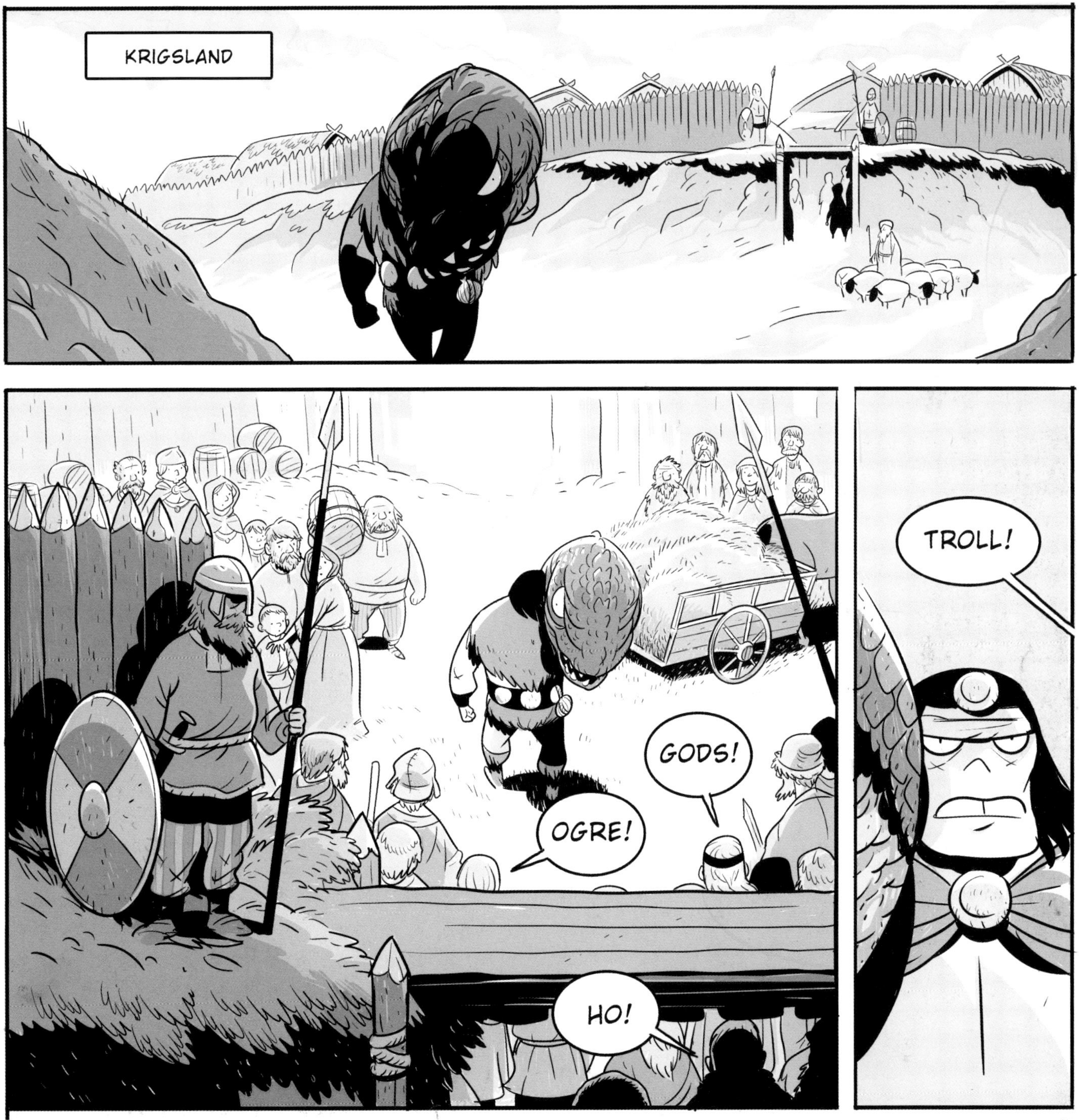
KRIGSLAND
OGRE!
GODS!
HO!
TROLL!

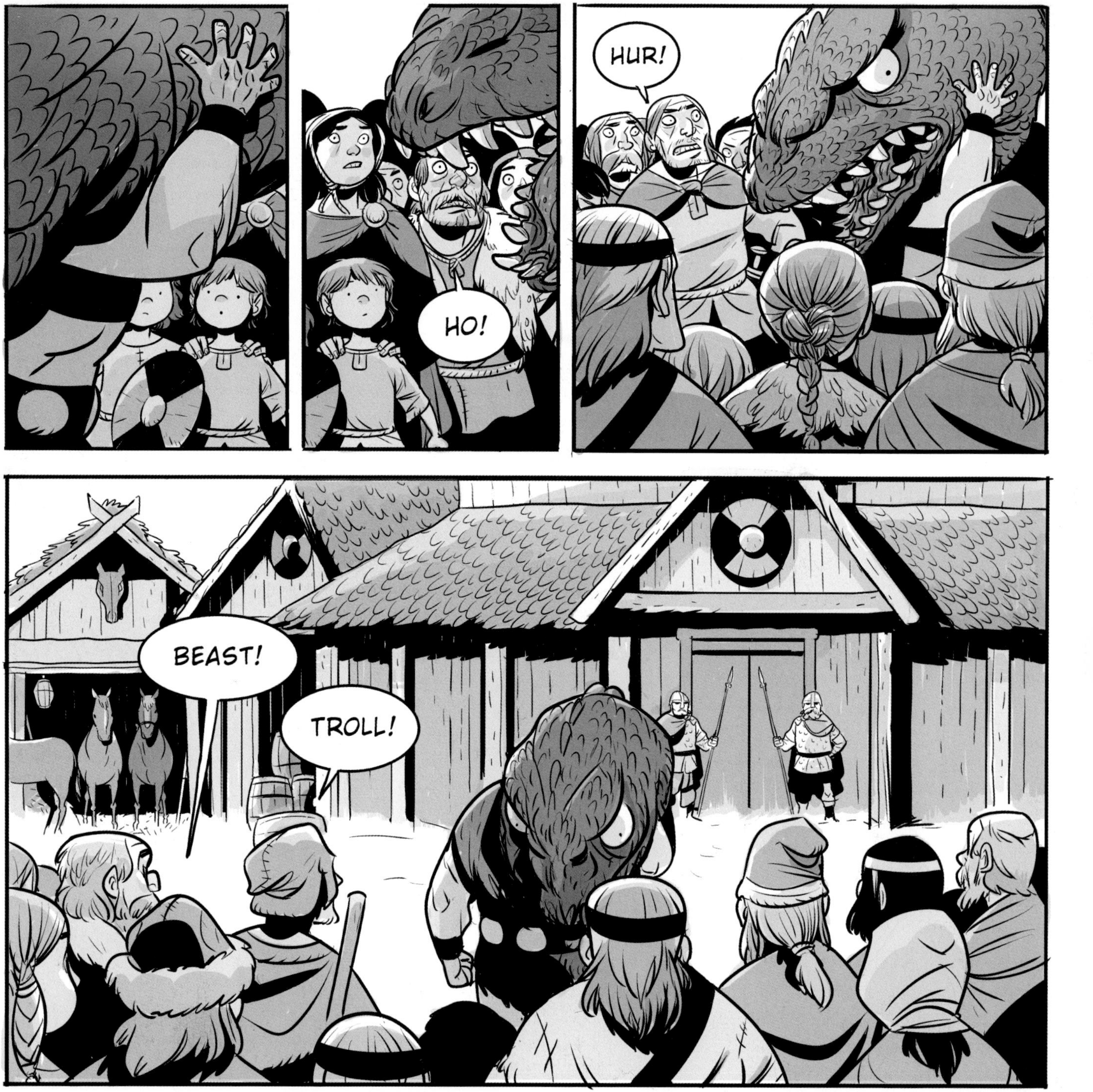
HO!
HUR!
BEAST!
TROLL!

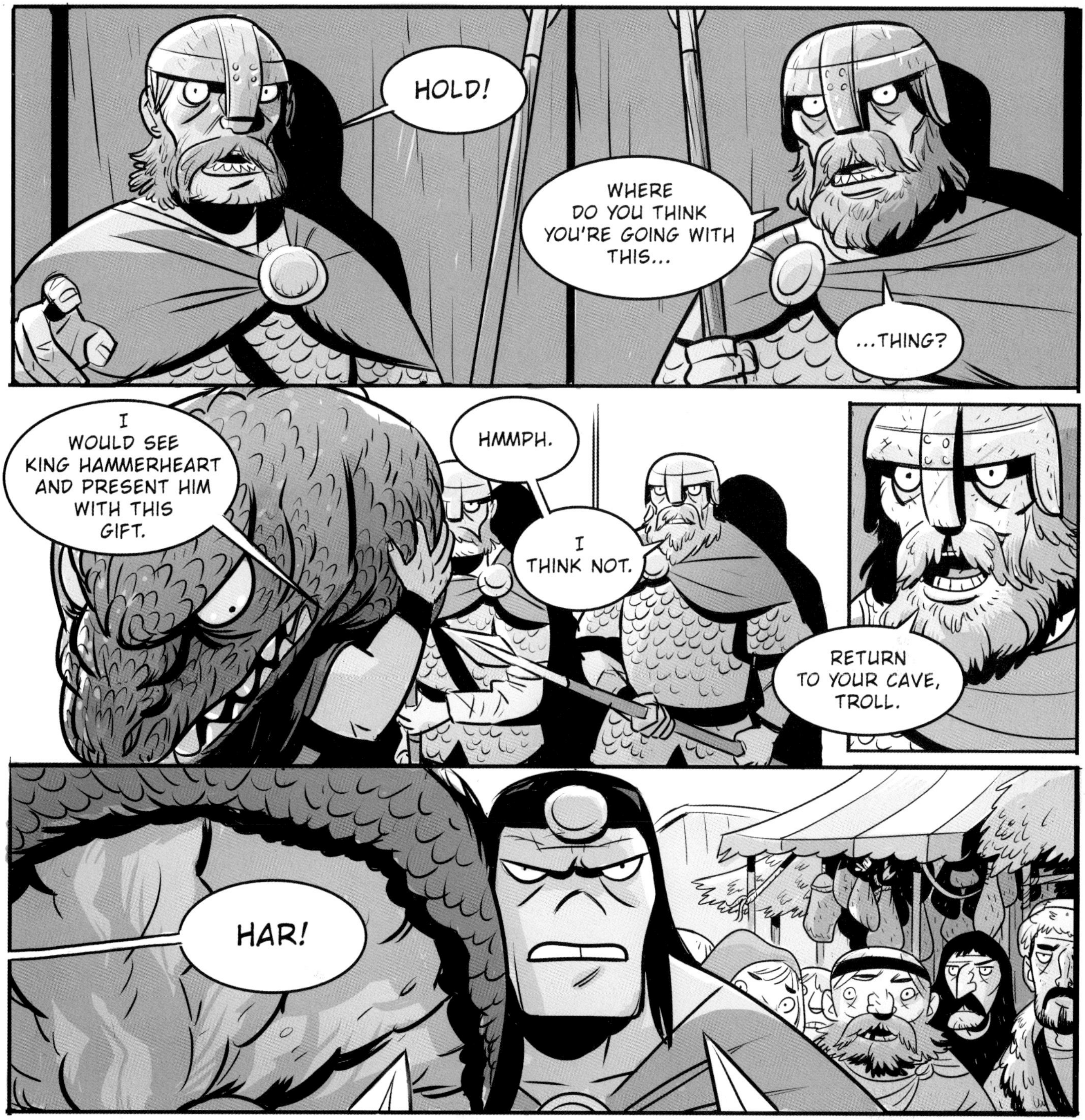
HOLD!
WHERE DO YOU THINK YOU'RE GOING WITH THIS...
...THING?
I WOULD SEE KING HAMMERHEART AND PRESENT HIM WITH THIS GIFT.
HMMPH.
I THINK NOT.
RETURN TO YOUR CAVE, TROLL.
HAR!

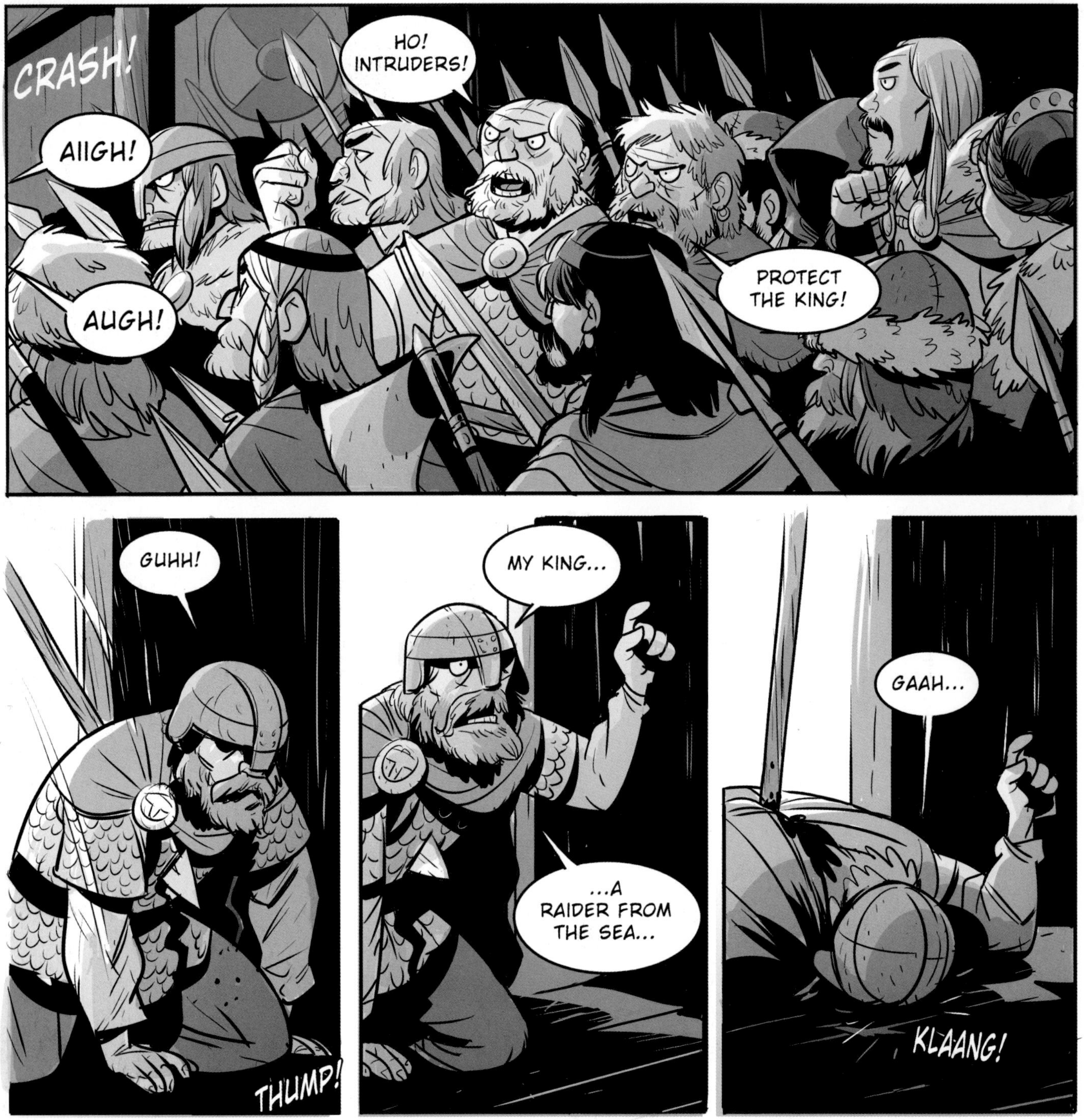
CRASH!
HO! INTRUDERS!
AIIGH!
AUGH!
PROTECT THE KING!
GUHH!
THUMP!
MY KING...
...A RAIDER FROM THE SEA...
GAAH...
KLAANG!

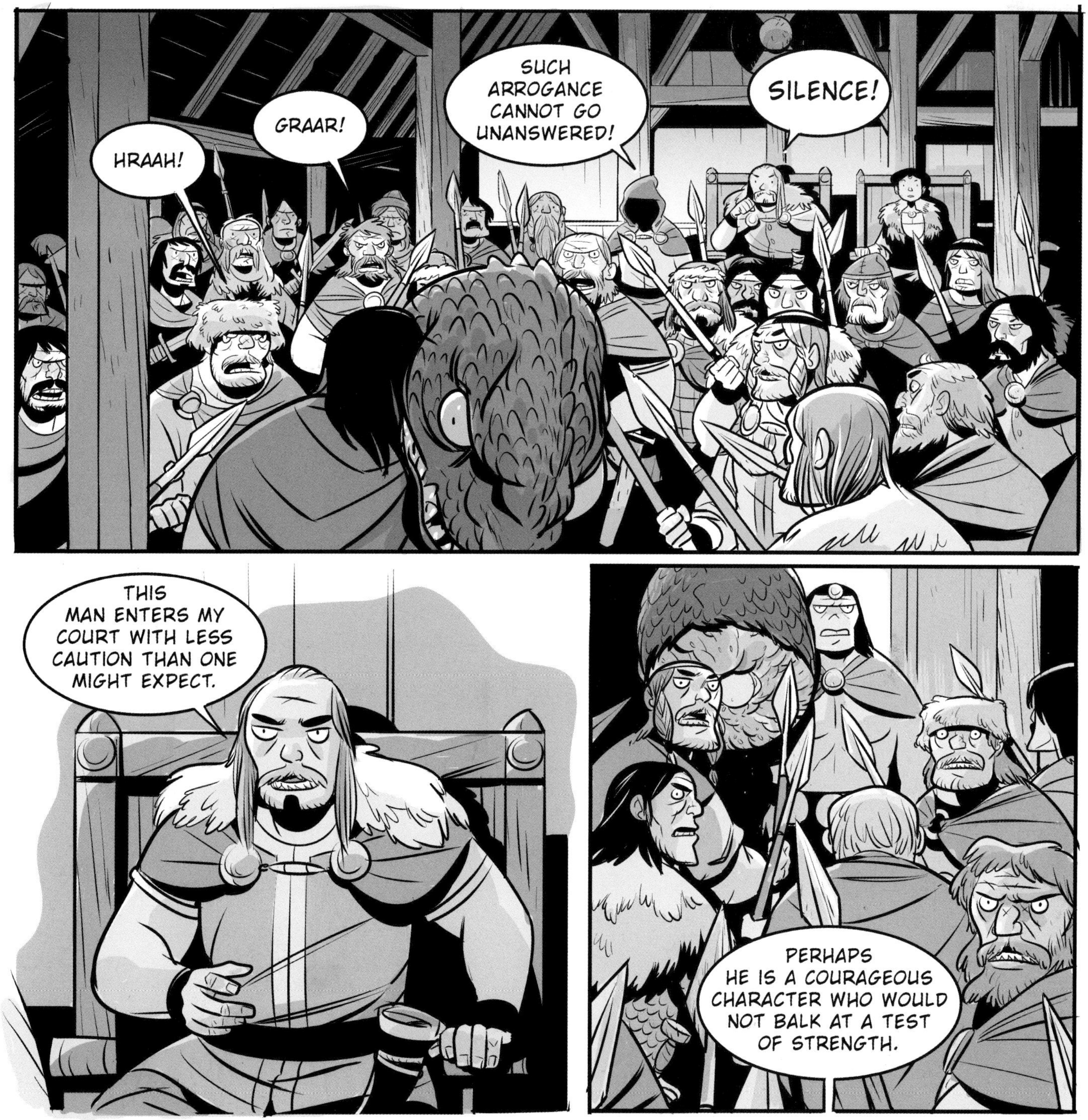
HRAAH!
GRAAR!
SUCH ARROGANCE CANNOT GO UNANSWERED!
SILENCE!
THIS MAN ENTERS MY COURT WITH LESS CAUTION THAN ONE MIGHT EXPECT.
PERHAPS HE IS A COURAGEOUS CHARACTER WHO WOULD NOT BALK AT A TEST OF STRENGTH.

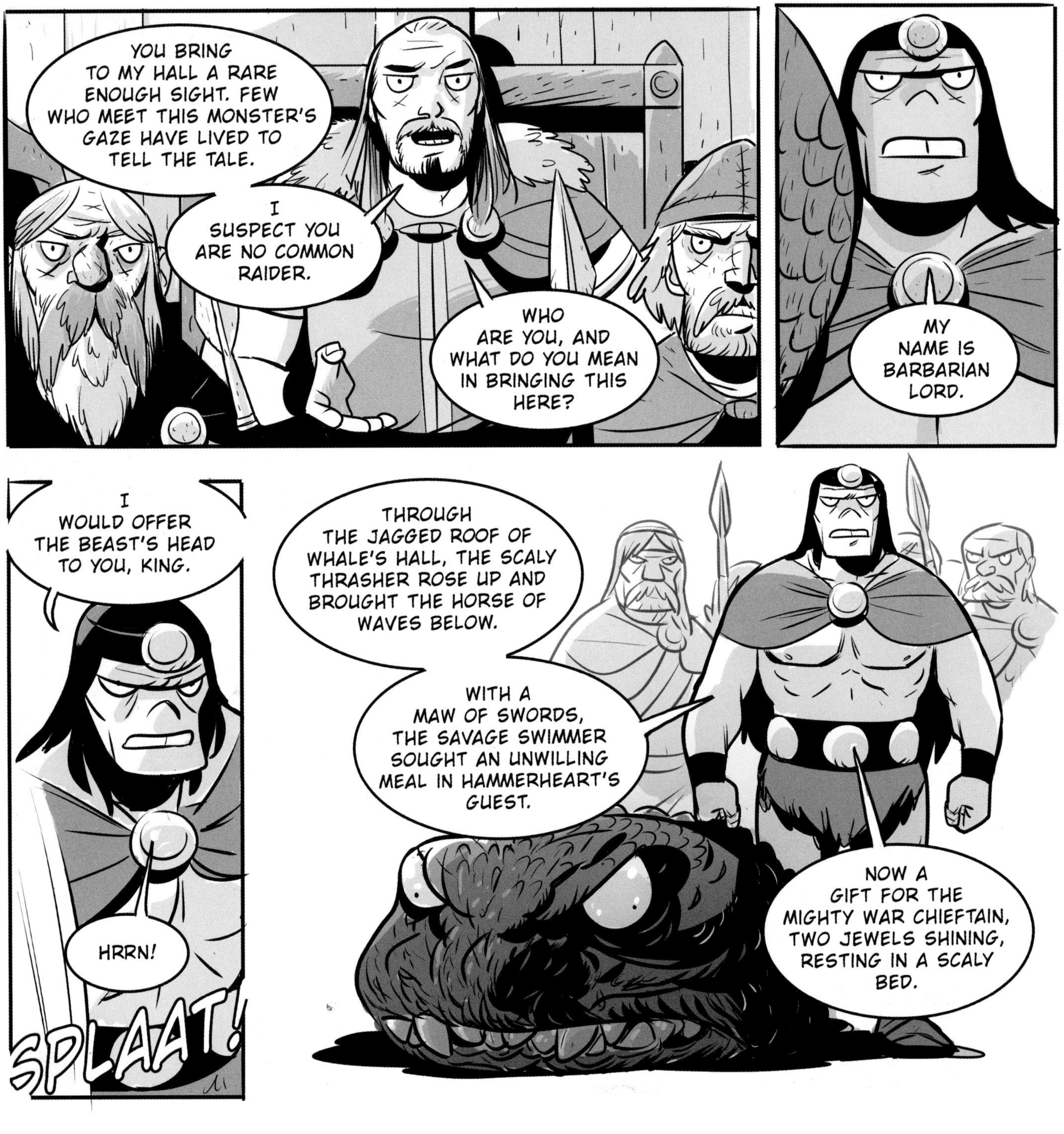
YOU BRING TO MY HALL A RARE ENOUGH SIGHT. FEW WHO MEET THIS MONSTER'S GAZE HAVE LIVED TO TELL THE TALE.
I SUSPECT YOU ARE NO COMMON RAIDER.
WHO ARE YOU, AND WHAT DO YOU MEAN IN BRINGING THIS HERE?
MY NAME IS BARBARIAN LORD.
I WOULD OFFER THE BEAST'S HEAD TO YOU, KING.
HRRN!
SPLAAT!
THROUGH THE JAGGED ROOF OF WHALE'S HALL, THE SCALY THRASHER ROSE UP AND BROUGHT THE HORSE OF WAVES BELOW.
WITH A MAW OF SWORDS, THE SAVAGE SWIMMER SOUGHT AN UNWILLING MEAL IN HAMMERHEART'S GUEST.
NOW A GIFT FOR THE MIGHTY WAR CHIEFTAIN, TWO JEWELS SHINING, RESTING IN A SCALY BED.

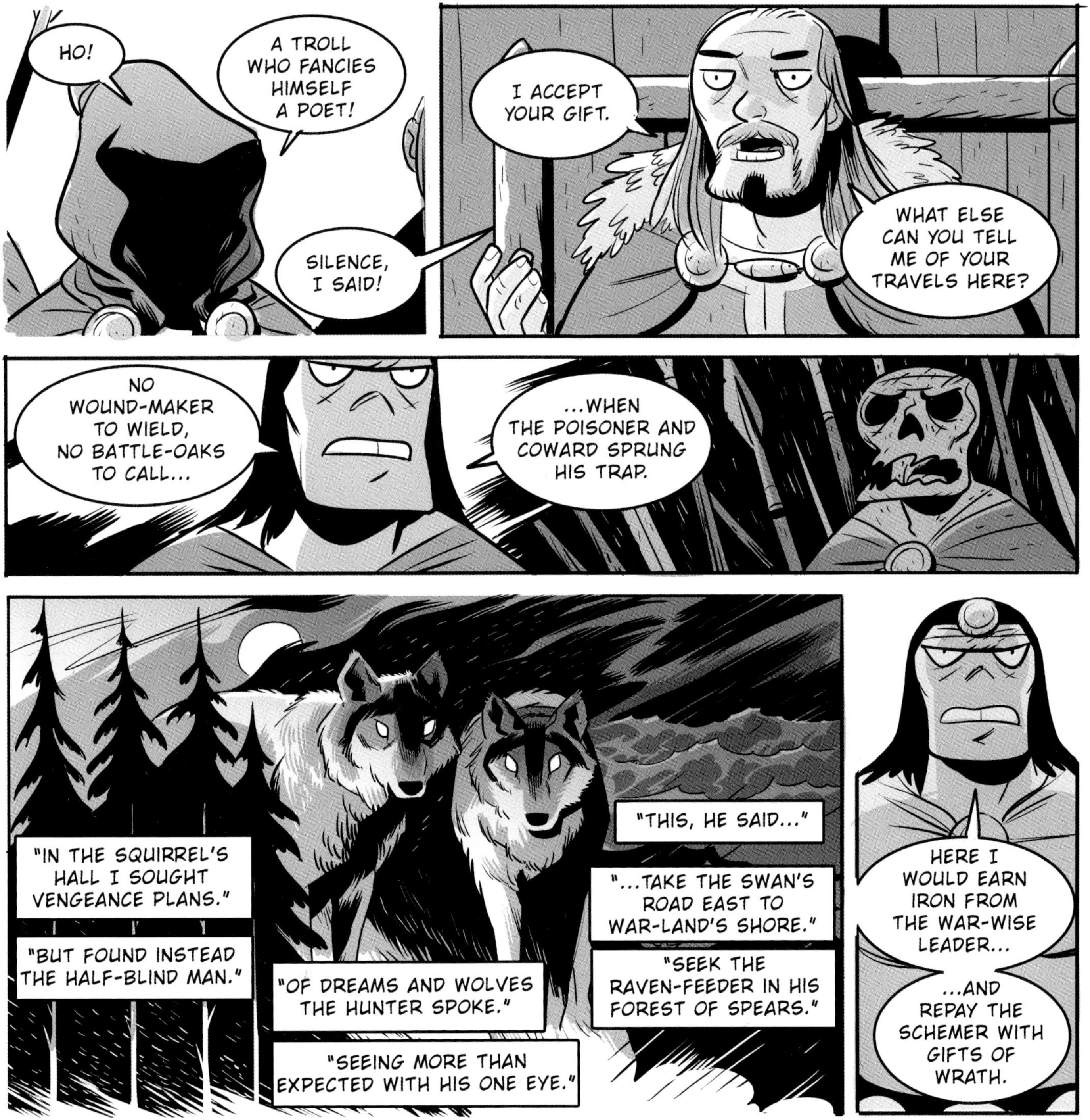
HO!
A TROLL WHO FANCIES HIMSELF A POET!
SILENCE, I SAID!
I ACCEPT YOUR GIFT.
WHAT ELSE CAN YOU TELL ME OF YOUR TRAVELS HERE?
NO WOUND-MAKER TO WIELD, NO BATTLE-OAKS TO CALL...
...WHEN THE POISONER AND COWARD SPRUNG HIS TRAP.
"IN THE SQUIRREL'S HALL I SOUGHT VENGEANCE PLANS."
"BUT FOUND INSTEAD THE HALF-BLIND MAN."
"OF DREAMS AND WOLVES THE HUNTER SPOKE."
"SEEING MORE THAN EXPECTED WITH HIS ONE EYE."
"THIS, HE SAID..."
"...TAKE THE SWAN'S ROAD EAST TO WAR-LAND'S SHORE."
"SEEK THE RAVEN-FEEDER IN HIS FOREST OF SPEARS."
HERE I WOULD EARN IRON FROM THE WAR-WISE LEADER...
...AND REPAY THE SCHEMER WITH GIFTS OF WRATH.

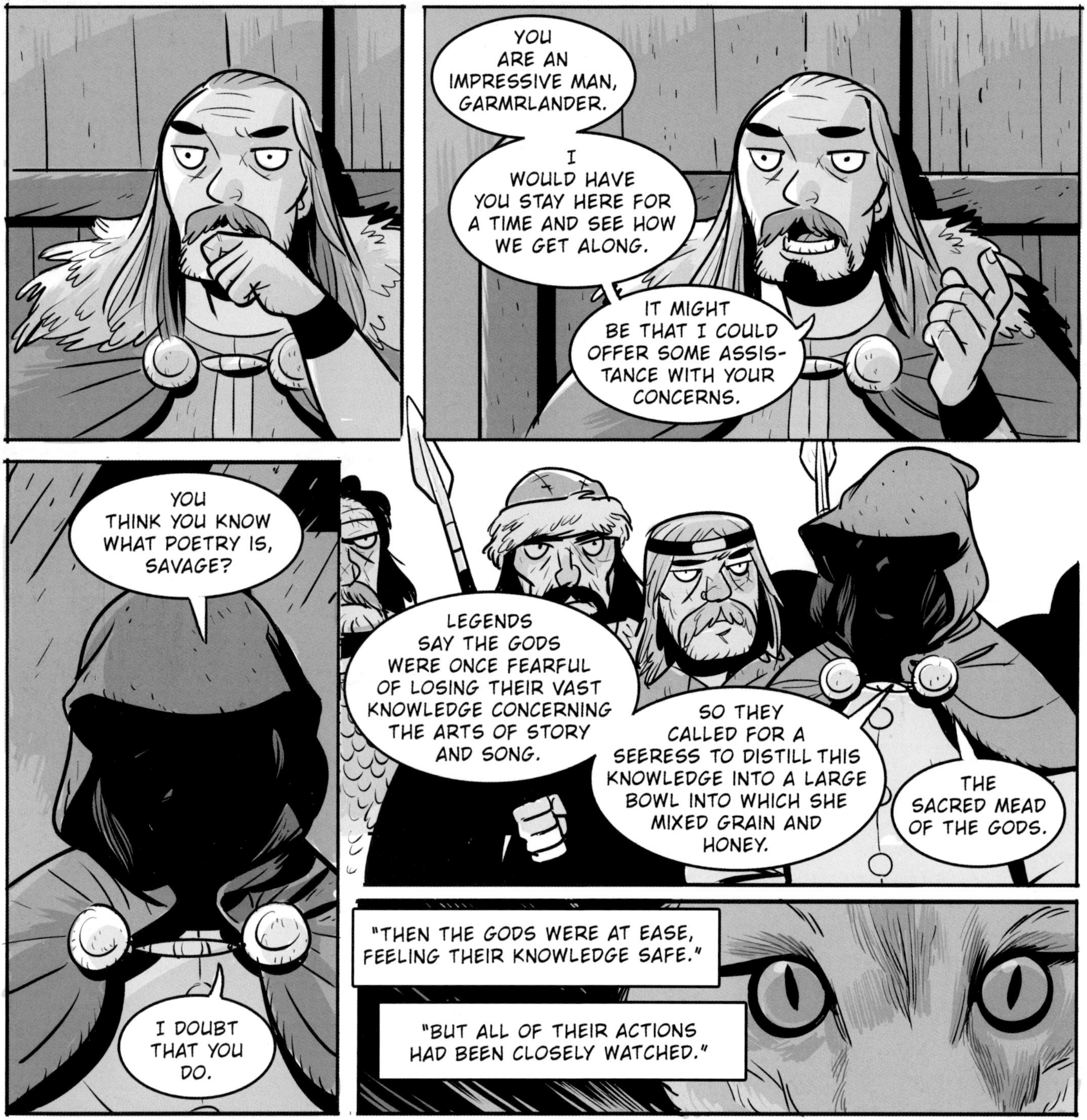
YOU ARE AN IMPRESSIVE MAN, GARMRLANDER.
I WOULD HAVE YOU STAY HERE FOR A TIME AND SEE HOW WE GET ALONG.
IT MIGHT BE THAT I COULD OFFER SOME ASSIS-TANCE WITH YOUR CONCERNS.
YOU THINK YOU KNOW WHAT POETRY IS, SAVAGE?
I DOUBT THAT YOU DO.
LEGENDS SAY THE GODS WERE ONCE FEARFUL OF LOSING THEIR VAST KNOWLEDGE CONCERNING THE ARTS OF STORY AND SONG.
SO THEY CALLED FOR A SEERESS TO DISTILL THIS KNOWLEDGE INTO A LARGE BOWL INTO WHICH SHE MIXED GRAIN AND HONEY.
THE SACRED MEAD OF THE GODS.
"THEN THE GODS WERE AT EASE, FEELING THEIR KNOWLEDGE SAFE."
"BUT ALL OF THEIR ACTIONS HAD BEEN CLOSELY WATCHED."

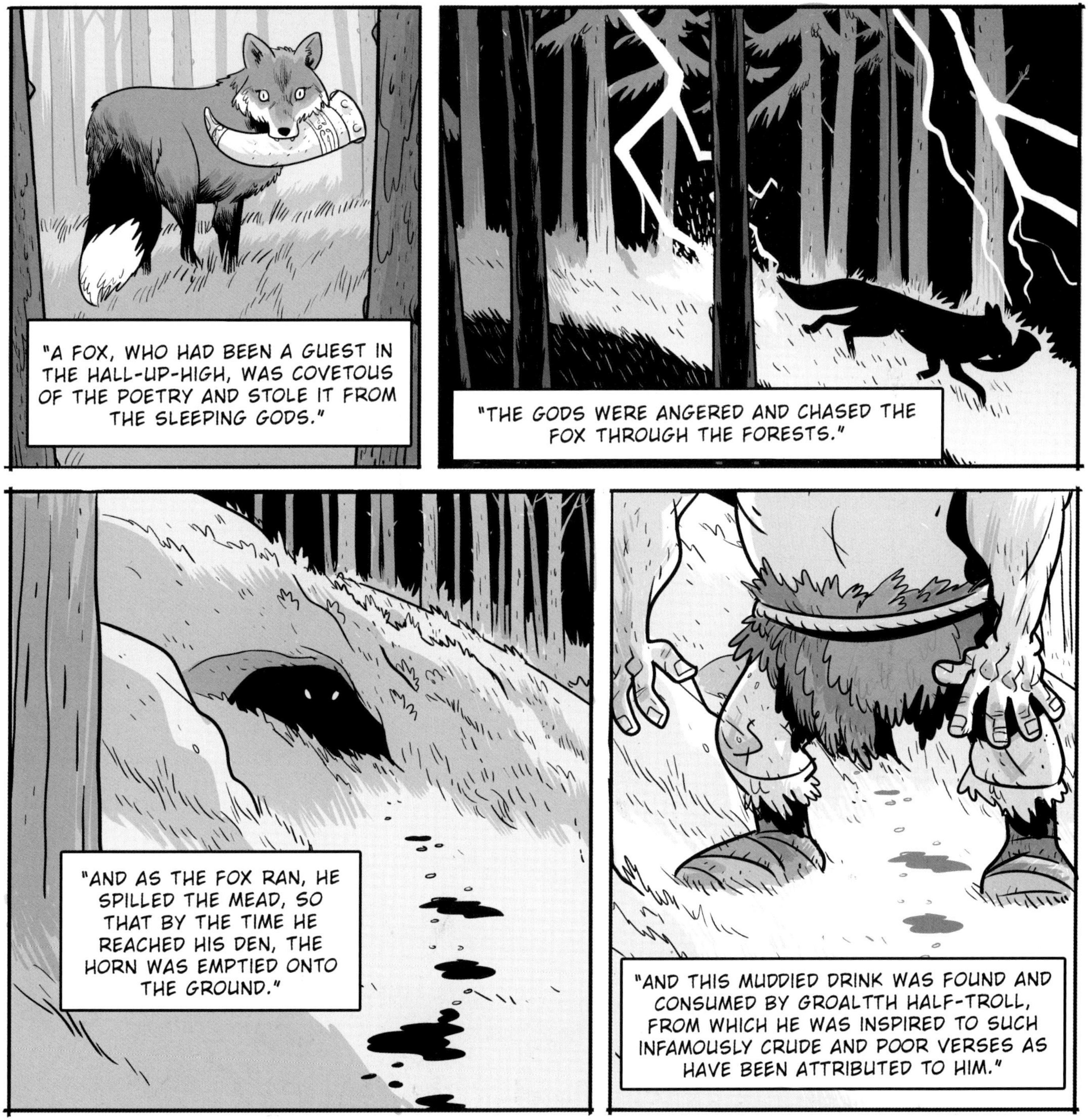
"A FOX, WHO HAD BEEN A GUEST IN THE HALL-UP-HIGH, WAS COVETOUS OF THE POETRY AND STOLE IT FROM THE SLEEPING GODS."
"THE GODS WERE ANGERED AND CHASED THE FOX THROUGH THE FORESTS."
"AND AS THE FOX RAN, HE SPILLED THE MEAD, SO THAT BY THE TIME HE REACHED HIS DEN, THE HORN WAS EMPTIED ONTO THE GROUND."
"AND THIS MUDDIED DRINK WAS FOUND AND CONSUMED BY GROALTTH HALF-TROLL, FROM WHICH HE WAS INSPIRED TO SUCH INFAMOUSLY CRUDE AND POOR VERSES AS HAVE BEEN ATTRIBUTED TO HIM."

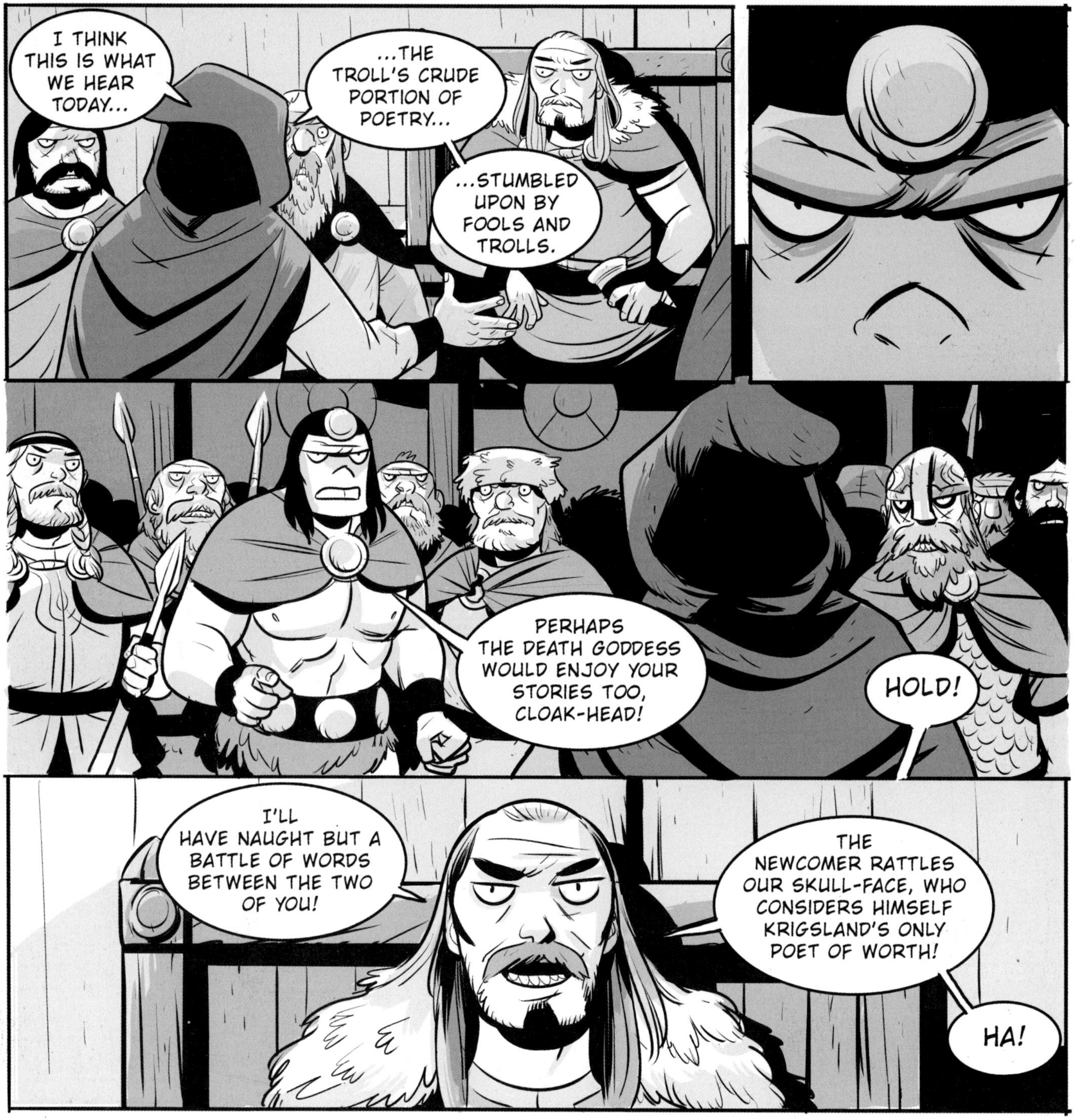
I THINK THIS IS WHAT WE HEAR TODAY...
...THE TROLL'S CRUDE PORTION OF POETRY...
...STUMBLED UPON BY FOOLS AND TROLLS.
PERHAPS THE DEATH GODDESS WOULD ENJOY YOUR STORIES TOO, CLOAK-HEAD!
HOLD!
I'LL HAVE NAUGHT BUT A BATTLE OF WORDS BETWEEN THE TWO OF YOU!
THE NEWCOMER RATTLES OUR SKULL-FACE, WHO CONSIDERS HIMSELF KRIGSLAND'S ONLY POET OF WORTH!
HA!

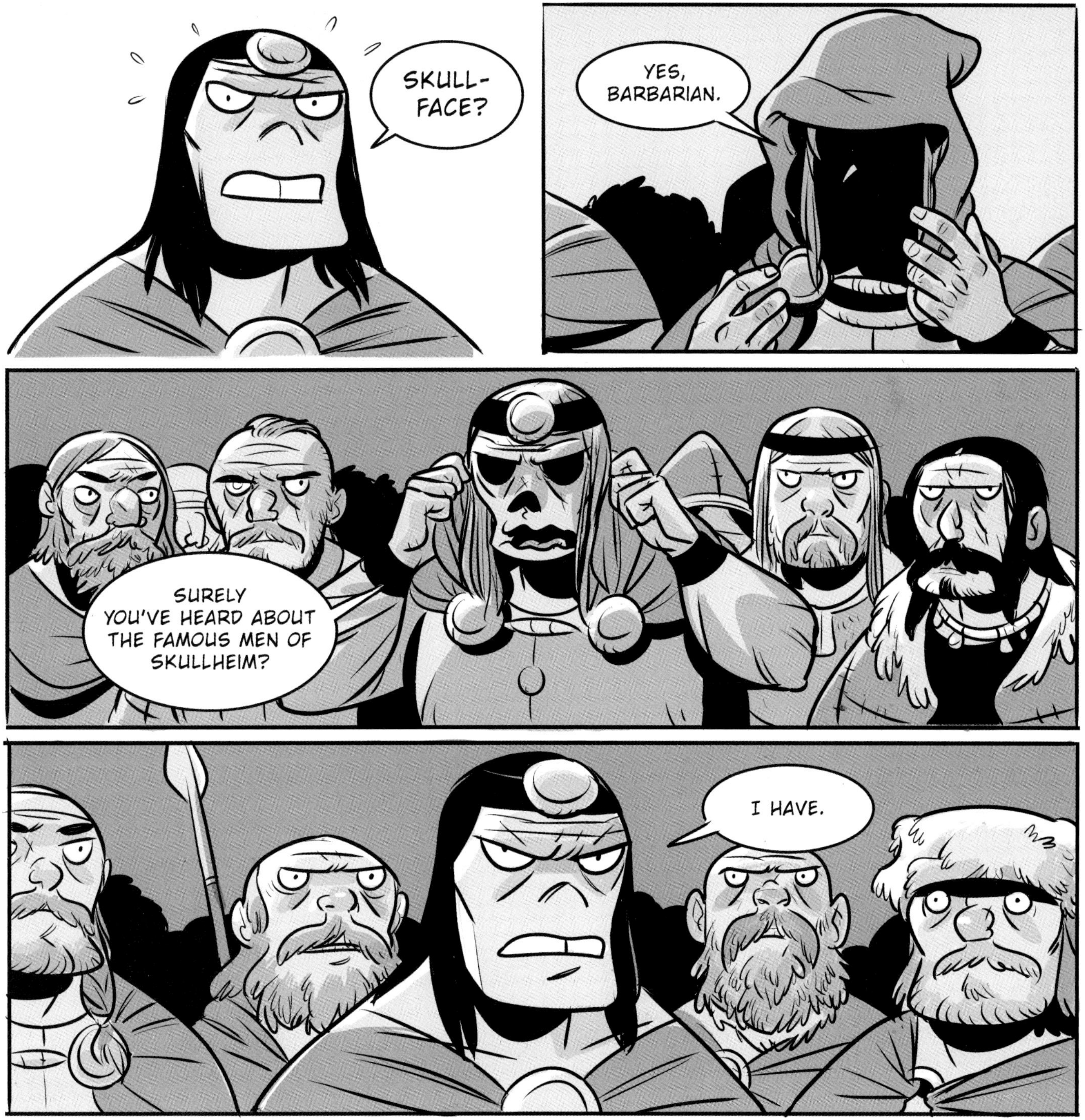
SKULL-
FACE?
YES,
BARBARIAN.
SURELY
YOU'VE HEARD ABOUT
THE FAMOUS MEN OF
SKULLHEIM?
I HAVE.

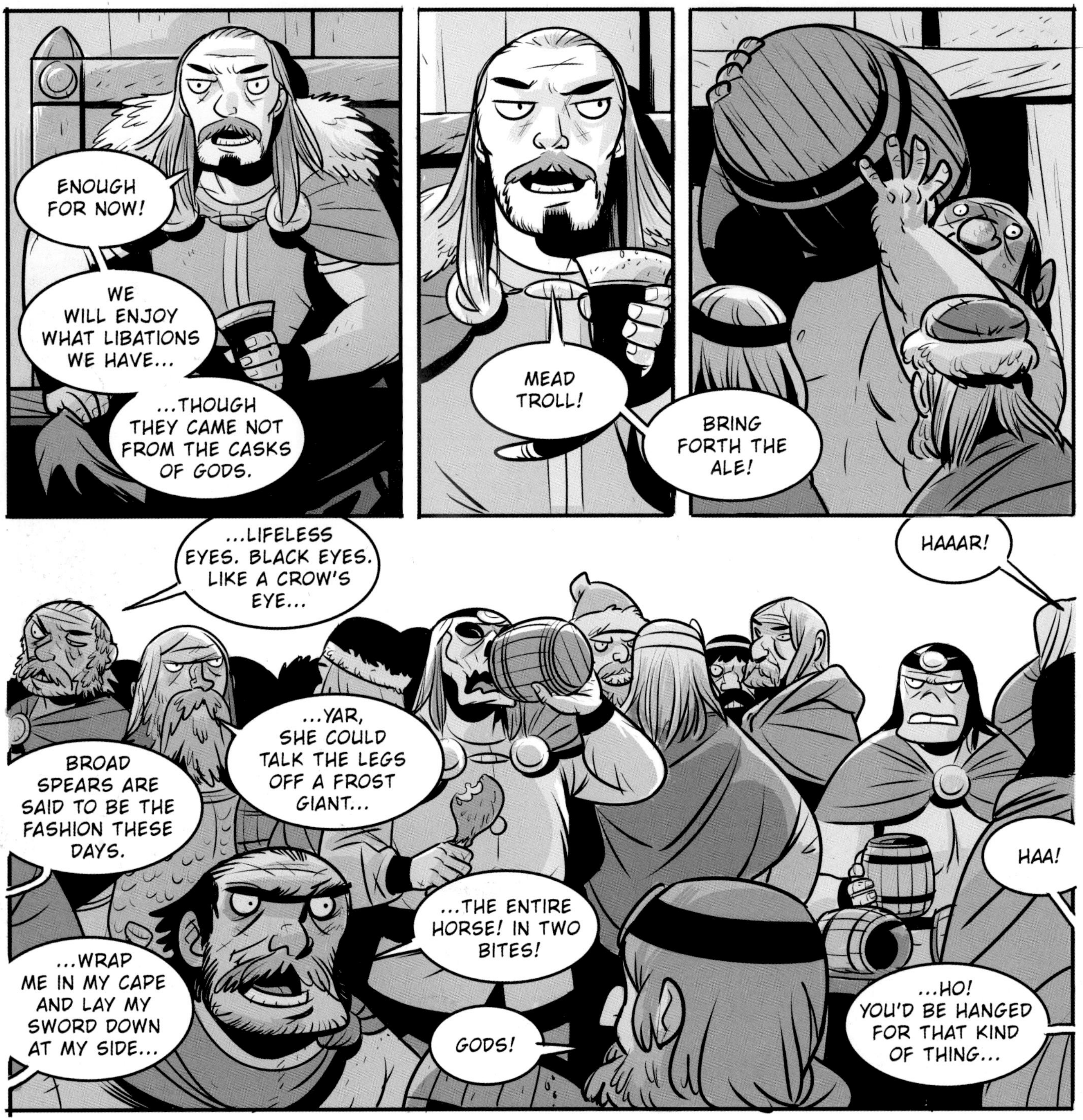
ENOUGH FOR NOW!
WE WILL ENJOY WHAT LIBATIONS WE HAVE...
...THOUGH THEY CAME NOT FROM THE CASKS OF GODS.
MEAD TROLL!
BRING FORTH THE ALE!
...LIFELESS EYES. BLACK EYES. LIKE A CROW'S EYE...
HAAAR!
...YAR, SHE COULD TALK THE LEGS OFF A FROST GIANT...
BROAD SPEARS ARE SAID TO BE THE FASHION THESE DAYS.
HAA!
...THE ENTIRE HORSE! IN TWO BITES!
...WRAP ME IN MY CAPE AND LAY MY SWORD DOWN AT MY SIDE...
GODS!
...HO! YOU'D BE HANGED FOR THAT KIND OF THING...

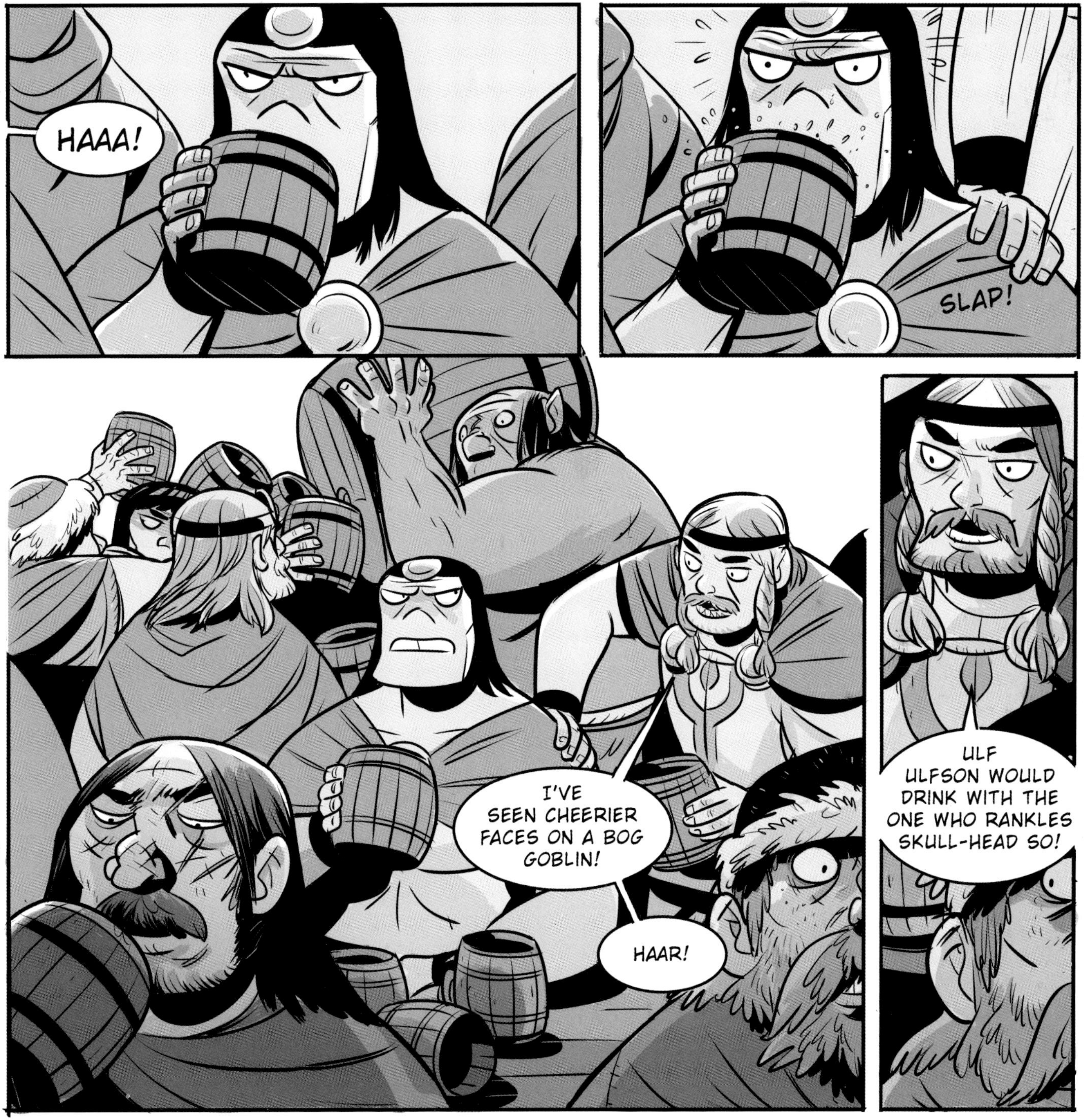
HAAA!
SLAP!
I'VE SEEN CHEERIER FACES ON A BOG GOBLIN!
HAAR!
ULF ULFSON WOULD DRINK WITH THE ONE WHO RANKLES SKULL-HEAD SO!

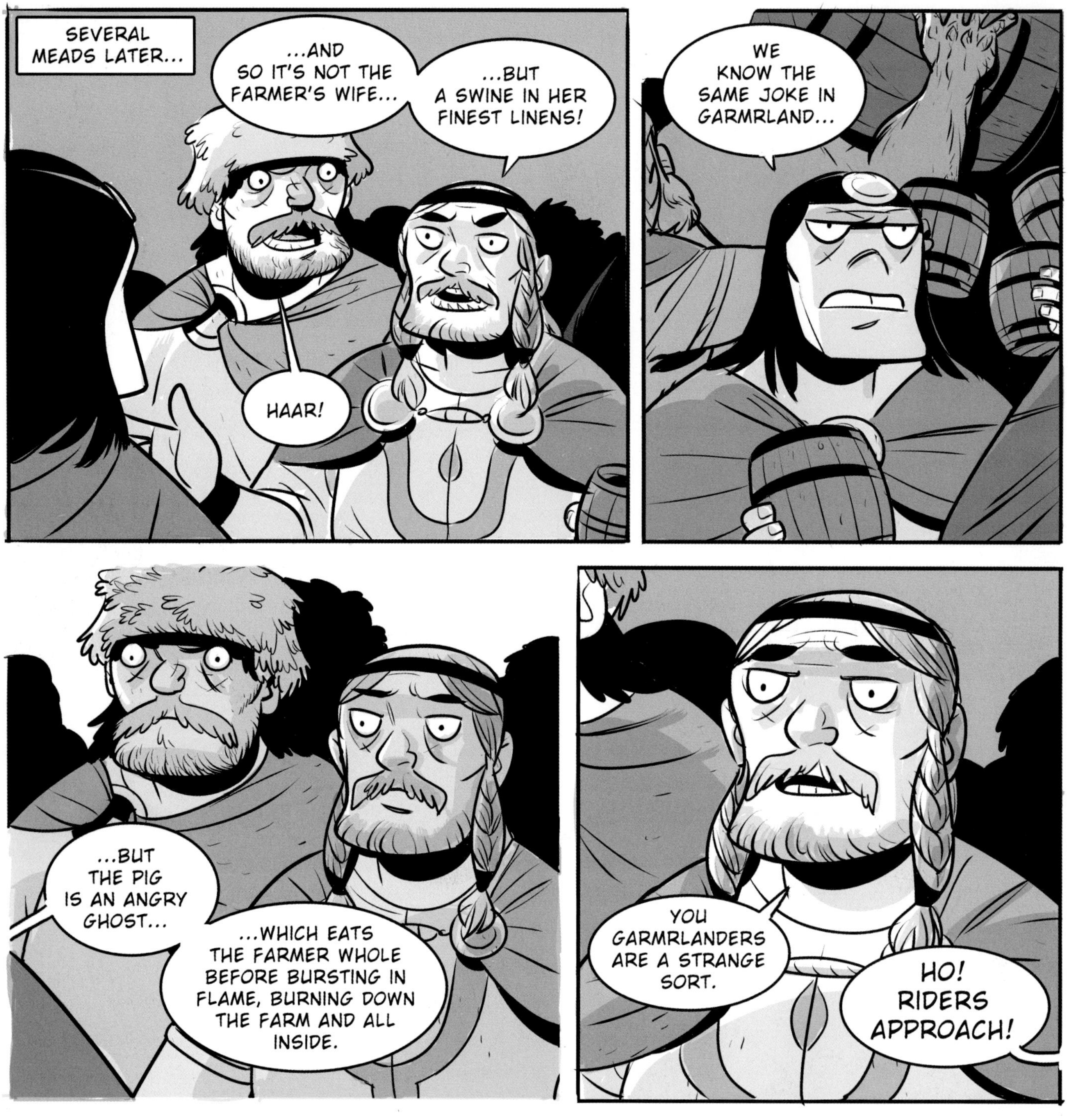

SEVERAL MEADS LATER...
...AND SO IT'S NOT THE FARMER'S WIFE...
...BUT A SWINE IN HER FINEST LINENS!
HAAR!
WE KNOW THE SAME JOKE IN GARMRLAND...
...BUT THE PIG IS AN ANGRY GHOST...
...WHICH EATS THE FARMER WHOLE BEFORE BURSTING IN FLAME, BURNING DOWN THE FARM AND ALL INSIDE.
YOU GARMRLANDERS ARE A STRANGE SORT.
HO! RIDERS APPROACH!

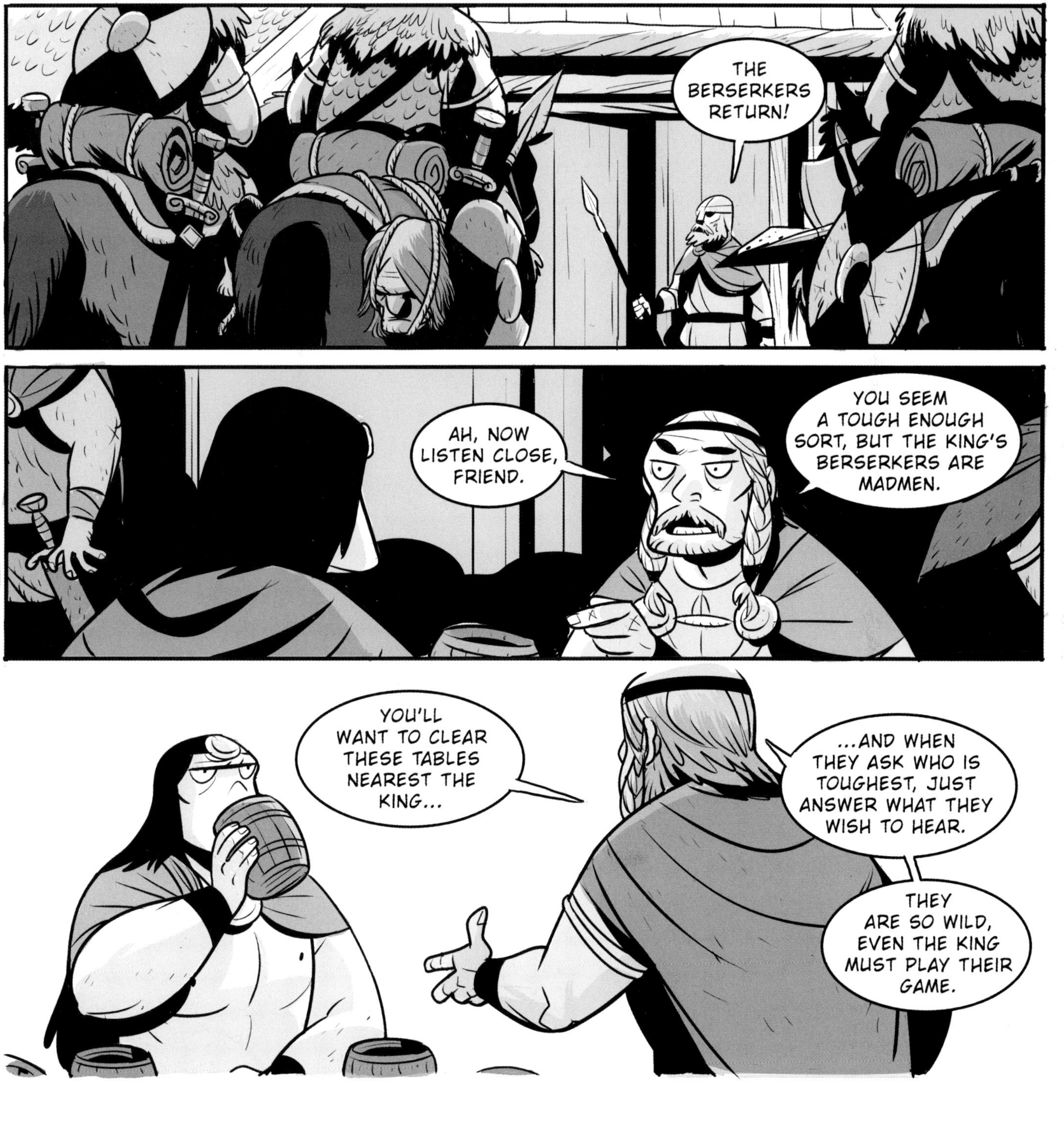
THE BERSERKERS RETURN!
AH, NOW LISTEN CLOSE, FRIEND.
YOU SEEM A TOUGH ENOUGH SORT, BUT THE KING'S BERSERKERS ARE MADMEN.
YOU'LL WANT TO CLEAR THESE TABLES NEAREST THE KING...
...AND WHEN THEY ASK WHO IS TOUGHEST, JUST ANSWER WHAT THEY WISH TO HEAR.
THEY ARE SO WILD, EVEN THE KING MUST PLAY THEIR GAME.

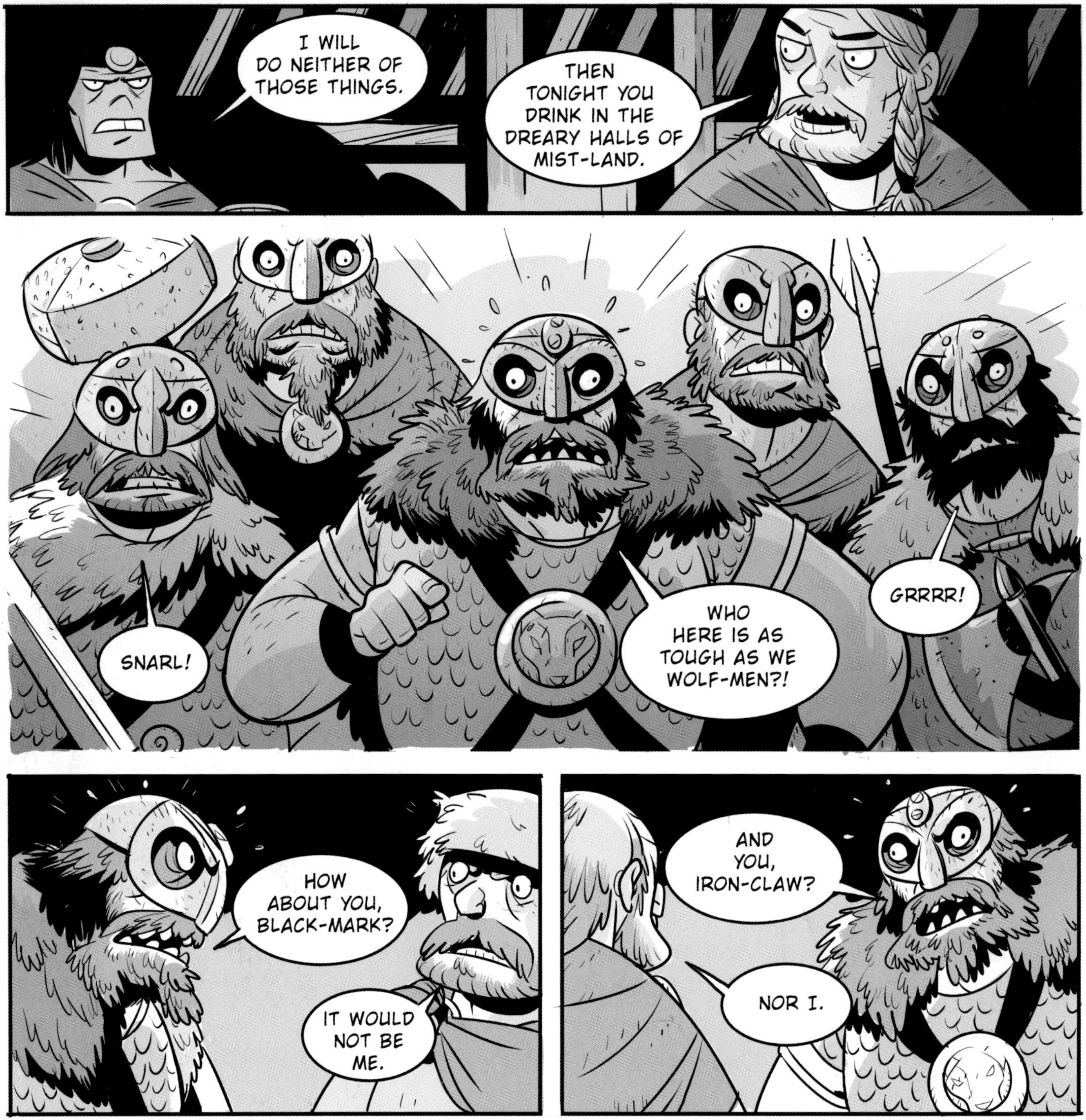
I WILL DO NEITHER OF THOSE THINGS.
THEN TONIGHT YOU DRINK IN THE DREARY HALLS OF MIST-LAND.
SNARL!
WHO HERE IS AS TOUGH AS WE WOLF-MEN?!
GRRRR!
HOW ABOUT YOU, BLACK-MARK?
IT WOULD NOT BE ME.
AND YOU, IRON-CLAW?
NOR I.

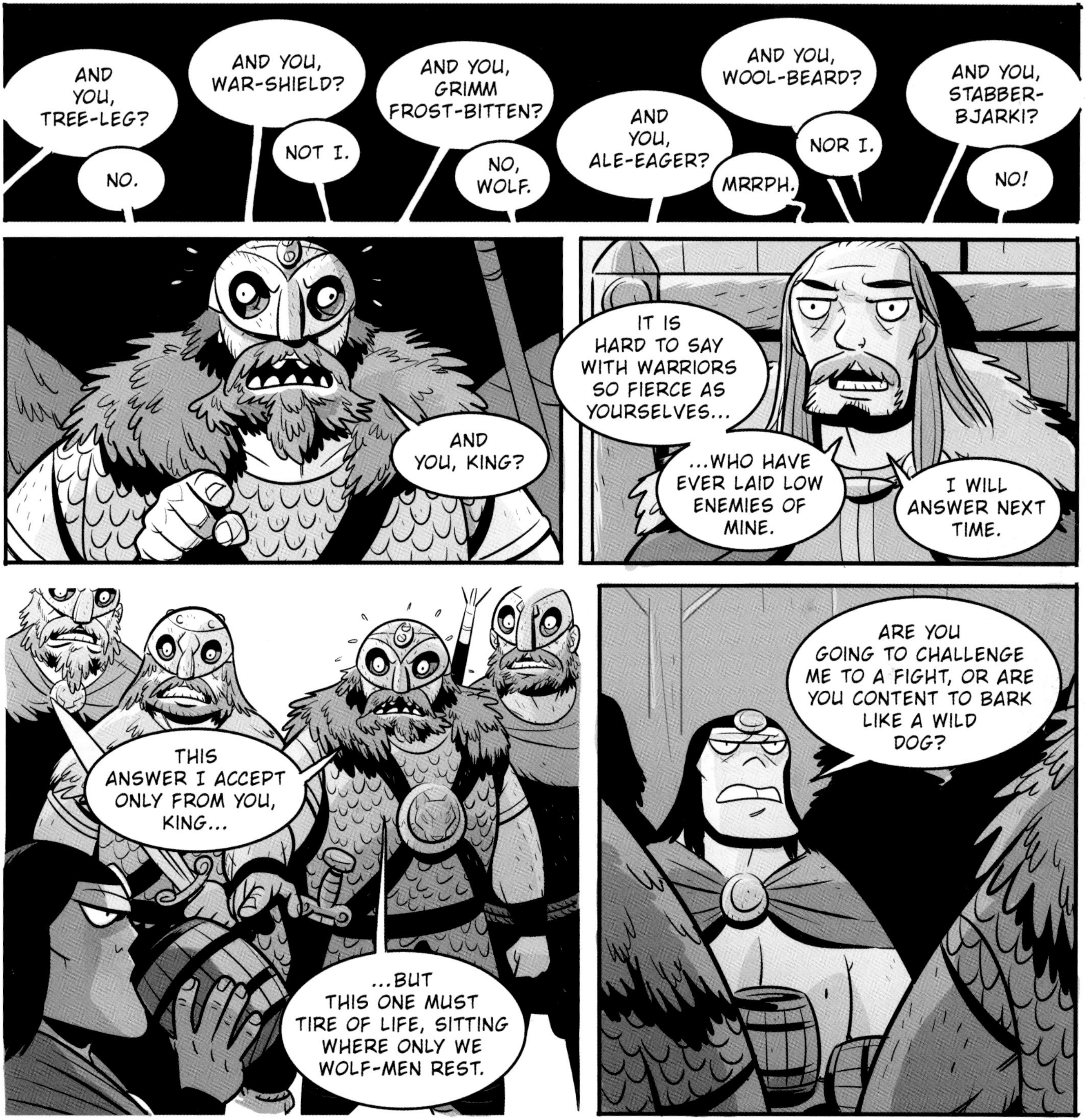
AND YOU, TREE-LEG?
NO.
AND YOU, WAR-SHIELD?
NOT I.
AND YOU, GRIMM FROST-BITTEN?
NO, WOLF.
AND YOU, ALE-EAGER?
MRRPH.
AND YOU, WOOL-BEARD?
NOR I.
AND YOU, STABBER-BJARKI?
NO!
AND YOU, KING?
IT IS HARD TO SAY WITH WARRIORS SO FIERCE AS YOURSELVES...
...WHO HAVE EVER LAID LOW ENEMIES OF MINE.
I WILL ANSWER NEXT TIME.
THIS ANSWER I ACCEPT ONLY FROM YOU, KING...
...BUT THIS ONE MUST TIRE OF LIFE, SITTING WHERE ONLY WE WOLF-MEN REST.
ARE YOU GOING TO CHALLENGE ME TO A FIGHT, OR ARE YOU CONTENT TO BARK LIKE A WILD DOG?

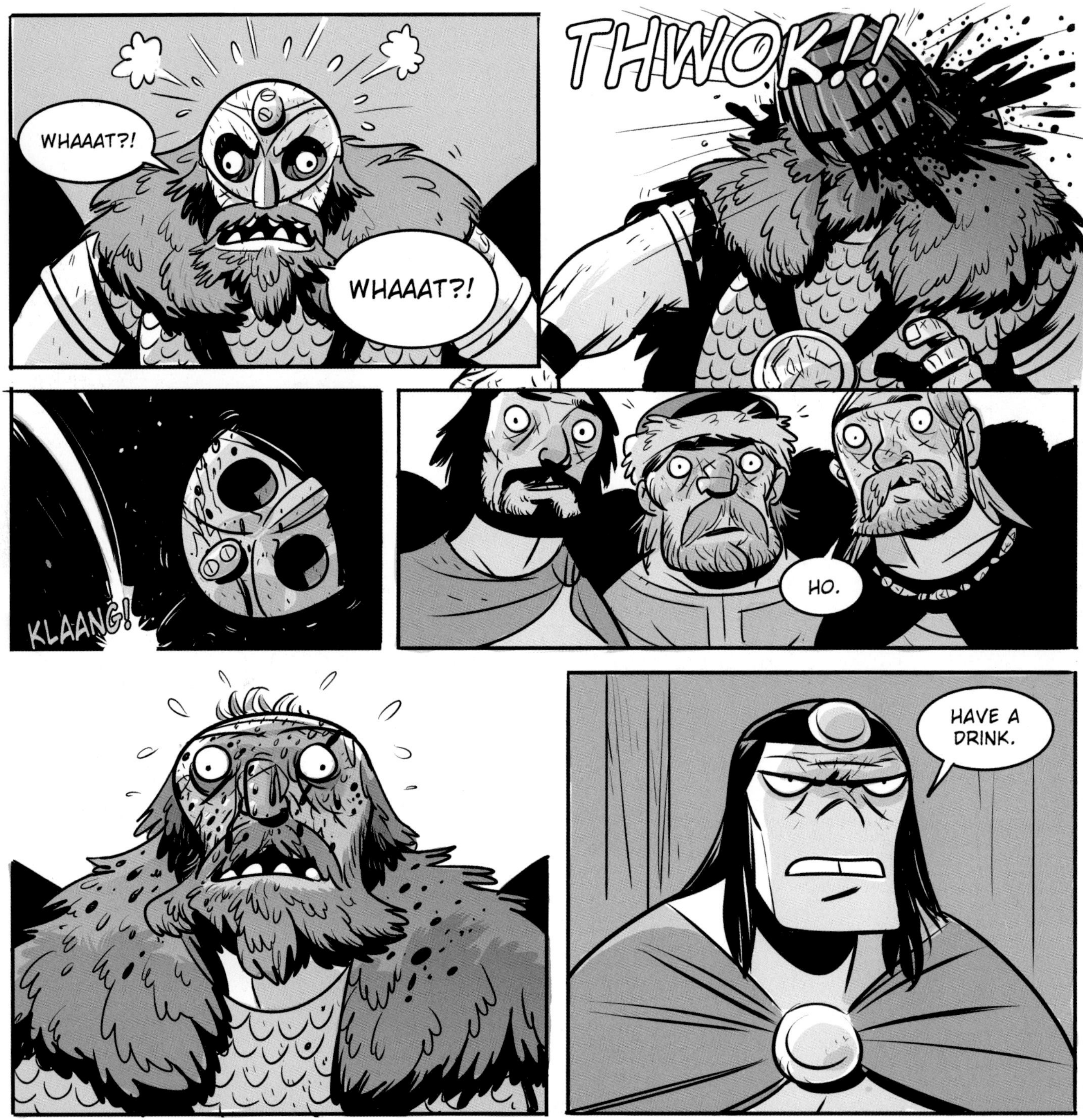
WHAAAT?!
WHAAAT?!
THWOK!!
KLAANG!
HO.
HAVE A DRINK.

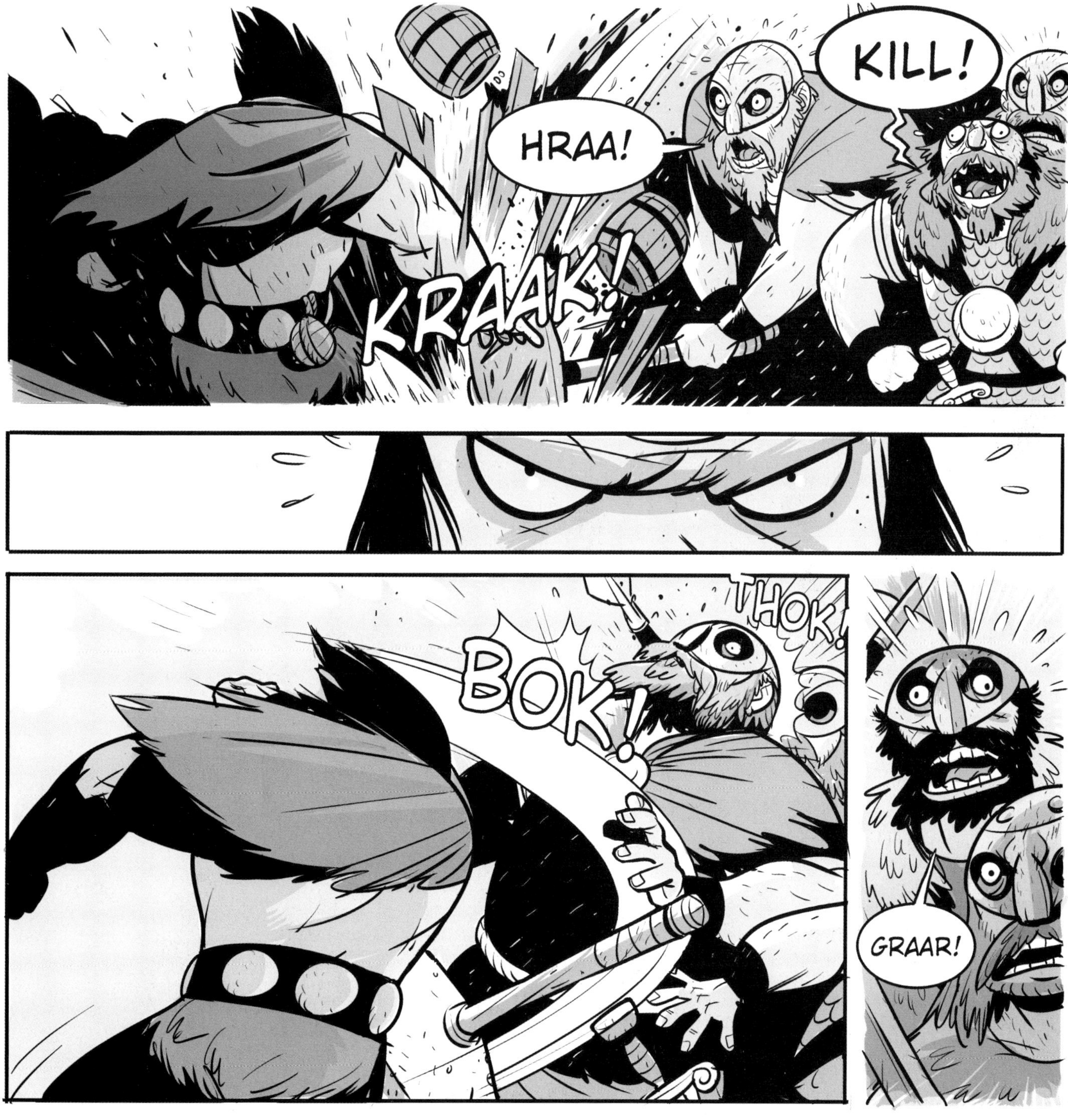
KILL!
HRAA!
KRAAK!
THOK!
BOK!
GRAAR!

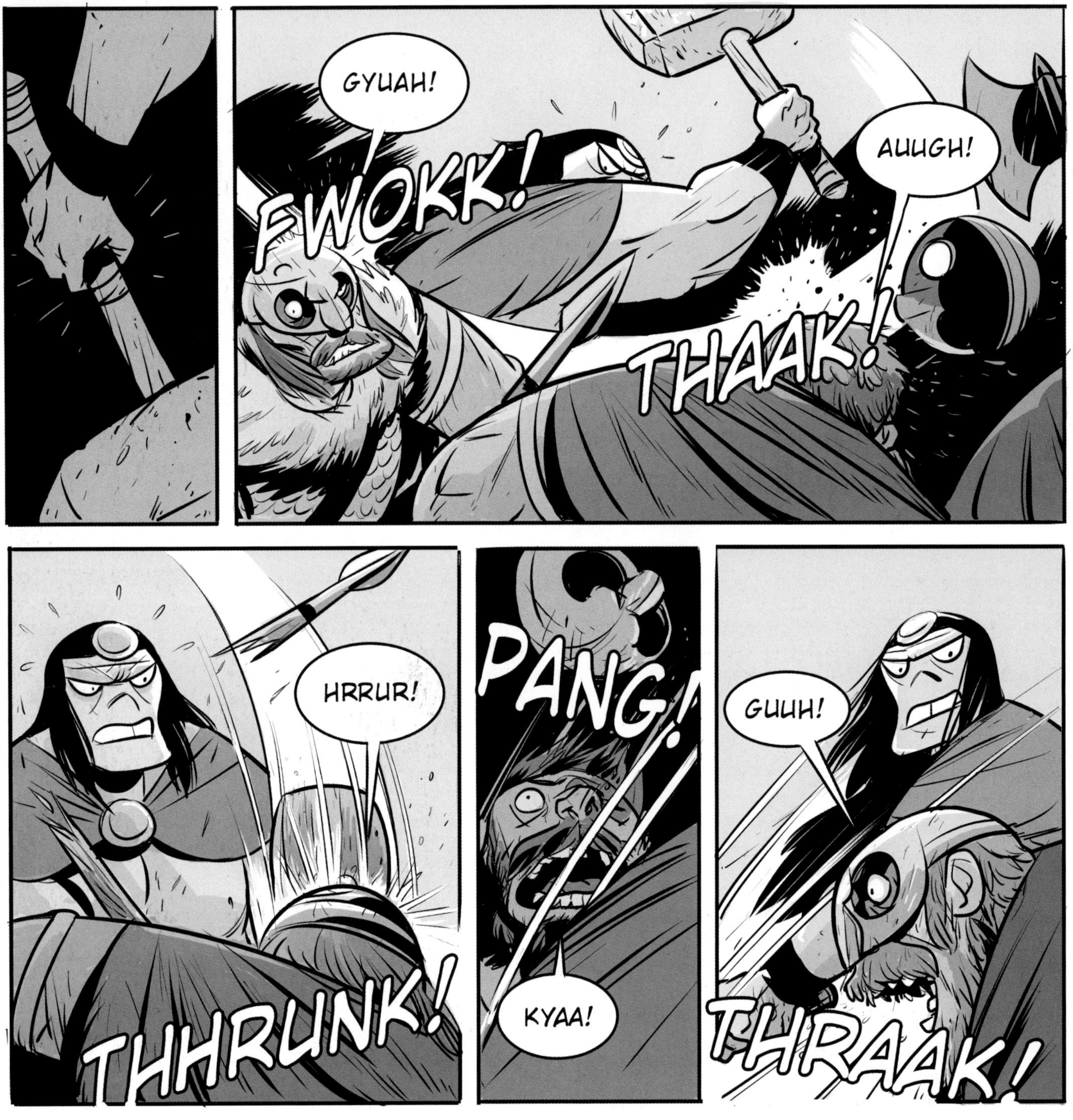
GYUAH!
FWOKK!
AUUGH!
THAAK!
HRRUR!
THHRUNK!
PANG!
KYAA!
GUUH!
THRAAK!

AHHHHHH!

HYAHR!

THROKK!

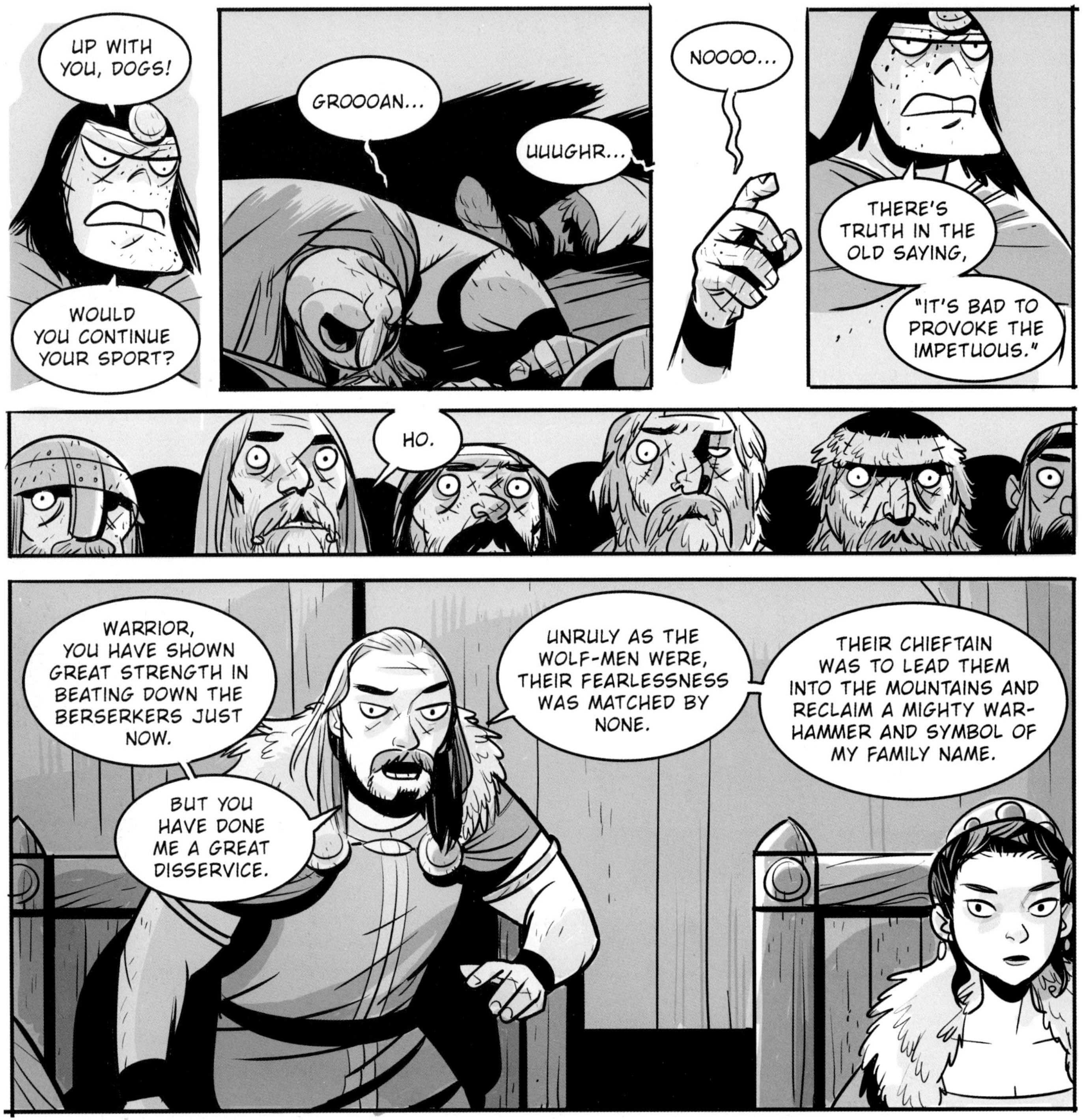
UP WITH YOU, DOGS!
WOULD YOU CONTINUE YOUR SPORT?
GROOOAN...
UUUGHR...
NOOOO...
THERE'S TRUTH IN THE OLD SAYING,
"IT'S BAD TO PROVOKE THE IMPETUOUS."
HO.
WARRIOR, YOU HAVE SHOWN GREAT STRENGTH IN BEATING DOWN THE BERSERKERS JUST NOW.
BUT YOU HAVE DONE ME A GREAT DISSERVICE.
UNRULY AS THE WOLF-MEN WERE, THEIR FEARLESSNESS WAS MATCHED BY NONE.
THEIR CHIEFTAIN WAS TO LEAD THEM INTO THE MOUNTAINS AND RECLAIM A MIGHTY WAR-HAMMER AND SYMBOL OF MY FAMILY NAME.

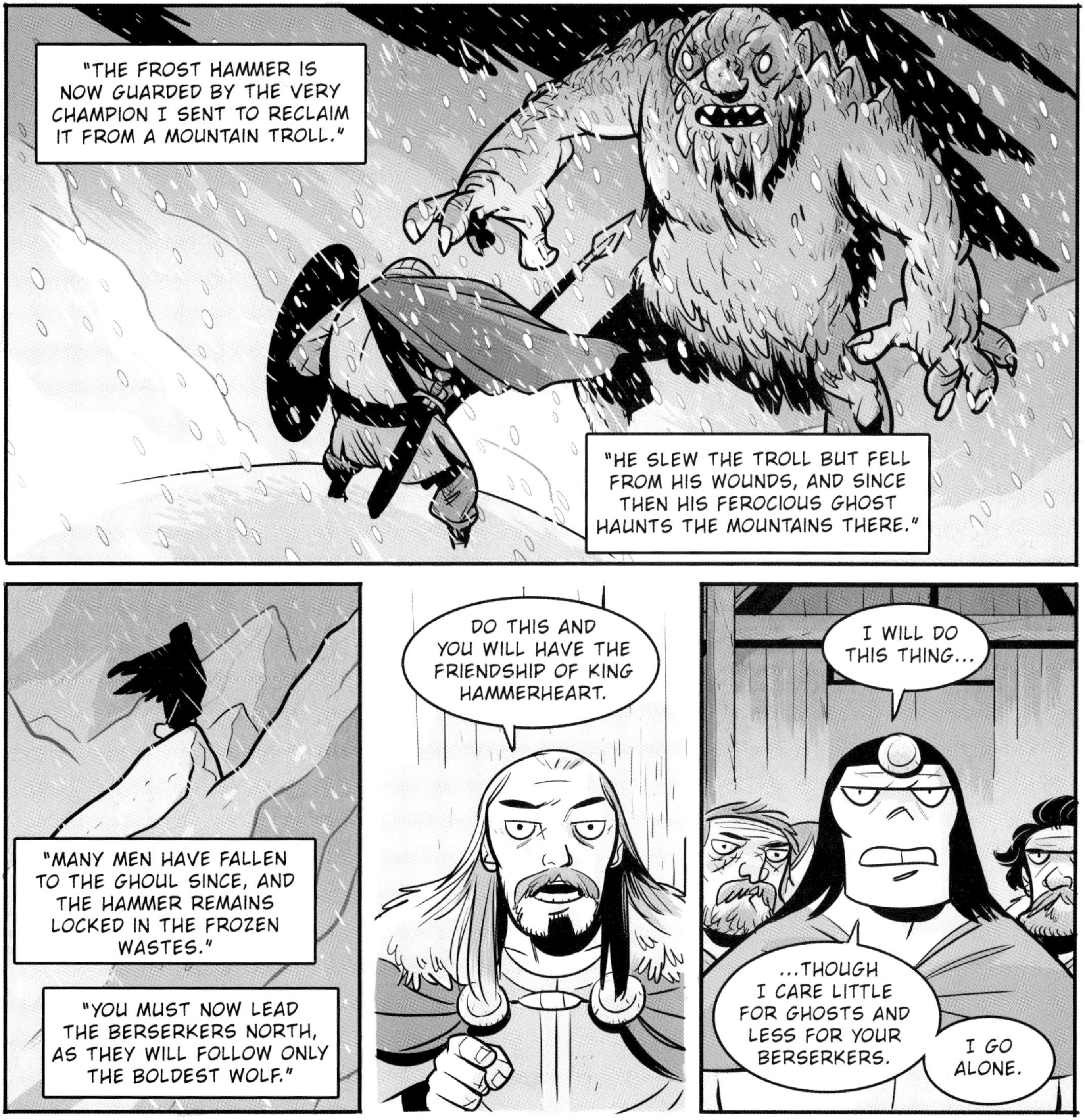
"THE FROST HAMMER IS NOW GUARDED BY THE VERY CHAMPION I SENT TO RECLAIM IT FROM A MOUNTAIN TROLL."
"HE SLEW THE TROLL BUT FELL FROM HIS WOUNDS, AND SINCE THEN HIS FEROCIOUS GHOST HAUNTS THE MOUNTAINS THERE."
"MANY MEN HAVE FALLEN TO THE GHOUL SINCE, AND THE HAMMER REMAINS LOCKED IN THE FROZEN WASTES."
"YOU MUST NOW LEAD THE BERSERKERS NORTH, AS THEY WILL FOLLOW ONLY THE BOLDEST WOLF."
DO THIS AND YOU WILL HAVE THE FRIENDSHIP OF KING HAMMERHEART.
I WILL DO THIS THING...
...THOUGH I CARE LITTLE FOR GHOSTS AND LESS FOR YOUR BERSERKERS.
I GO ALONE.

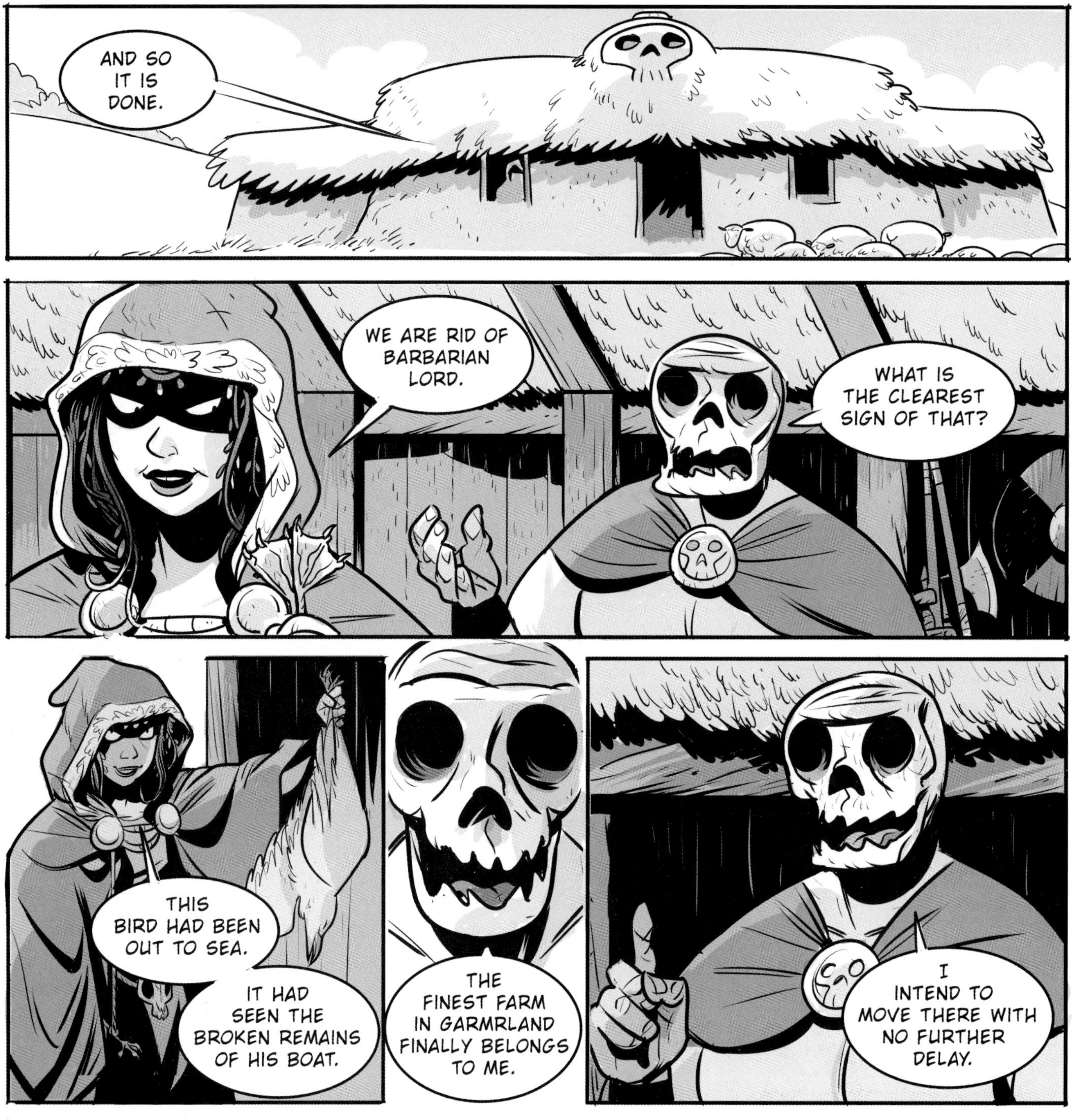
AND SO IT IS DONE.
WE ARE RID OF BARBARIAN LORD.
WHAT IS THE CLEAREST SIGN OF THAT?
THIS BIRD HAD BEEN OUT TO SEA.
IT HAD SEEN THE BROKEN REMAINS OF HIS BOAT.
THE FINEST FARM IN GARMRLAND FINALLY BELONGS TO ME.
I INTEND TO MOVE THERE WITH NO FURTHER DELAY.

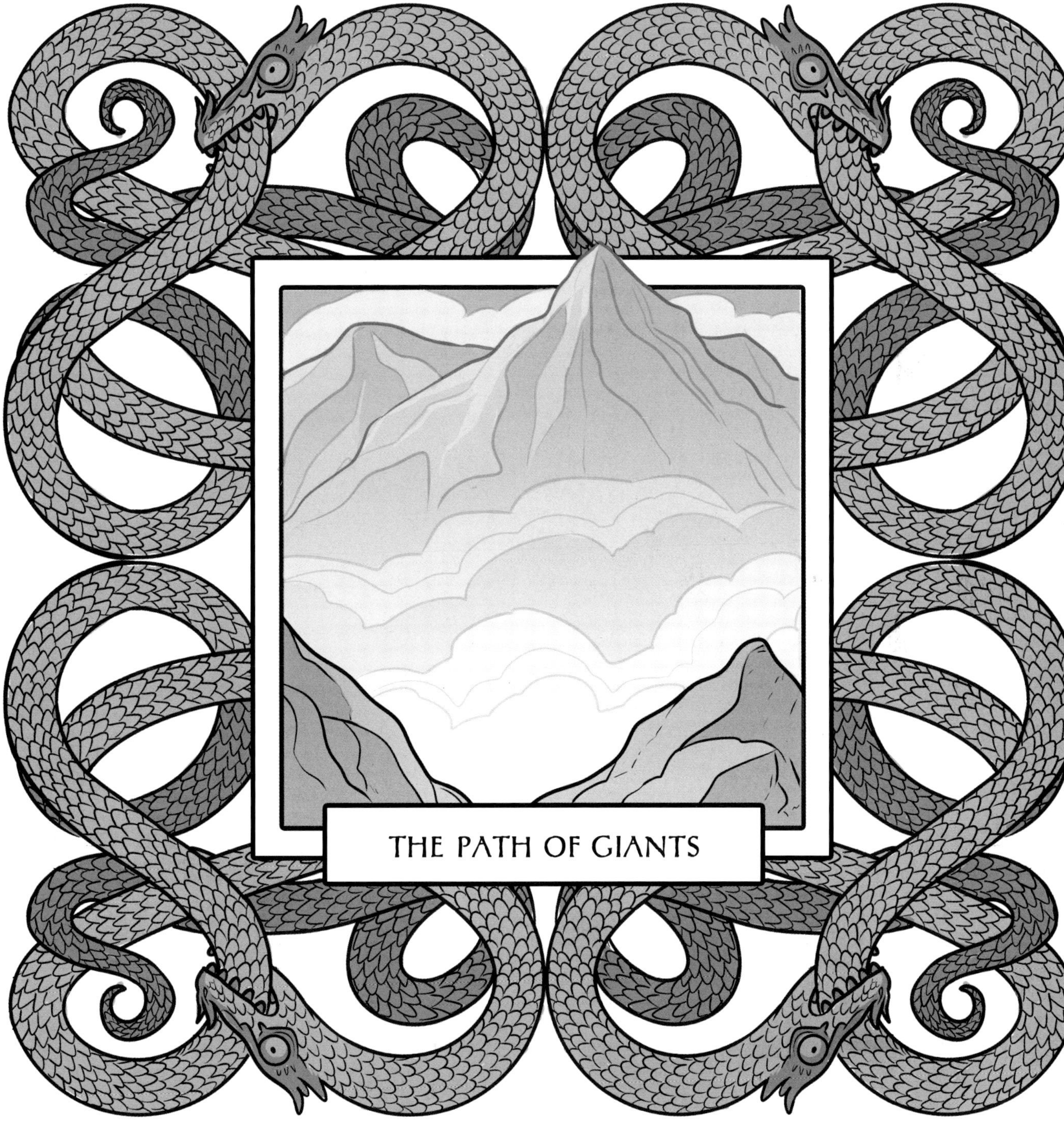
THE PATH OF GIANTS

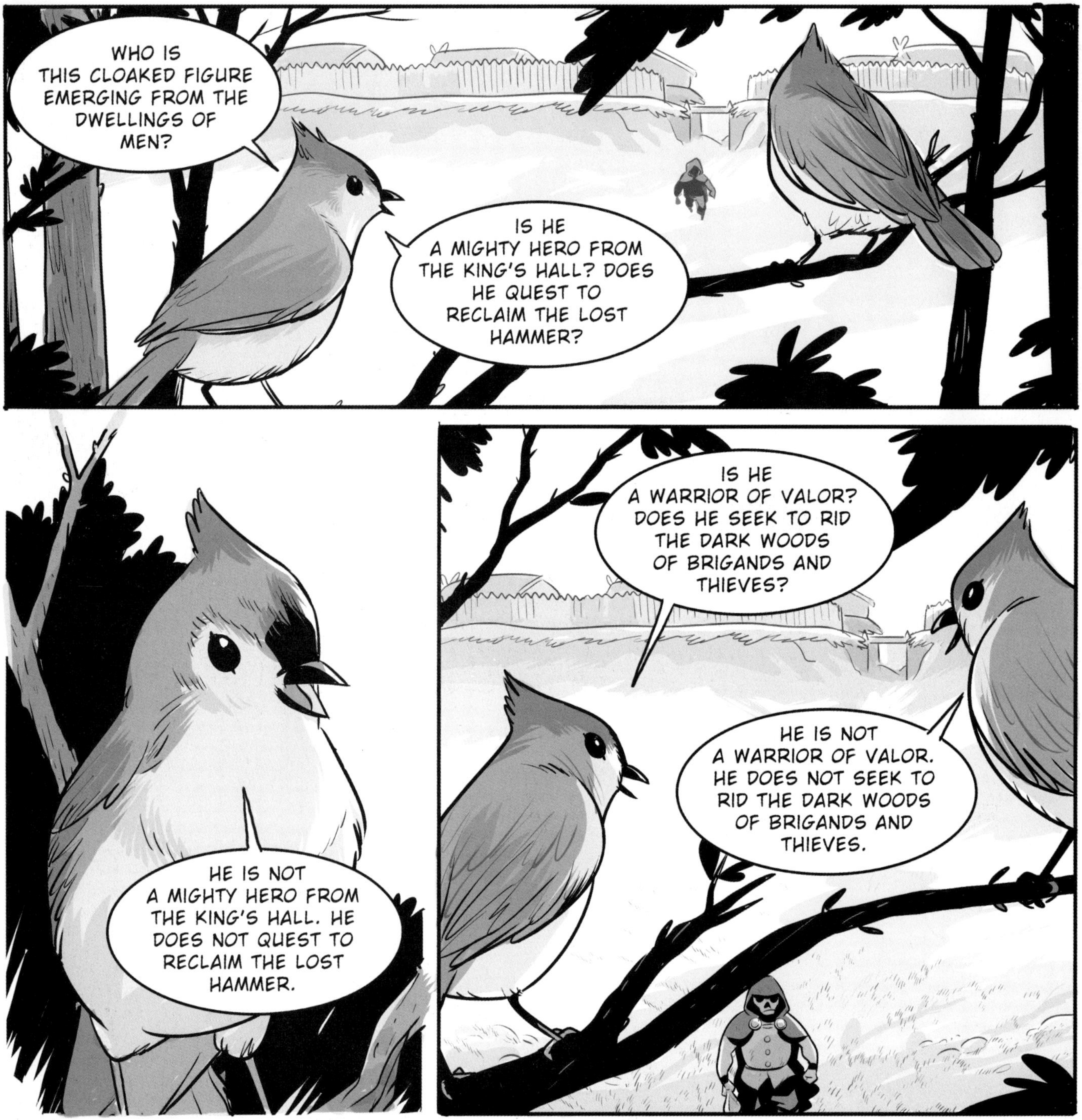
WHO IS THIS CLOAKED FIGURE EMERGING FROM THE DWELLINGS OF MEN?
IS HE A MIGHTY HERO FROM THE KING'S HALL? DOES HE QUEST TO RECLAIM THE LOST HAMMER?
HE IS NOT A MIGHTY HERO FROM THE KING'S HALL. HE DOES NOT QUEST TO RECLAIM THE LOST HAMMER.
IS HE A WARRIOR OF VALOR? DOES HE SEEK TO RID THE DARK WOODS OF BRIGANDS AND THIEVES?
HE IS NOT A WARRIOR OF VALOR. HE DOES NOT SEEK TO RID THE DARK WOODS OF BRIGANDS AND THIEVES.

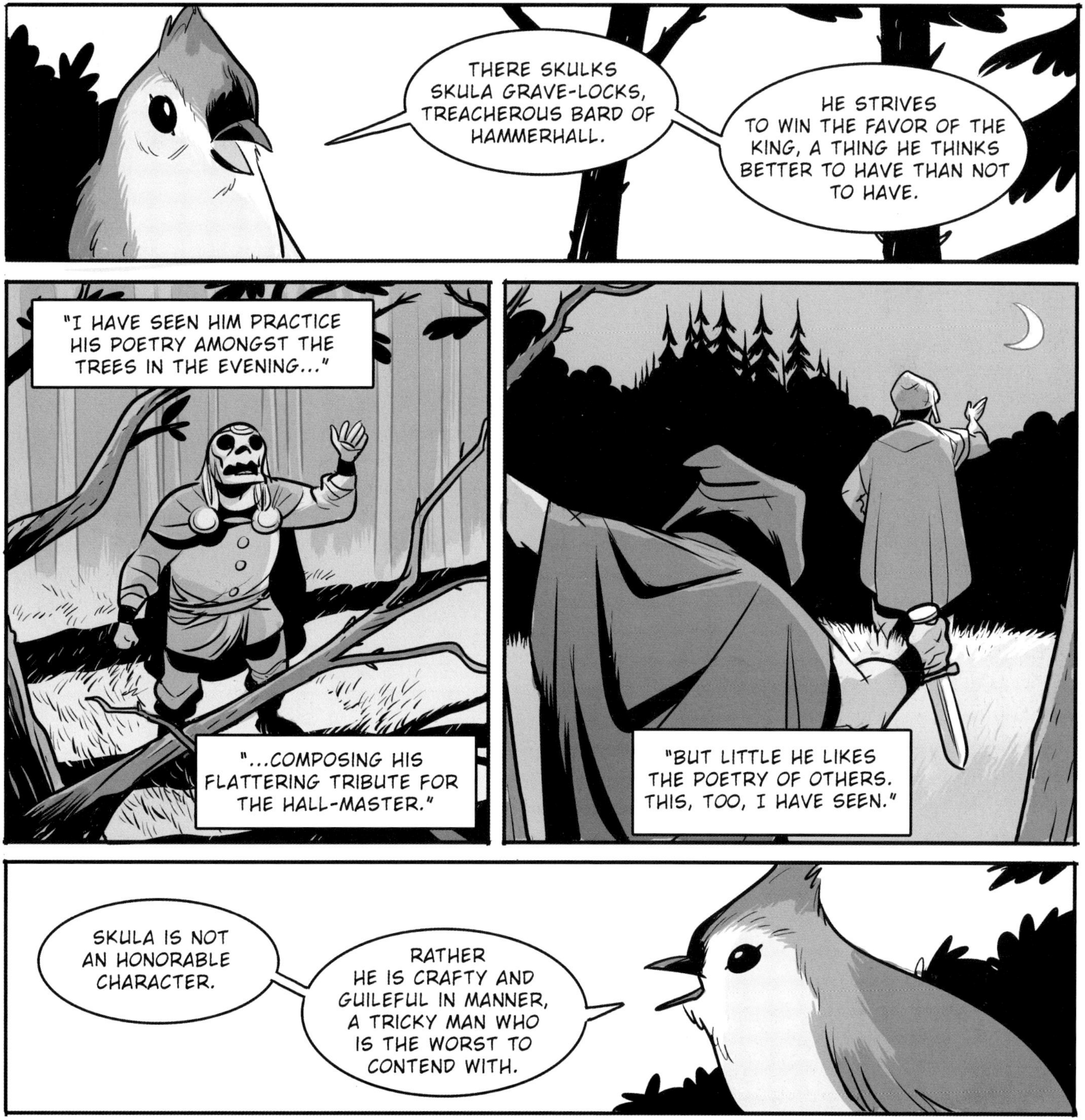
THERE SKULKS SKULA GRAVE-LOCKS, TREACHEROUS BARD OF HAMMERHALL.
HE STRIVES TO WIN THE FAVOR OF THE KING, A THING HE THINKS BETTER TO HAVE THAN NOT TO HAVE.
"I HAVE SEEN HIM PRACTICE HIS POETRY AMONGST THE TREES IN THE EVENING..."
"...COMPOSING HIS FLATTERING TRIBUTE FOR THE HALL-MASTER."
"BUT LITTLE HE LIKES THE POETRY OF OTHERS. THIS, TOO, I HAVE SEEN."
SKULA IS NOT AN HONORABLE CHARACTER.
RATHER HE IS CRAFTY AND GUILEFUL IN MANNER, A TRICKY MAN WHO IS THE WORST TO CONTEND WITH.

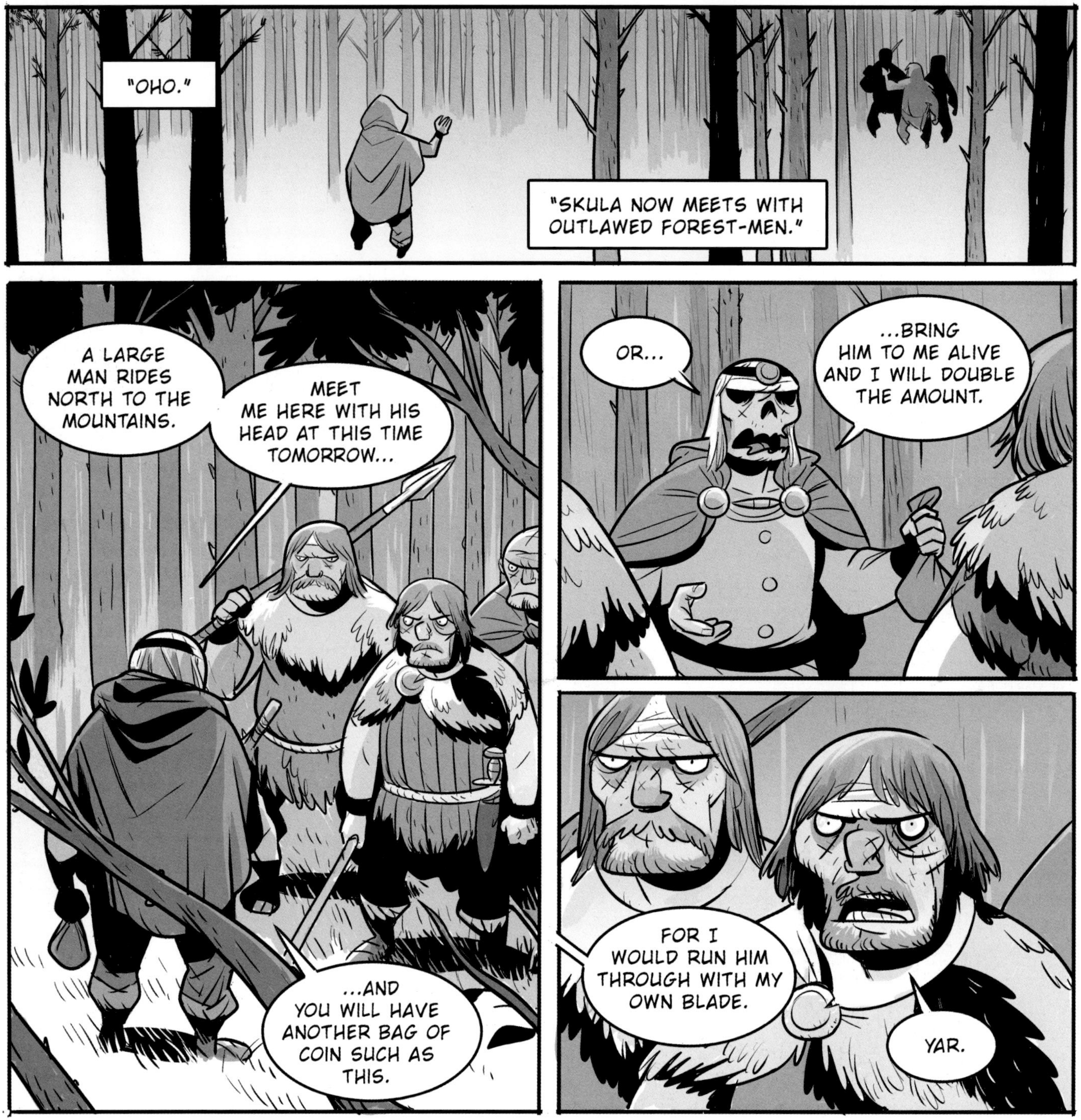
"OHO."
"SKULA NOW MEETS WITH OUTLAWED FOREST-MEN."
A LARGE MAN RIDES NORTH TO THE MOUNTAINS.
MEET ME HERE WITH HIS HEAD AT THIS TIME TOMORROW...
...AND YOU WILL HAVE ANOTHER BAG OF COIN SUCH AS THIS.
OR...
...BRING HIM TO ME ALIVE AND I WILL DOUBLE THE AMOUNT.
FOR I WOULD RUN HIM THROUGH WITH MY OWN BLADE.
YAR.

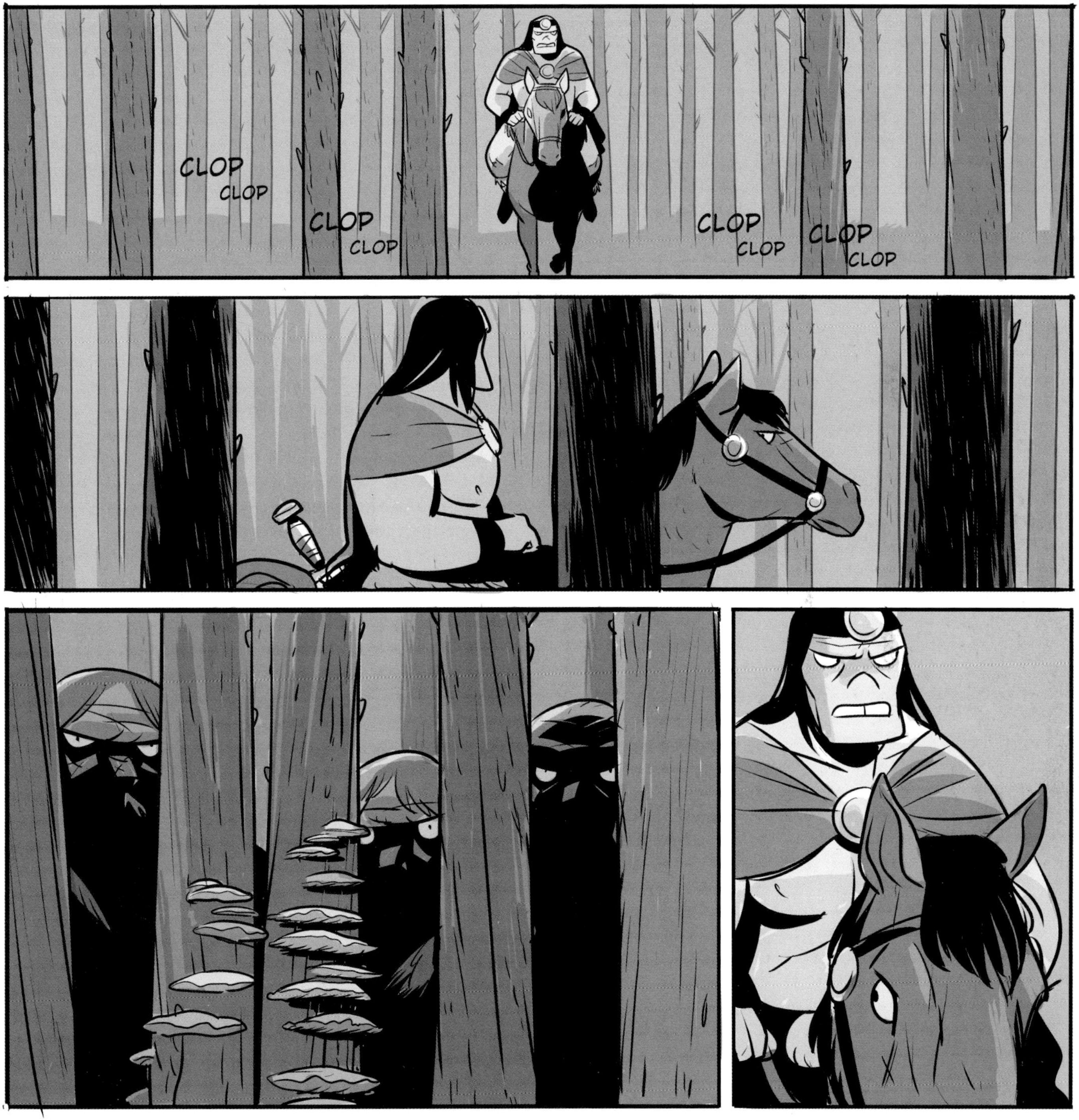
CLOP
CLOP
CLOP
CLOP
CLOP
CLOP
CLOP
CLOP

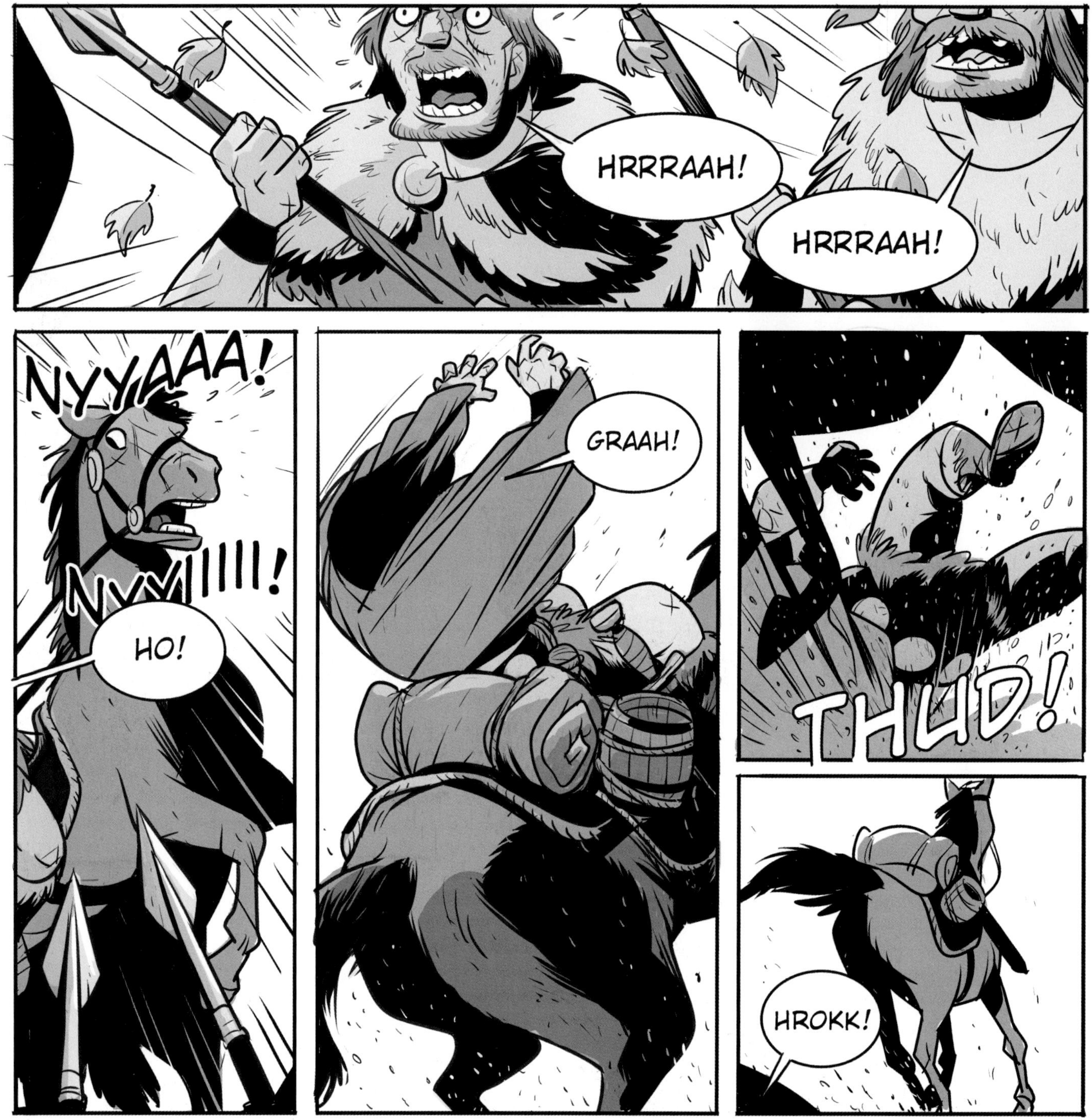
HRRRAAH!
HRRRAAH!
NYYAAA!
NYYIIIIII!
HO!
GRAAH!
THUD!
HROKK!

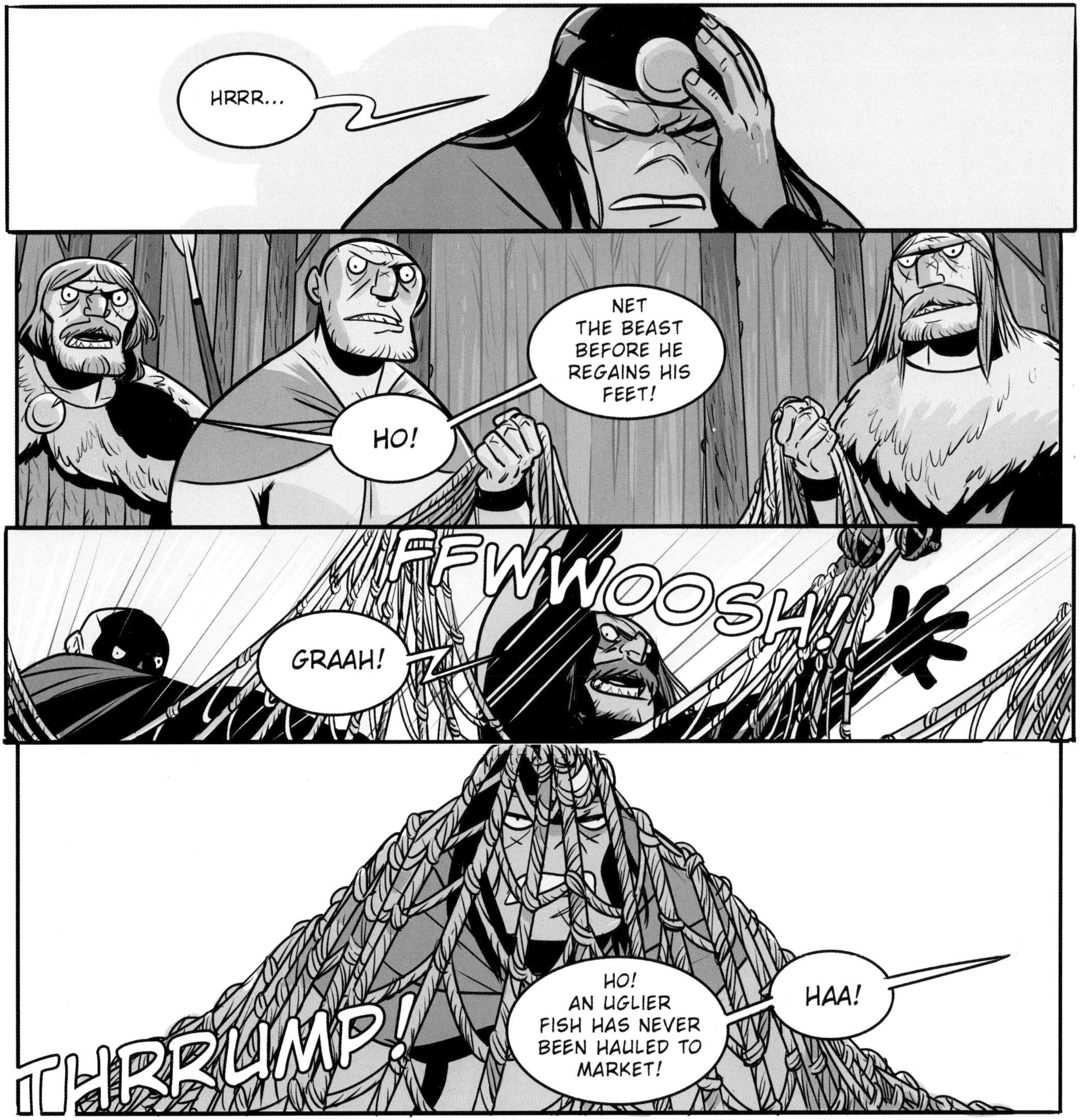
HRRR...
NET THE BEAST BEFORE HE REGAINS HIS FEET!
HO!
FFWWOOSH!
GRAAH!
THRRUMP!
HO! AN UGLIER FISH HAS NEVER BEEN HAULED TO MARKET!
HAA!

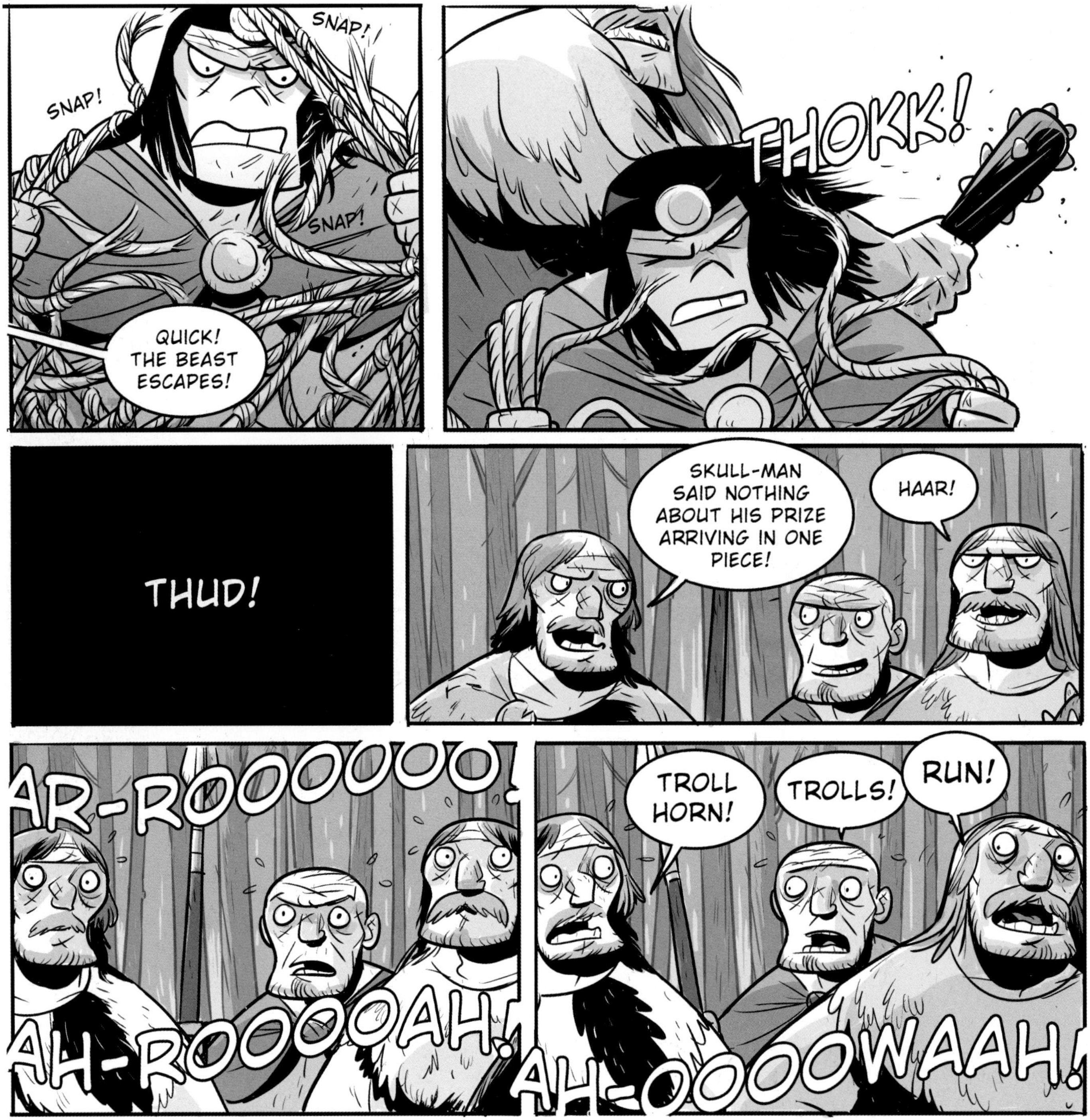
SNAP!
SNAP!
SNAP!
QUICK! THE BEAST ESCAPES!
THOKK!
THUD!
SKULL-MAN SAID NOTHING ABOUT HIS PRIZE ARRIVING IN ONE PIECE!
HAAR!
AR-ROOOOOOO!
AH-ROOOOOAH!
TROLL HORN!
TROLLS!
RUN!
AH-OOOOOWAAH!

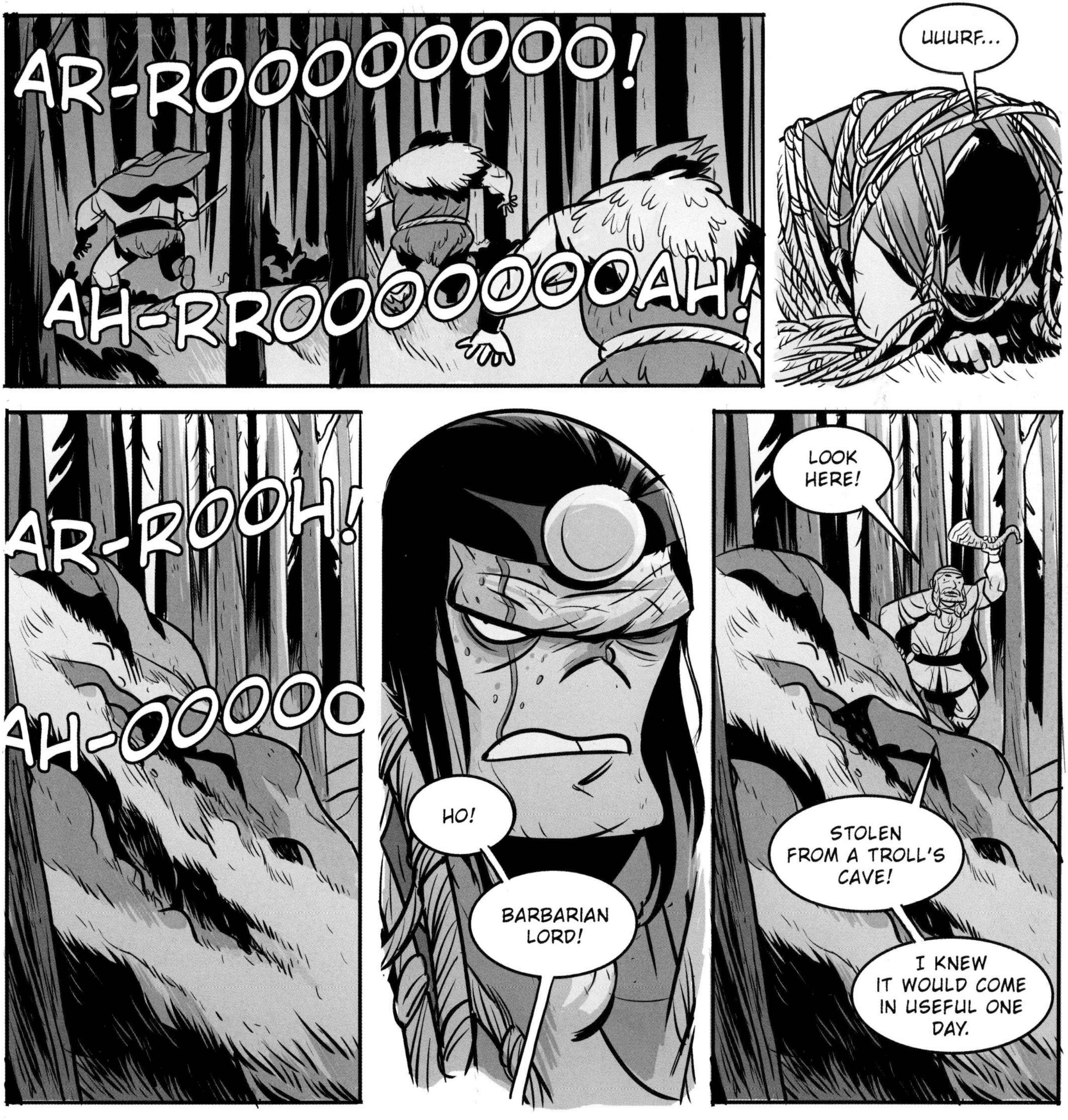

AR-ROOOOOOOOO!
AH-RROOOOOOOOAH!
UUURF...
AR-ROOH!
AH-OOOOO
HO!
BARBARIAN LORD!
LOOK HERE!
STOLEN FROM A TROLL'S CAVE!
I KNEW IT WOULD COME IN USEFUL ONE DAY.

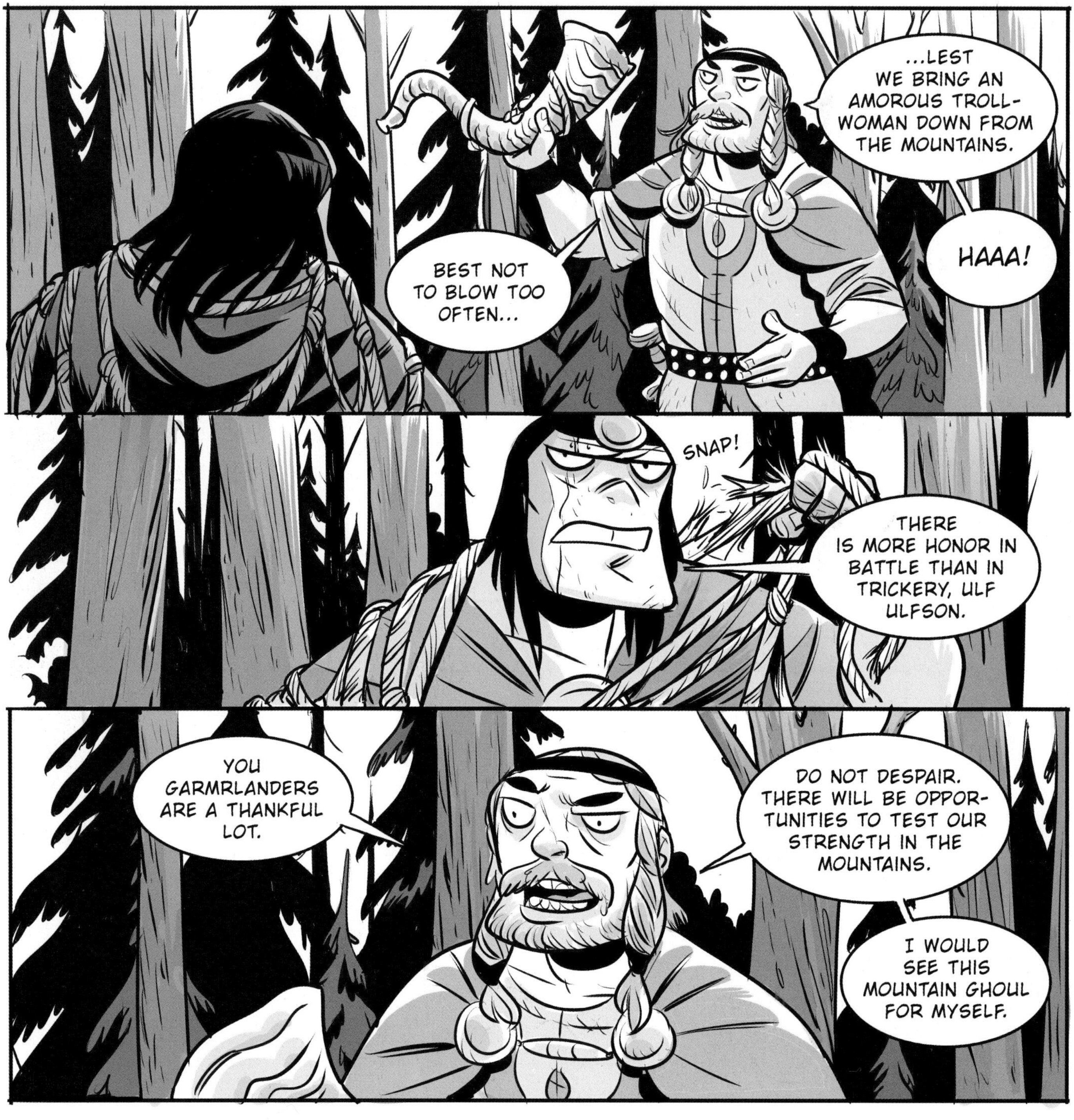
BEST NOT TO BLOW TOO OFTEN...
...LEST WE BRING AN AMOROUS TROLL-WOMAN DOWN FROM THE MOUNTAINS.
HAAA!
SNAP!
THERE IS MORE HONOR IN BATTLE THAN IN TRICKERY, ULF ULFSON.
YOU GARMRLANDERS ARE A THANKFUL LOT.
DO NOT DESPAIR. THERE WILL BE OPPOR-TUNITIES TO TEST OUR STRENGTH IN THE MOUNTAINS.
I WOULD SEE THIS MOUNTAIN GHOUL FOR MYSELF.

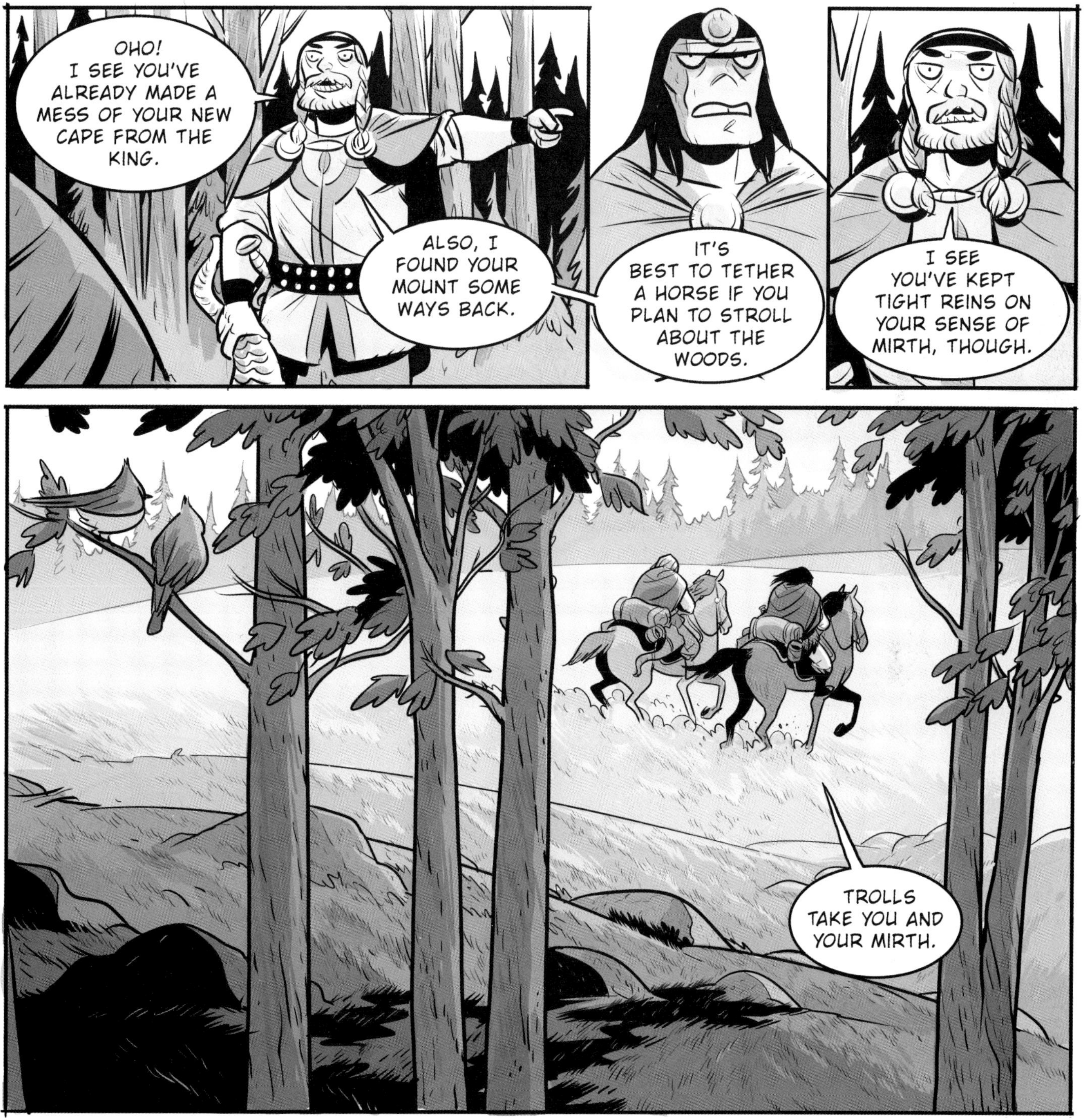
OHO! I SEE YOU'VE ALREADY MADE A MESS OF YOUR NEW CAPE FROM THE KING.
ALSO, I FOUND YOUR MOUNT SOME WAYS BACK.
IT'S BEST TO TETHER A HORSE IF YOU PLAN TO STROLL ABOUT THE WOODS.
I SEE YOU'VE KEPT TIGHT REINS ON YOUR SENSE OF MIRTH, THOUGH.
TROLLS TAKE YOU AND YOUR MIRTH.

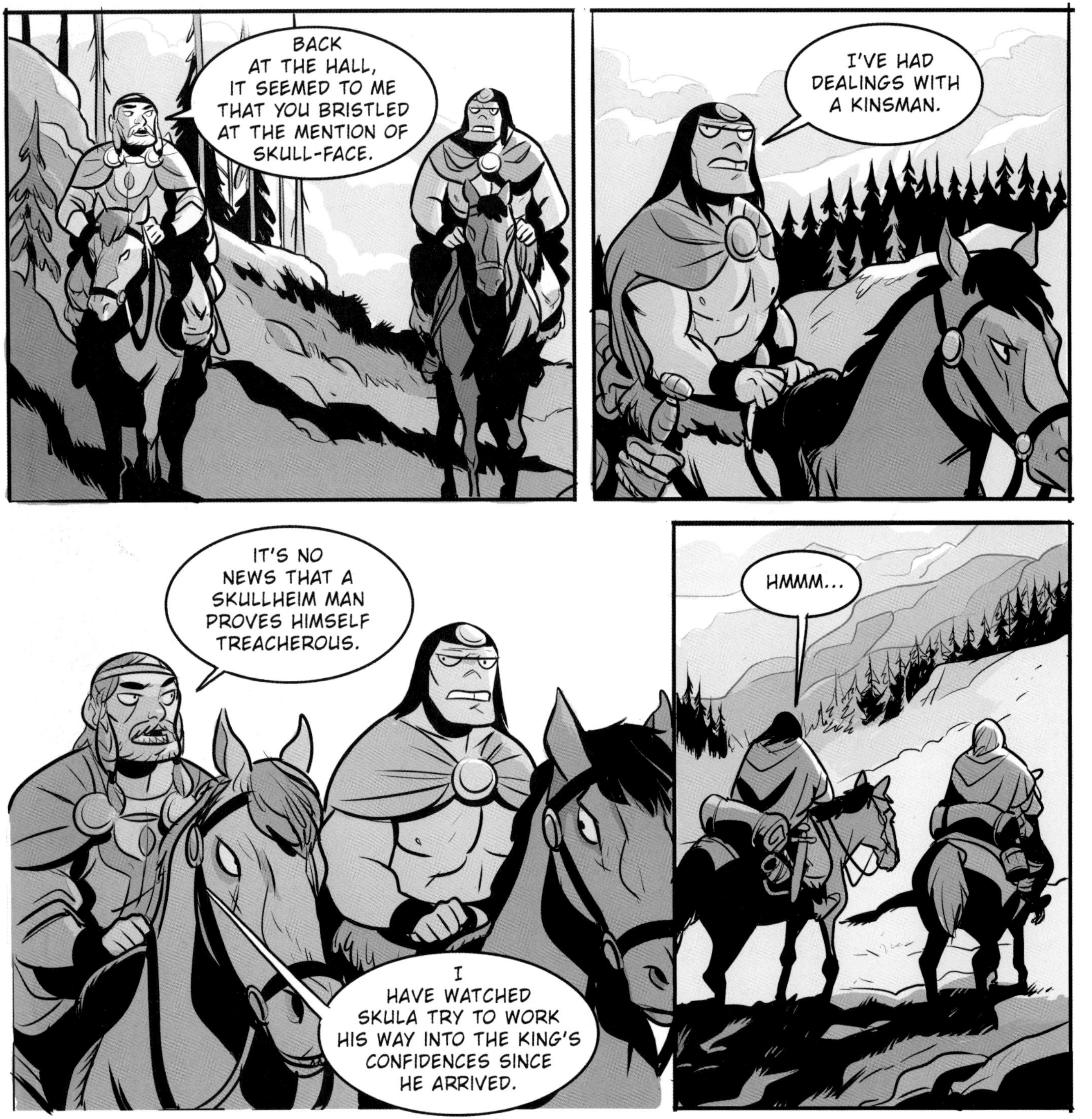
BACK AT THE HALL, IT SEEMED TO ME THAT YOU BRISTLED AT THE MENTION OF SKULL-FACE.
I'VE HAD DEALINGS WITH A KINSMAN.
IT'S NO NEWS THAT A SKULLHEIM MAN PROVES HIMSELF TREACHEROUS.
I HAVE WATCHED SKULA TRY TO WORK HIS WAY INTO THE KING'S CONFIDENCES SINCE HE ARRIVED.
HMMM...

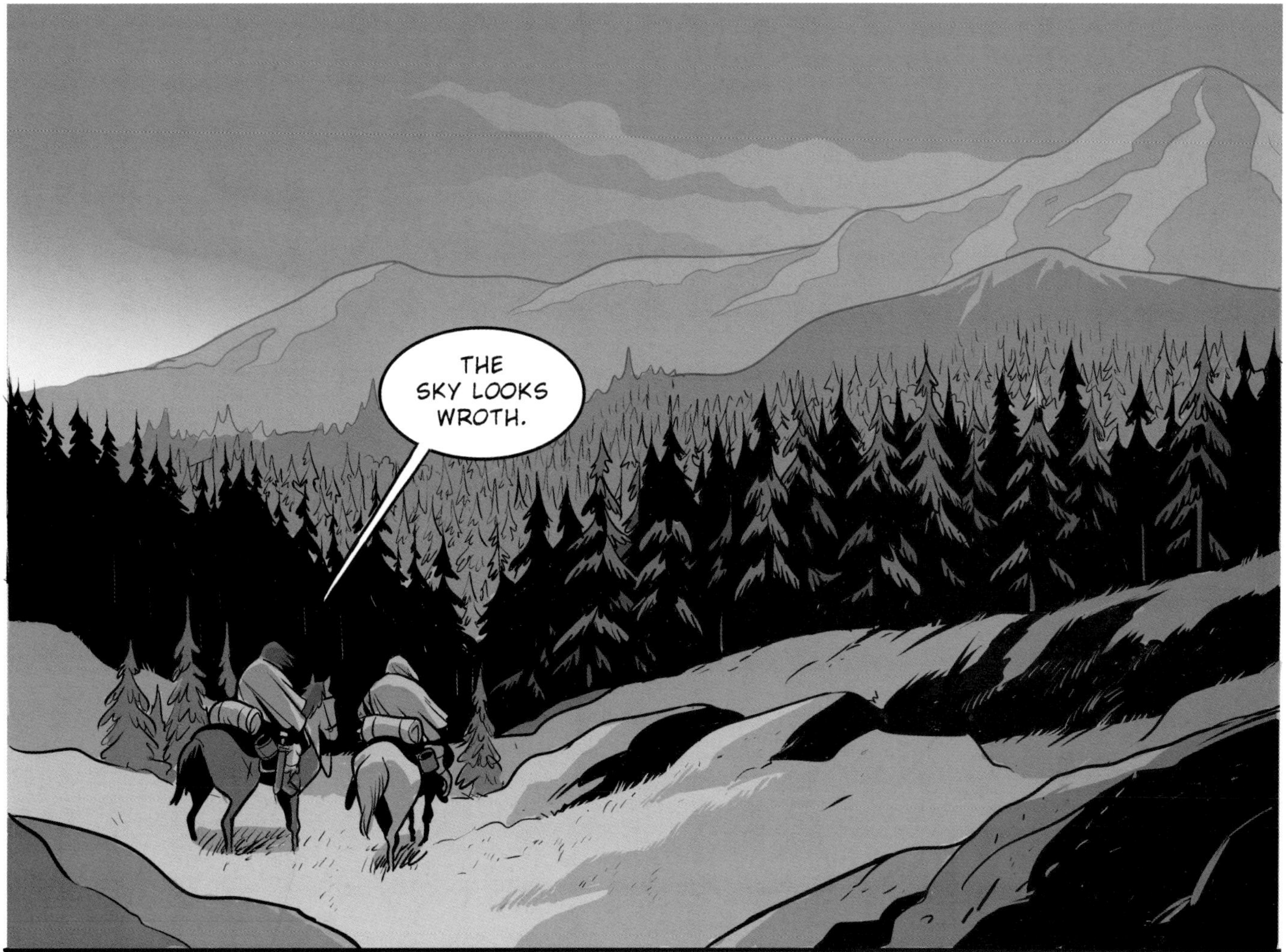
THE SKY LOOKS WROTH.

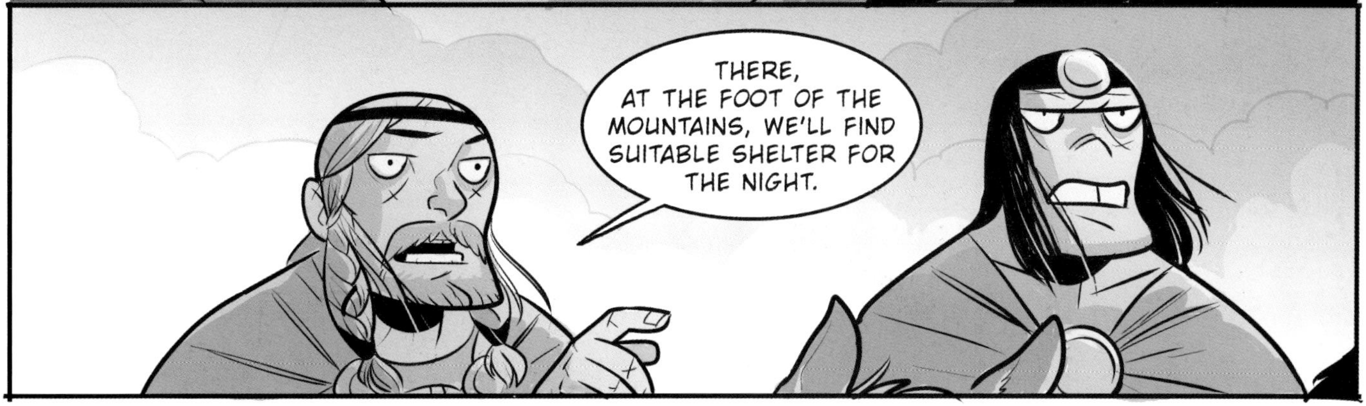
THERE, AT THE FOOT OF THE MOUNTAINS, WE'LL FIND SUITABLE SHELTER FOR THE NIGHT.

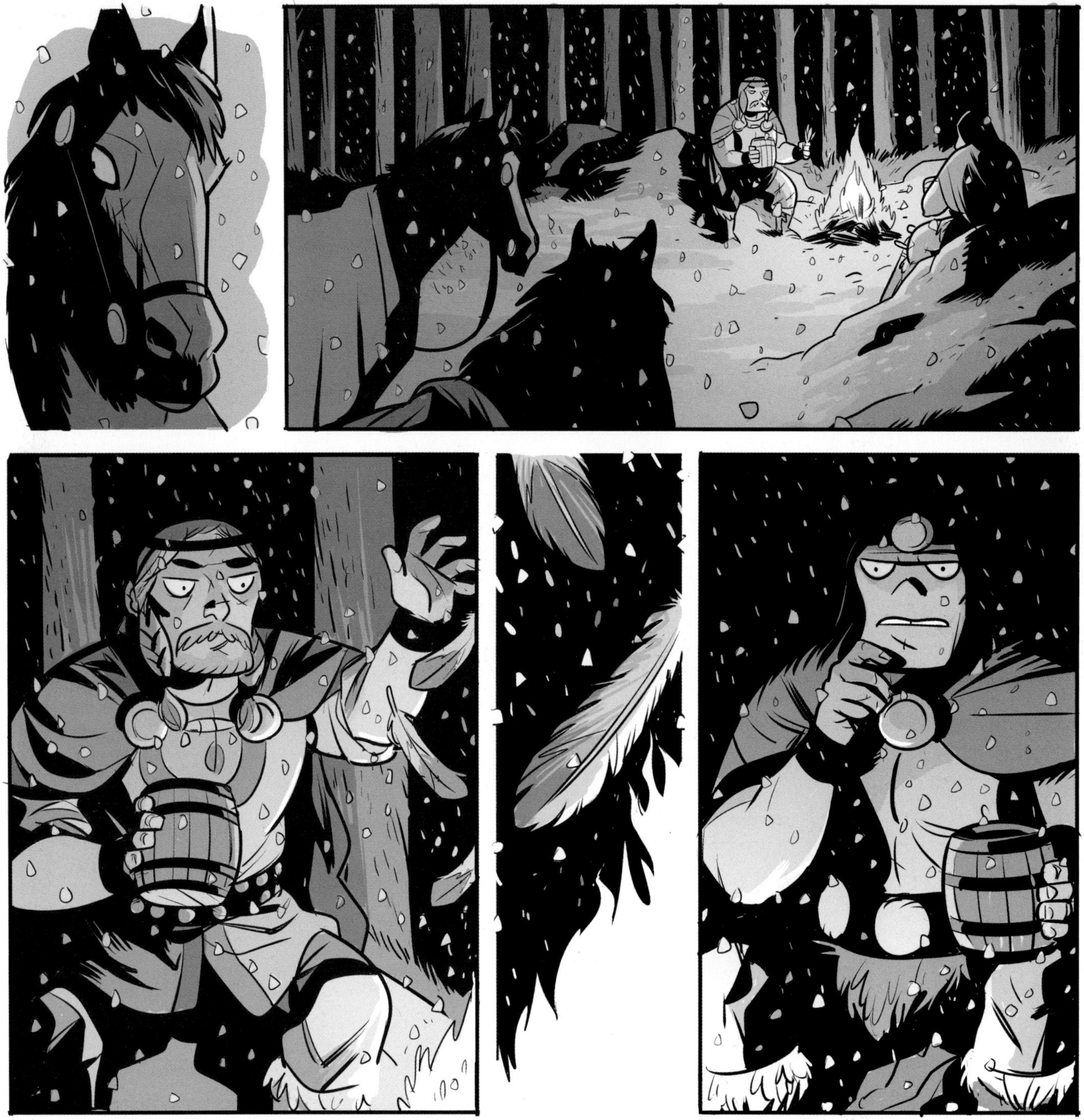

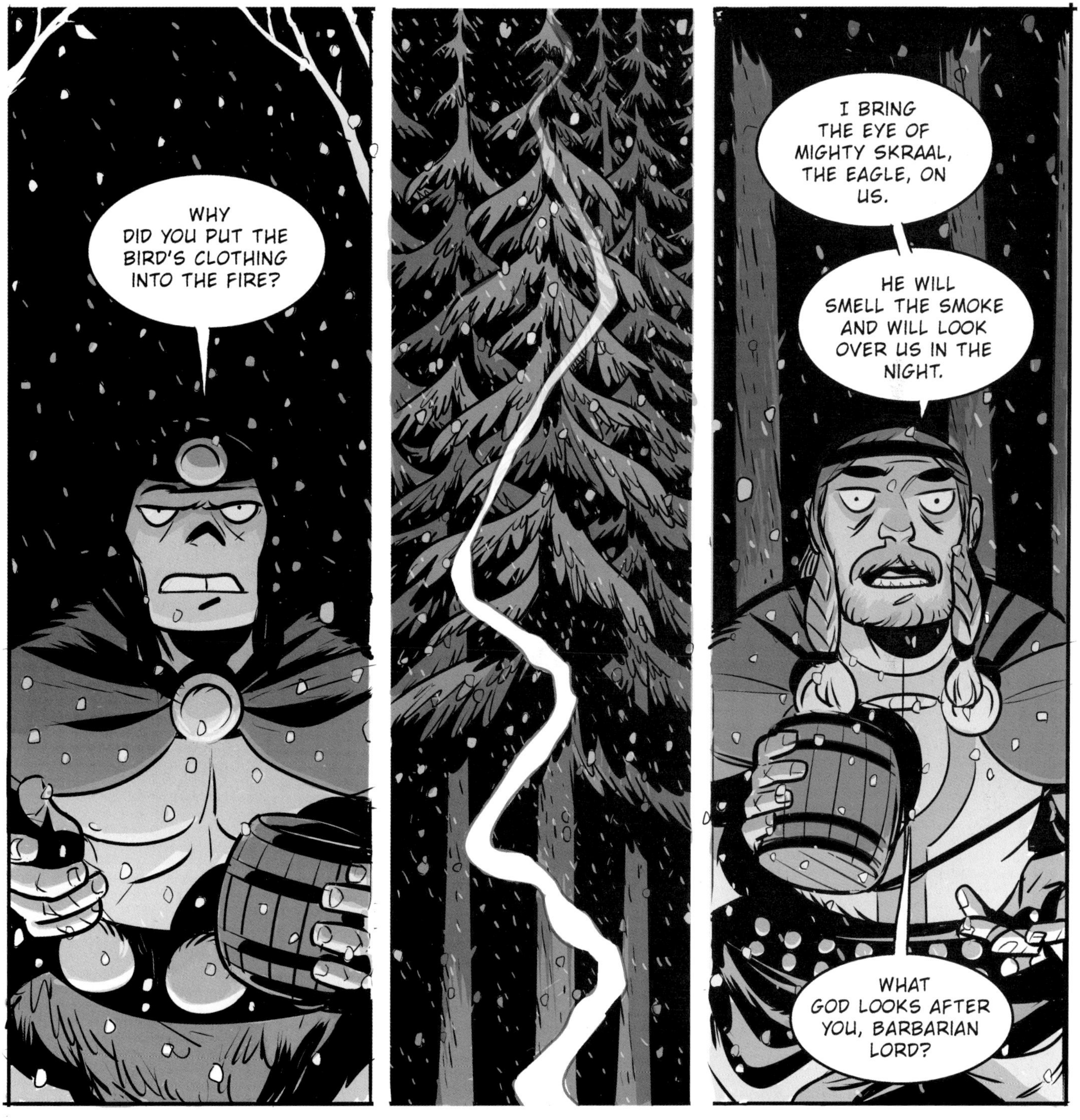
WHY DID YOU PUT THE BIRD'S CLOTHING INTO THE FIRE?
I BRING THE EYE OF MIGHTY SKRAAL, THE EAGLE, ON US.
HE WILL SMELL THE SMOKE AND WILL LOOK OVER US IN THE NIGHT.
WHAT GOD LOOKS AFTER YOU, BARBARIAN LORD?

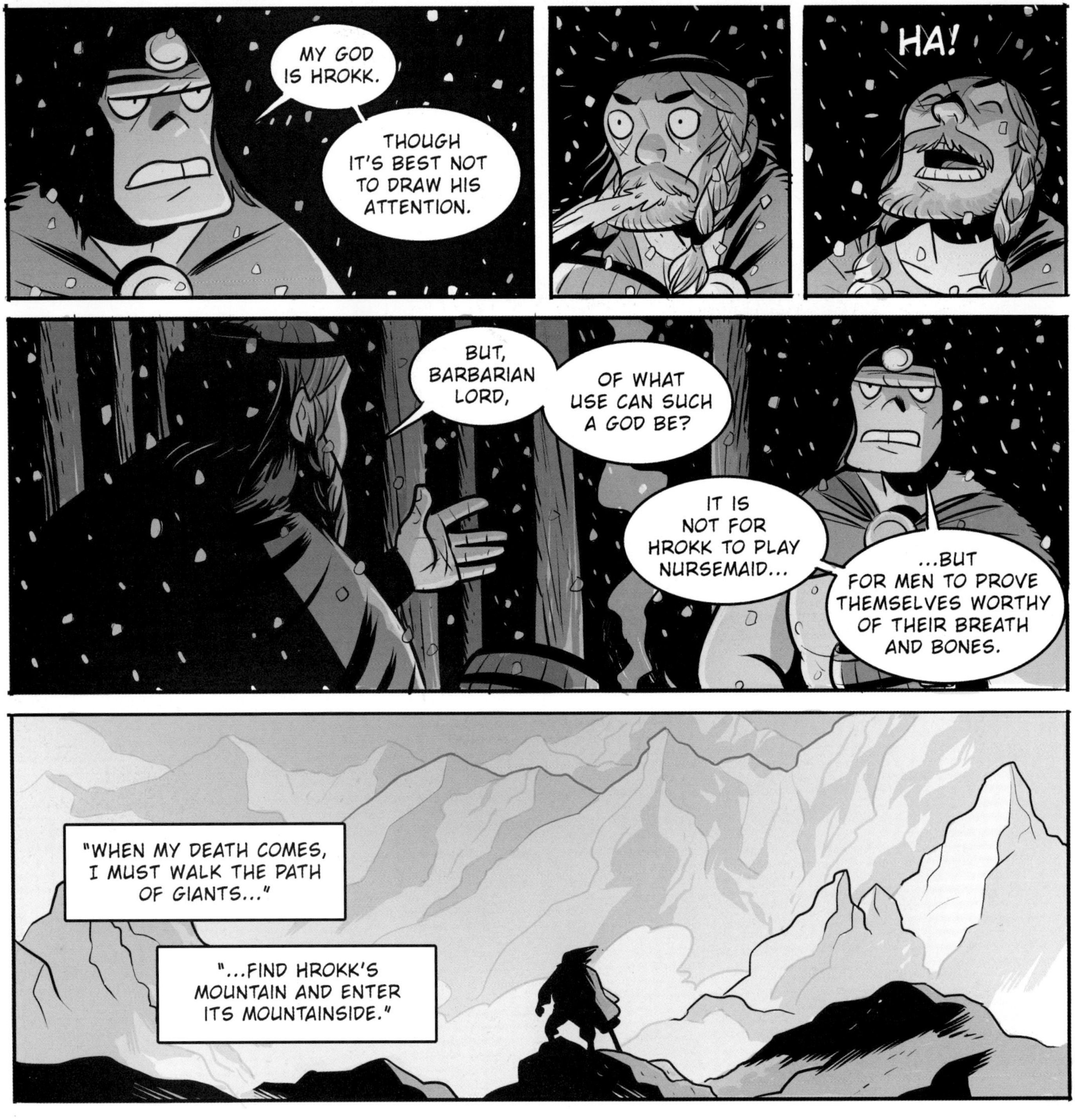
MY GOD IS HROKK.
THOUGH IT'S BEST NOT TO DRAW HIS ATTENTION.
HA!
BUT, BARBARIAN LORD,
OF WHAT USE CAN SUCH A GOD BE?
IT IS NOT FOR HROKK TO PLAY NURSEMAID...
...BUT FOR MEN TO PROVE THEMSELVES WORTHY OF THEIR BREATH AND BONES.
"WHEN MY DEATH COMES, I MUST WALK THE PATH OF GIANTS..."
"...FIND HROKK'S MOUNTAIN AND ENTER ITS MOUNTAINSIDE."

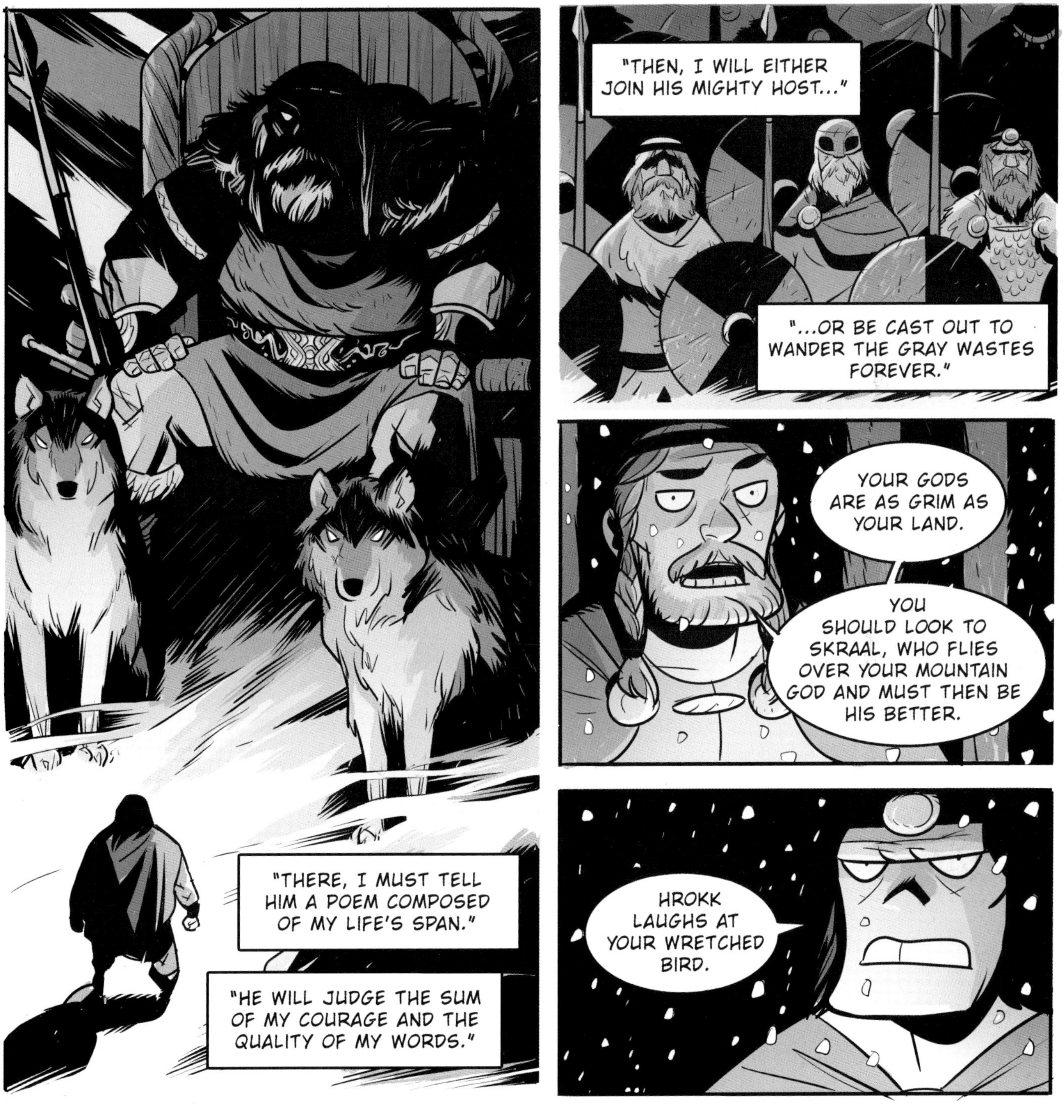
"THERE, I MUST TELL HIM A POEM COMPOSED OF MY LIFE'S SPAN."
"HE WILL JUDGE THE SUM OF MY COURAGE AND THE QUALITY OF MY WORDS."
"THEN, I WILL EITHER JOIN HIS MIGHTY HOST..."
"...OR BE CAST OUT TO WANDER THE GRAY WASTES FOREVER."
YOUR GODS ARE AS GRIM AS YOUR LAND.
YOU SHOULD LOOK TO SKRAAL, WHO FLIES OVER YOUR MOUNTAIN GOD AND MUST THEN BE HIS BETTER.
HROKK LAUGHS AT YOUR WRETCHED BIRD.

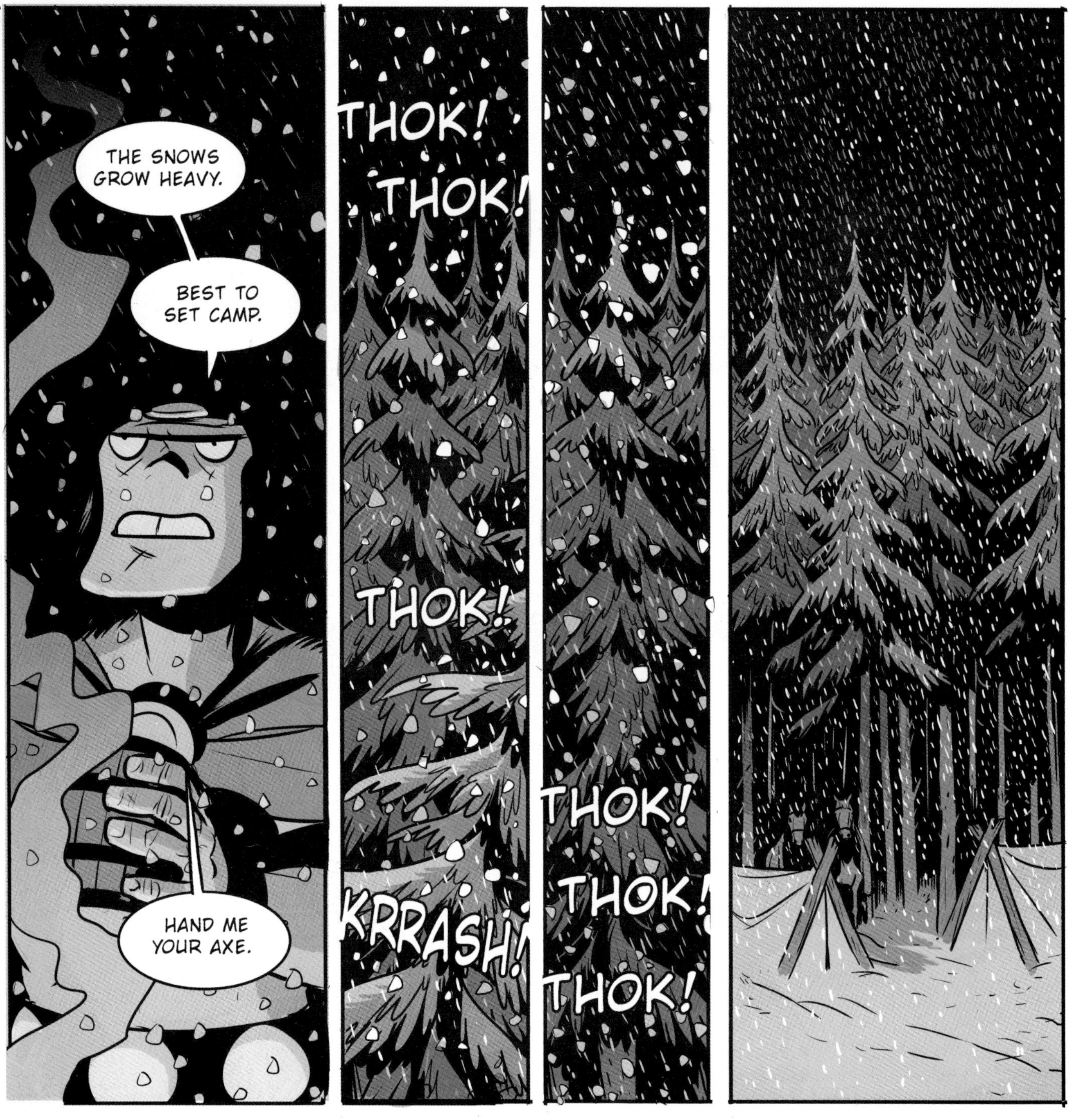
THE SNOWS GROW HEAVY.
BEST TO SET CAMP.
HAND ME YOUR AXE.
THOK!
THOK!
THOK!
KRRASH!
THOK!
THOK!
THOK!

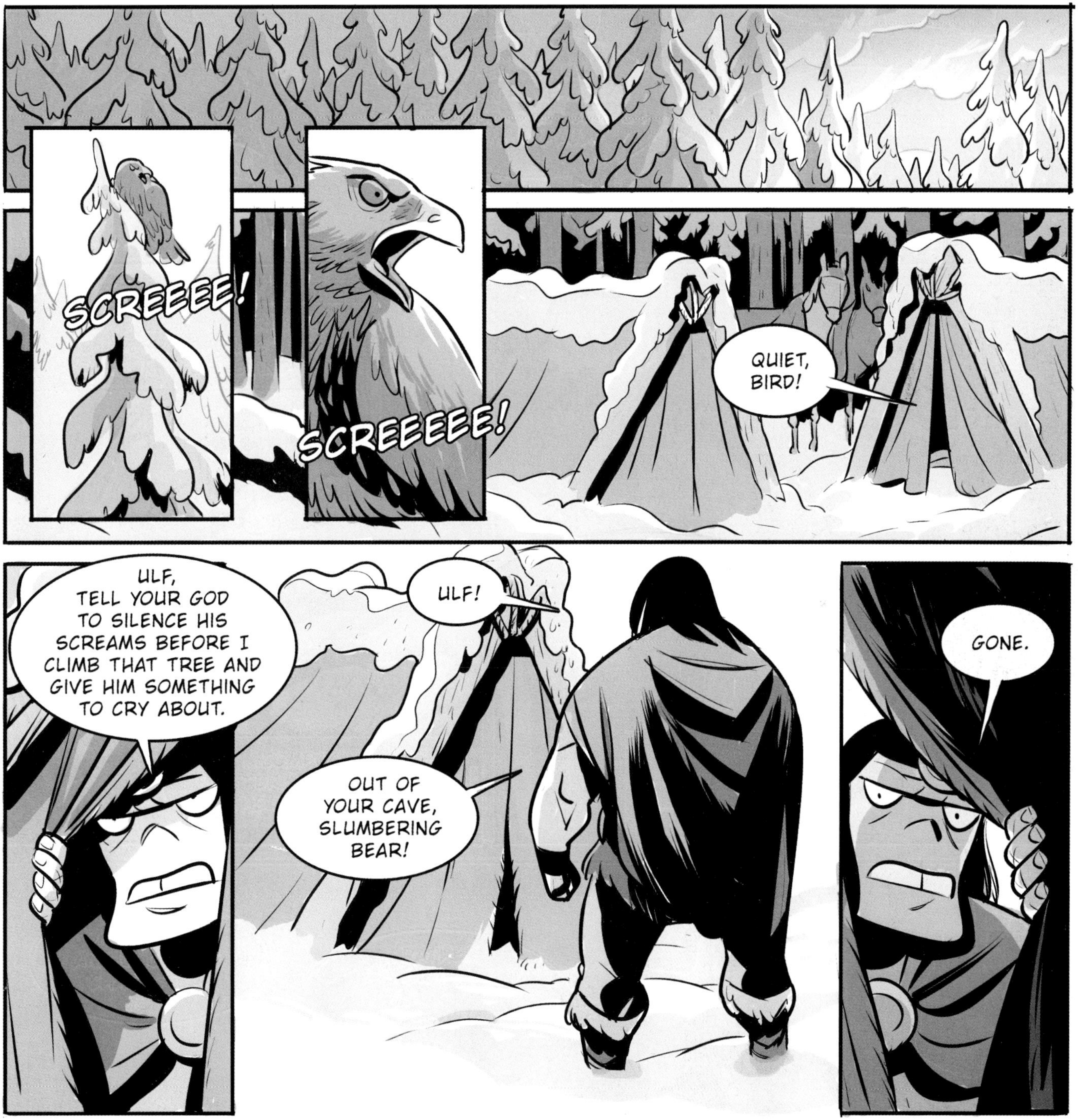
SCREEEEE!
SCREEEEEE!
QUIET, BIRD!
ULF, TELL YOUR GOD TO SILENCE HIS SCREAMS BEFORE I CLIMB THAT TREE AND GIVE HIM SOMETHING TO CRY ABOUT.
ULF!
OUT OF YOUR CAVE, SLUMBERING BEAR!
GONE.

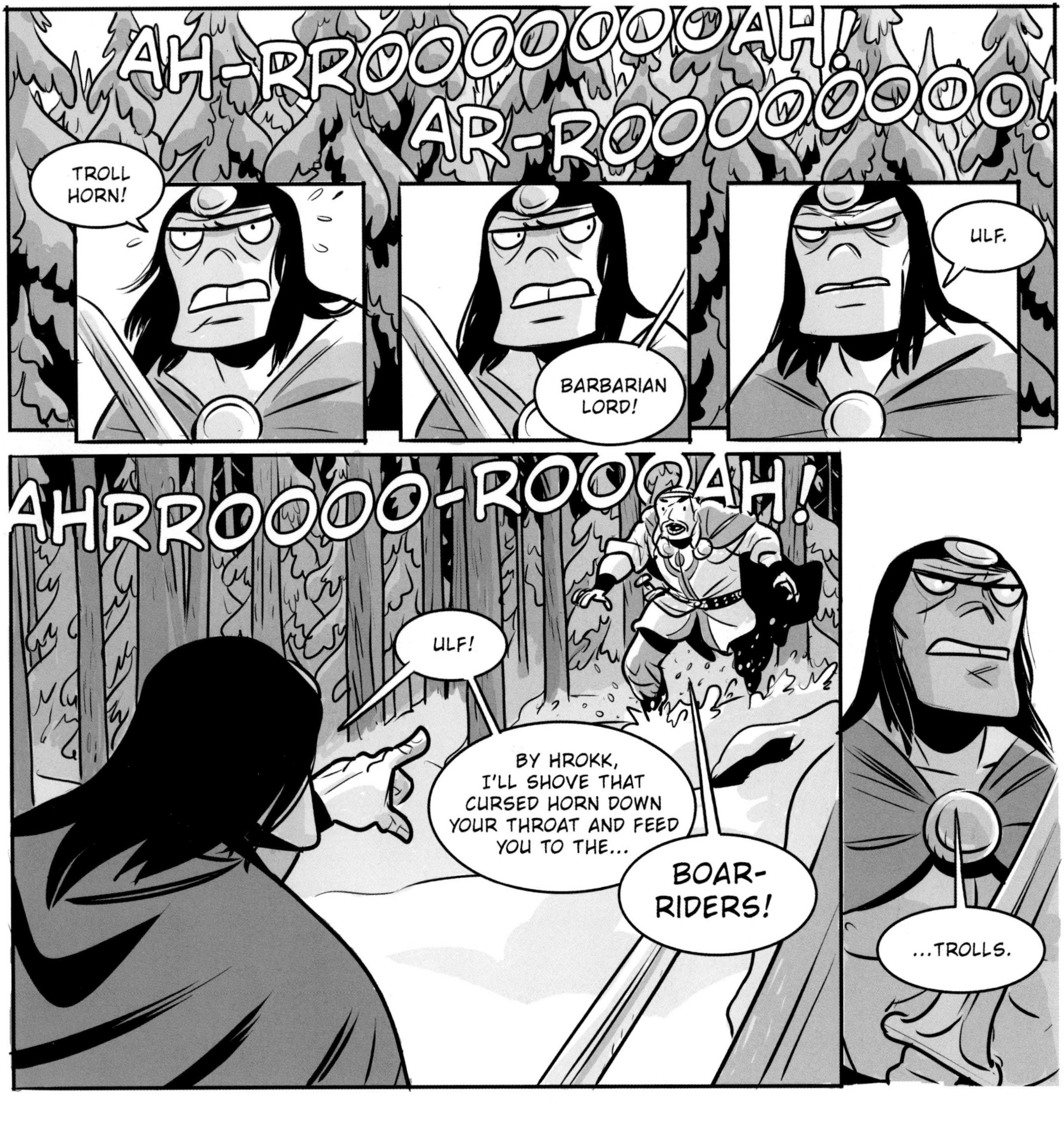
AH-RROOOOOOOOAH!
AR-ROOOOOOOOOO!
TROLL HORN!
BARBARIAN LORD!
ULF.
AHRROOOO-ROOOOAH!
ULF!
BY HROKK, I'LL SHOVE THAT CURSED HORN DOWN YOUR THROAT AND FEED YOU TO THE...
BOAR-RIDERS!
...TROLLS.

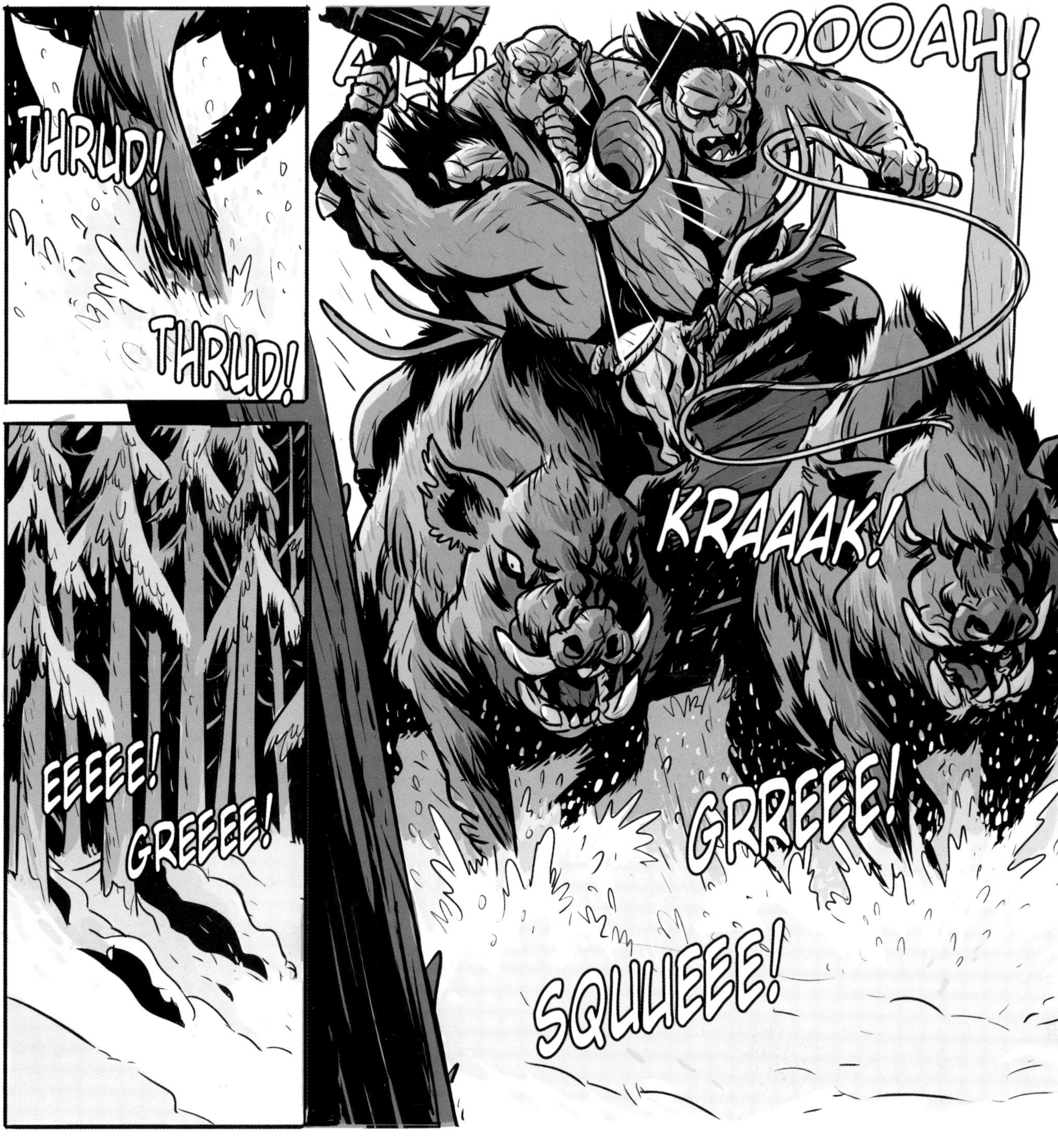
THRUD!
THRUD!
OOOOAH!
KRAAAK!
GRREEE!
SQUEEE!
EEEEE!
GREEEE!

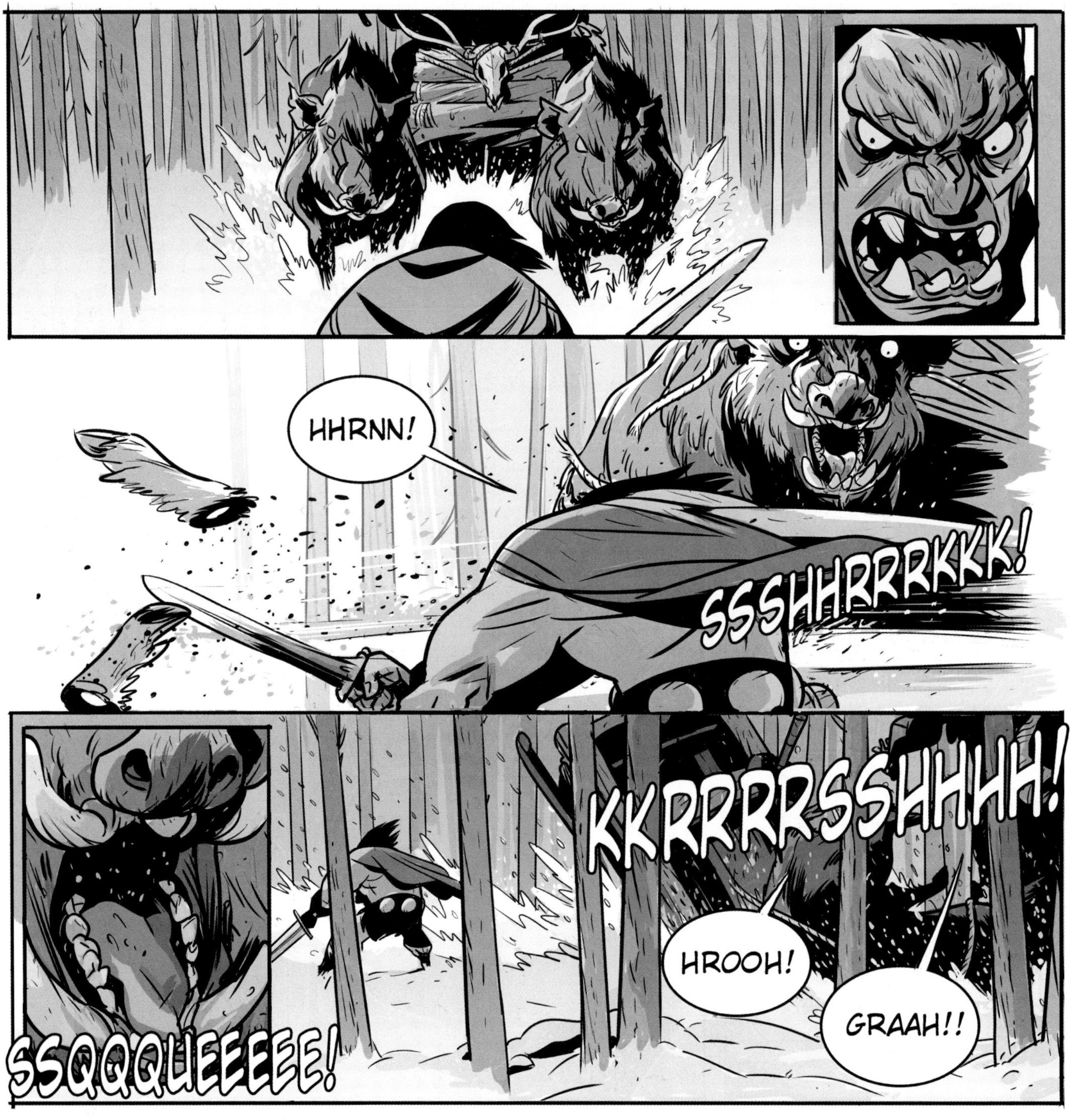
HHRNN!
SSSHHRRRKKK!
SSQQQUEEEEEE!
KKRRRRRSSHHHH!
HROOH!
GRAAH!!

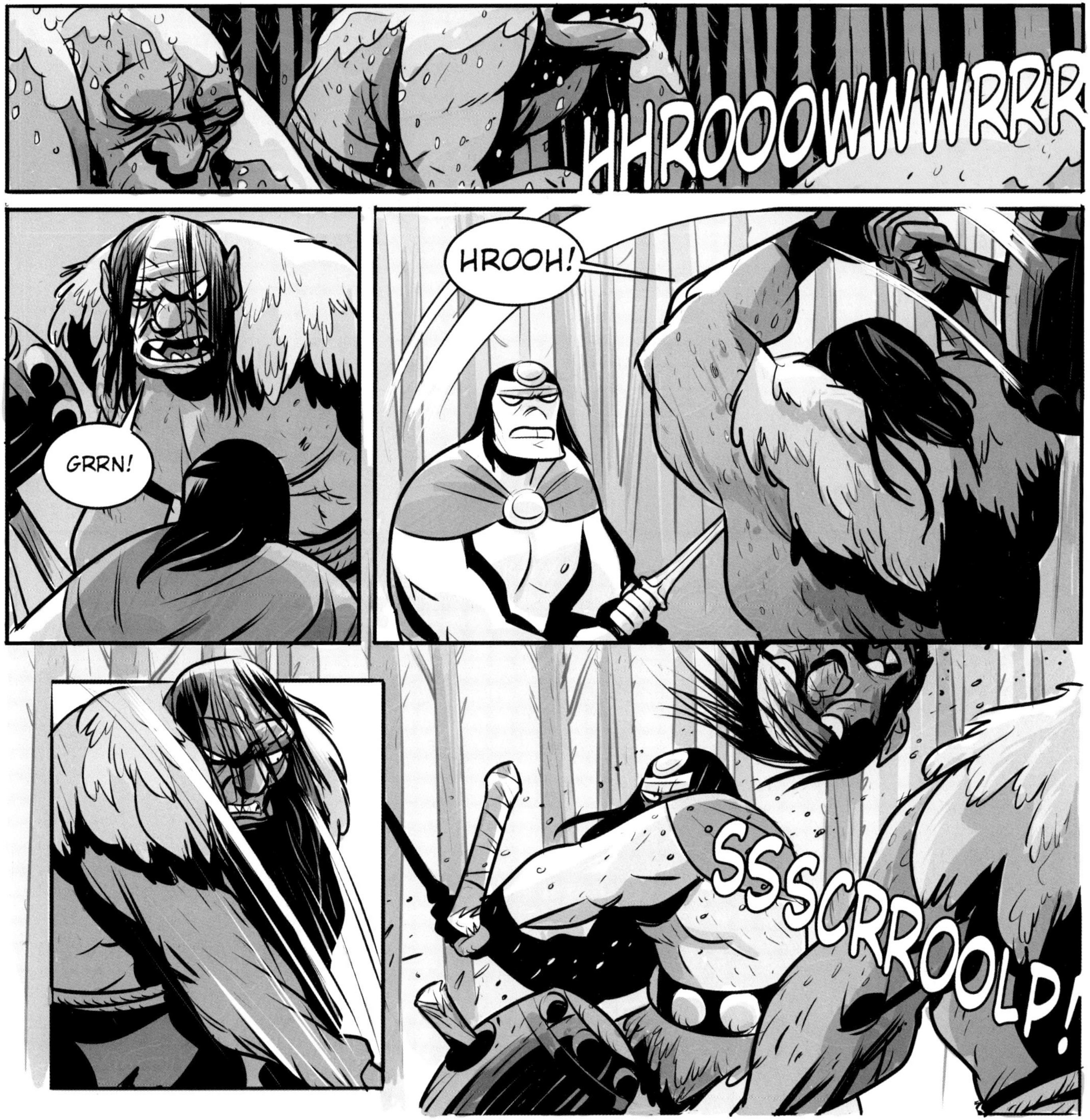
HHROOOWWWRRR
GRRN!
HROOH!
SSSCRROOLP!

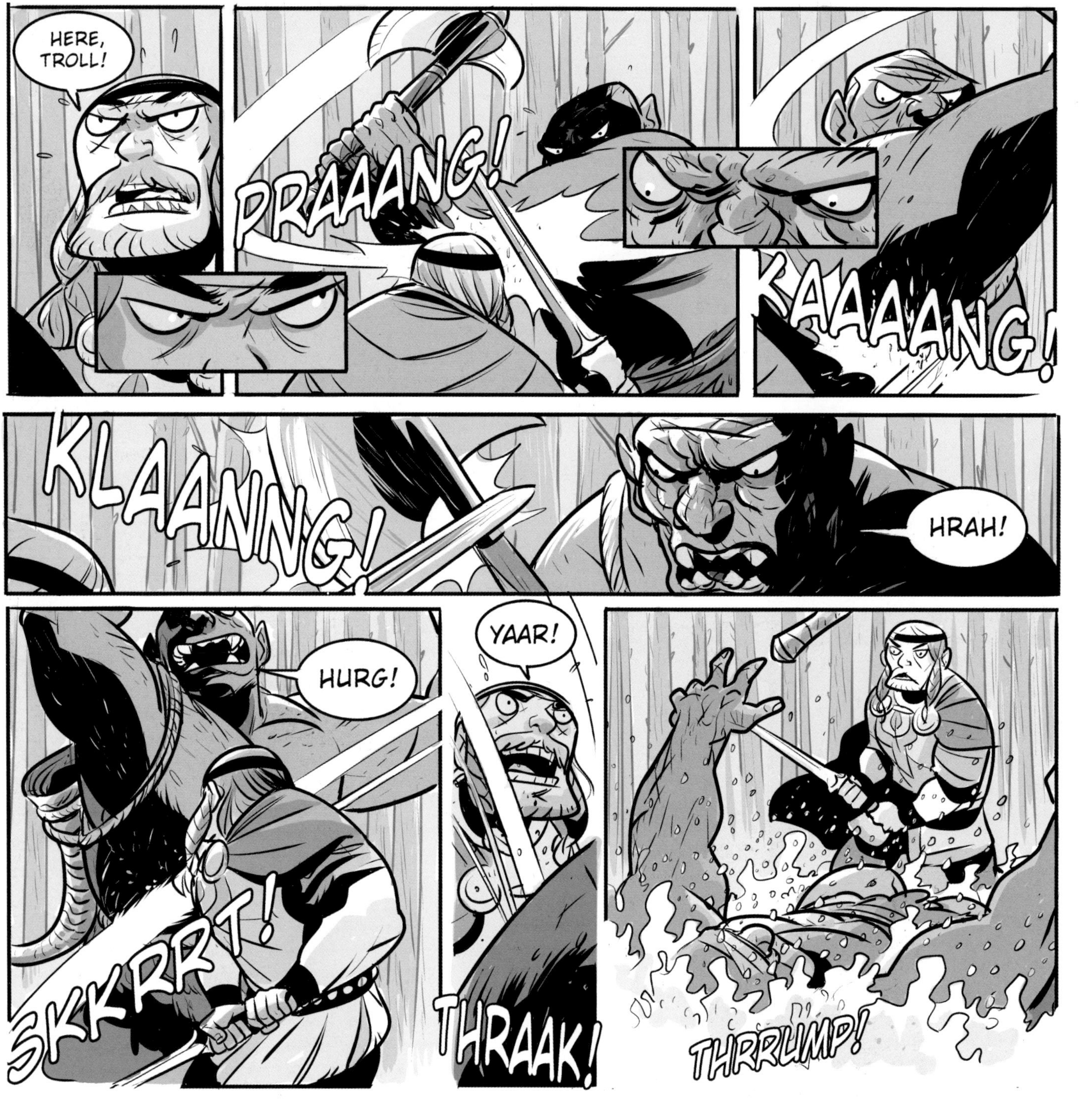
HERE, TROLL!
PRAAANG!
KAAAAANG!
KLAANNG!
HRAH!
HURG!
SKKRRRT!
YAAR!
THRAAK!
THRRUMP!

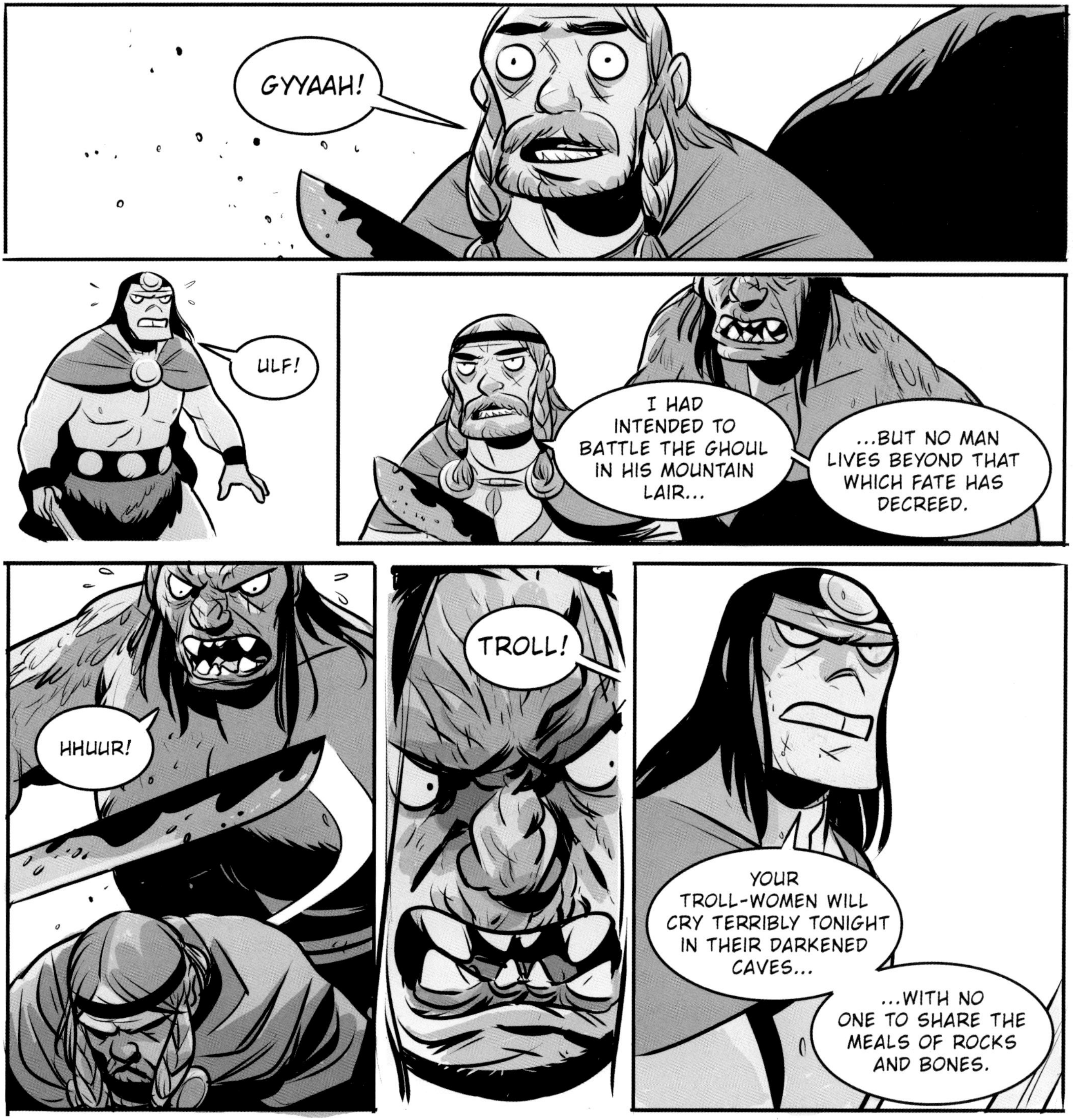
GYYAAH!
ULF!
I HAD INTENDED TO BATTLE THE GHOUL IN HIS MOUNTAIN LAIR...
...BUT NO MAN LIVES BEYOND THAT WHICH FATE HAS DECREED.
HHUUR!
TROLL!
YOUR TROLL-WOMEN WILL CRY TERRIBLY TONIGHT IN THEIR DARKENED CAVES...
...WITH NO ONE TO SHARE THE MEALS OF ROCKS AND BONES.

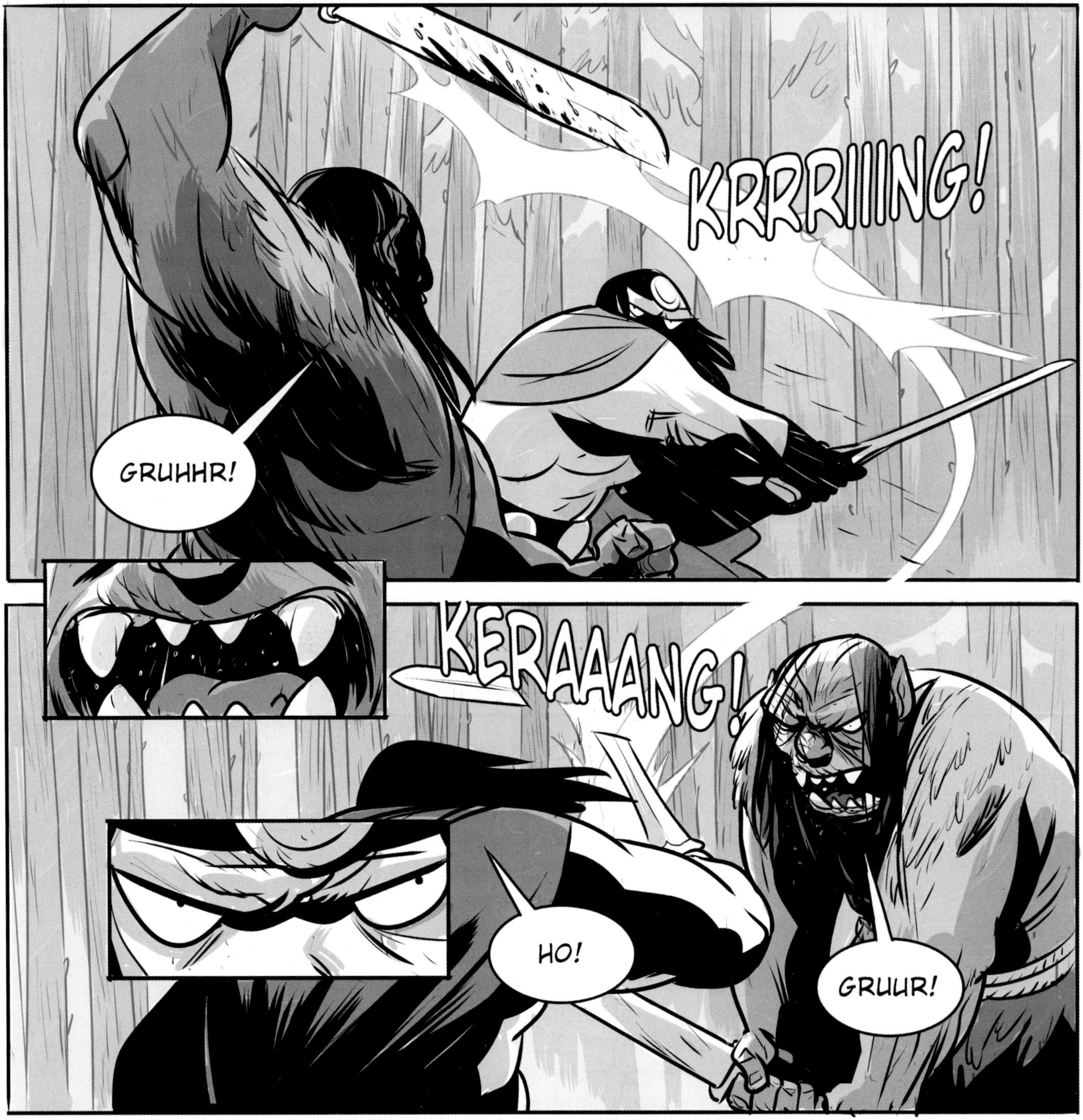
KRRRIIING!
GRUHHR!
KERAAANG!
HO!
GRUUR!

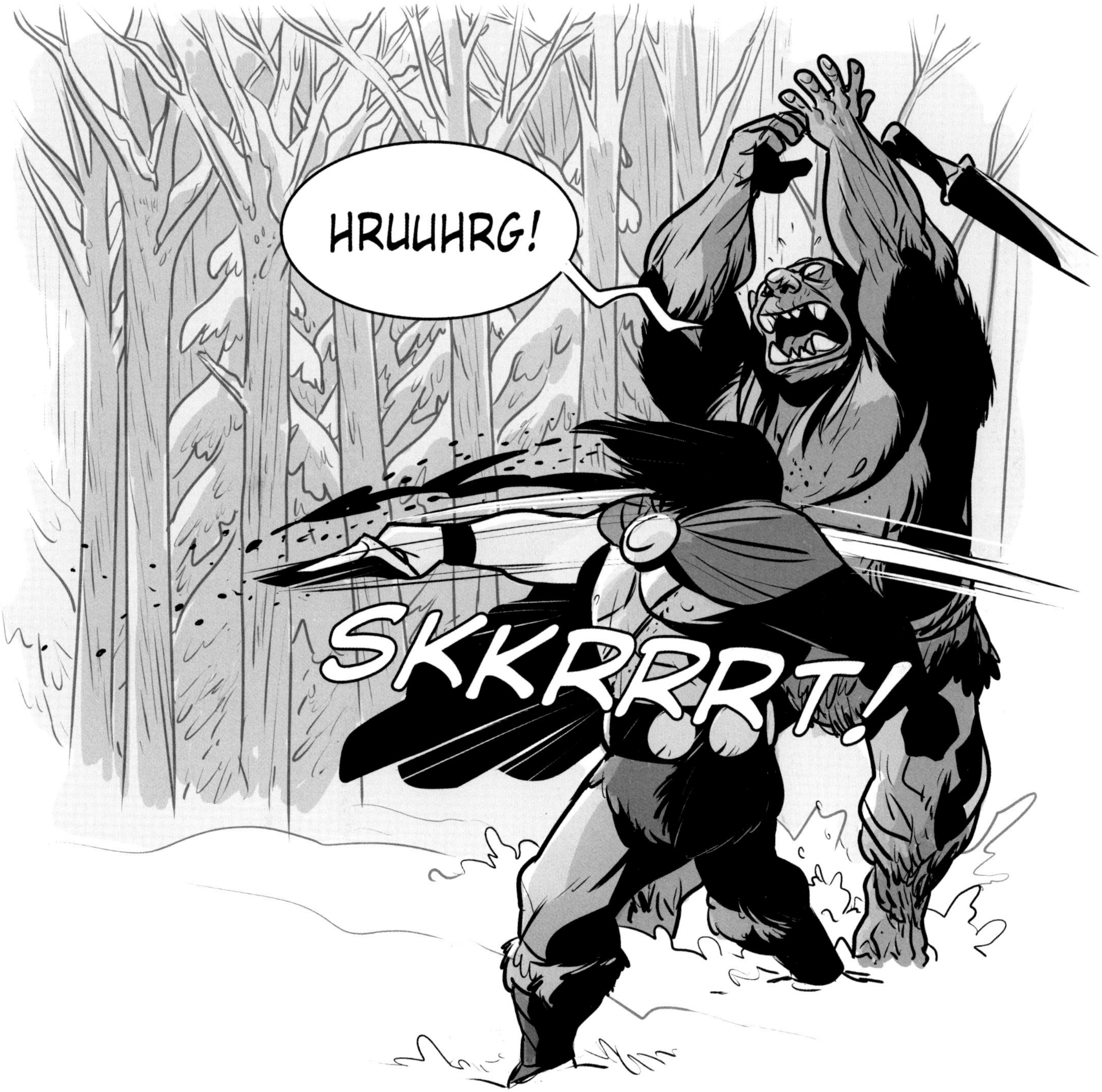
HRUUHRG!
SKKRRRT!

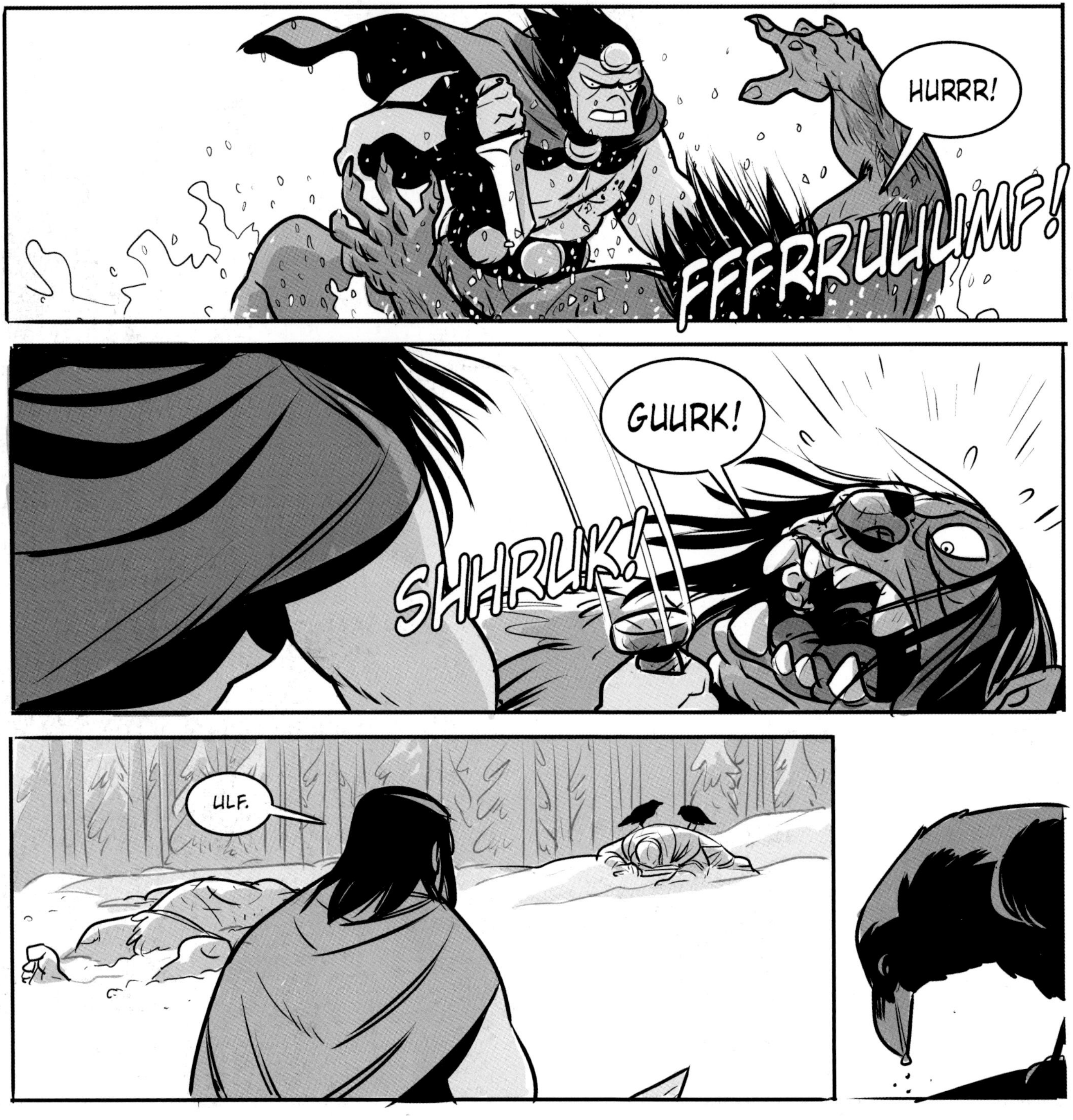
HURRR!
FFFRRUULUMF!
GUURK!
SHHRUK!
ULF.

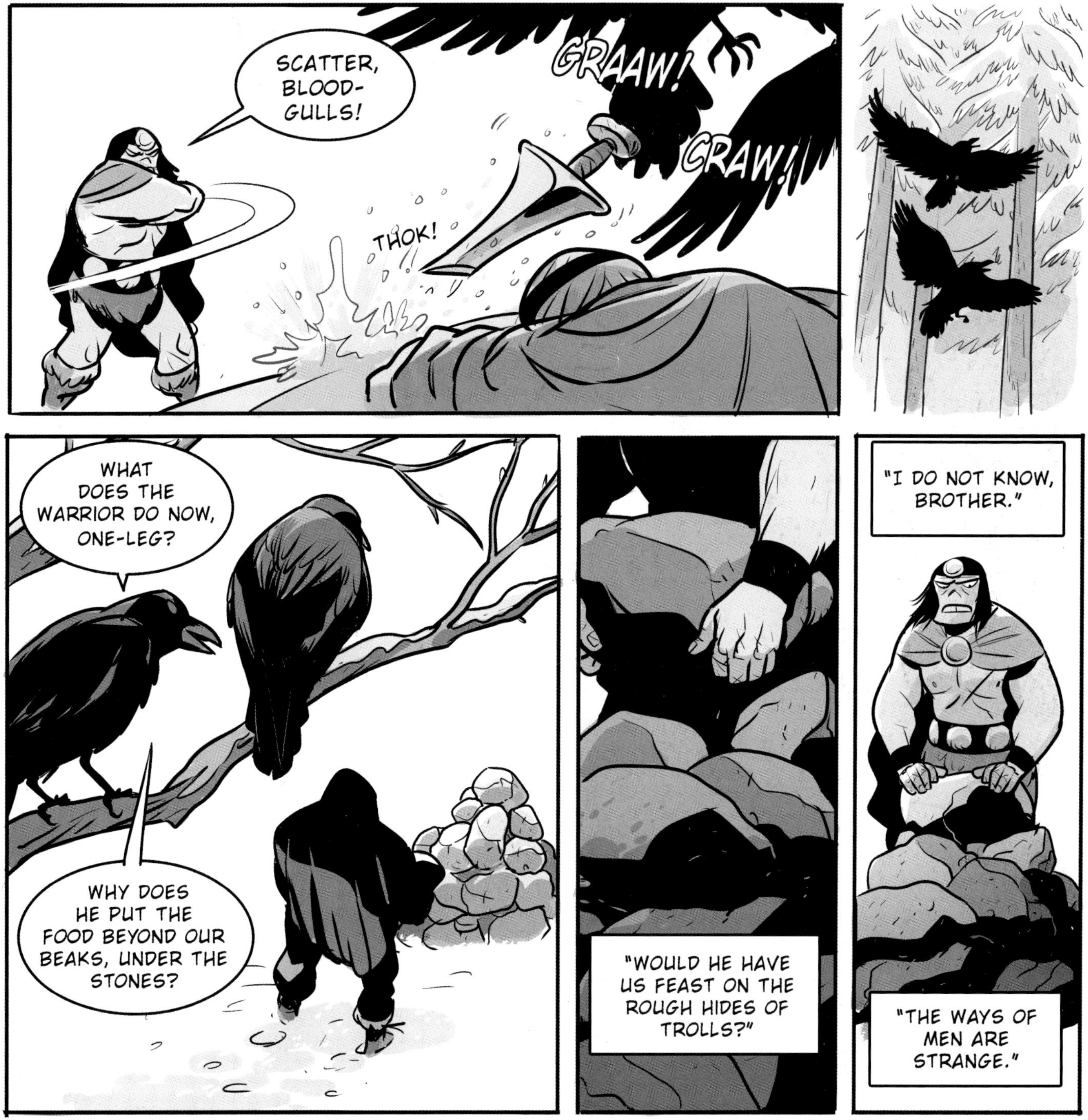
SCATTER, BLOOD-GULLS!
GRAAW!
CRAW!
THOK!
WHAT DOES THE WARRIOR DO NOW, ONE-LEG?
WHY DOES HE PUT THE FOOD BEYOND OUR BEAKS, UNDER THE STONES?
"WOULD HE HAVE US FEAST ON THE ROUGH HIDES OF TROLLS?"
"I DO NOT KNOW, BROTHER."
"THE WAYS OF MEN ARE STRANGE."

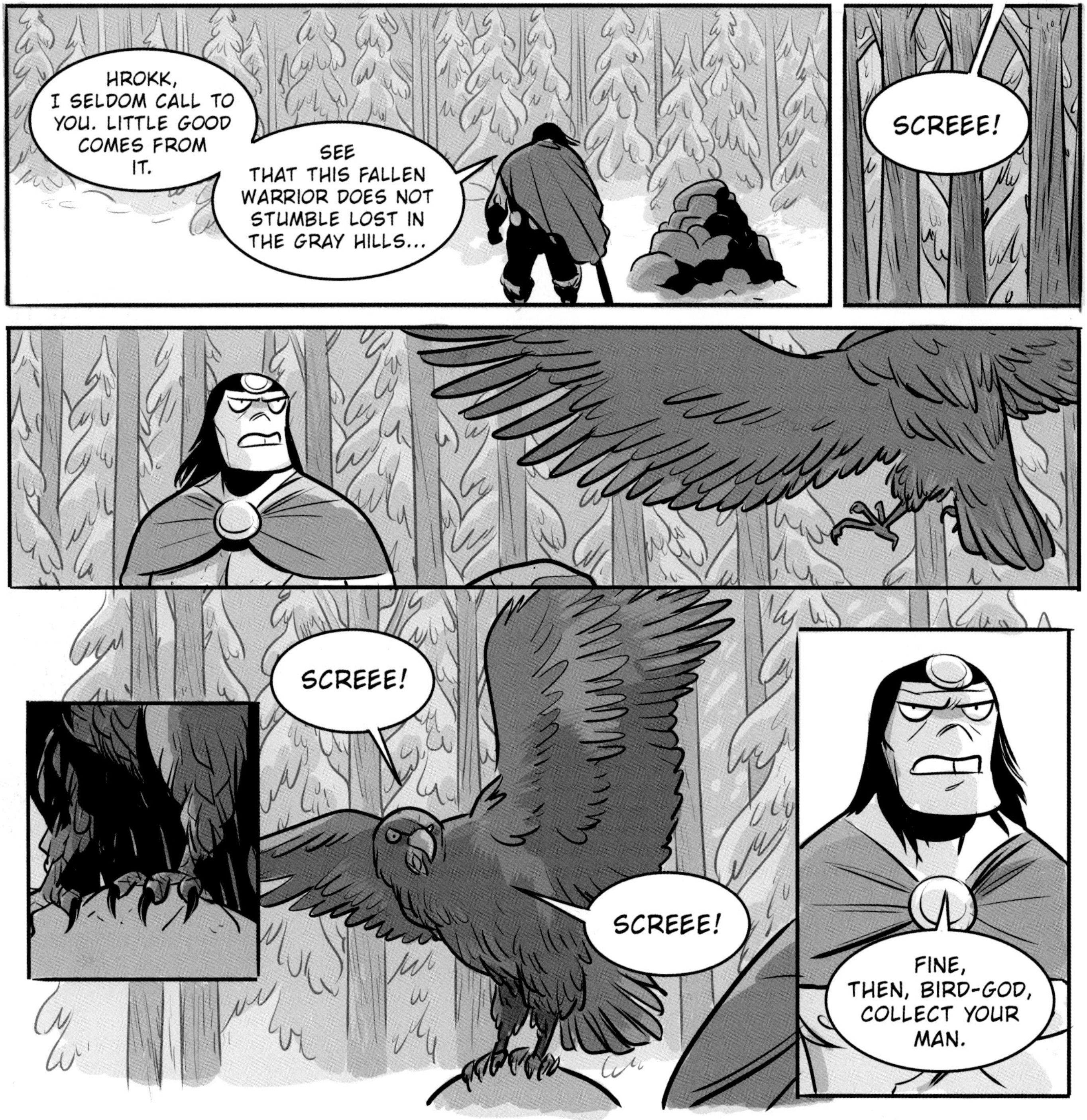
HROKK, I SELDOM CALL TO YOU. LITTLE GOOD COMES FROM IT.
SEE THAT THIS FALLEN WARRIOR DOES NOT STUMBLE LOST IN THE GRAY HILLS...
SCREEE!
SCREEE!
SCREEE!
FINE, THEN, BIRD-GOD, COLLECT YOUR MAN.

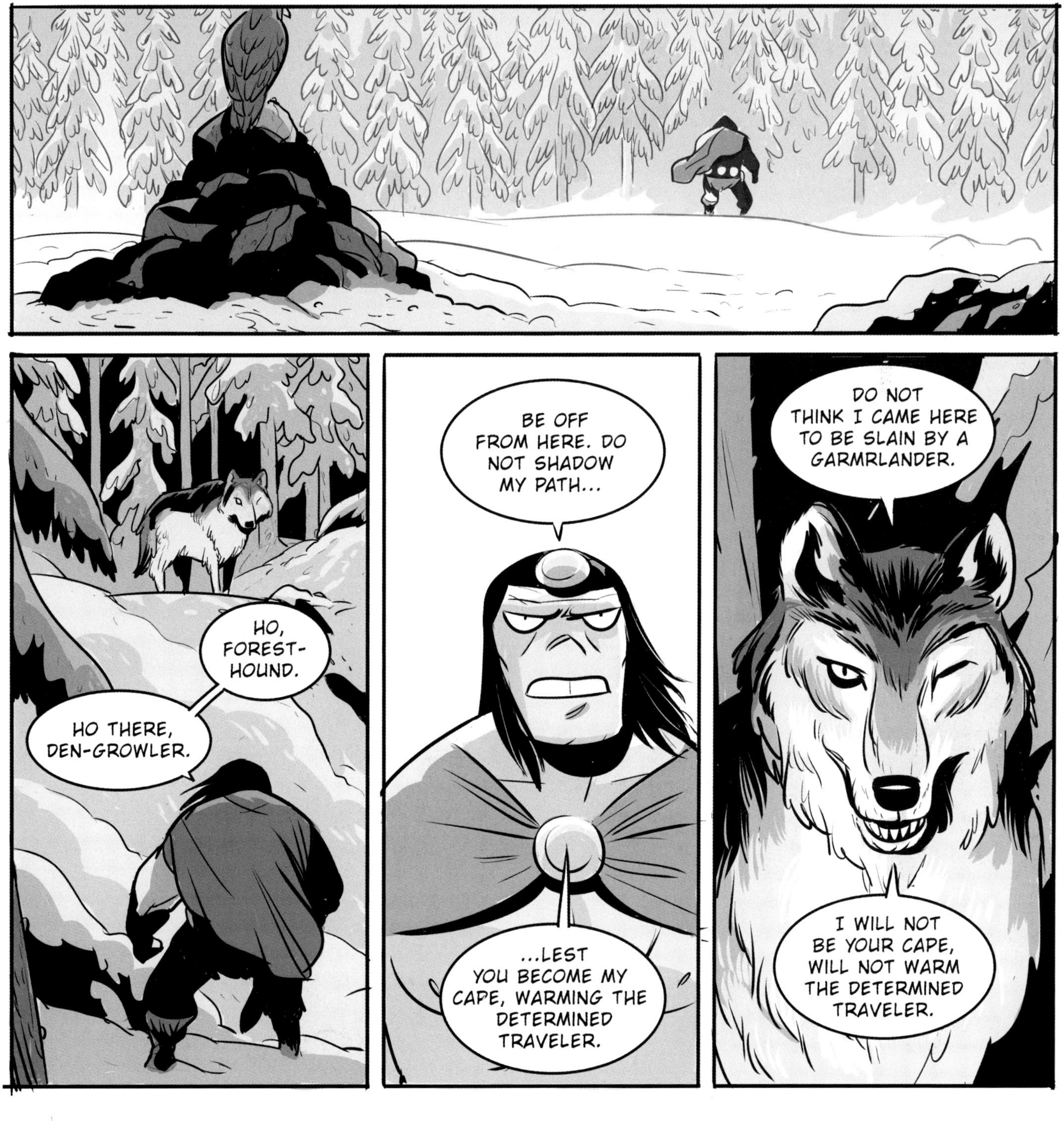
HO THERE, DEN-GROWLER.
HO, FOREST-HOUND.
BE OFF FROM HERE. DO NOT SHADOW MY PATH...
...LEST YOU BECOME MY CAPE, WARMING THE DETERMINED TRAVELER.
DO NOT THINK I CAME HERE TO BE SLAIN BY A GARMRLANDER.
I WILL NOT BE YOUR CAPE, WILL NOT WARM THE DETERMINED TRAVELER.

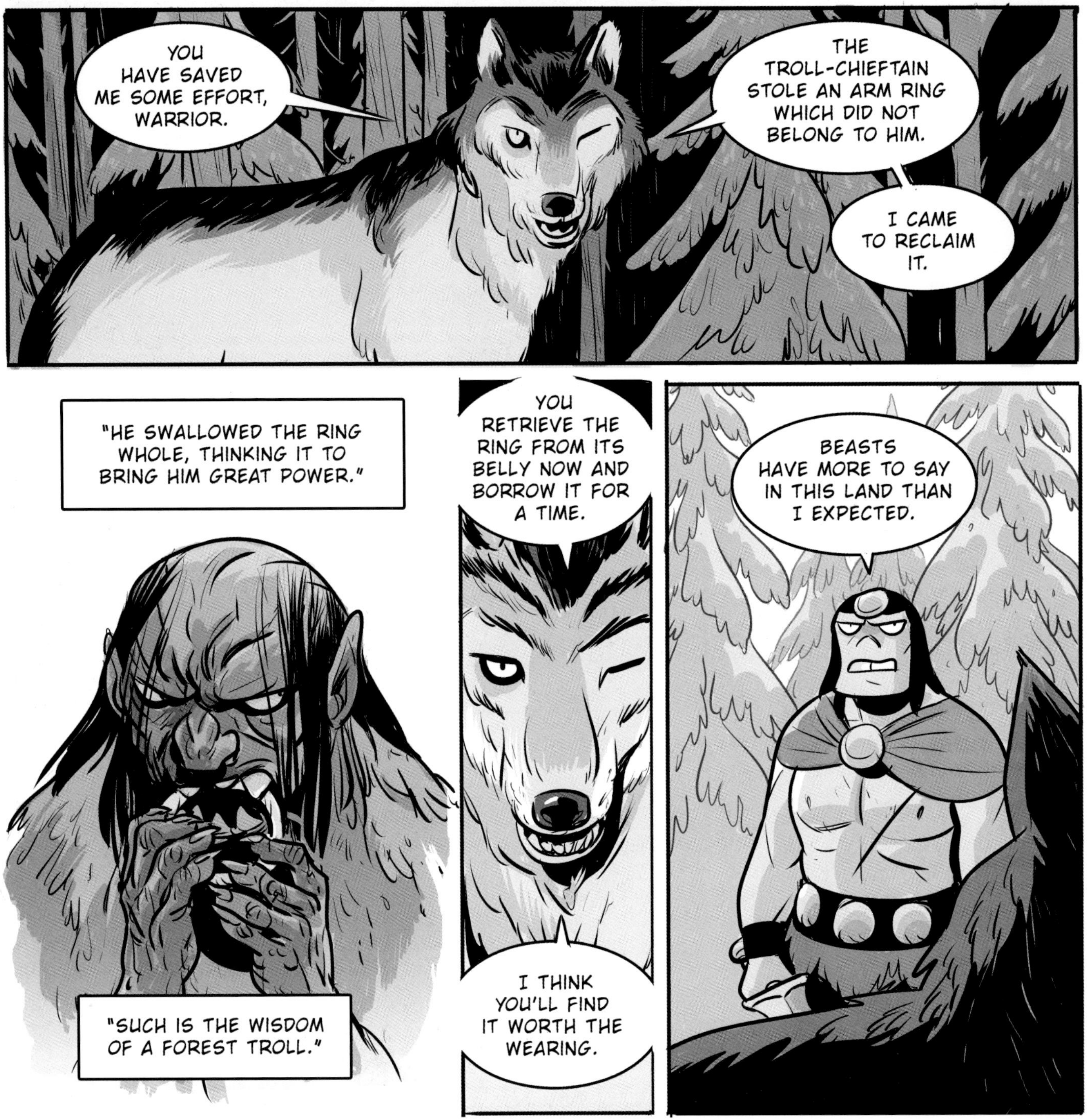
YOU HAVE SAVED ME SOME EFFORT, WARRIOR.
THE TROLL-CHIEFTAIN STOLE AN ARM RING WHICH DID NOT BELONG TO HIM.
I CAME TO RECLAIM IT.
"HE SWALLOWED THE RING WHOLE, THINKING IT TO BRING HIM GREAT POWER."
"SUCH IS THE WISDOM OF A FOREST TROLL."
YOU RETRIEVE THE RING FROM ITS BELLY NOW AND BORROW IT FOR A TIME.
I THINK YOU'LL FIND IT WORTH THE WEARING.
BEASTS HAVE MORE TO SAY IN THIS LAND THAN I EXPECTED.

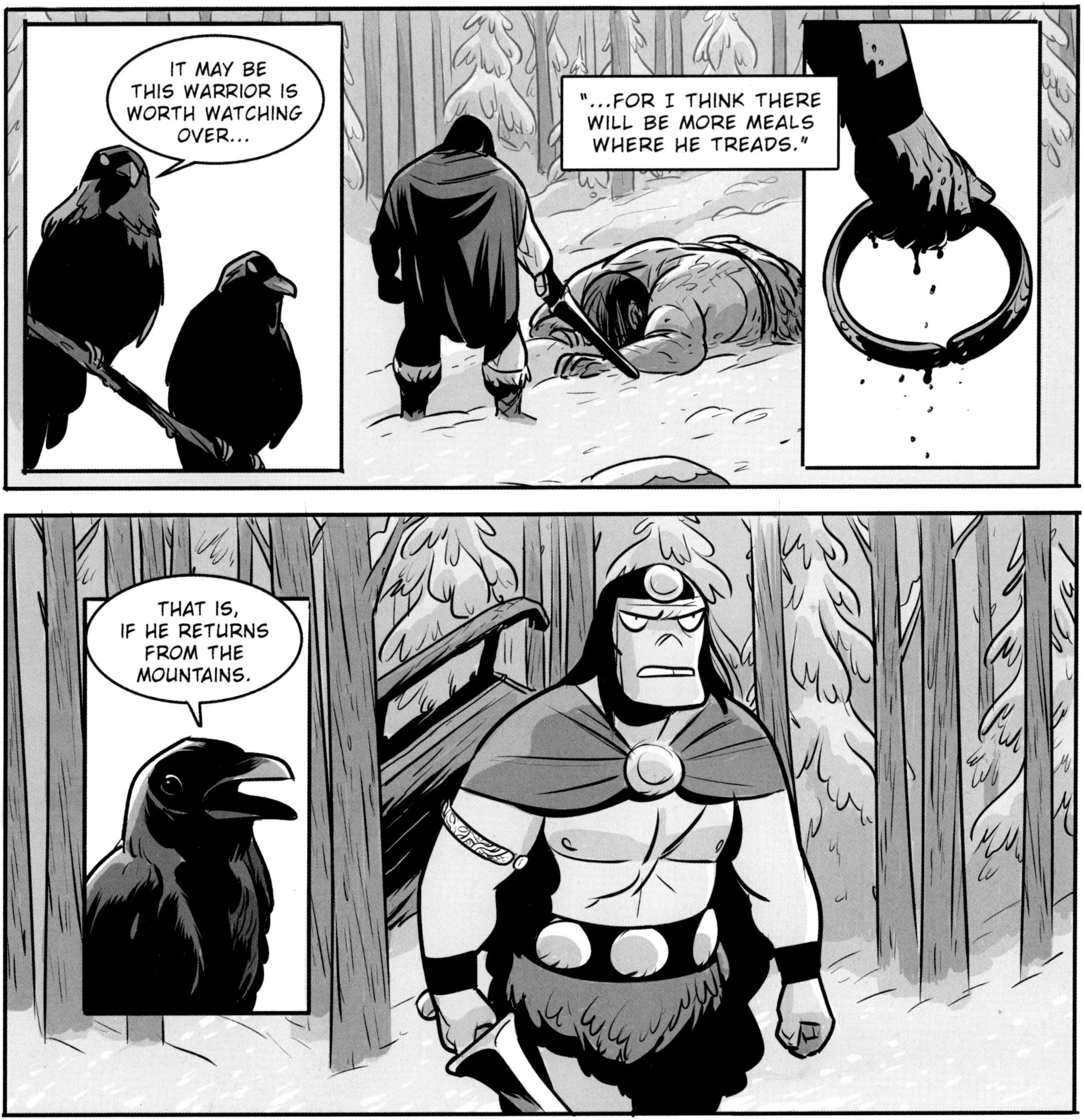
IT MAY BE THIS WARRIOR IS WORTH WATCHING OVER...
"...FOR I THINK THERE WILL BE MORE MEALS WHERE HE TREADS."
THAT IS, IF HE RETURNS FROM THE MOUNTAINS.

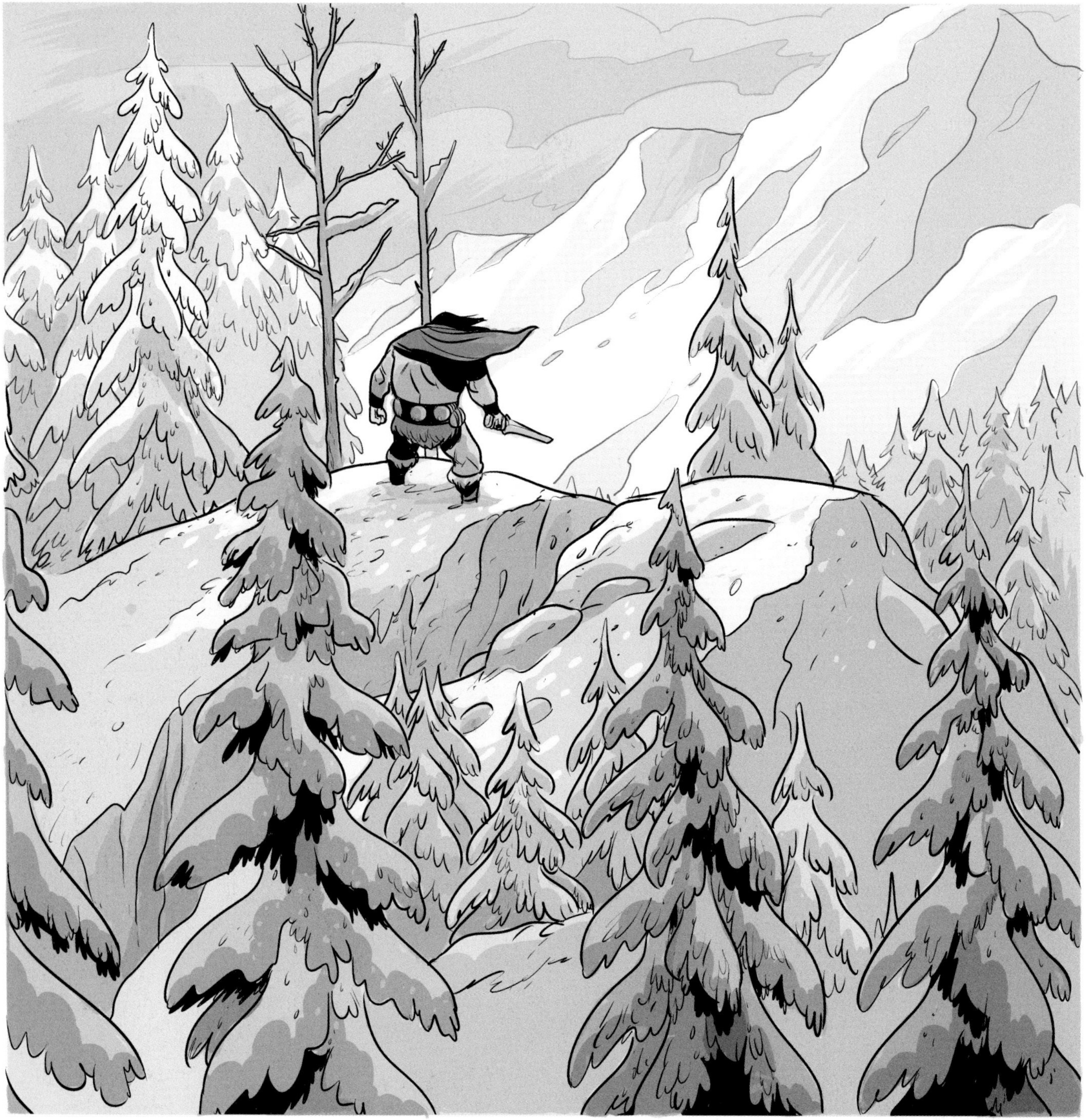

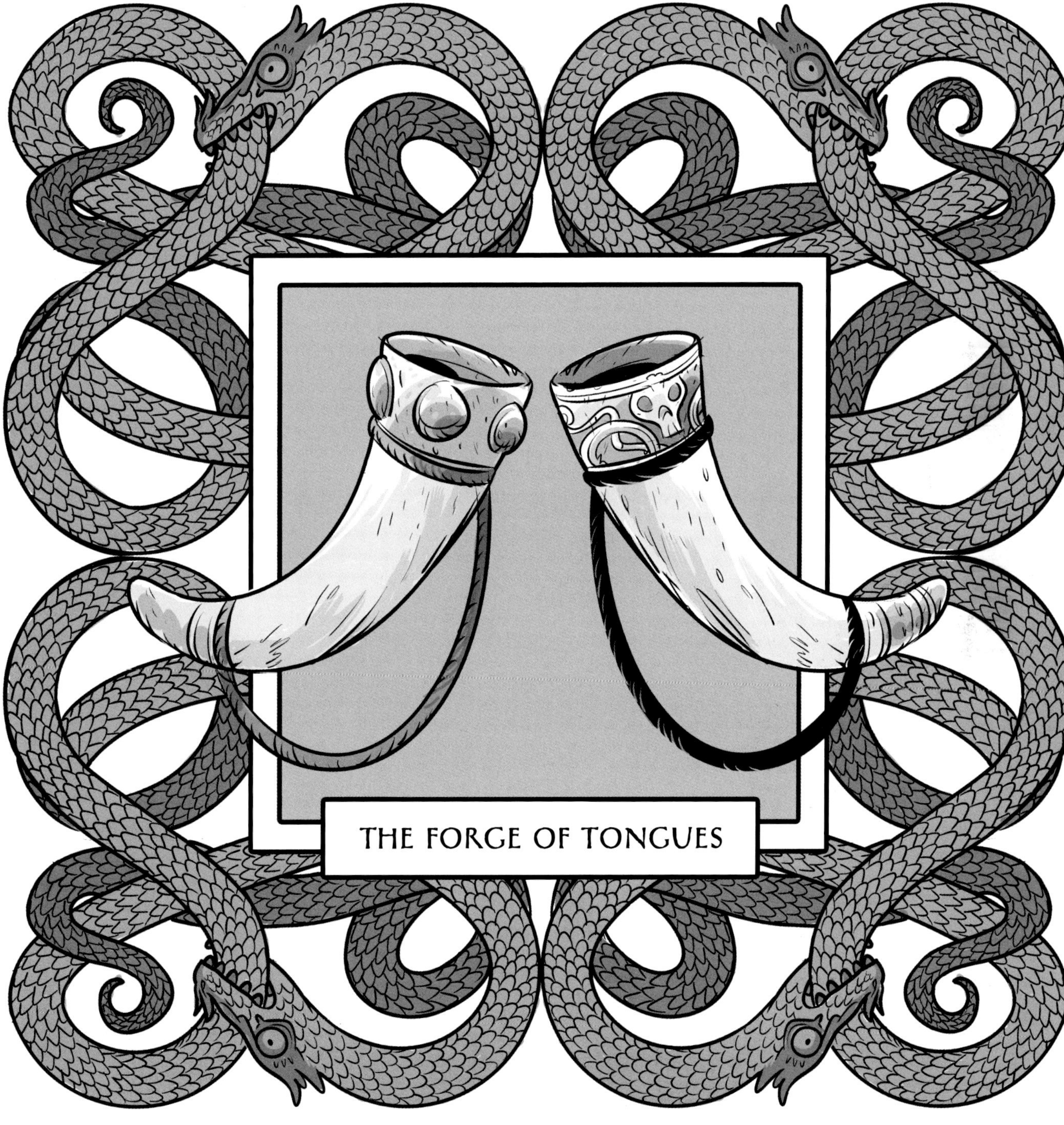

THE FORGE OF TONGUES

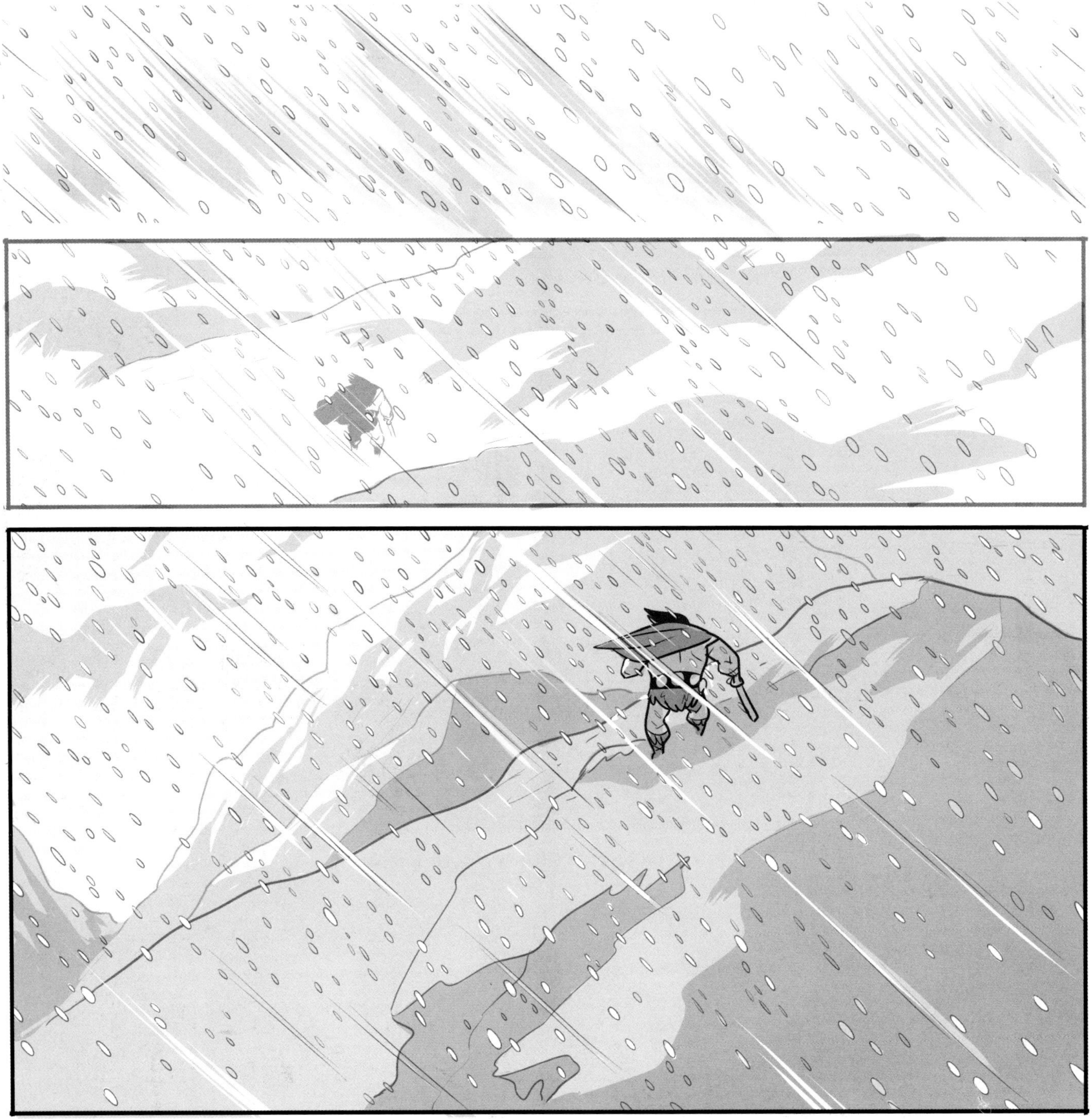

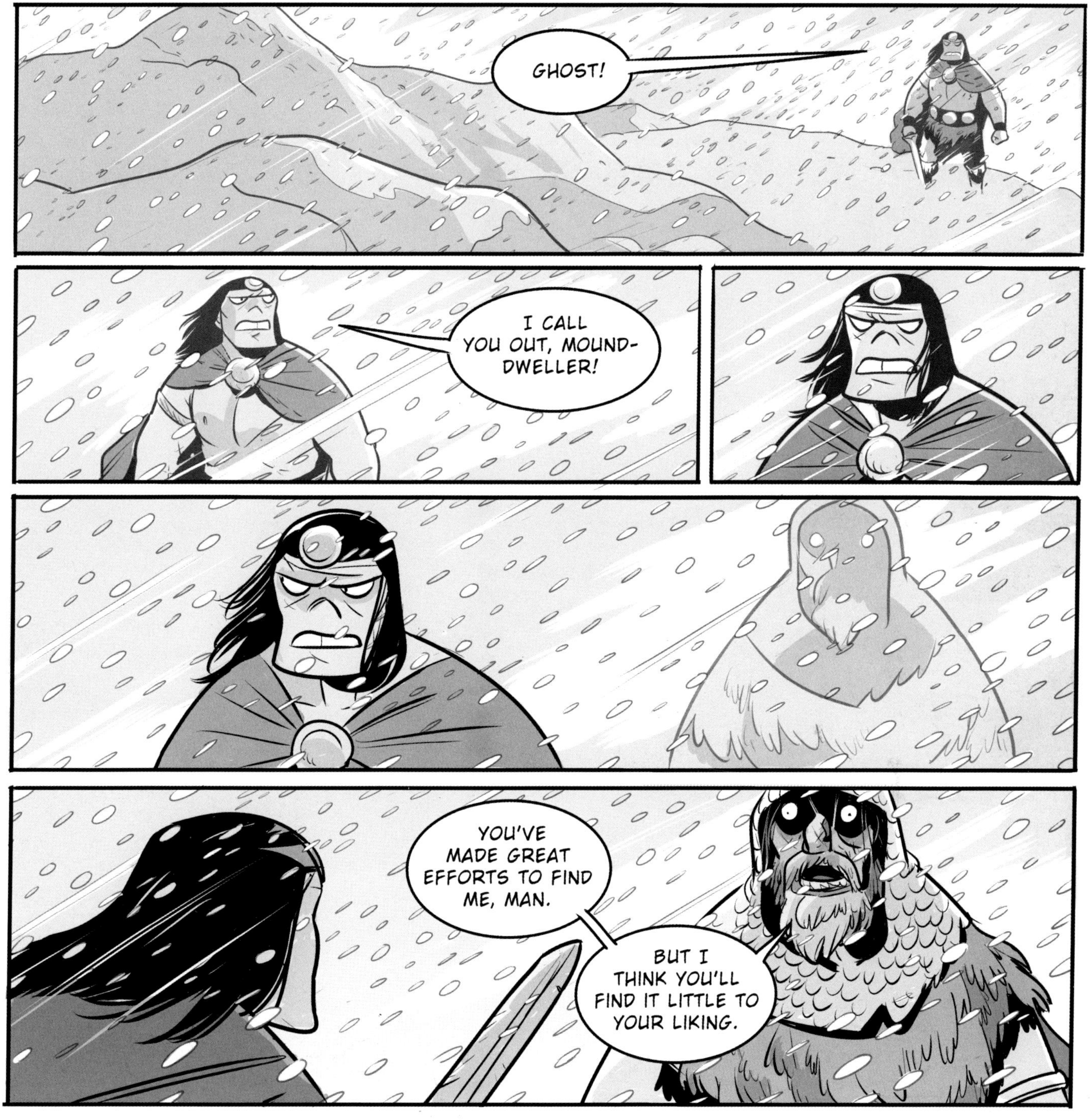
GHOST!
I CALL YOU OUT, MOUND-DWELLER!
YOU'VE MADE GREAT EFFORTS TO FIND ME, MAN.
BUT I THINK YOU'LL FIND IT LITTLE TO YOUR LIKING.

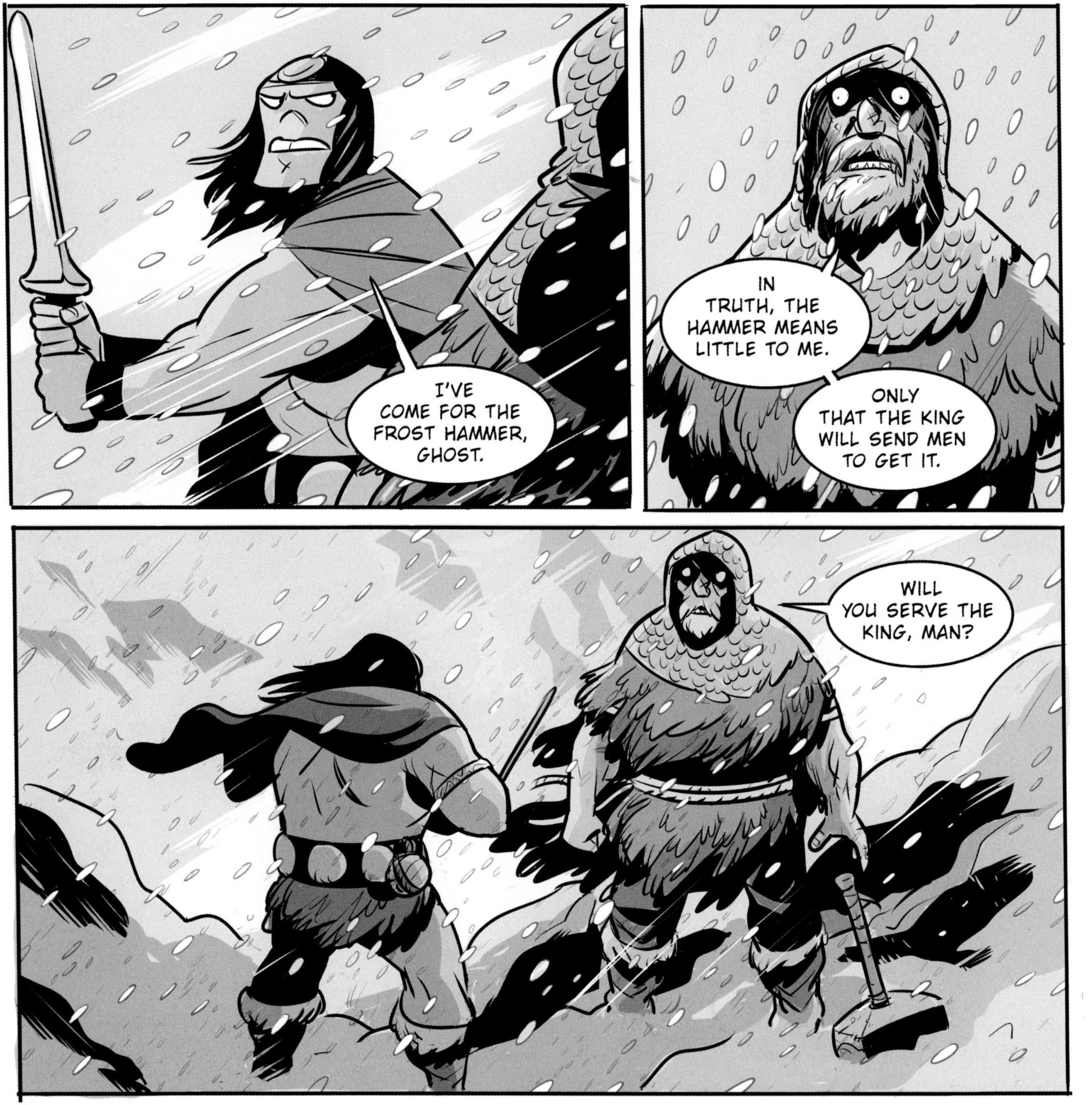
I'VE COME FOR THE FROST HAMMER, GHOST.
IN TRUTH, THE HAMMER MEANS LITTLE TO ME.
ONLY THAT THE KING WILL SEND MEN TO GET IT.
WILL YOU SERVE THE KING, MAN?

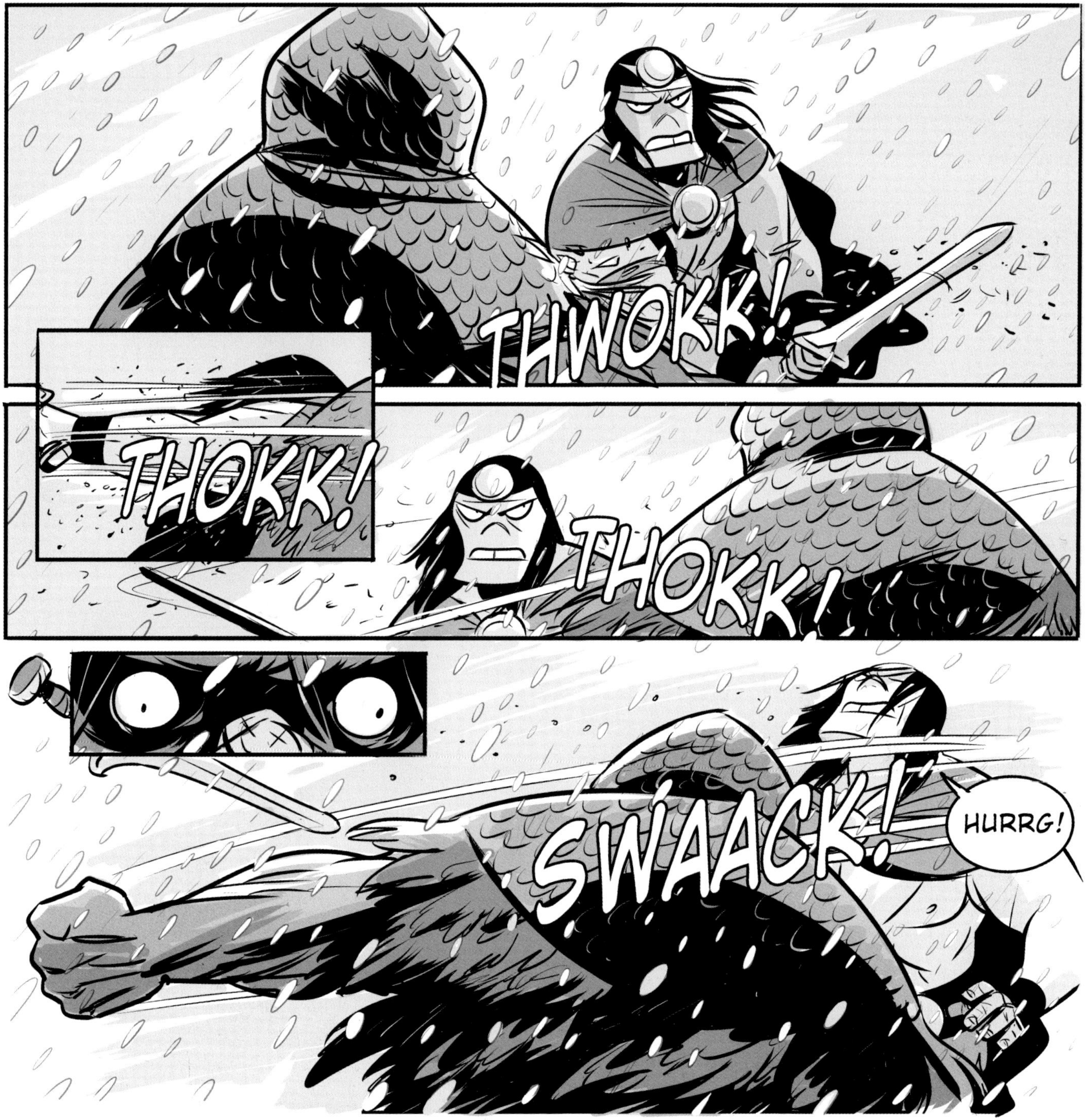
THWOKK!
THOKK!
THOKK!
SWAACK!
HURRG!

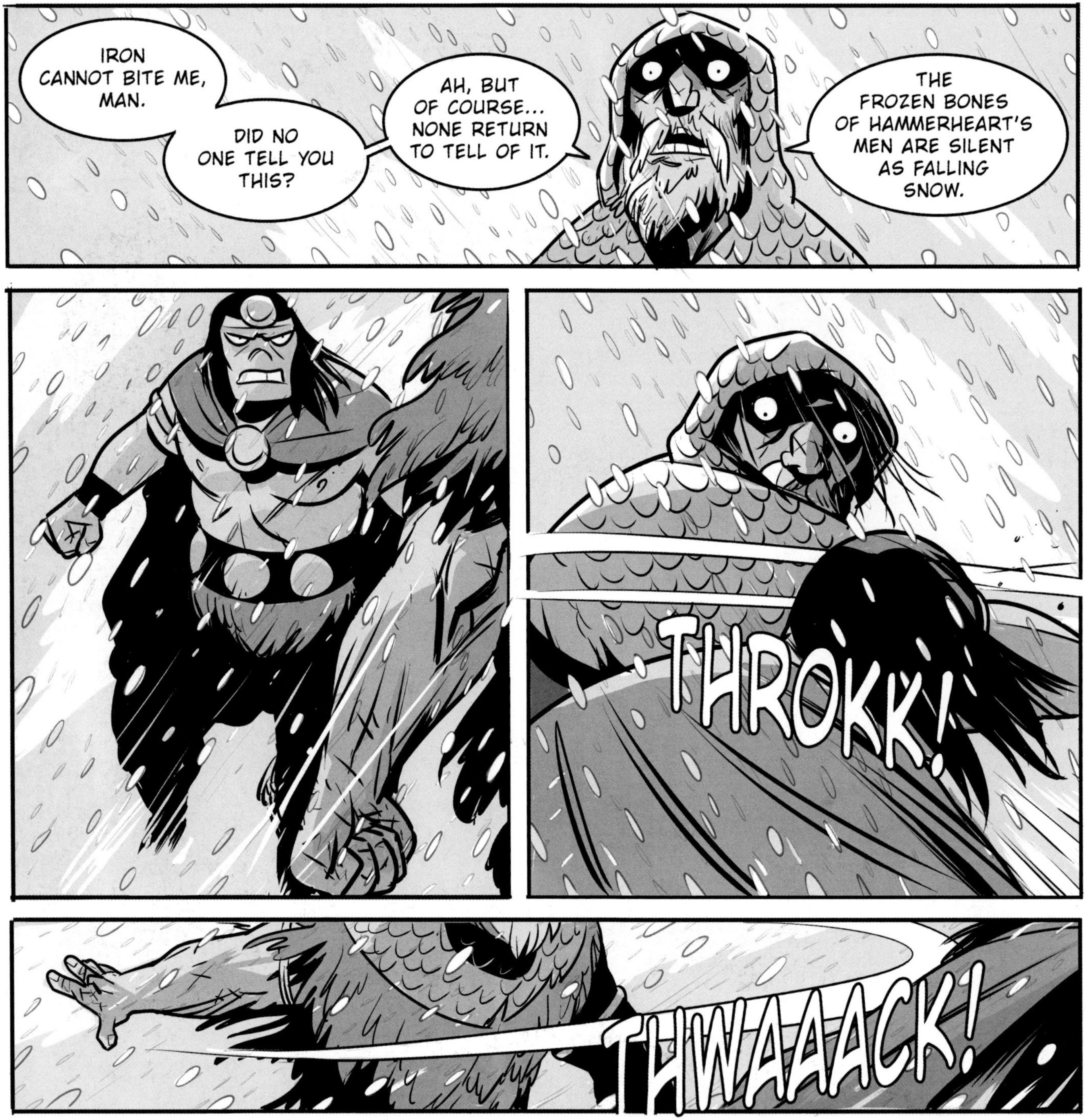
IRON CANNOT BITE ME, MAN.
DID NO ONE TELL YOU THIS?
AH, BUT OF COURSE... NONE RETURN TO TELL OF IT.
THE FROZEN BONES OF HAMMERHEART'S MEN ARE SILENT AS FALLING SNOW.
THROKK!
THWAAACK!

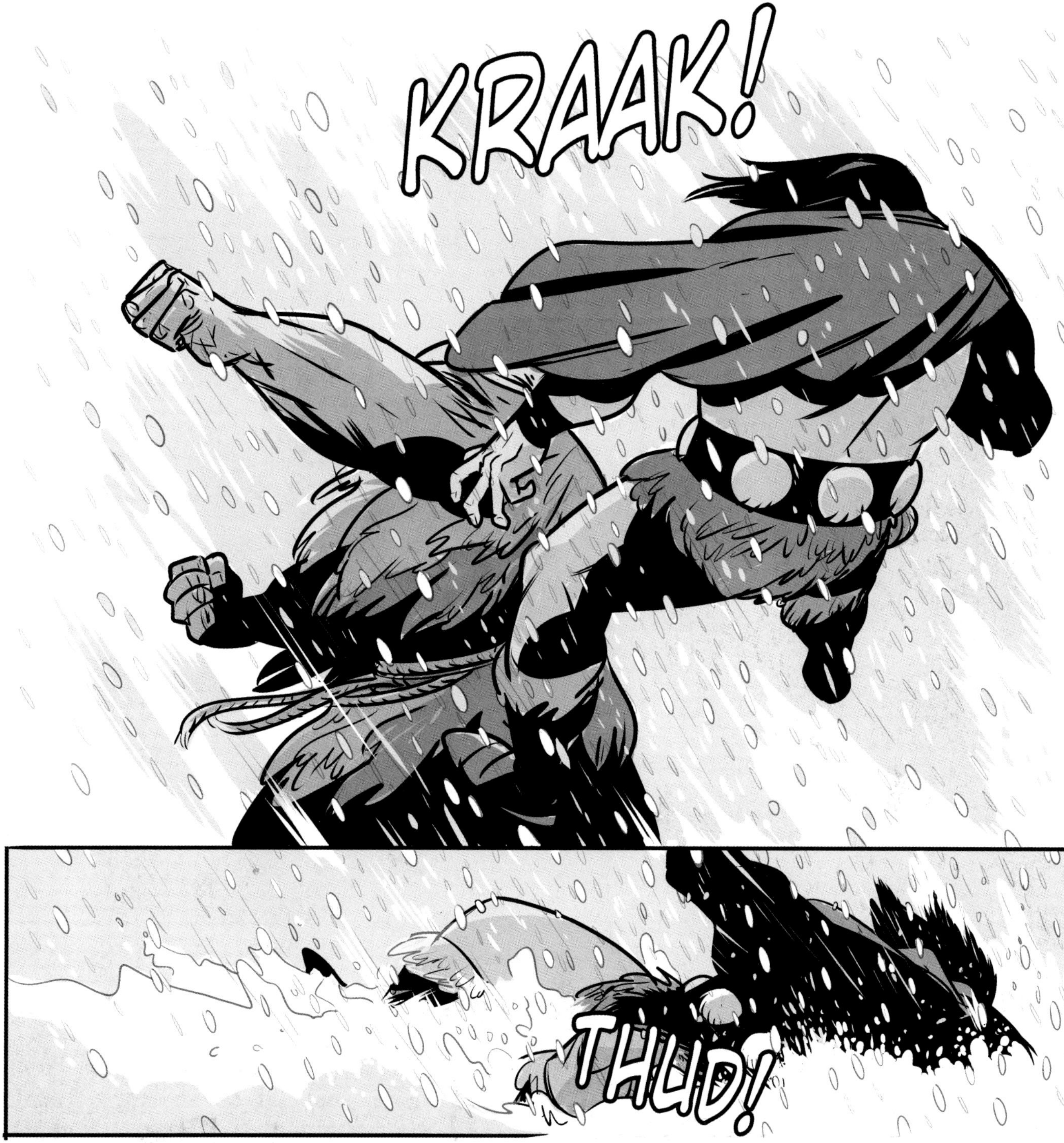
KRAAK!
THUD!

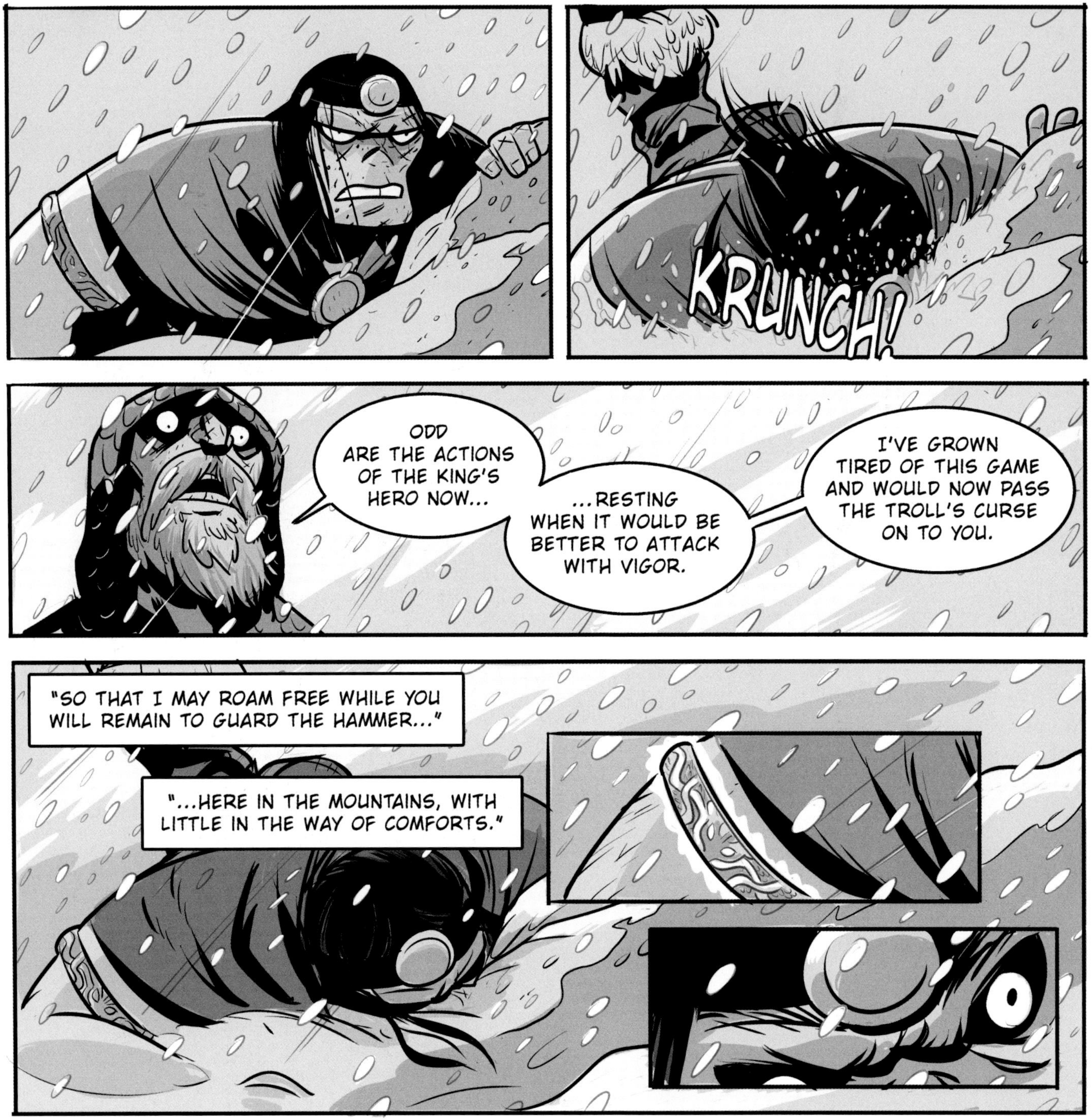
KRUNCH!
ODD ARE THE ACTIONS OF THE KING'S HERO NOW...
...RESTING WHEN IT WOULD BE BETTER TO ATTACK WITH VIGOR.
I'VE GROWN TIRED OF THIS GAME AND WOULD NOW PASS THE TROLL'S CURSE ON TO YOU.
"SO THAT I MAY ROAM FREE WHILE YOU WILL REMAIN TO GUARD THE HAMMER..."
"...HERE IN THE MOUNTAINS, WITH LITTLE IN THE WAY OF COMFORTS."

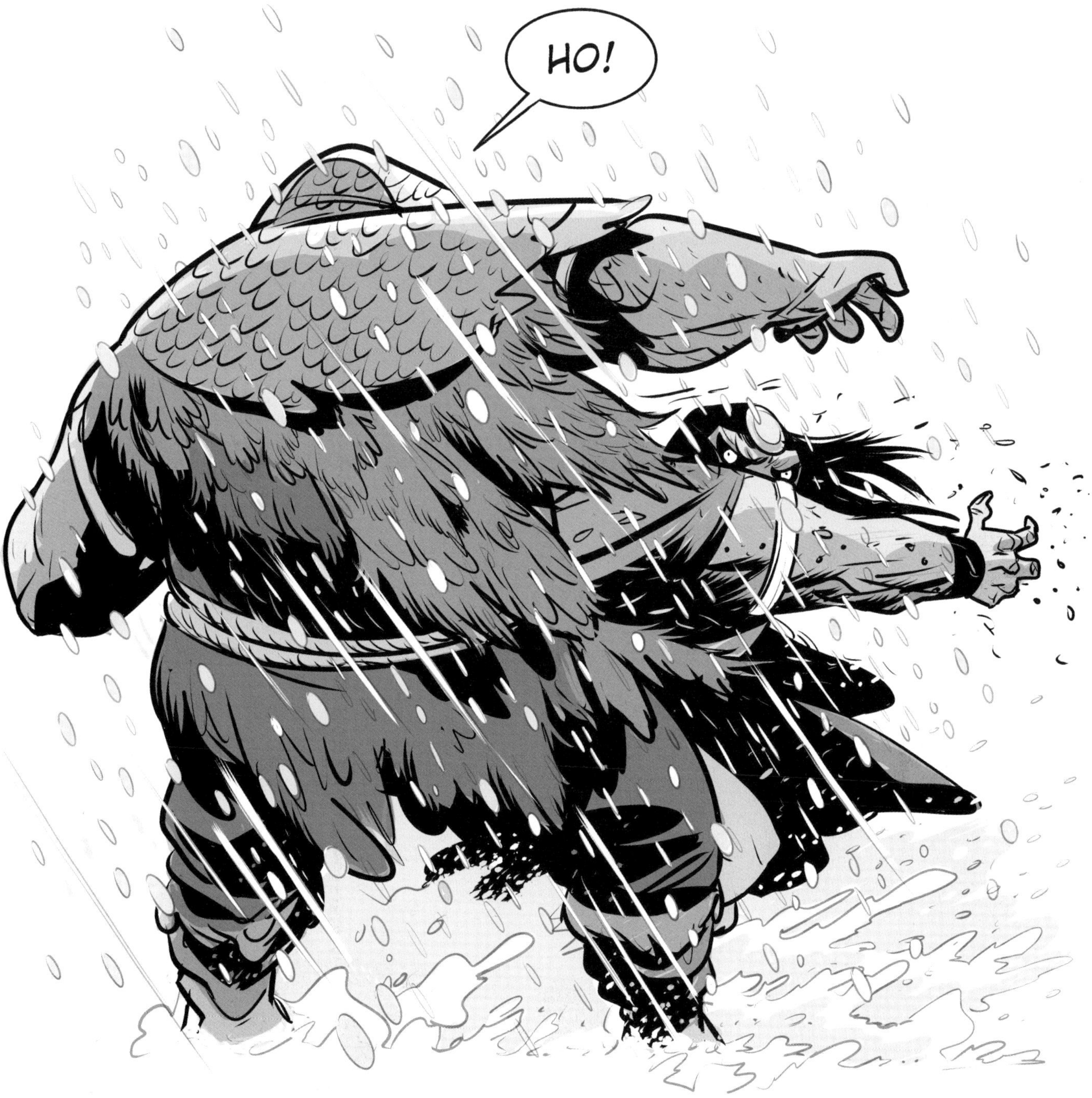
HO!

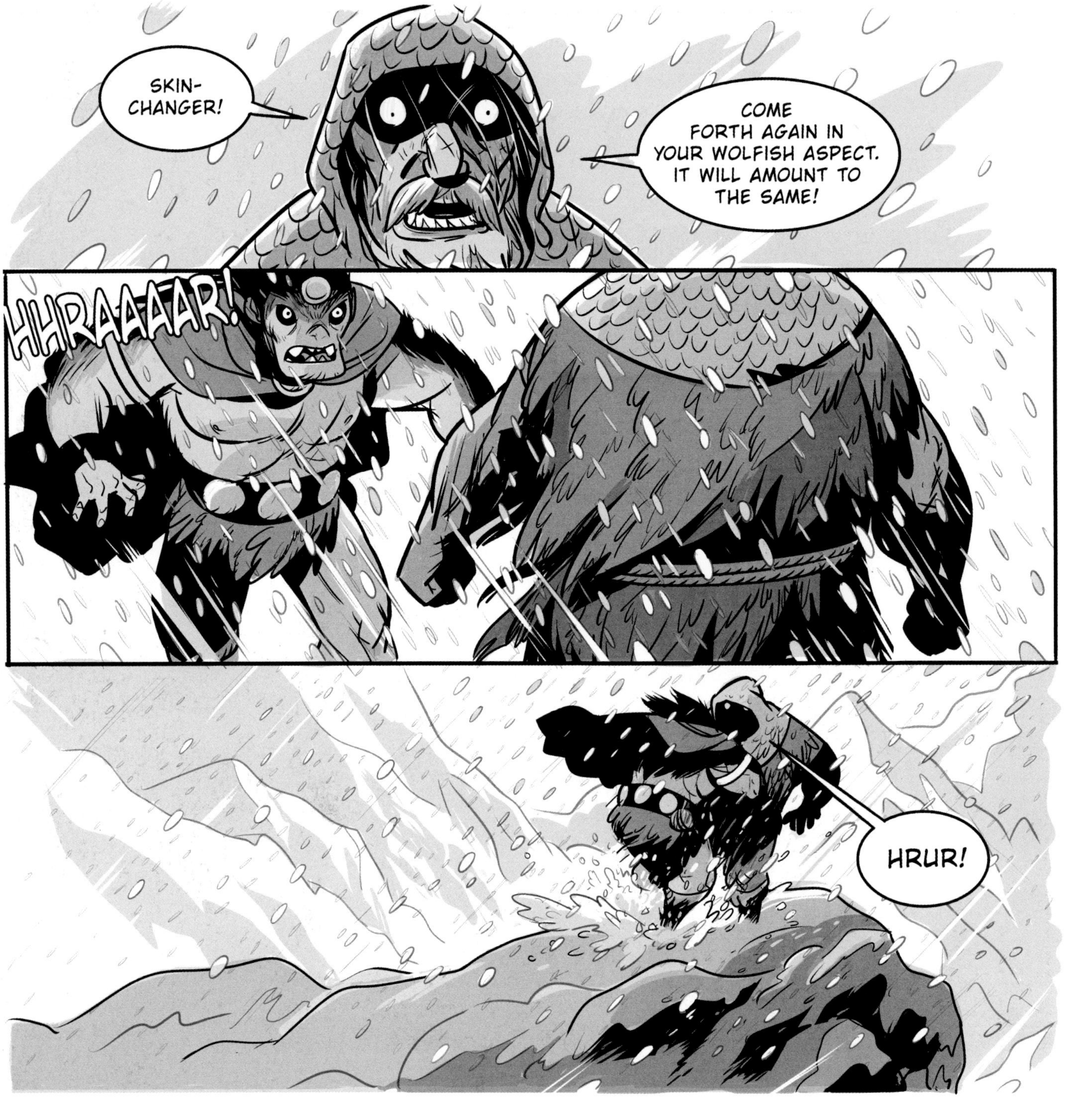
SKIN-CHANGER!
COME FORTH AGAIN IN YOUR WOLFISH ASPECT. IT WILL AMOUNT TO THE SAME!
HHRAAAAR!
HRUR!

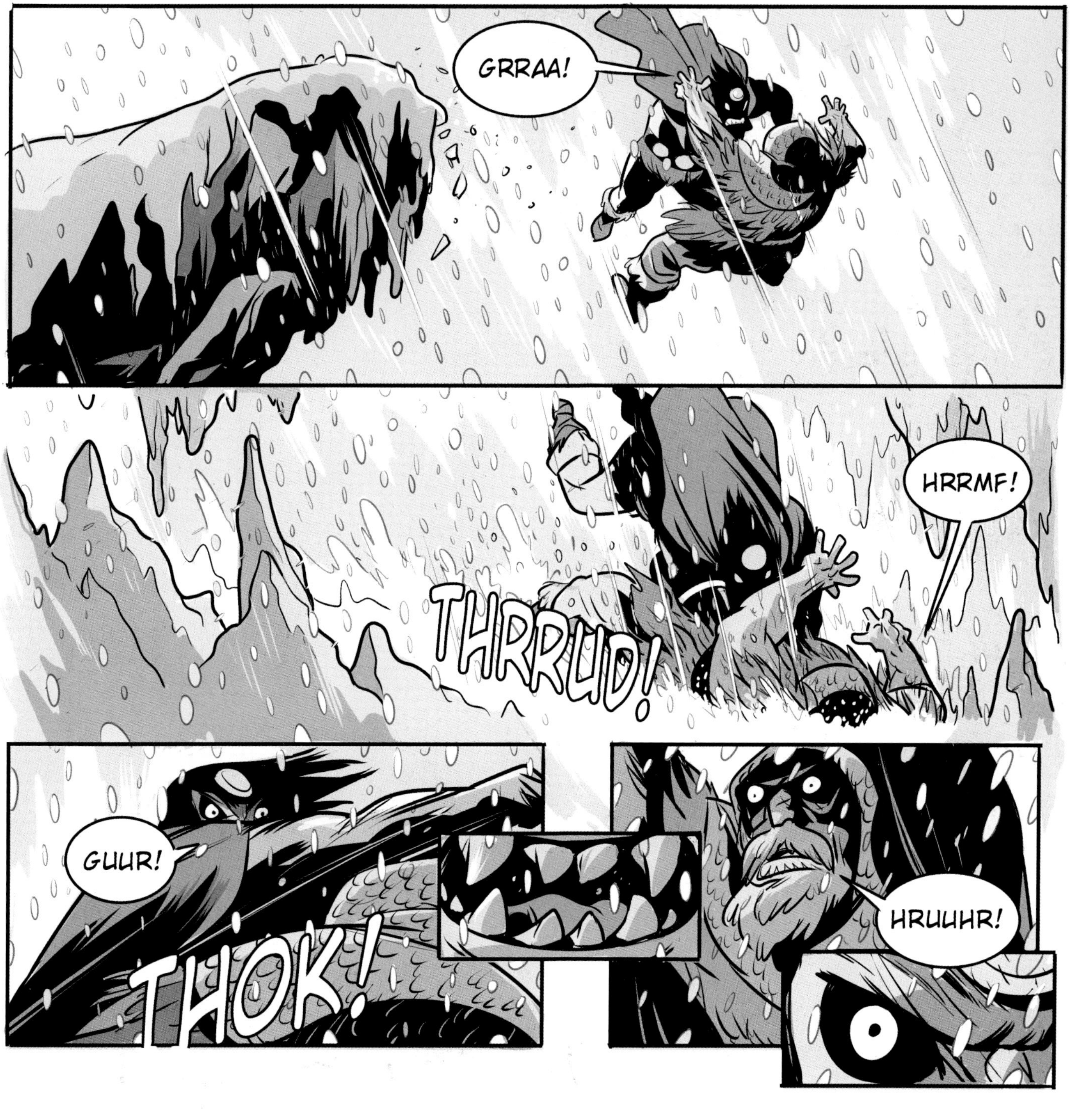
GRRAA!
THRRUD!
HRRMF!
GUUR!
THOK!
HRUUHR!

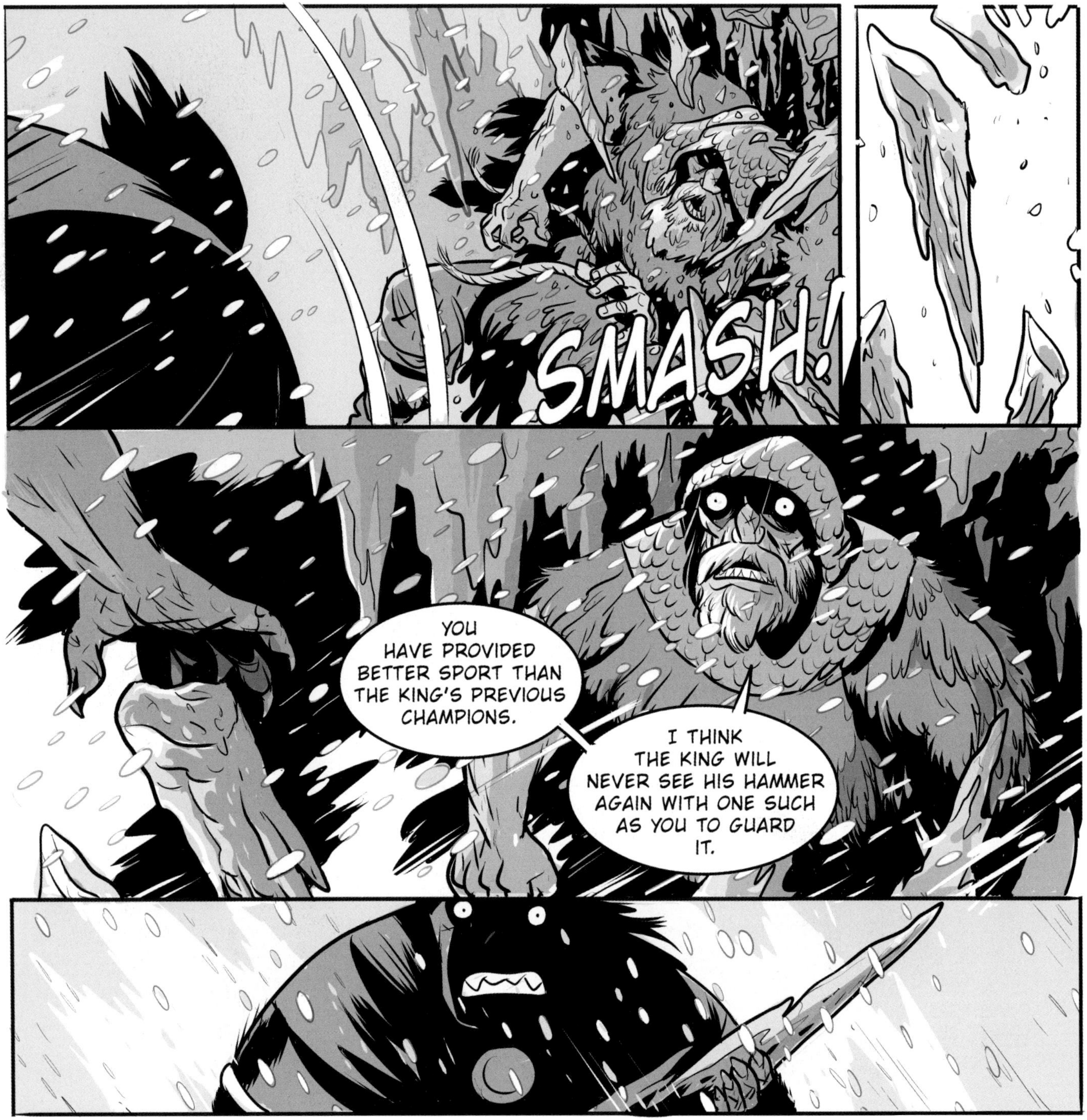
SMASH!!
YOU HAVE PROVIDED BETTER SPORT THAN THE KING'S PREVIOUS CHAMPIONS.
I THINK THE KING WILL NEVER SEE HIS HAMMER AGAIN WITH ONE SUCH AS YOU TO GUARD IT.

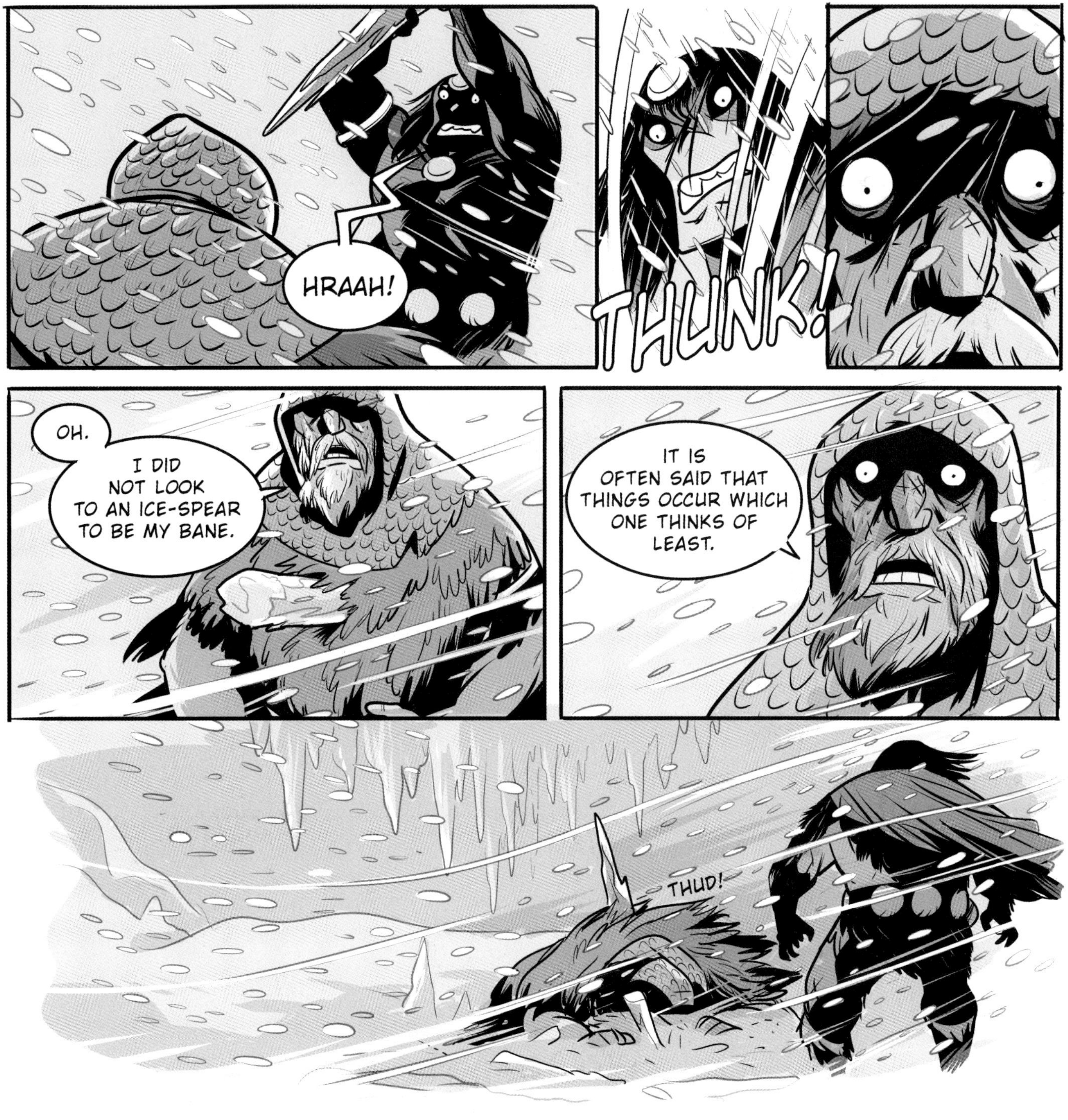
HRAAH!
THUNK!
OH.
I DID NOT LOOK TO AN ICE-SPEAR TO BE MY BANE.
IT IS OFTEN SAID THAT THINGS OCCUR WHICH ONE THINKS OF LEAST.
THUD!

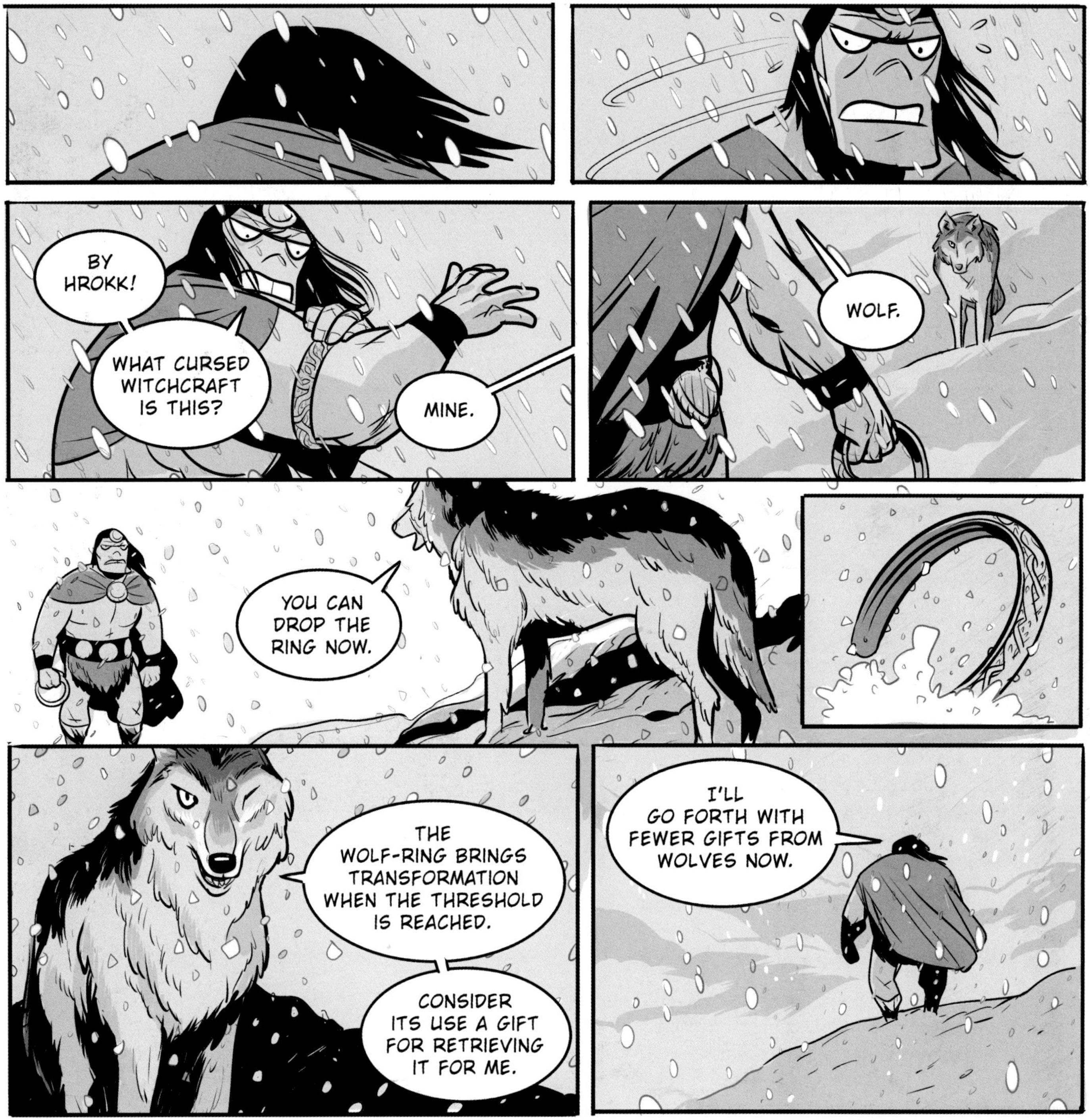
BY HROKK!
WHAT CURSED WITCHCRAFT IS THIS?
MINE.
WOLF.
YOU CAN DROP THE RING NOW.
THE WOLF-RING BRINGS TRANSFORMATION WHEN THE THRESHOLD IS REACHED.
CONSIDER ITS USE A GIFT FOR RETRIEVING IT FOR ME.
I'LL GO FORTH WITH FEWER GIFTS FROM WOLVES NOW.

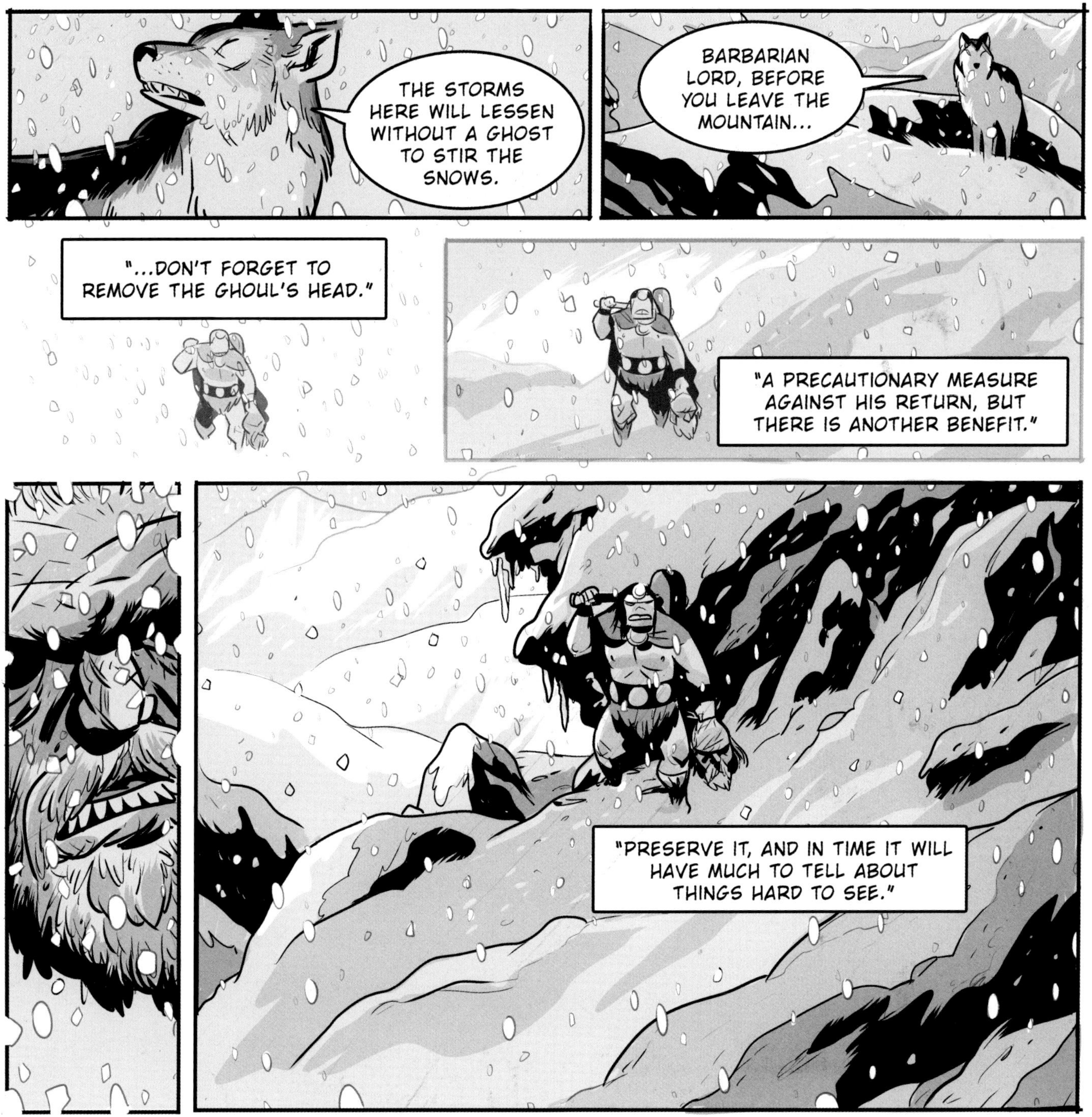
THE STORMS HERE WILL LESSEN WITHOUT A GHOST TO STIR THE SNOWS.
BARBARIAN LORD, BEFORE YOU LEAVE THE MOUNTAIN...
"...DON'T FORGET TO REMOVE THE GHOUL'S HEAD."
"A PRECAUTIONARY MEASURE AGAINST HIS RETURN, BUT THERE IS ANOTHER BENEFIT."
"PRESERVE IT, AND IN TIME IT WILL HAVE MUCH TO TELL ABOUT THINGS HARD TO SEE."

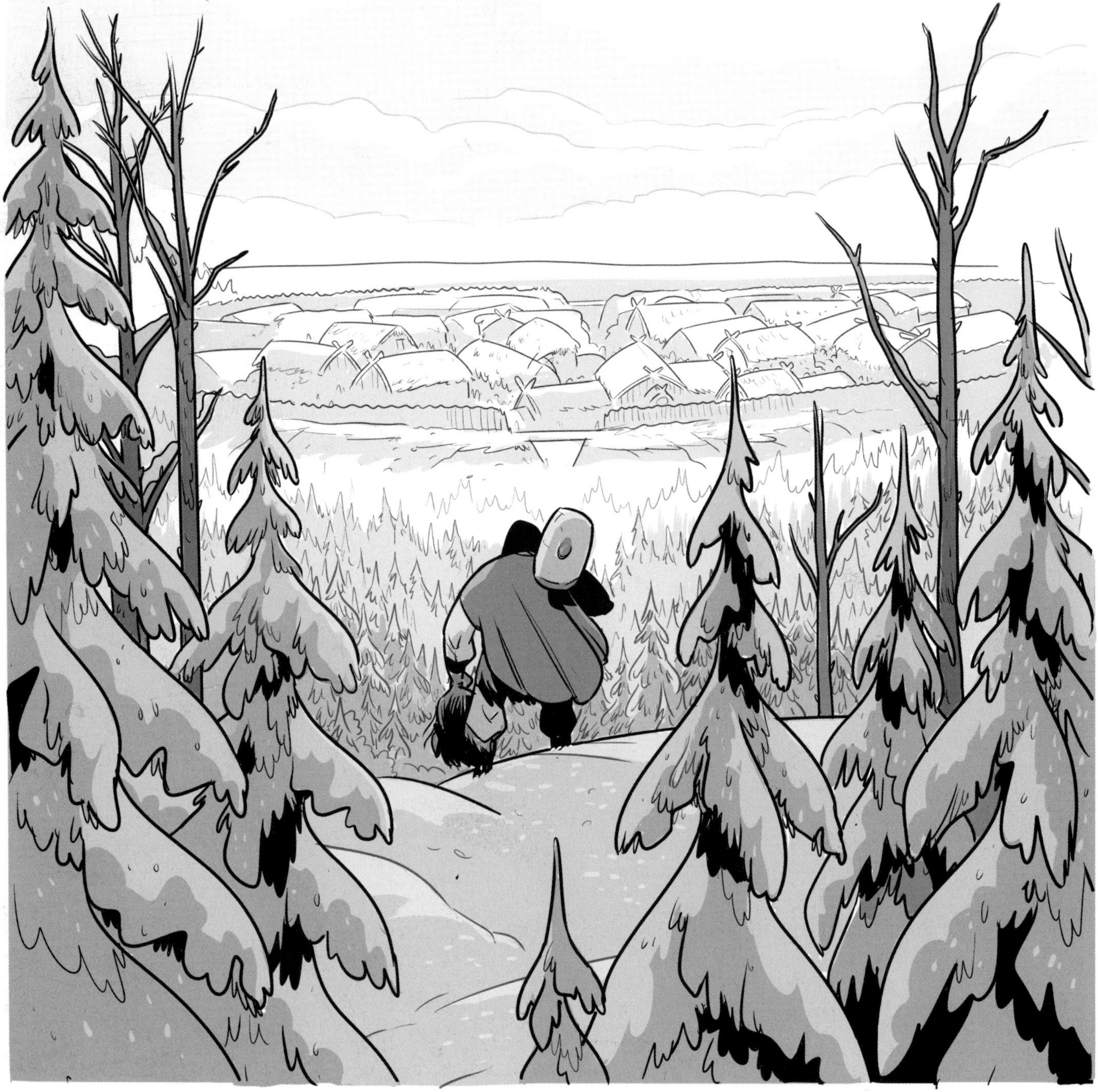

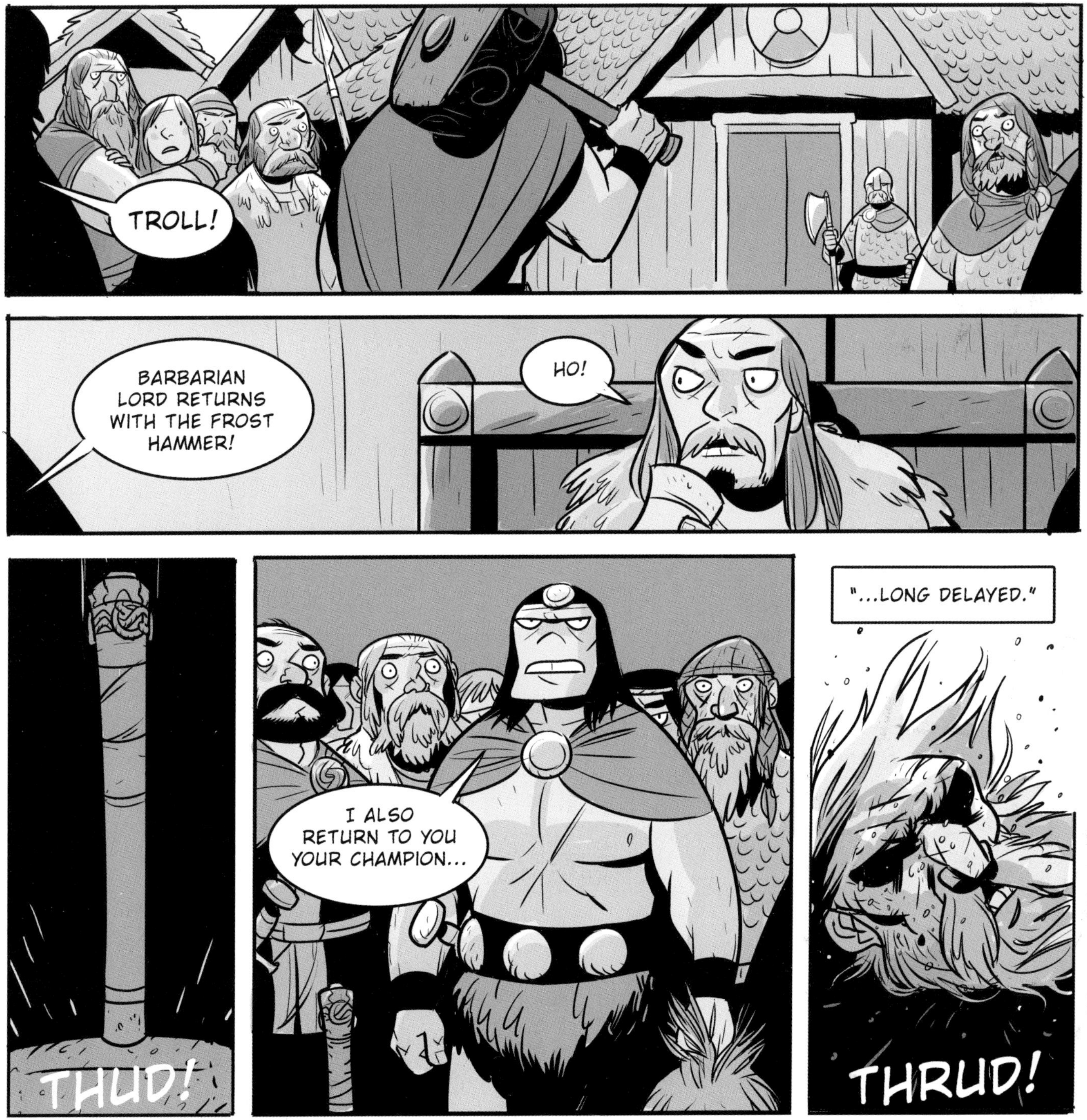
TROLL!
BARBARIAN LORD RETURNS WITH THE FROST HAMMER!
HO!
THUD!
I ALSO RETURN TO YOU YOUR CHAMPION...
"...LONG DELAYED."
THRUD!

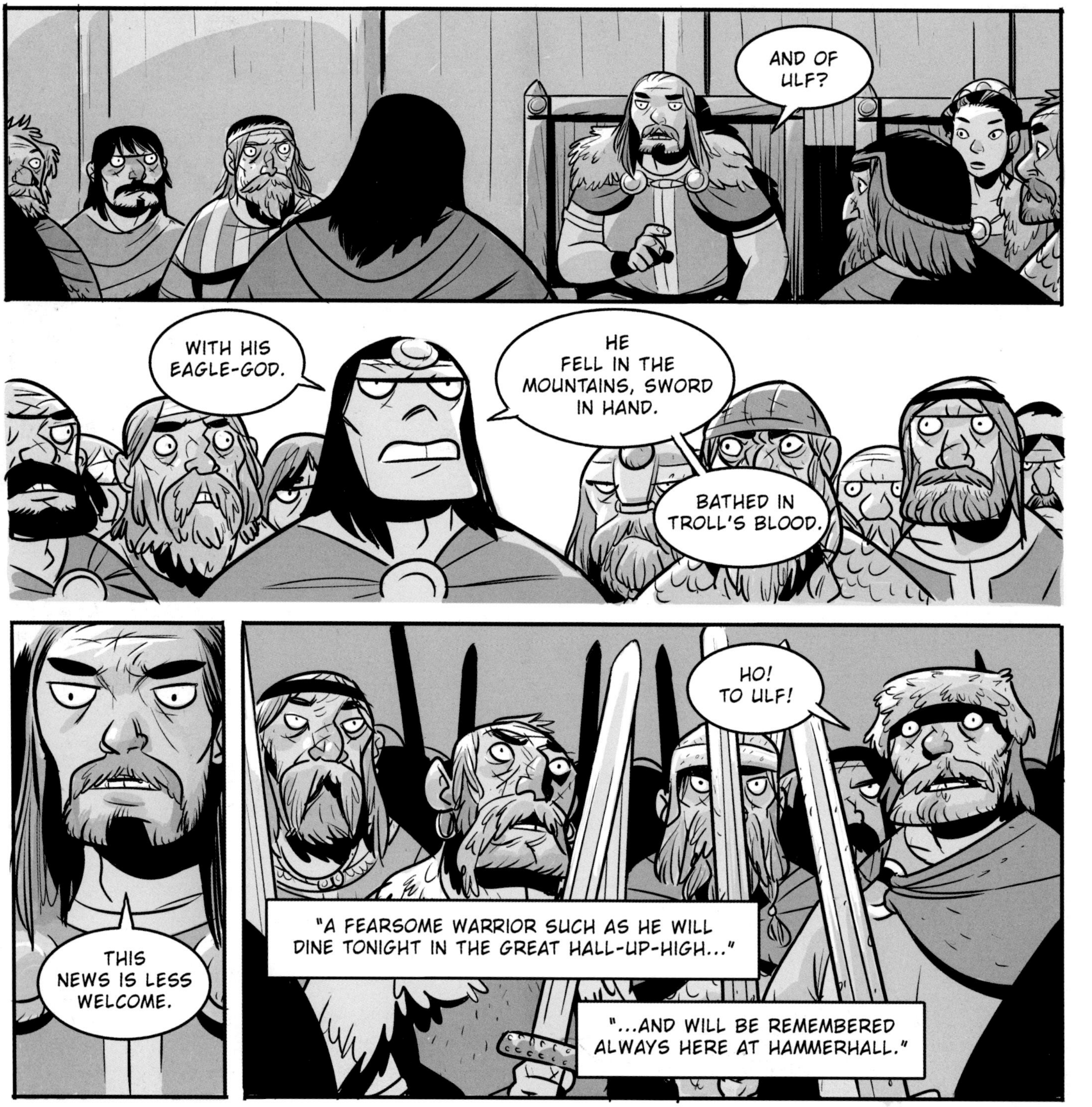
AND OF ULF?
WITH HIS EAGLE-GOD.
HE FELL IN THE MOUNTAINS, SWORD IN HAND.
BATHED IN TROLL'S BLOOD.
THIS NEWS IS LESS WELCOME.
HO! TO ULF!
"A FEARSOME WARRIOR SUCH AS HE WILL DINE TONIGHT IN THE GREAT HALL-UP-HIGH..."
"...AND WILL BE REMEMBERED ALWAYS HERE AT HAMMERHALL."

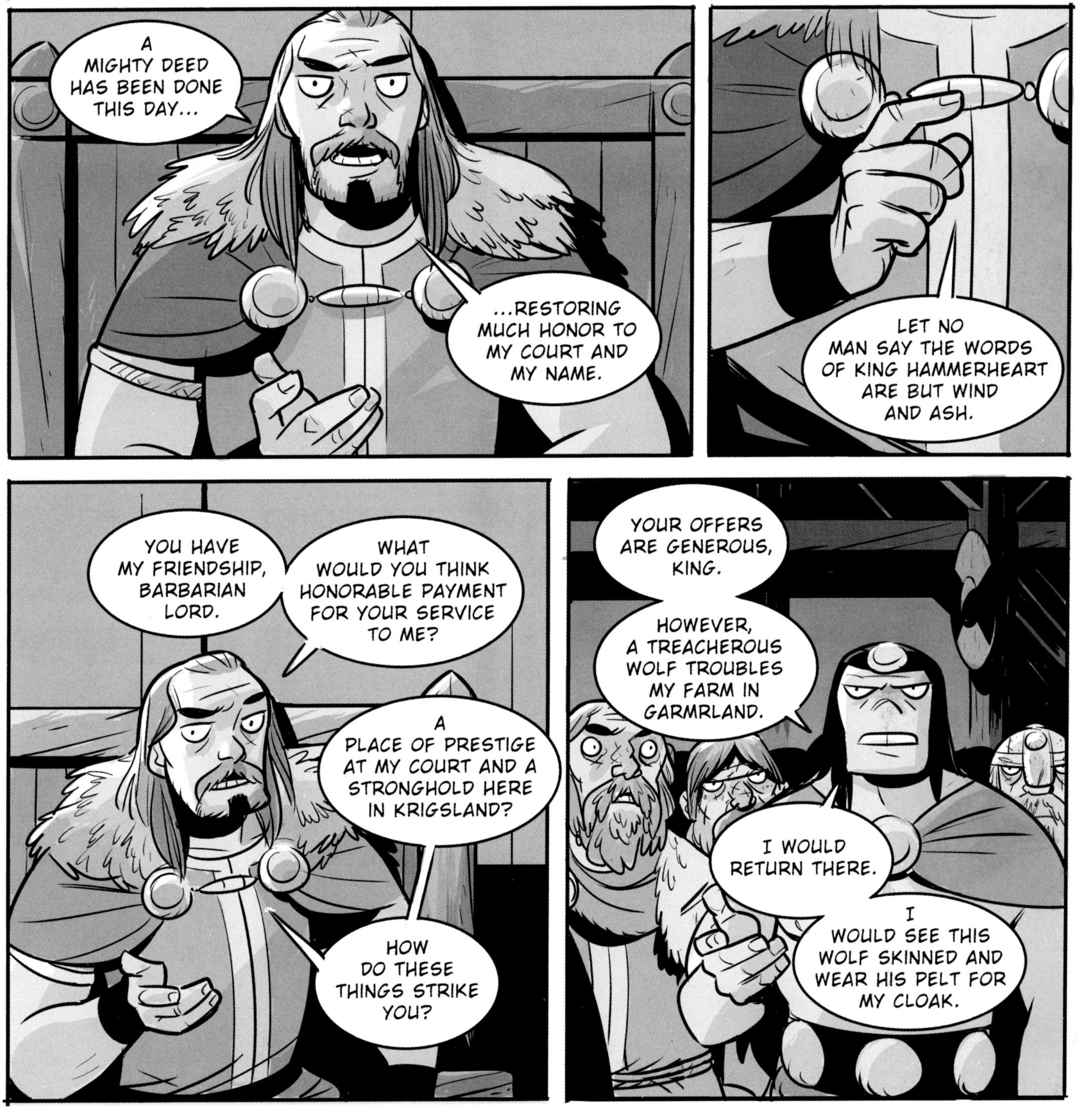
A MIGHTY DEED HAS BEEN DONE THIS DAY...
...RESTORING MUCH HONOR TO MY COURT AND MY NAME.
LET NO MAN SAY THE WORDS OF KING HAMMERHEART ARE BUT WIND AND ASH.
YOU HAVE MY FRIENDSHIP, BARBARIAN LORD.
WHAT WOULD YOU THINK HONORABLE PAYMENT FOR YOUR SERVICE TO ME?
A PLACE OF PRESTIGE AT MY COURT AND A STRONGHOLD HERE IN KRIGSLAND?
HOW DO THESE THINGS STRIKE YOU?
YOUR OFFERS ARE GENEROUS, KING.
HOWEVER, A TREACHEROUS WOLF TROUBLES MY FARM IN GARMRLAND.
I WOULD RETURN THERE.
I WOULD SEE THIS WOLF SKINNED AND WEAR HIS PELT FOR MY CLOAK.

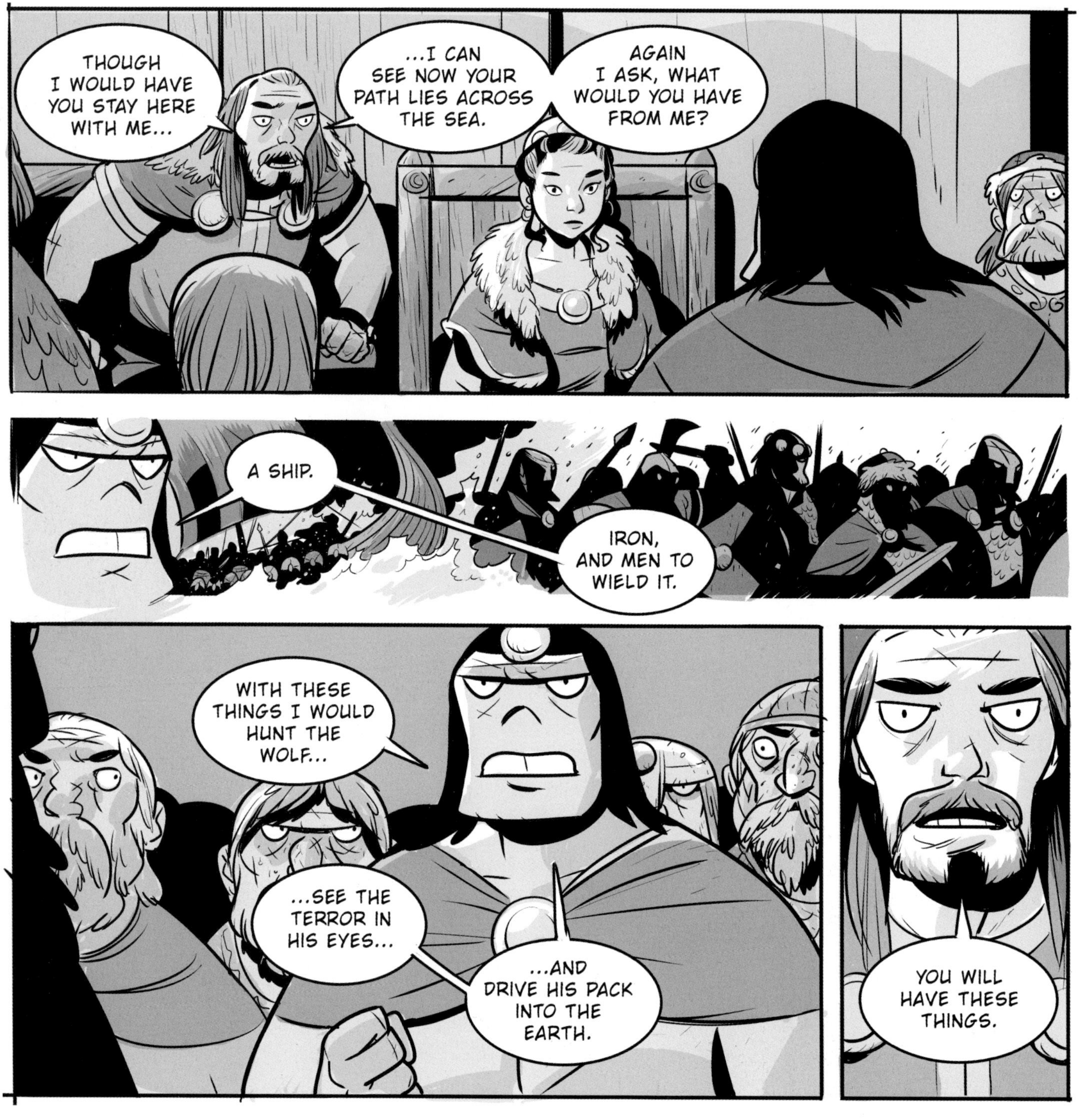
THOUGH I WOULD HAVE YOU STAY HERE WITH ME...
...I CAN SEE NOW YOUR PATH LIES ACROSS THE SEA.
AGAIN I ASK, WHAT WOULD YOU HAVE FROM ME?
A SHIP.
IRON, AND MEN TO WIELD IT.
WITH THESE THINGS I WOULD HUNT THE WOLF...
...SEE THE TERROR IN HIS EYES...
...AND DRIVE HIS PACK INTO THE EARTH.
YOU WILL HAVE THESE THINGS.

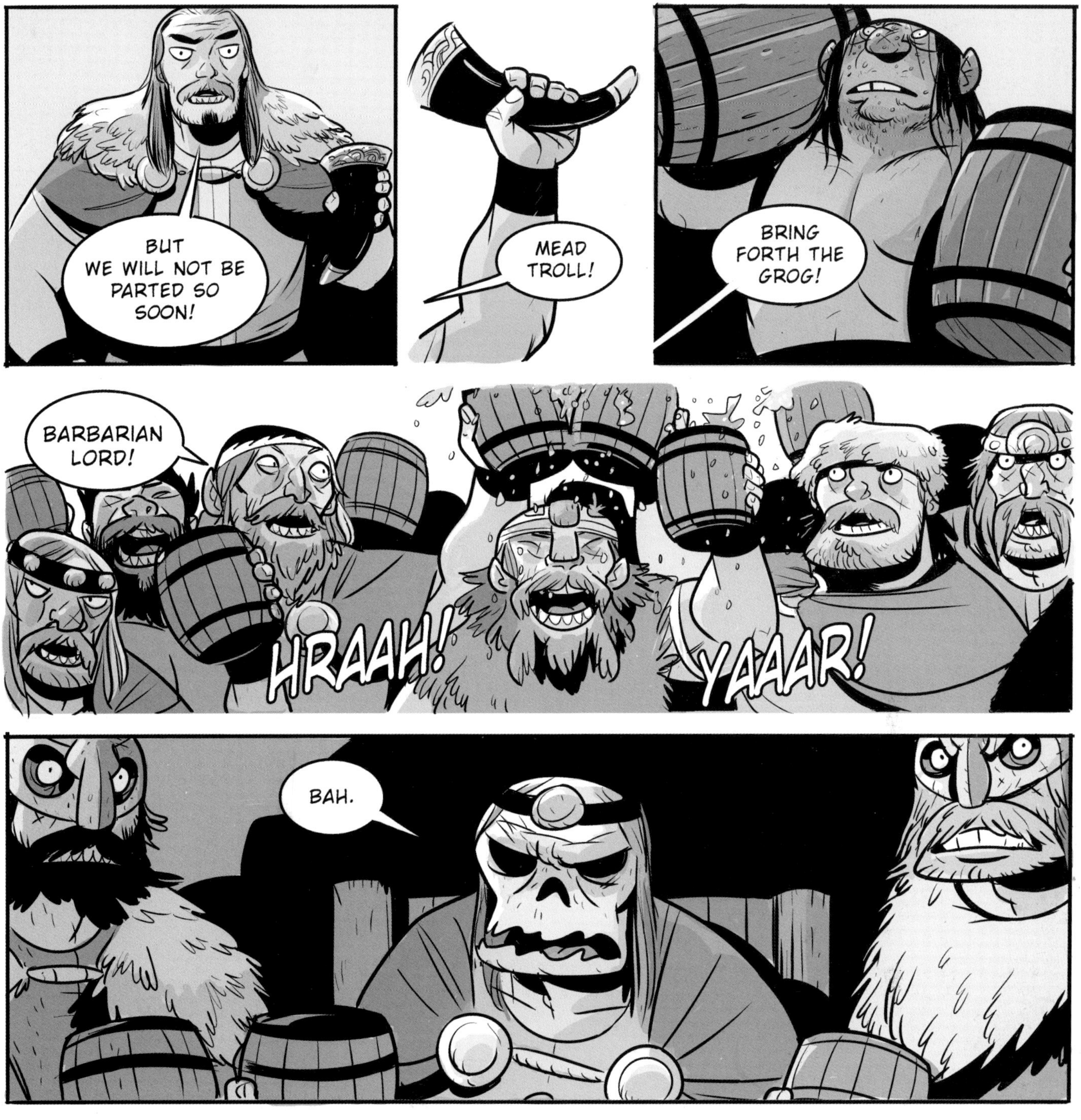
BUT WE WILL NOT BE PARTED SO SOON!
MEAD TROLL!
BRING FORTH THE GROG!
BARBARIAN LORD!
HRAAH!
YAAAR!
BAH.

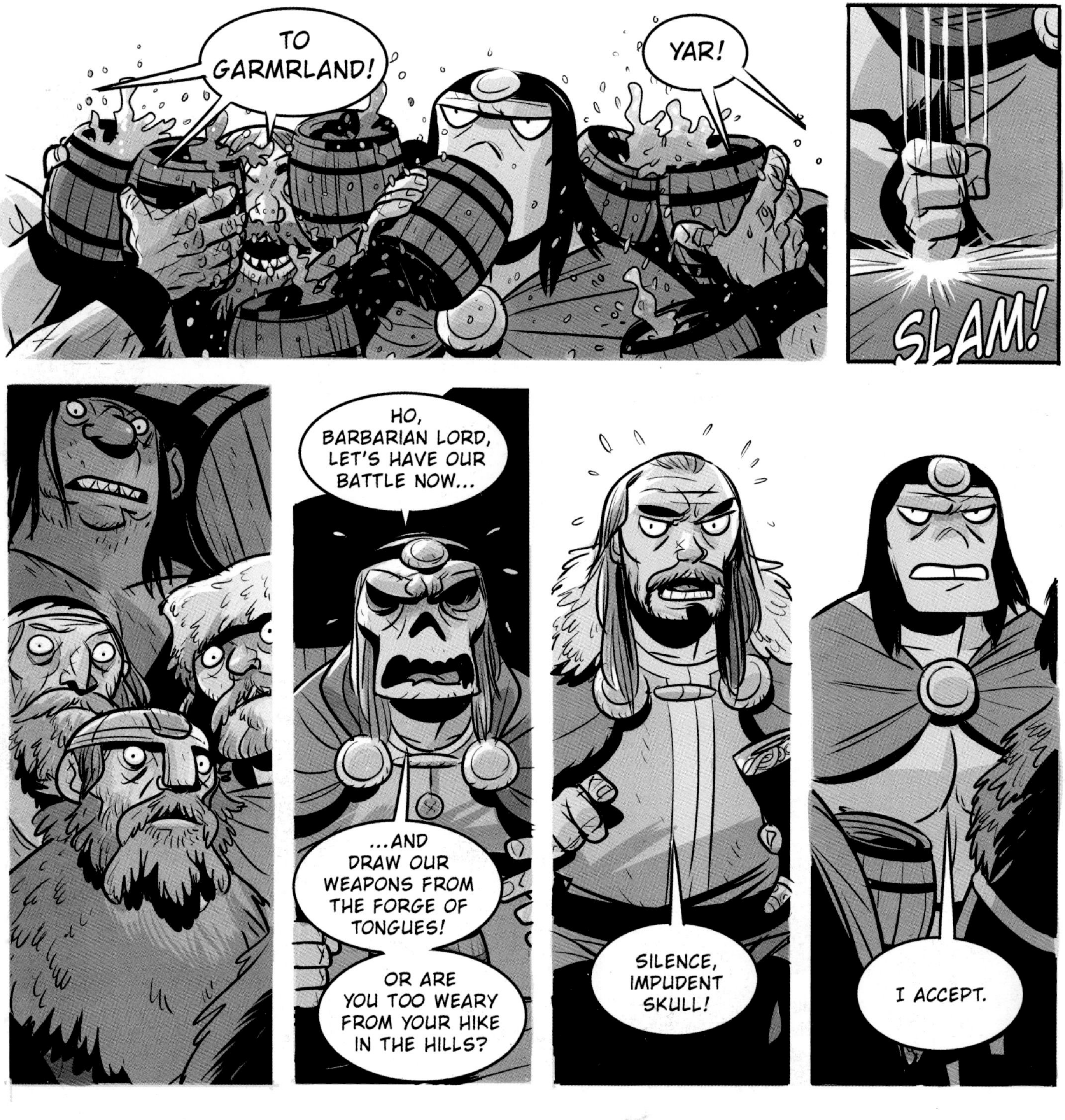
TO GARMRLAND!
YAR!
SLAM!
HO, BARBARIAN LORD, LET'S HAVE OUR BATTLE NOW...
...AND DRAW OUR WEAPONS FROM THE FORGE OF TONGUES!
OR ARE YOU TOO WEARY FROM YOUR HIKE IN THE HILLS?
SILENCE, IMPUDENT SKULL!
I ACCEPT.

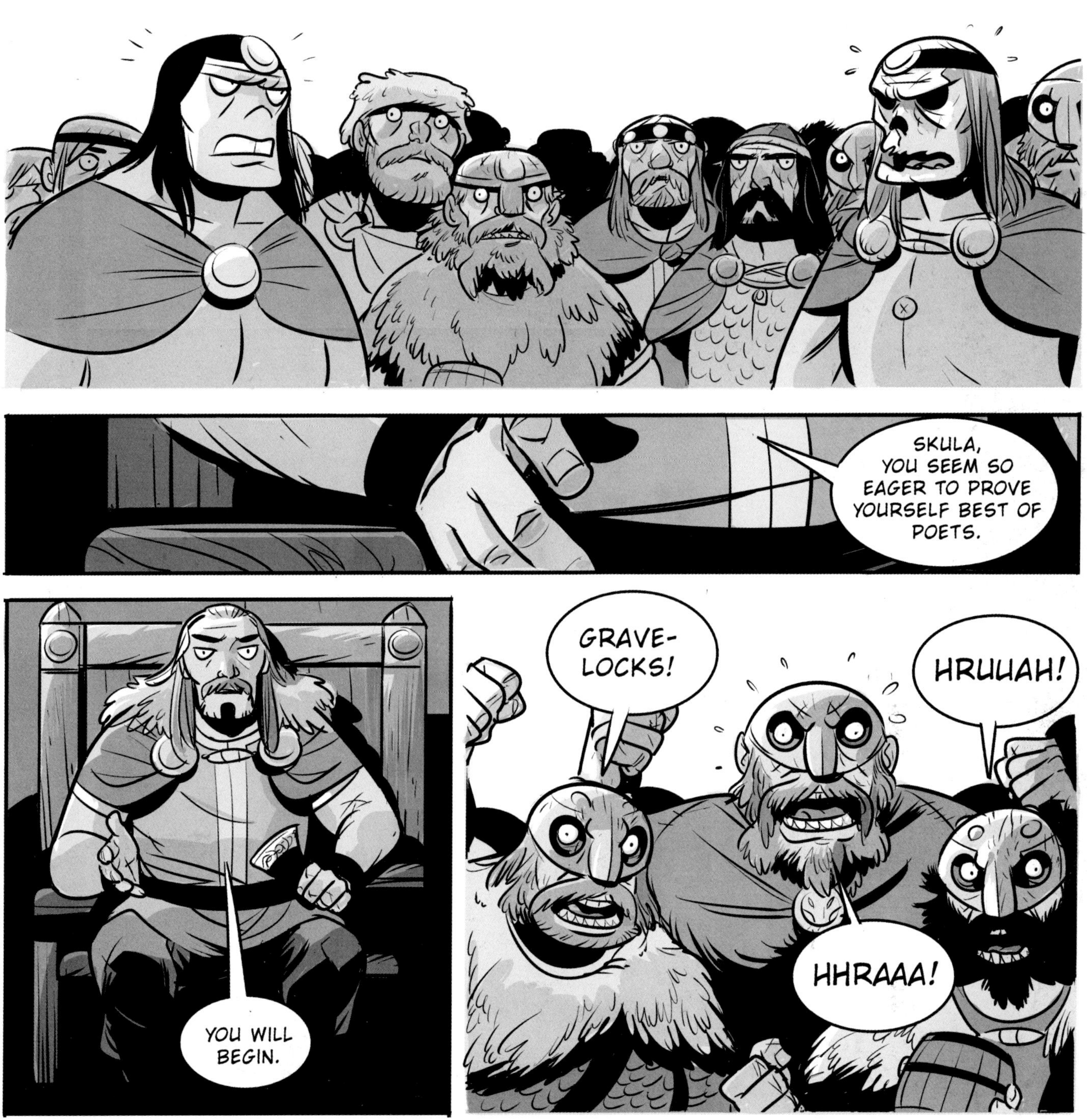
SKULA, YOU SEEM SO EAGER TO PROVE YOURSELF BEST OF POETS.
YOU WILL BEGIN.
GRAVE-LOCKS!
HRUUAH!
HHRAAA!

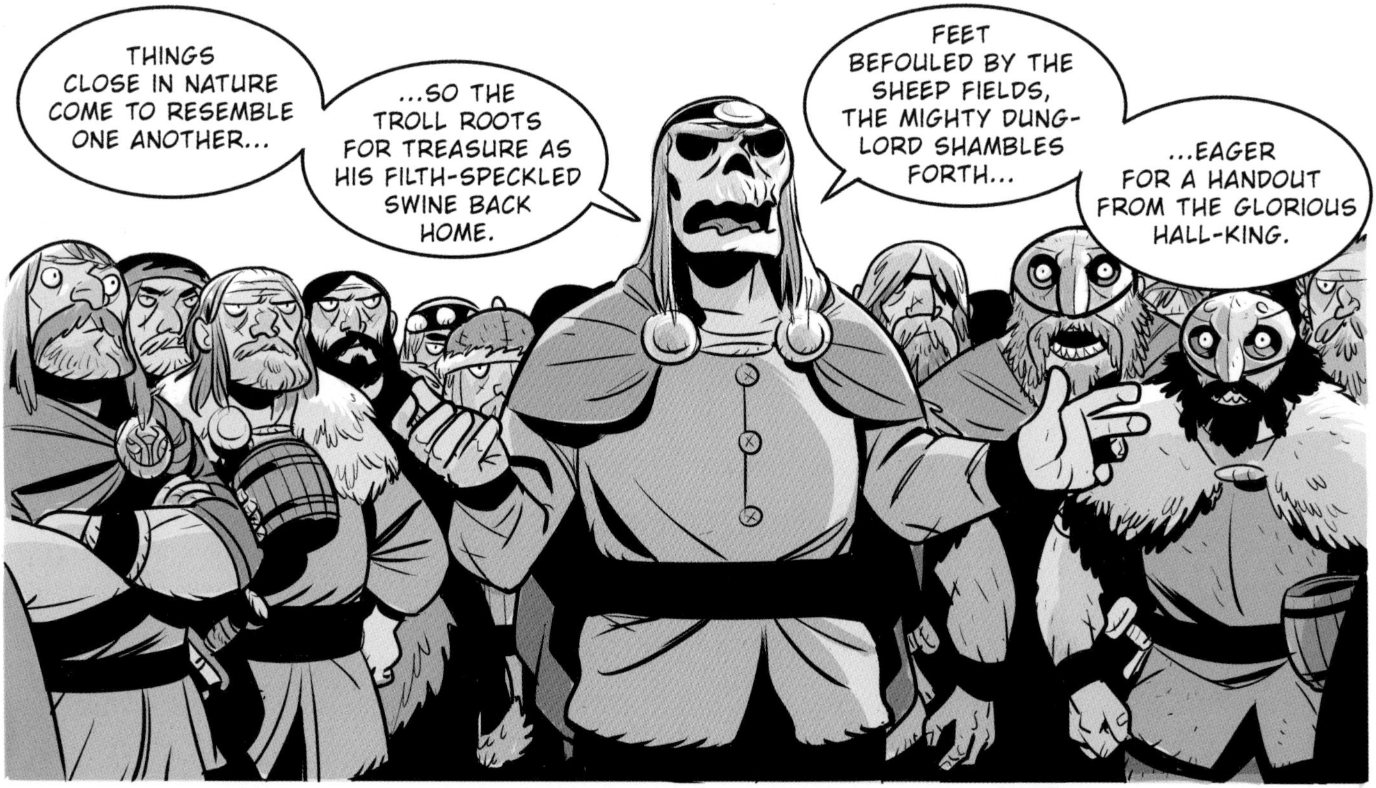
THINGS CLOSE IN NATURE COME TO RESEMBLE ONE ANOTHER...
...SO THE TROLL ROOTS FOR TREASURE AS HIS FILTH-SPECKLED SWINE BACK HOME.
FEET BEFOULED BY THE SHEEP FIELDS, THE MIGHTY DUNG-LORD SHAMBLES FORTH...
...EAGER FOR A HANDOUT FROM THE GLORIOUS HALL-KING.

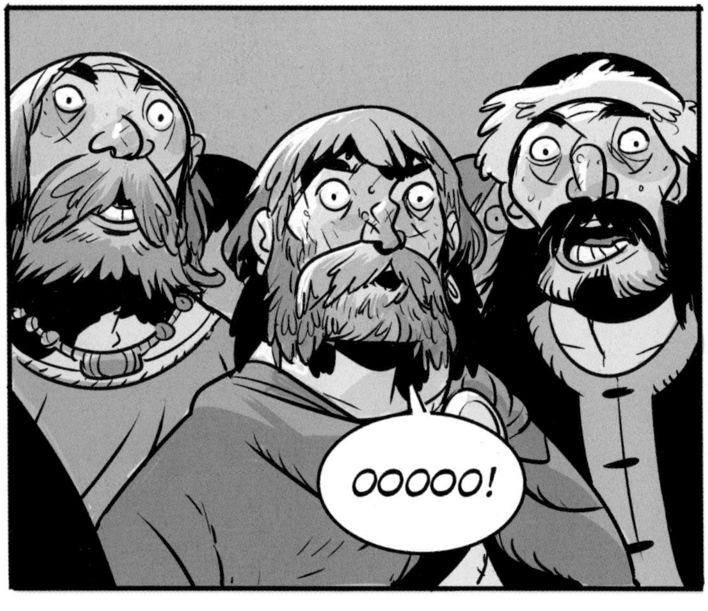
OOOOO!

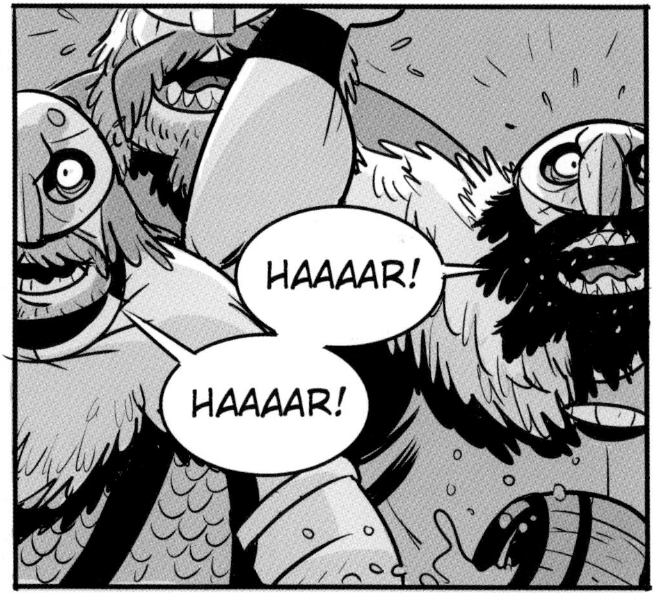
HAAAAR!
HAAAAR!

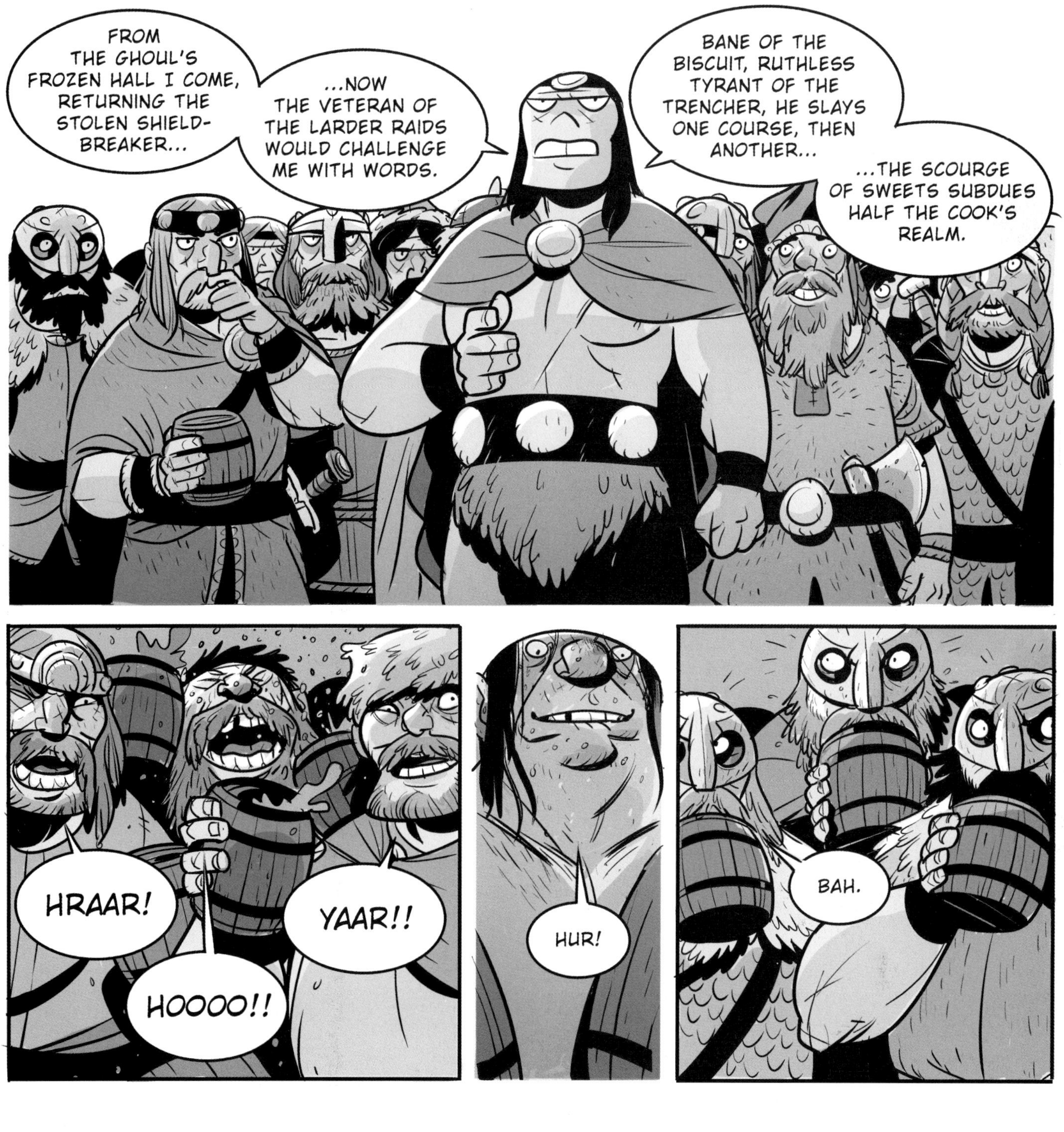
FROM THE GHOUL'S FROZEN HALL I COME, RETURNING THE STOLEN SHIELD-BREAKER...
...NOW THE VETERAN OF THE LARDER RAIDS WOULD CHALLENGE ME WITH WORDS.
BANE OF THE BISCUIT, RUTHLESS TYRANT OF THE TRENCHER, HE SLAYS ONE COURSE, THEN ANOTHER...
...THE SCOURGE OF SWEETS SUBDUES HALF THE COOK'S REALM.
HRAAR!
HOOOO!!
YAAR!!
HUR!
BAH.

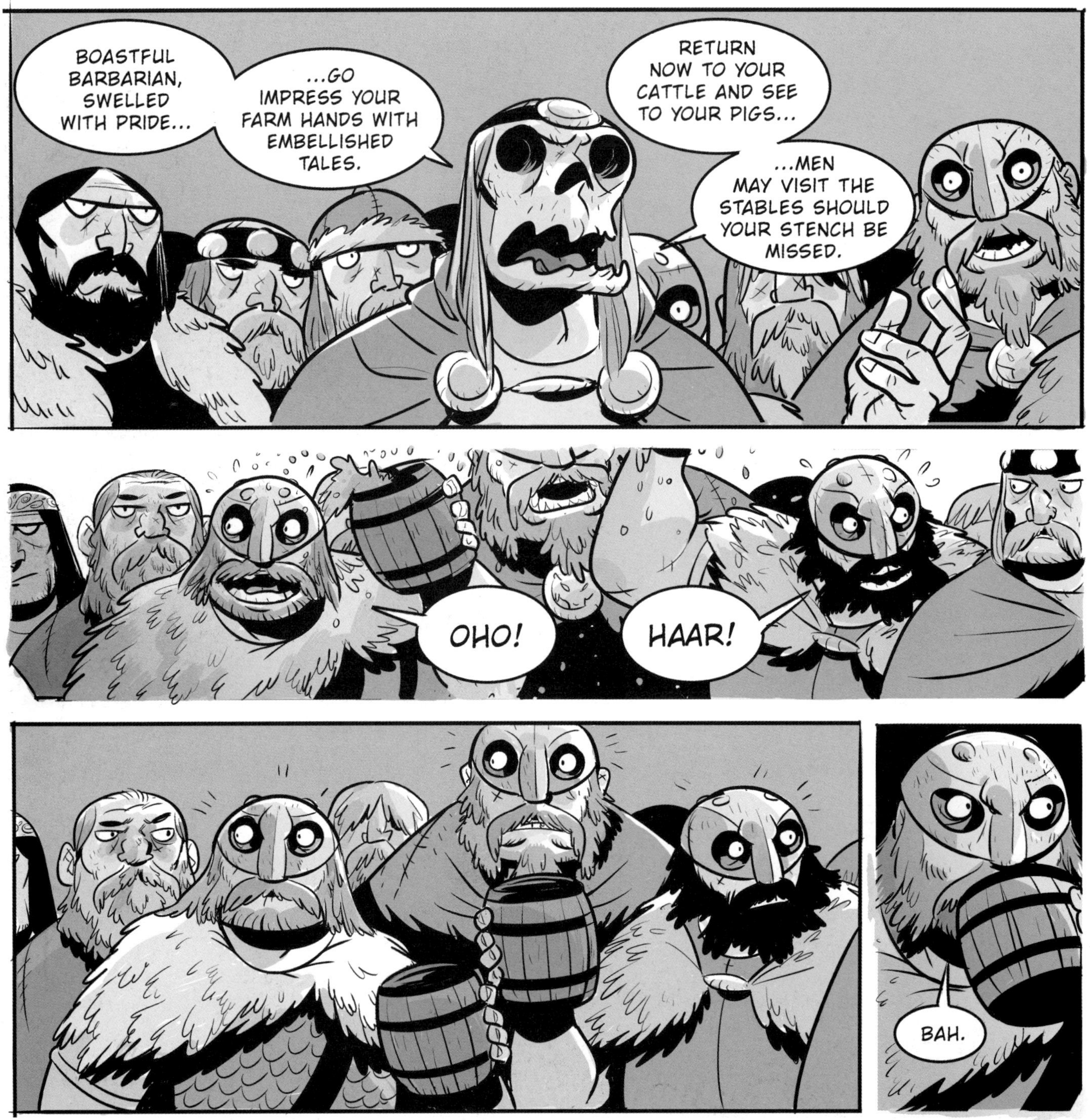
BOASTFUL BARBARIAN, SWELLED WITH PRIDE...
...GO IMPRESS YOUR FARM HANDS WITH EMBELLISHED TALES.
RETURN NOW TO YOUR CATTLE AND SEE TO YOUR PIGS...
...MEN MAY VISIT THE STABLES SHOULD YOUR STENCH BE MISSED.
OHO!
HAAR!
BAH.

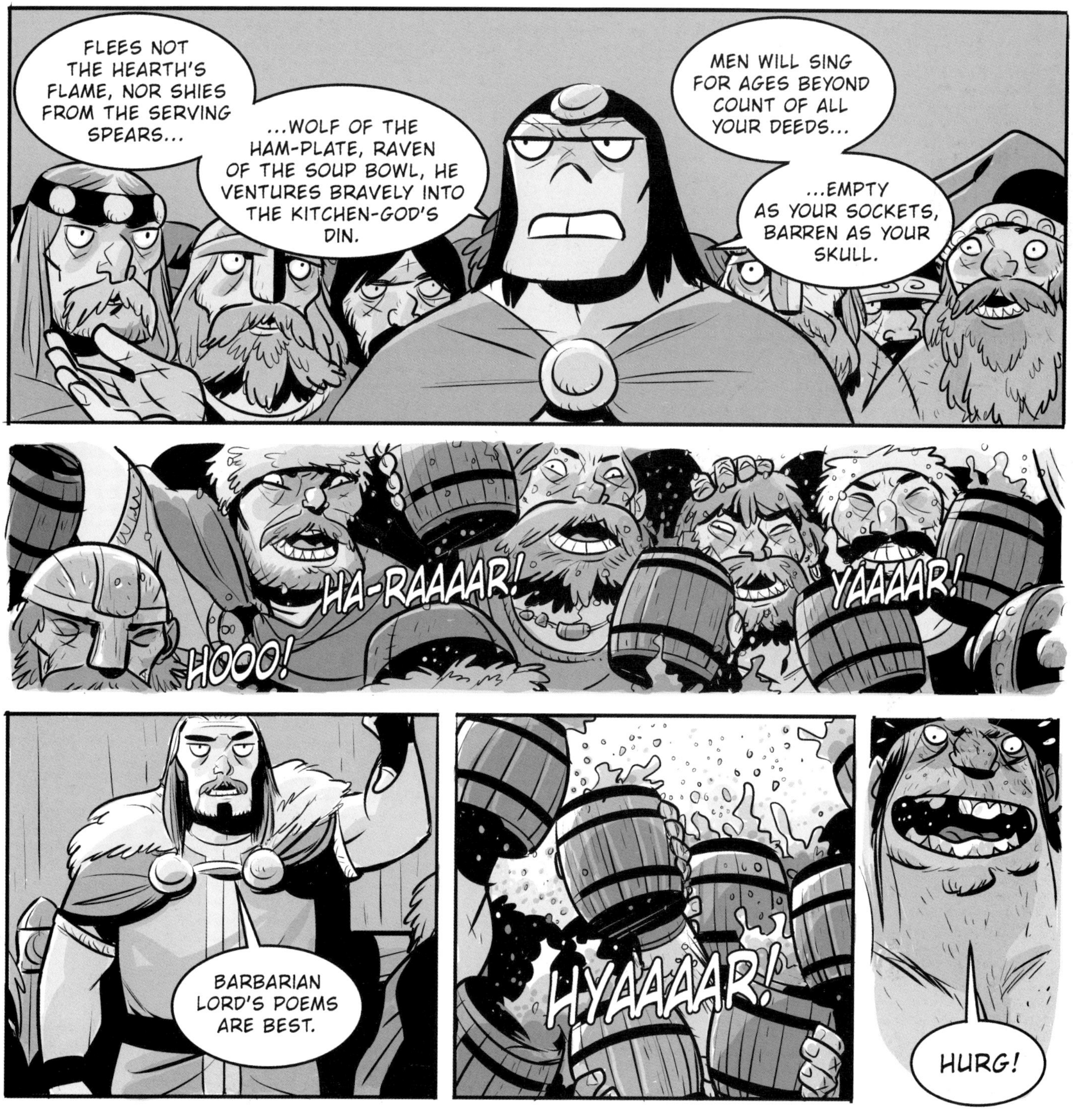
FLEES NOT THE HEARTH'S FLAME, NOR SHIES FROM THE SERVING SPEARS...
...WOLF OF THE HAM-PLATE, RAVEN OF THE SOUP BOWL, HE VENTURES BRAVELY INTO THE KITCHEN-GOD'S DIN.
MEN WILL SING FOR AGES BEYOND COUNT OF ALL YOUR DEEDS...
...EMPTY AS YOUR SOCKETS, BARREN AS YOUR SKULL.
HA-RAAAAR!
YAAAAR!
HOOO!
BARBARIAN LORD'S POEMS ARE BEST.
HYAAAAR!
HURG!

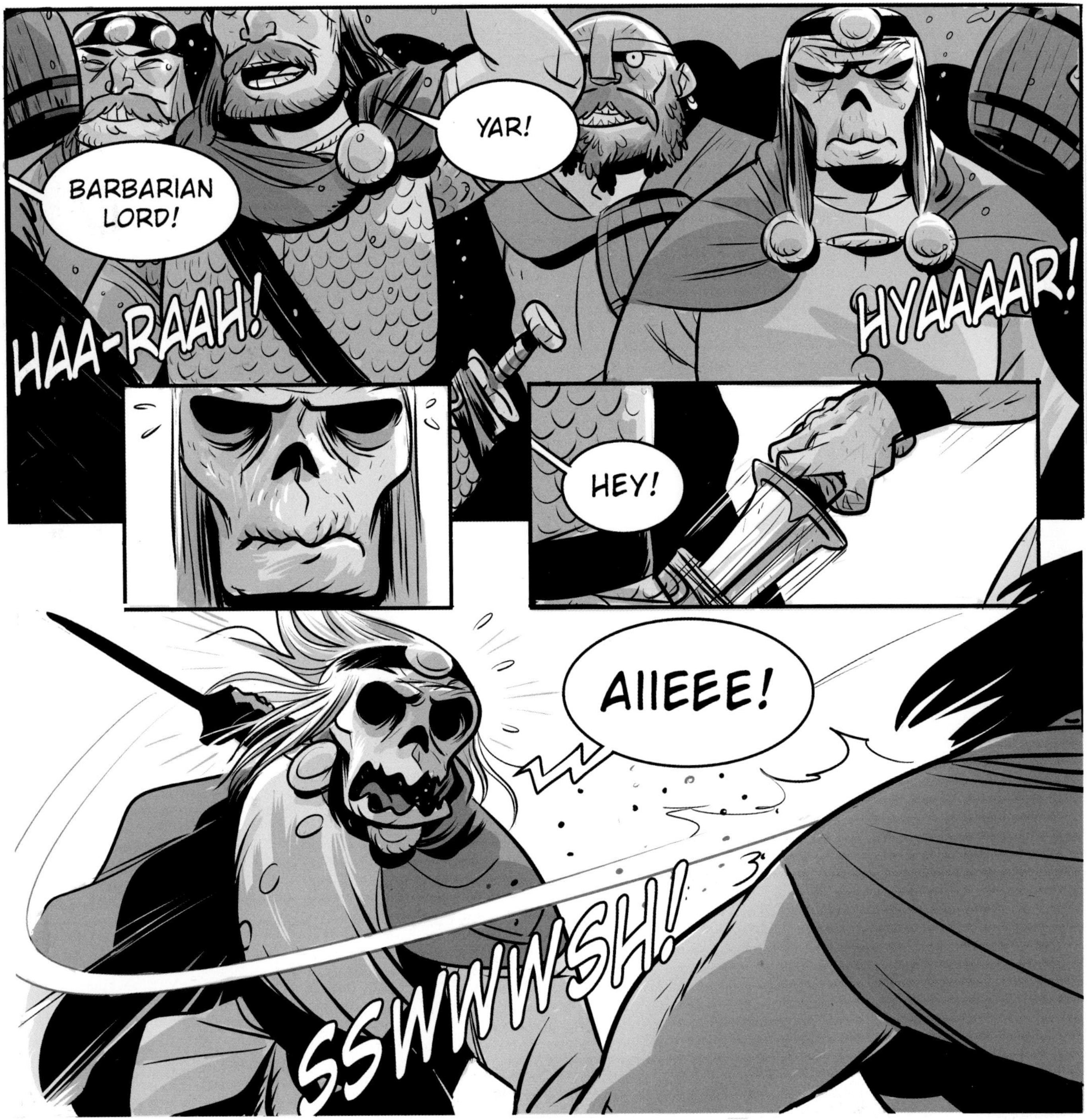
BARBARIAN LORD!
YAR!
HAA-RAAH!
HYAAAAR!
HEY!
AIIEEE!
SSWWWWSH!

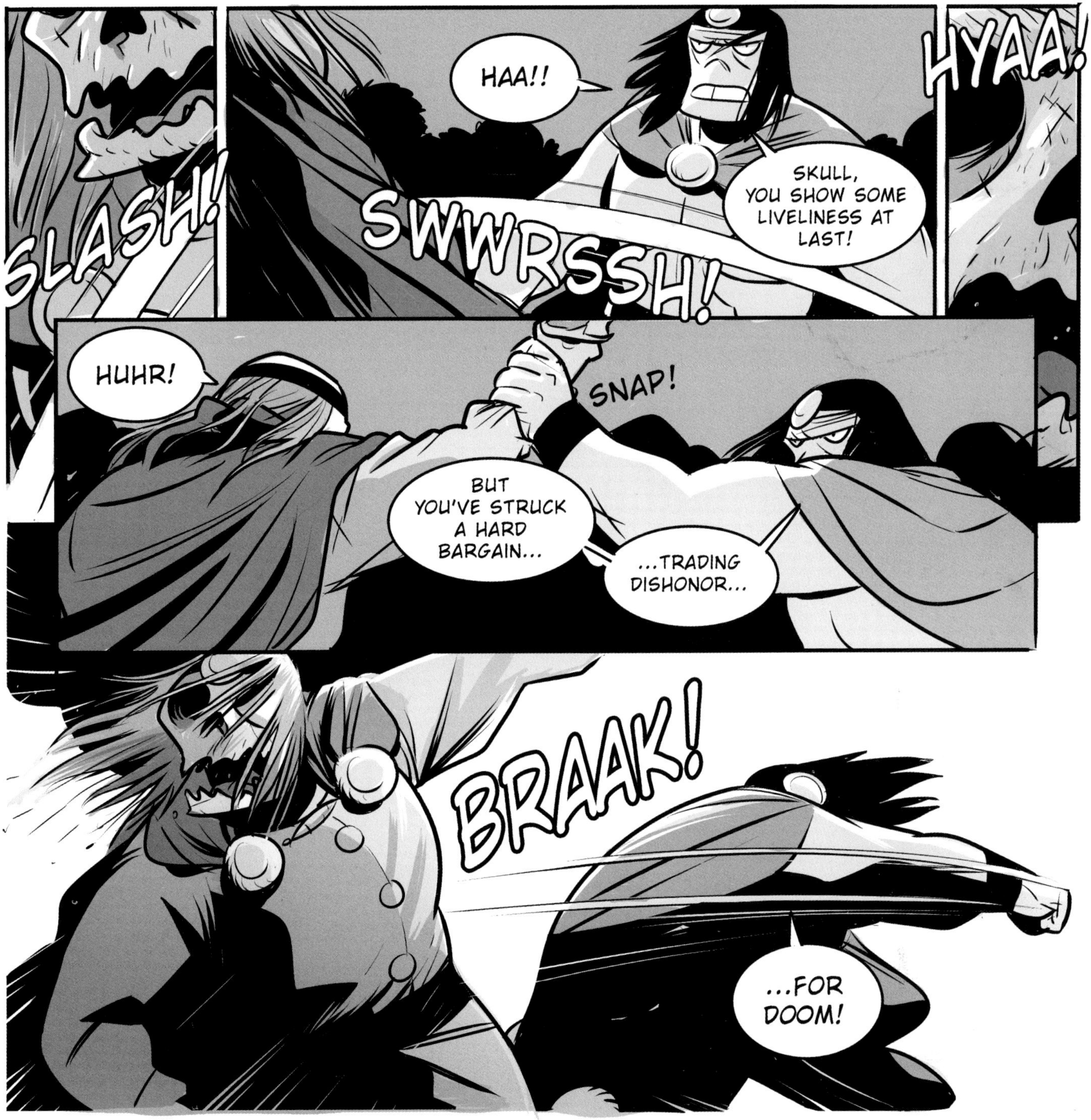
SLASH!
HAA!!
SWWRSSH!
SKULL, YOU SHOW SOME LIVELINESS AT LAST!
HYAA!
HUHR!
SNAP!
BUT YOU'VE STRUCK A HARD BARGAIN...
...TRADING DISHONOR...
BRAAK!
...FOR DOOM!

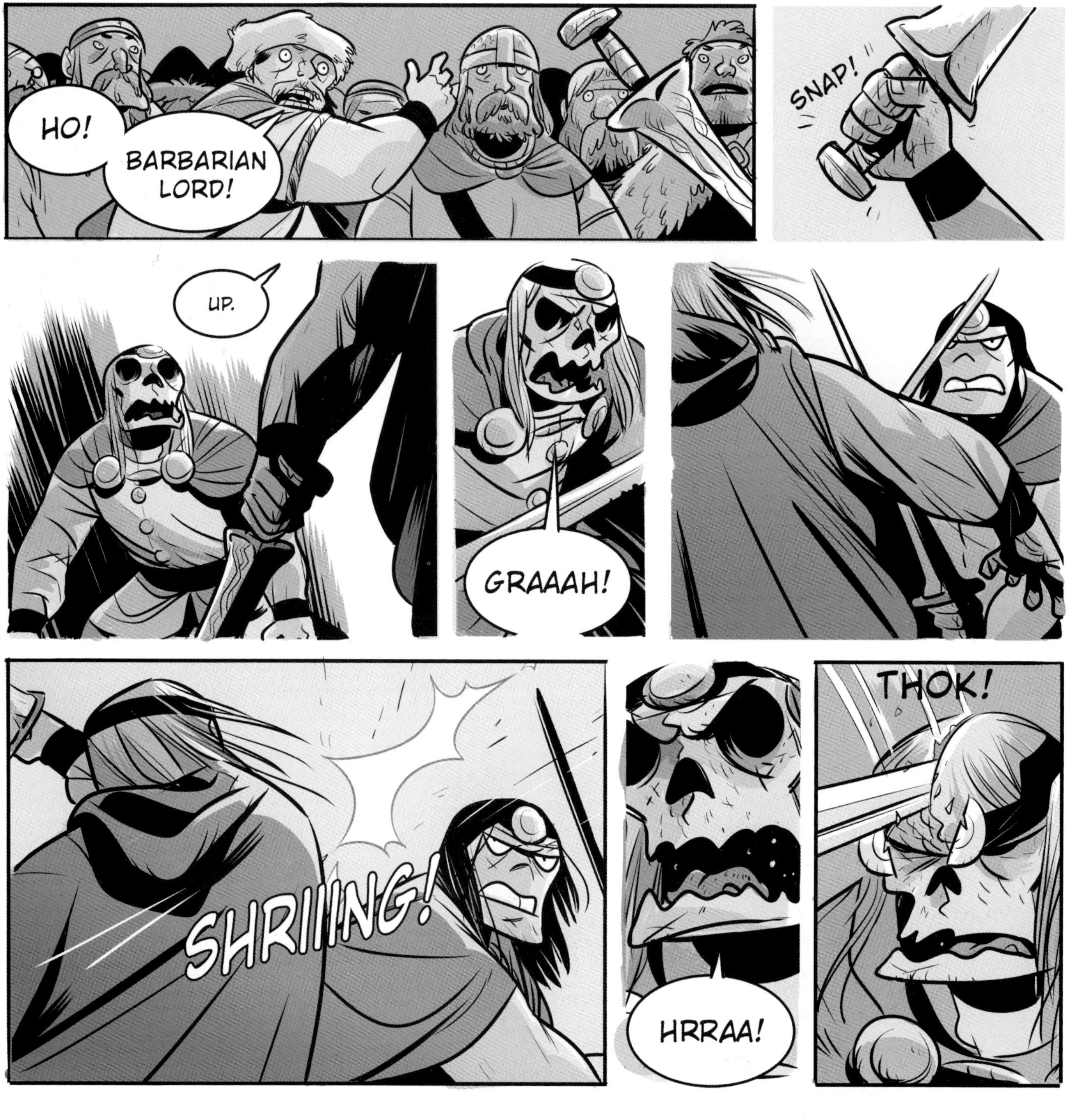
HO!
BARBARIAN LORD!
SNAP!
UP.
GRAAAH!
SHRIIING!
HRRAA!
THOK!

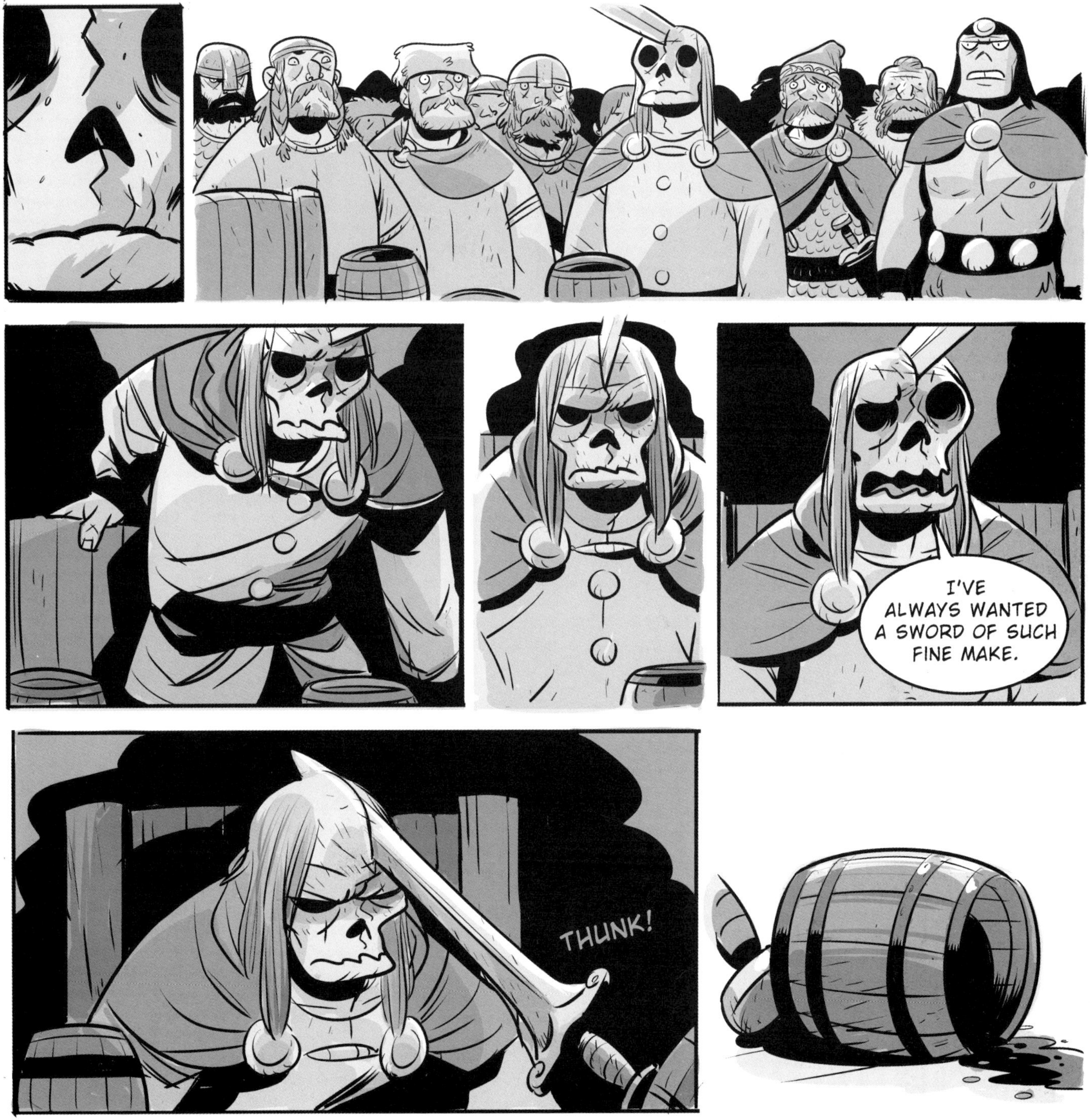
I'VE ALWAYS WANTED A SWORD OF SUCH FINE MAKE.
THUNK!

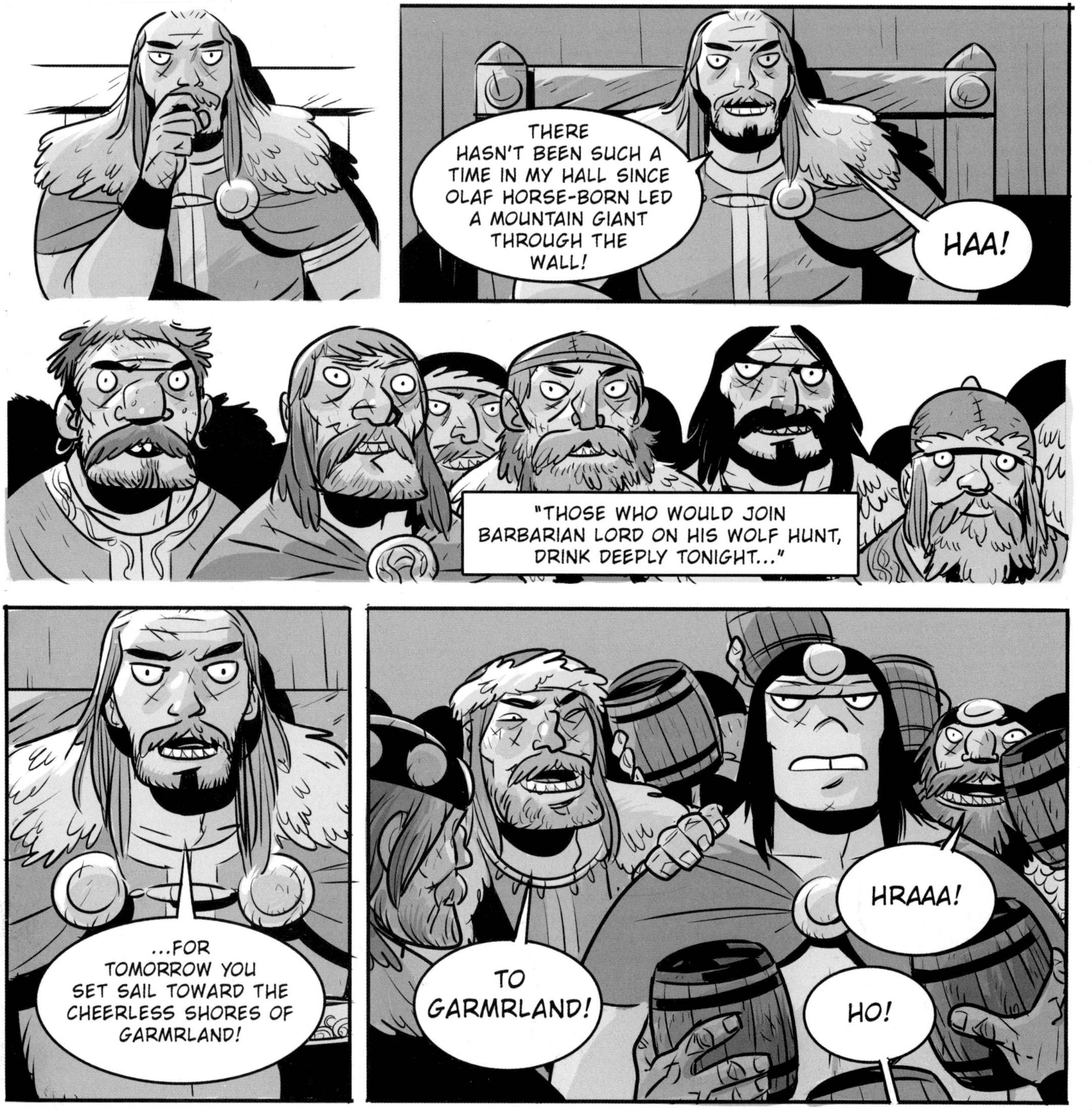
THERE HASN'T BEEN SUCH A TIME IN MY HALL SINCE OLAF HORSE-BORN LED A MOUNTAIN GIANT THROUGH THE WALL!
HAA!
"THOSE WHO WOULD JOIN BARBARIAN LORD ON HIS WOLF HUNT, DRINK DEEPLY TONIGHT..."
...FOR TOMORROW YOU SET SAIL TOWARD THE CHEERLESS SHORES OF GARMRLAND!
TO GARMRLAND!
HRAAA!
HO!

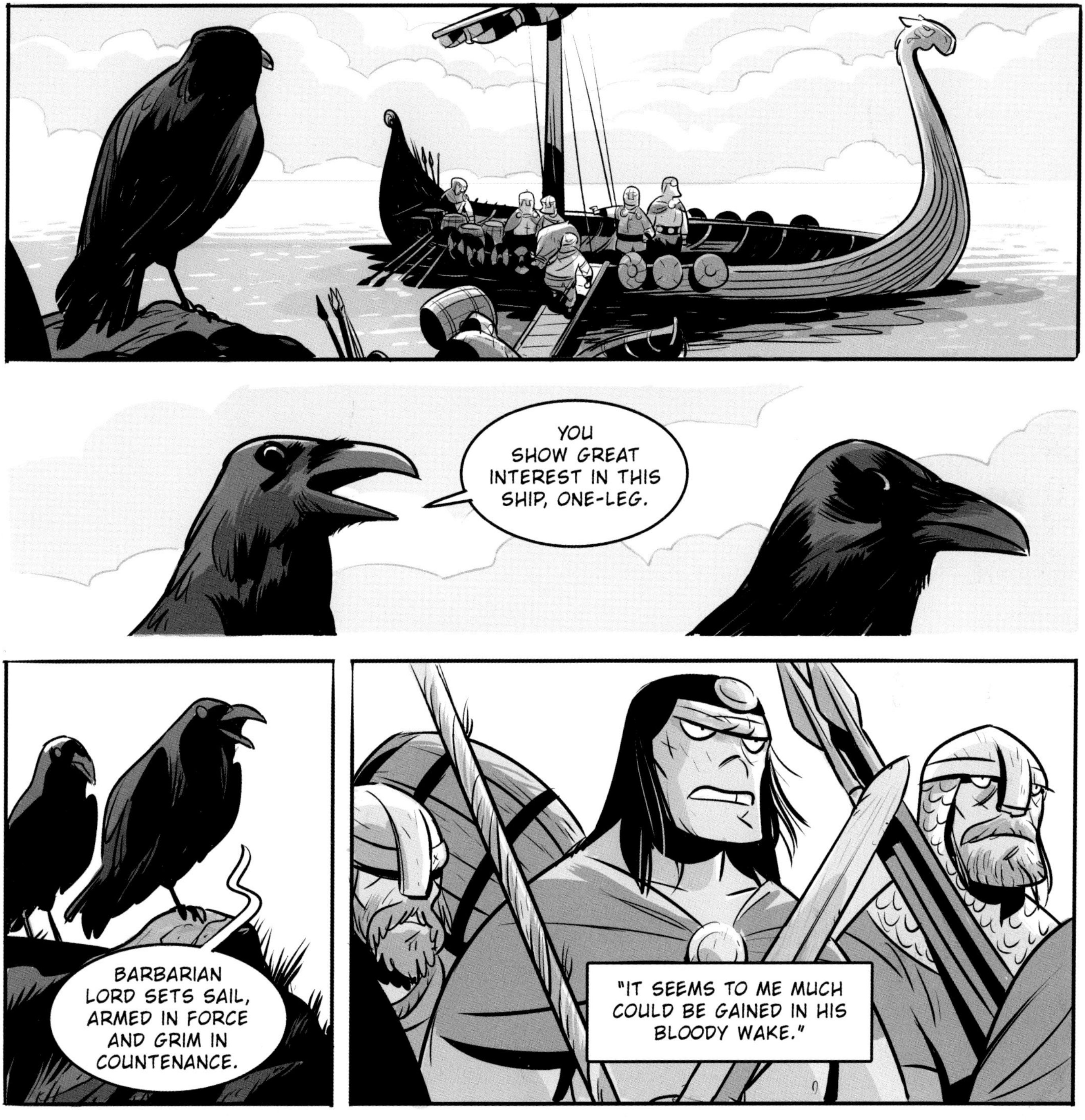
YOU SHOW GREAT INTEREST IN THIS SHIP, ONE-LEG.
BARBARIAN LORD SETS SAIL, ARMED IN FORCE AND GRIM IN COUNTENANCE.
"IT SEEMS TO ME MUCH COULD BE GAINED IN HIS BLOODY WAKE."

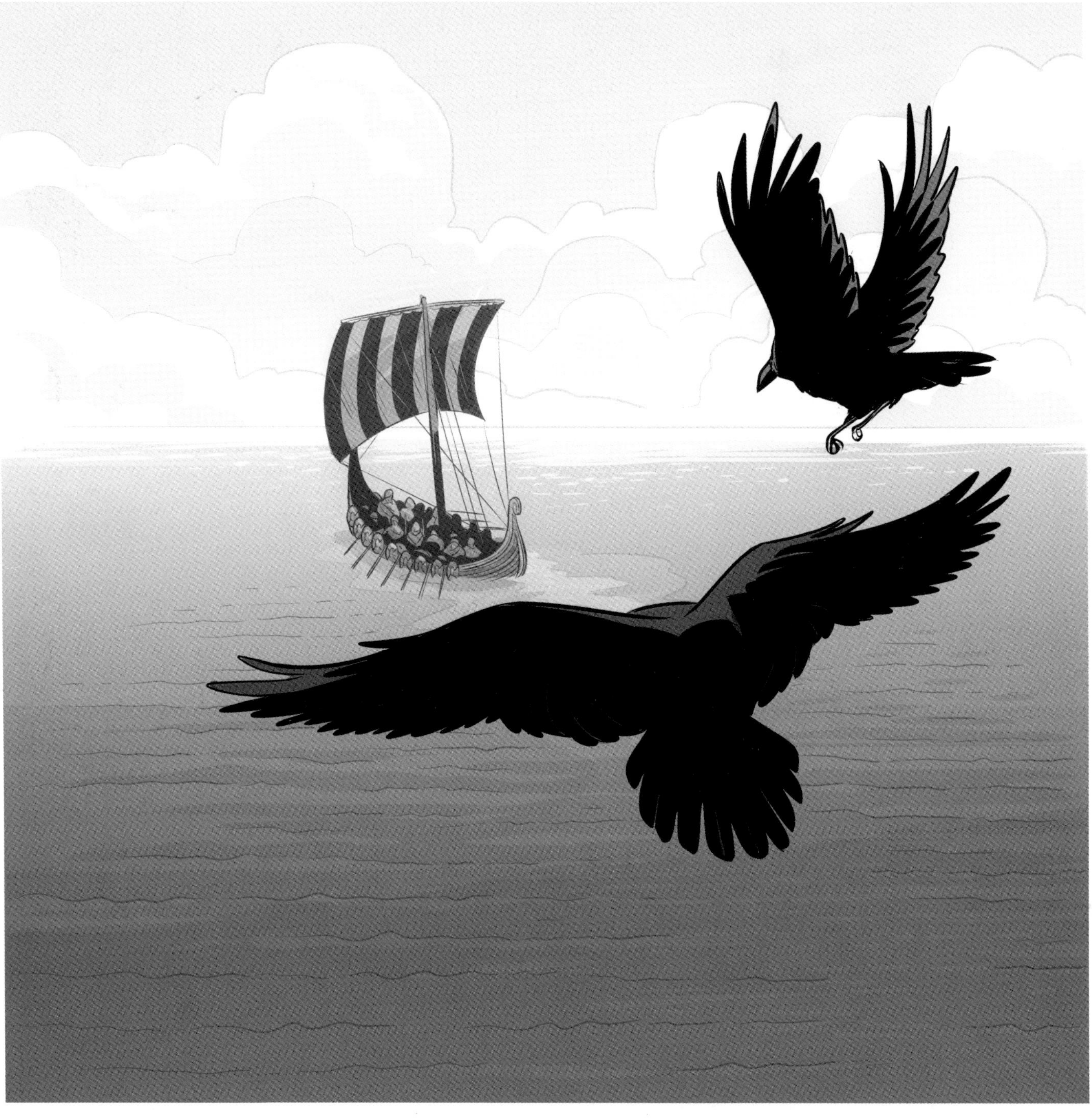

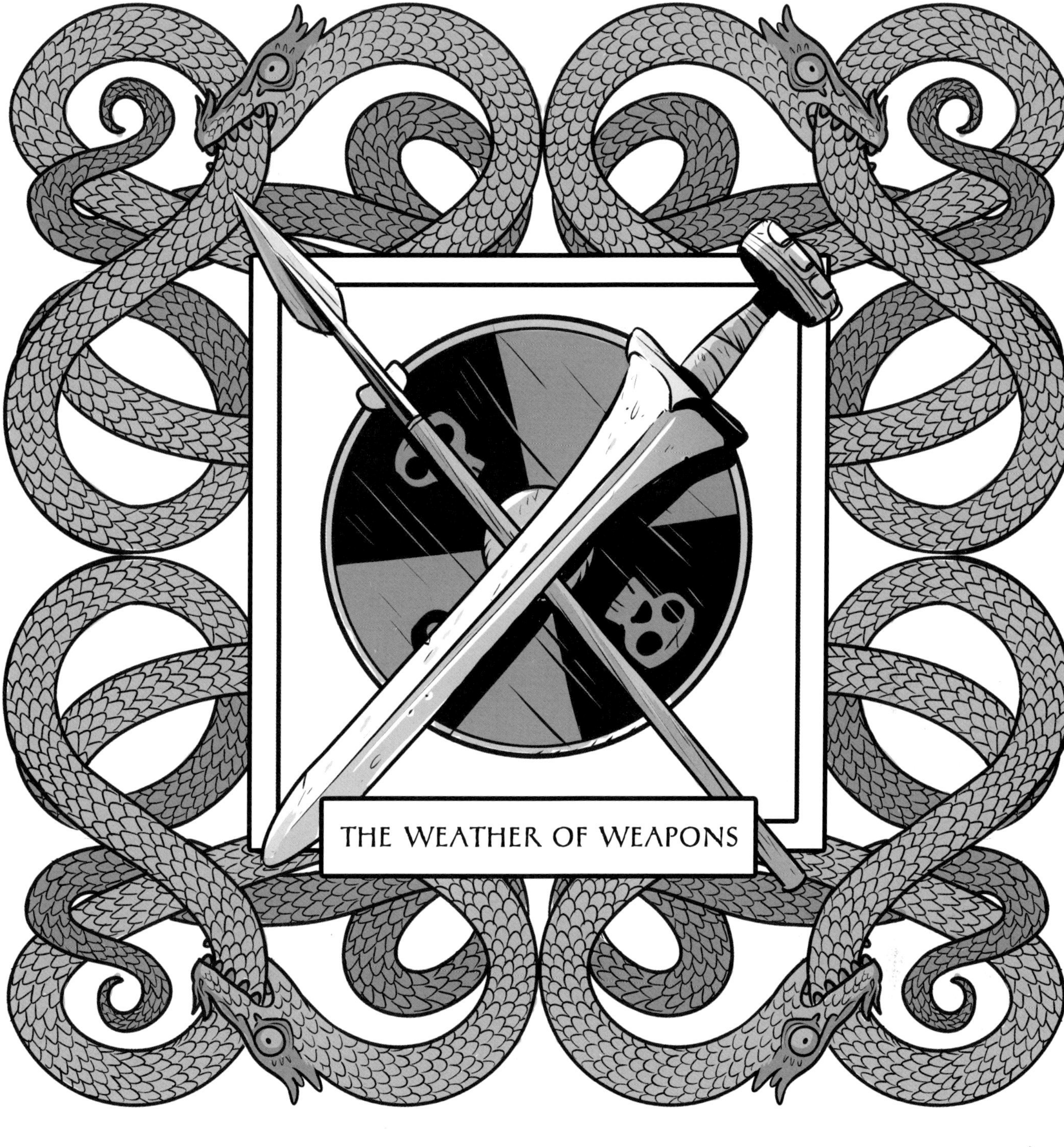
THE WEATHER OF WEAPONS

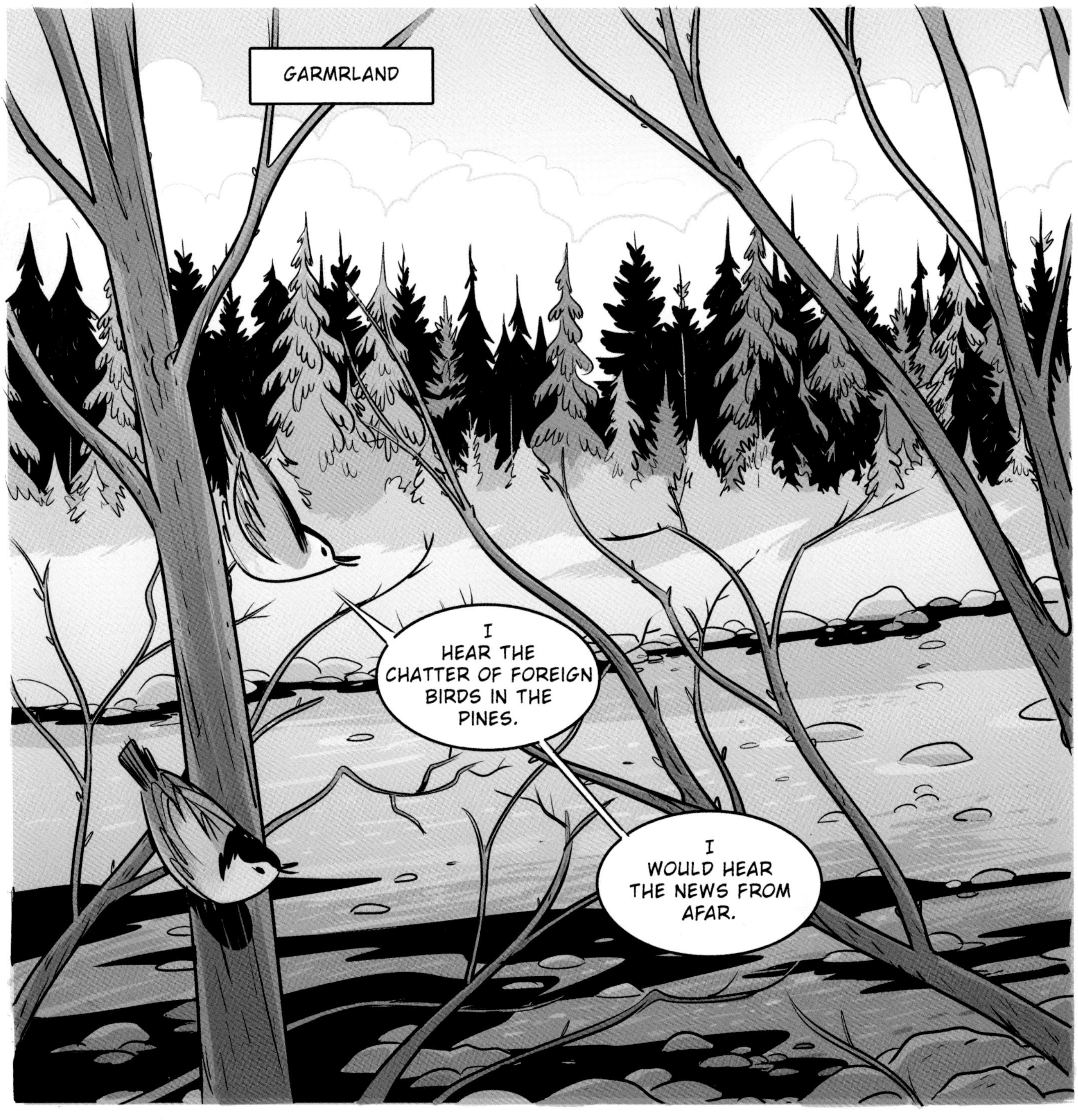
GARMRLAND
I HEAR THE CHATTER OF FOREIGN BIRDS IN THE PINES.
I WOULD HEAR THE NEWS FROM AFAR.

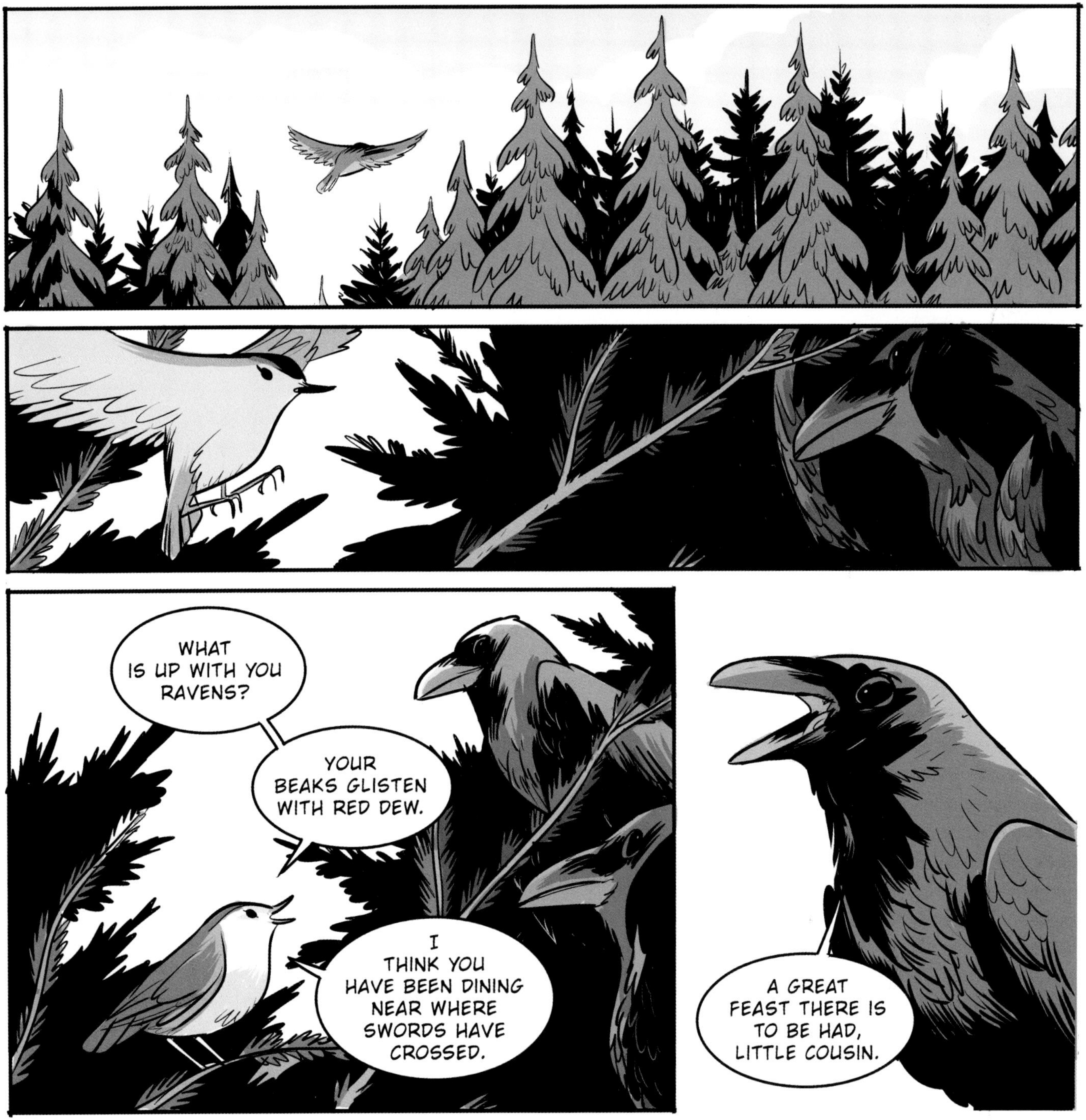
WHAT IS UP WITH YOU RAVENS?
YOUR BEAKS GLISTEN WITH RED DEW.
I THINK YOU HAVE BEEN DINING NEAR WHERE SWORDS HAVE CROSSED.
A GREAT FEAST THERE IS TO BE HAD, LITTLE COUSIN.

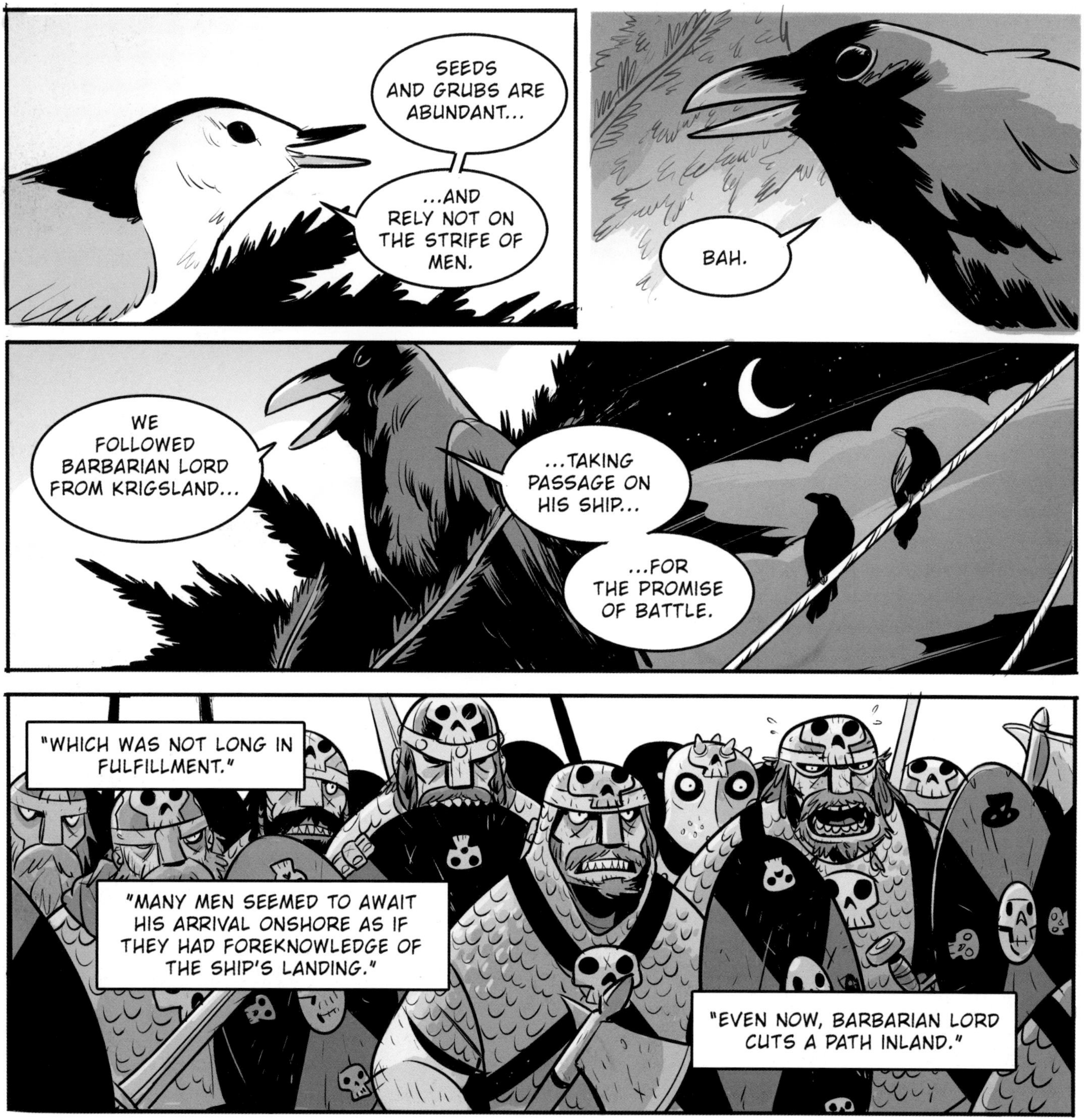
SEEDS AND GRUBS ARE ABUNDANT...
...AND RELY NOT ON THE STRIFE OF MEN.
BAH.
WE FOLLOWED BARBARIAN LORD FROM KRIGSLAND...
...TAKING PASSAGE ON HIS SHIP...
...FOR THE PROMISE OF BATTLE.
"WHICH WAS NOT LONG IN FULFILLMENT."
"MANY MEN SEEMED TO AWAIT HIS ARRIVAL ONSHORE AS IF THEY HAD FOREKNOWLEDGE OF THE SHIP'S LANDING."
"EVEN NOW, BARBARIAN LORD CUTS A PATH INLAND."

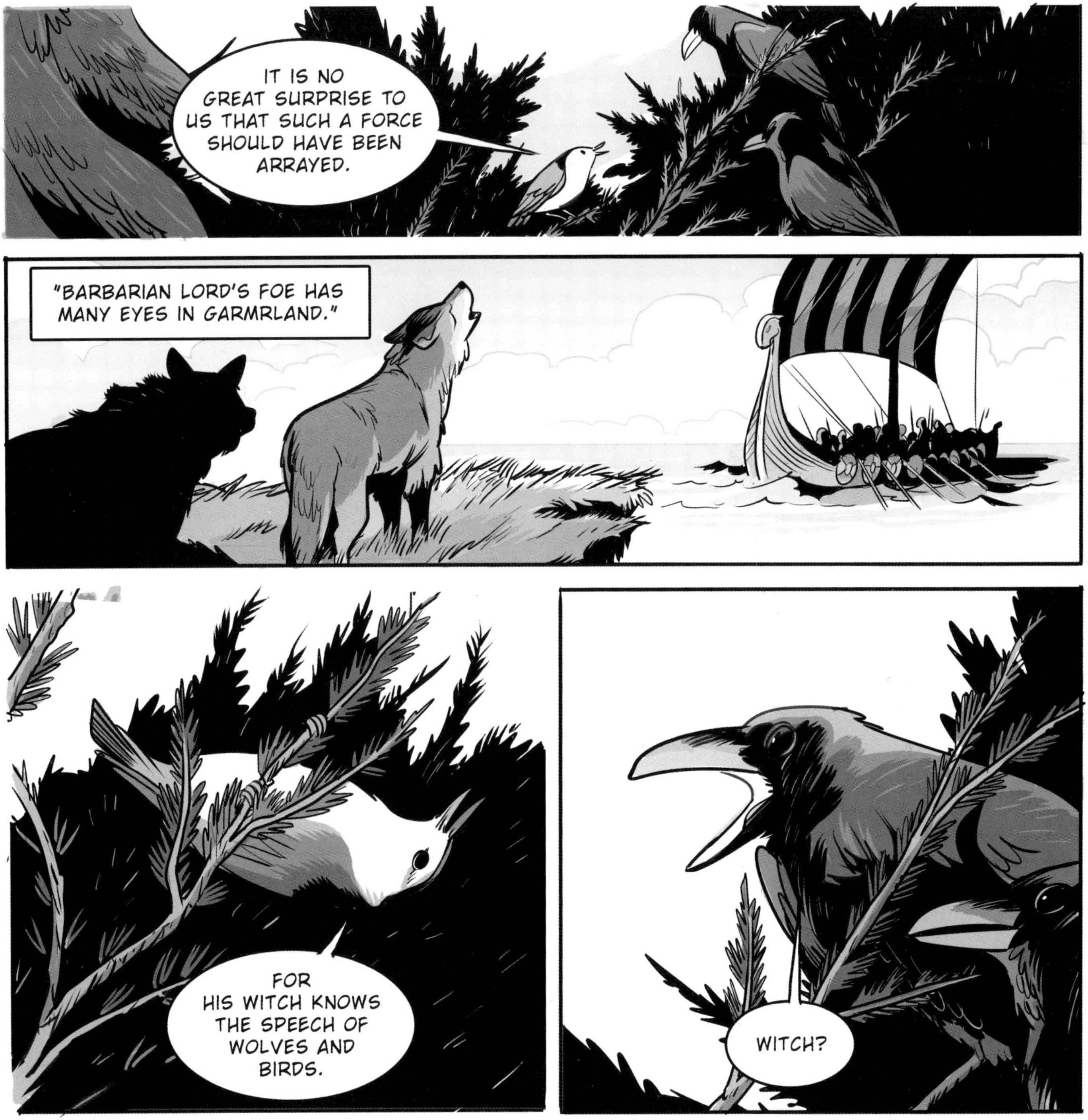
IT IS NO GREAT SURPRISE TO US THAT SUCH A FORCE SHOULD HAVE BEEN ARRAYED.
"BARBARIAN LORD'S FOE HAS MANY EYES IN GARMRLAND."
FOR HIS WITCH KNOWS THE SPEECH OF WOLVES AND BIRDS.
WITCH?

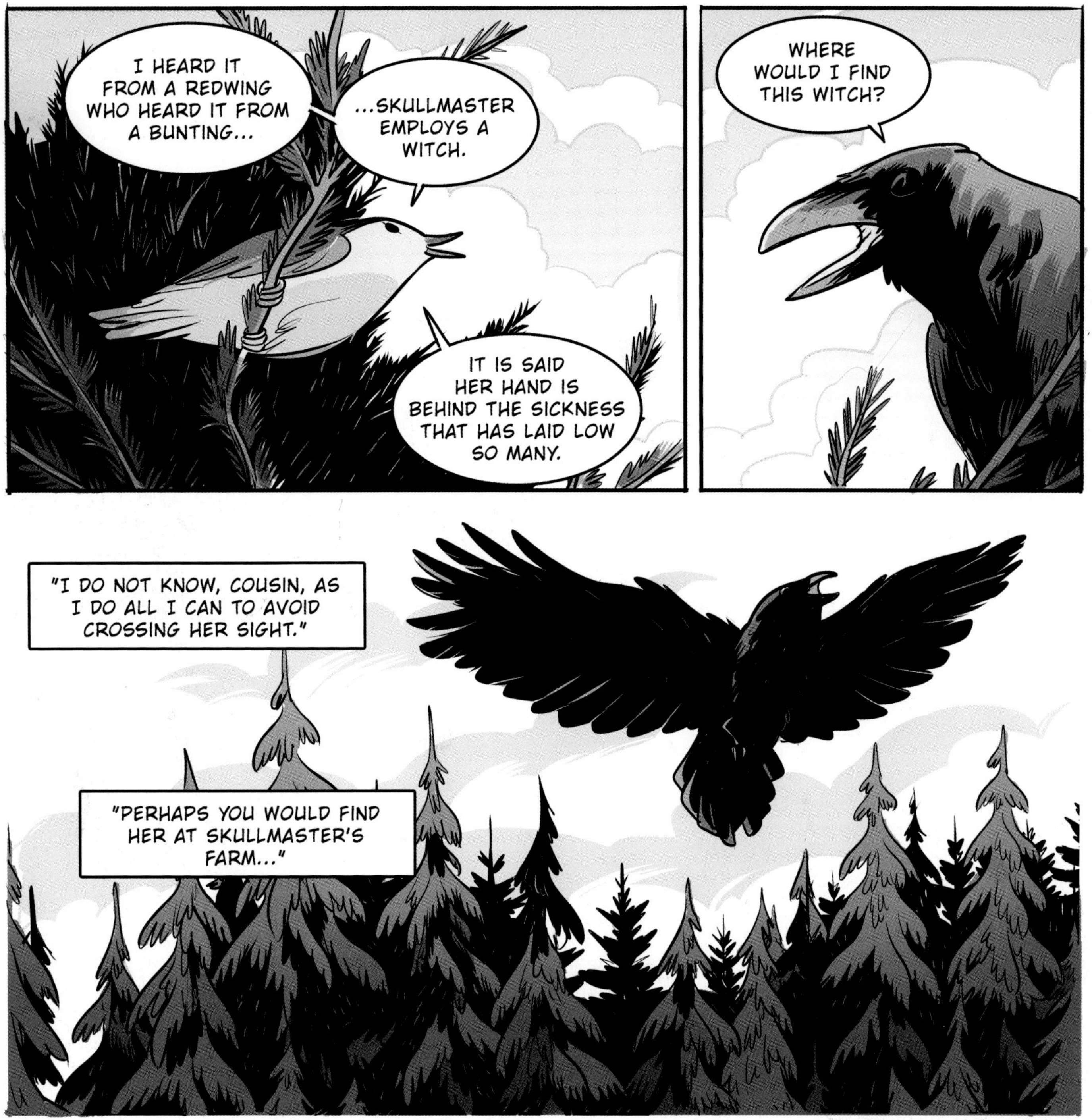
I HEARD IT FROM A REDWING WHO HEARD IT FROM A BUNTING...
...SKULLMASTER EMPLOYS A WITCH.
IT IS SAID HER HAND IS BEHIND THE SICKNESS THAT HAS LAID LOW SO MANY.
WHERE WOULD I FIND THIS WITCH?
"I DO NOT KNOW, COUSIN, AS I DO ALL I CAN TO AVOID CROSSING HER SIGHT."
"PERHAPS YOU WOULD FIND HER AT SKULLMASTER'S FARM..."

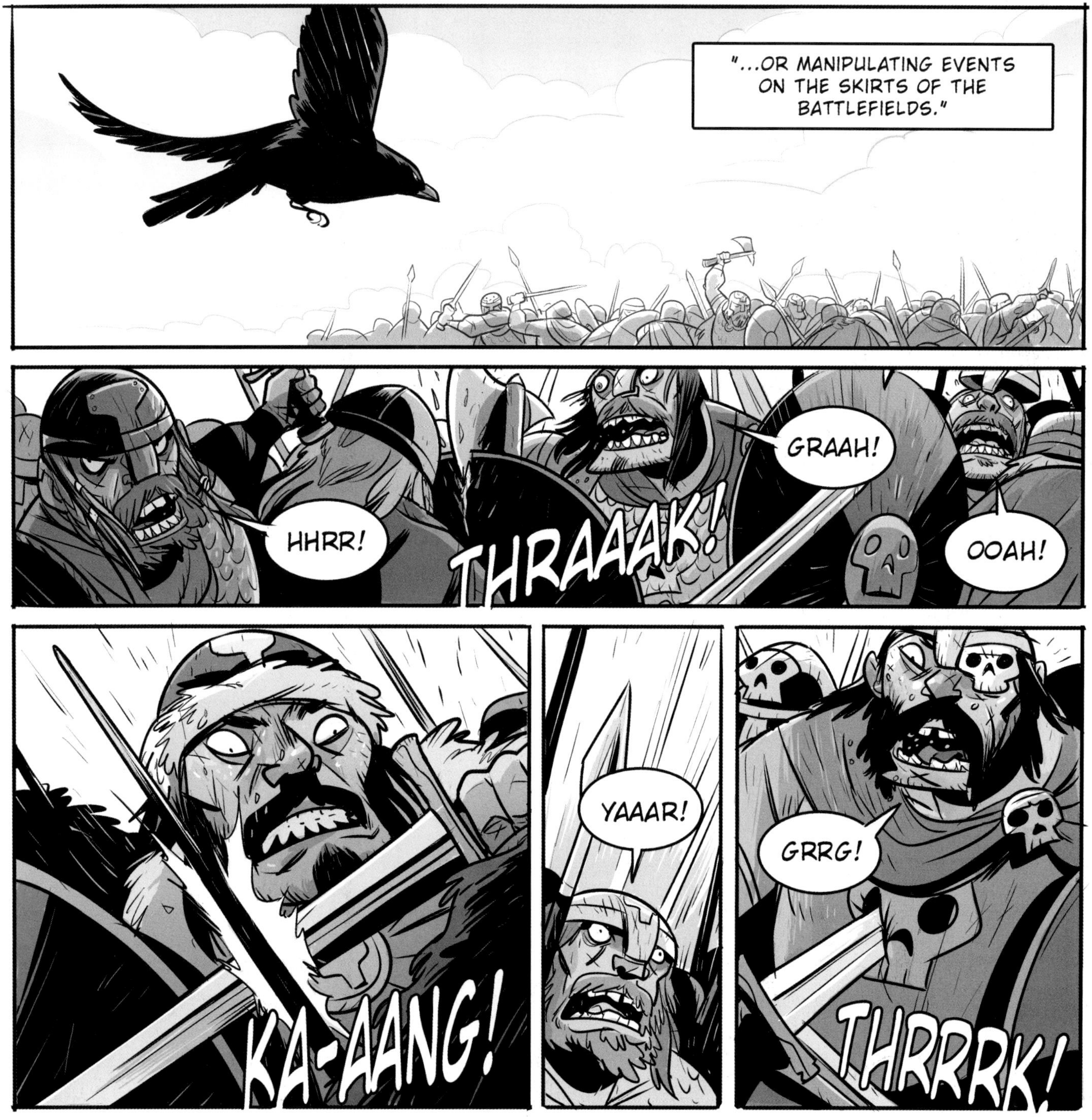
"...OR MANIPULATING EVENTS ON THE SKIRTS OF THE BATTLEFIELDS."
HHRR!
THRAAAK!
GRAAH!
OOAH!
KA-AANG!
YAAAR!
GRRG!
THRRRK!

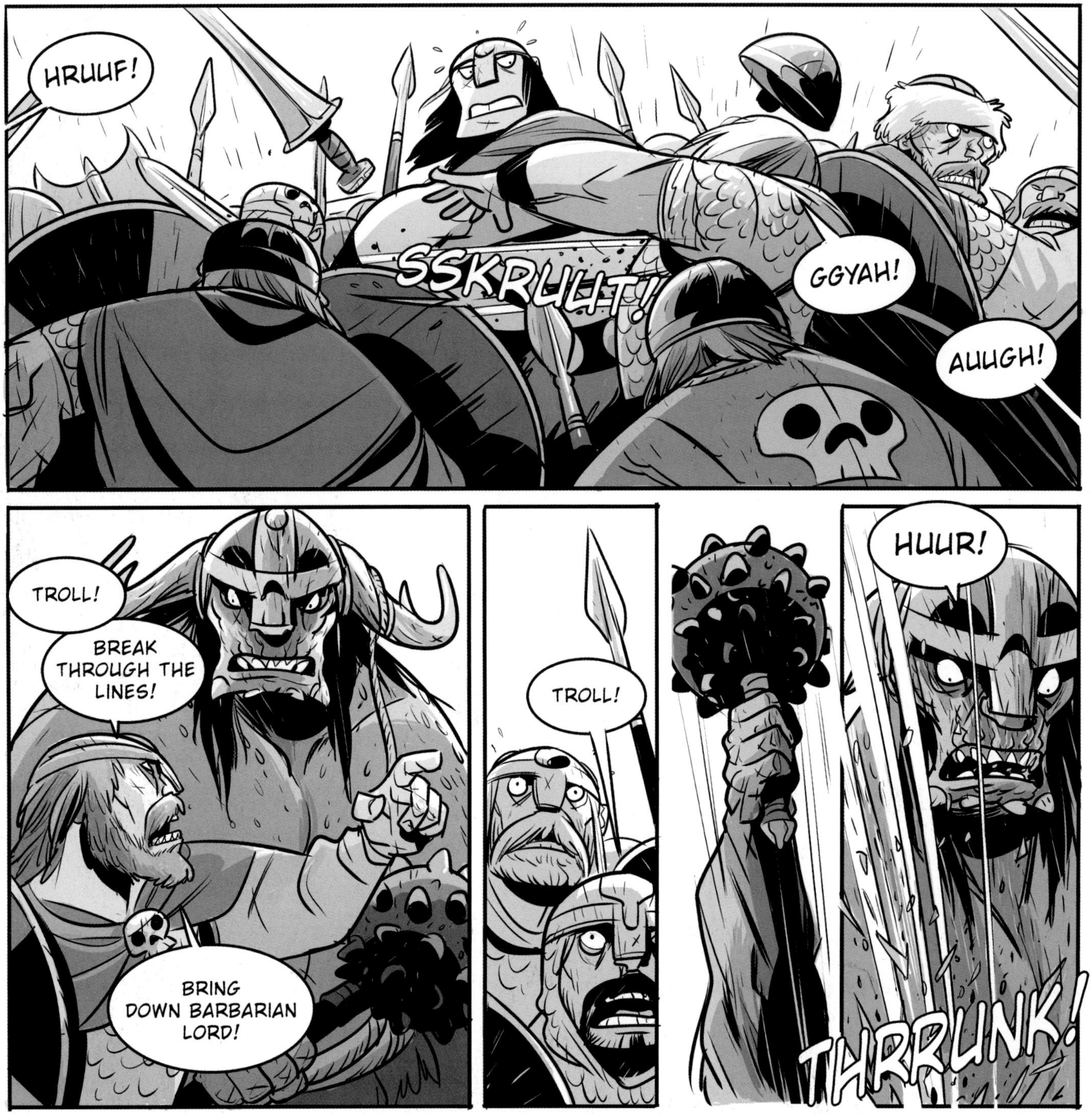
HRUUF!
SSKRUUT!
GGYAH!
AUUGH!
TROLL!
BREAK THROUGH THE LINES!
BRING DOWN BARBARIAN LORD!
TROLL!
HUUR!
THRRUNK!

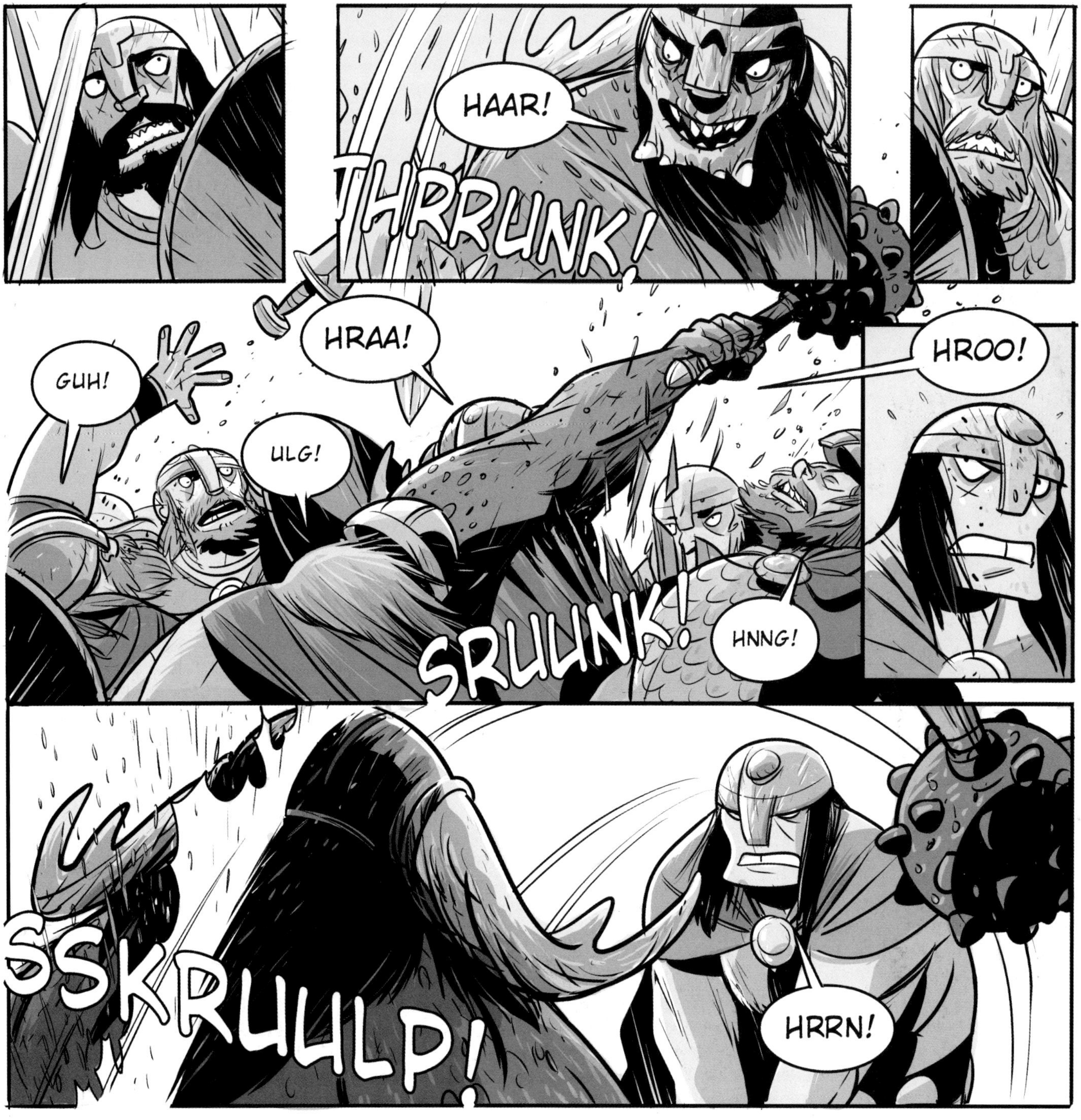
HAAR!
THRRUNK!
HRAA!
GUH!
ULG!
HROO!
SRUUNK!
HNNG!
SSKRUULP!
HRRN!

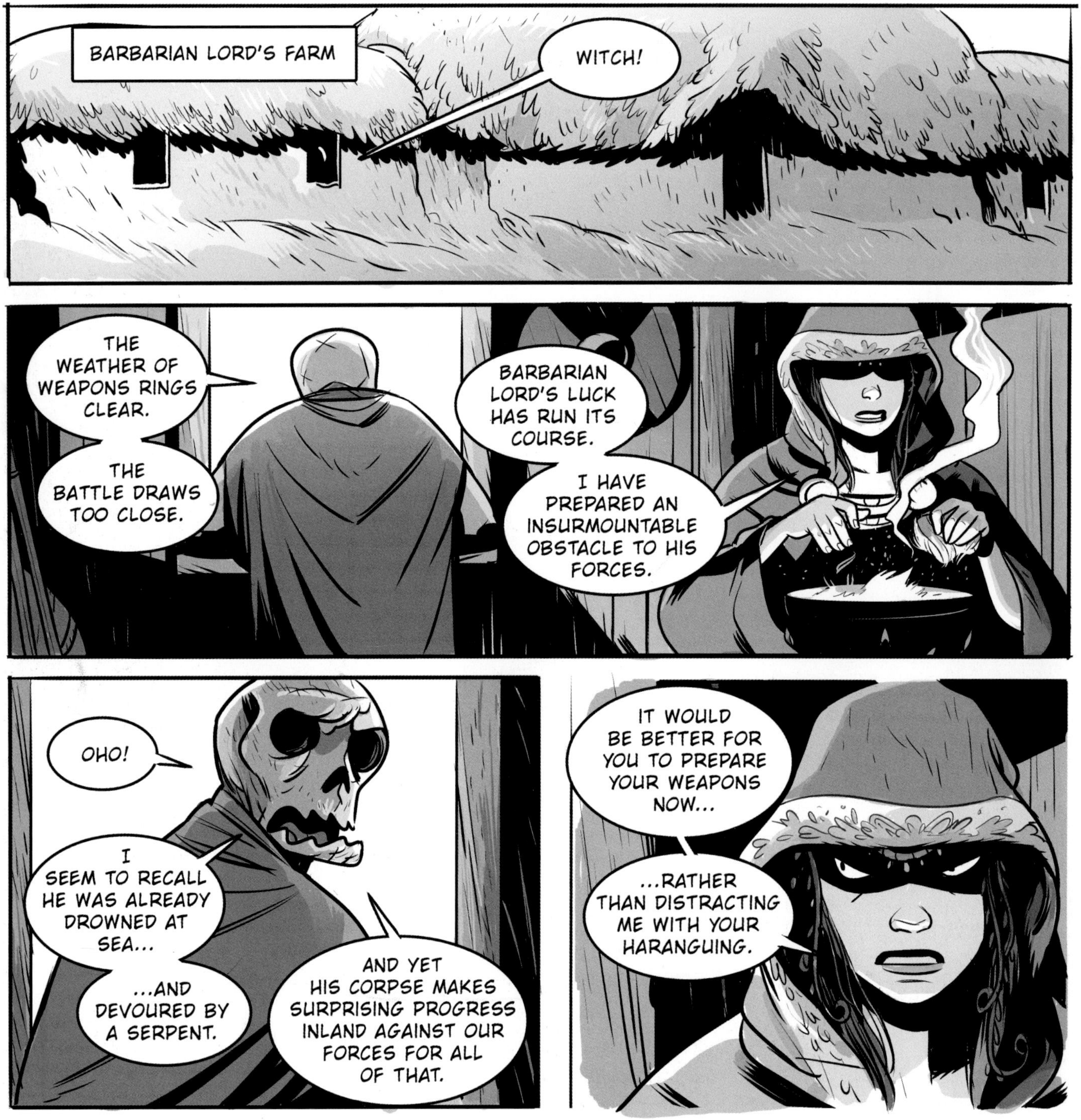

BARBARIAN LORD'S FARM
WITCH!
THE WEATHER OF WEAPONS RINGS CLEAR.
THE BATTLE DRAWS TOO CLOSE.
BARBARIAN LORD'S LUCK HAS RUN ITS COURSE.
I HAVE PREPARED AN INSURMOUNTABLE OBSTACLE TO HIS FORCES.
OHO!
I SEEM TO RECALL HE WAS ALREADY DROWNED AT SEA...
...AND DEVOURED BY A SERPENT.
AND YET HIS CORPSE MAKES SURPRISING PROGRESS INLAND AGAINST OUR FORCES FOR ALL OF THAT.
IT WOULD BE BETTER FOR YOU TO PREPARE YOUR WEAPONS NOW...
...RATHER THAN DISTRACTING ME WITH YOUR HARANGUING.

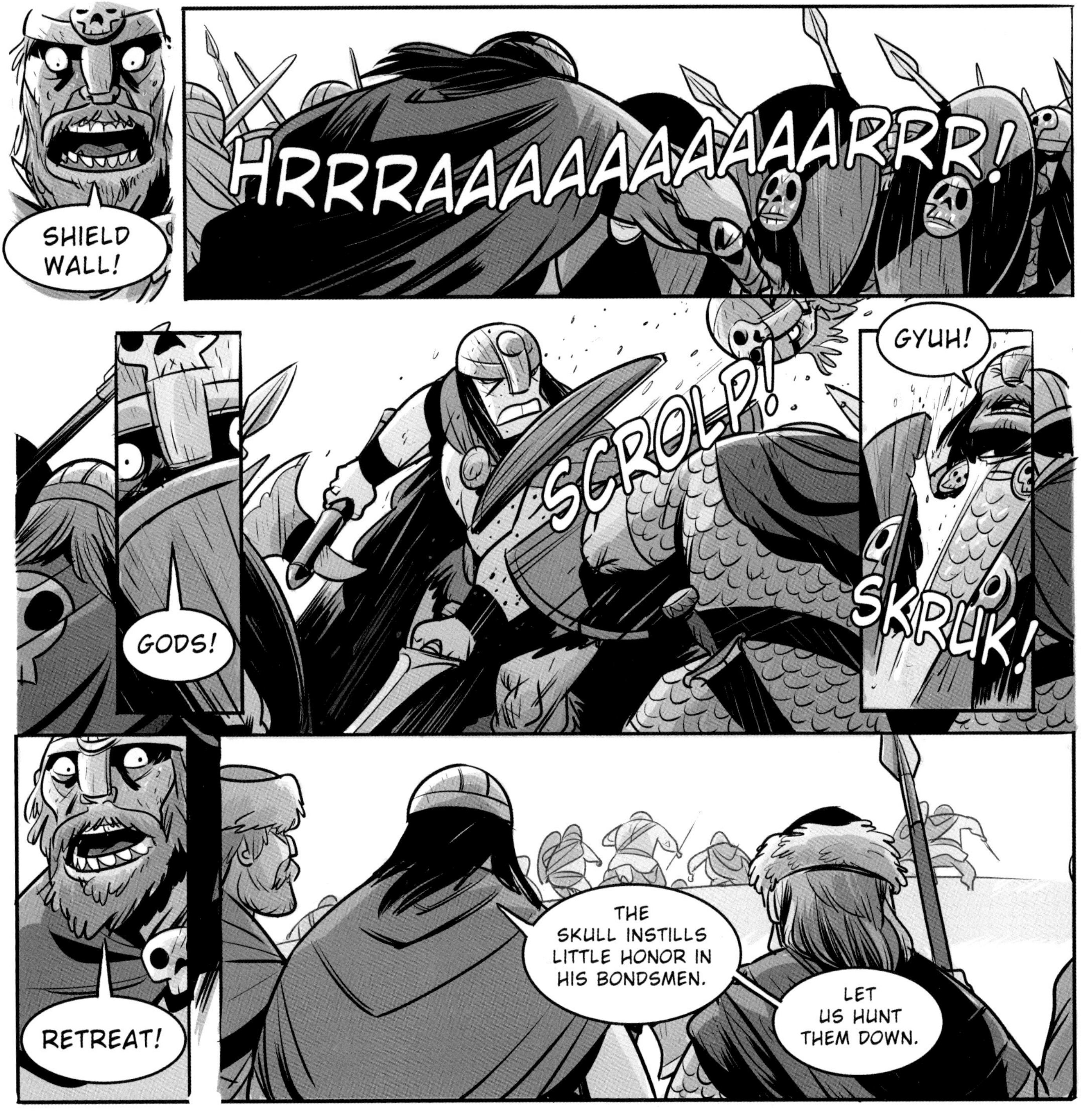
SHIELD WALL!
HRRRAAAAAAAAAARRRR!
GODS!
SCROLP!
GYUH!
SKRUK!
RETREAT!
THE SKULL INSTILLS LITTLE HONOR IN HIS BONDSMEN.
LET US HUNT THEM DOWN.

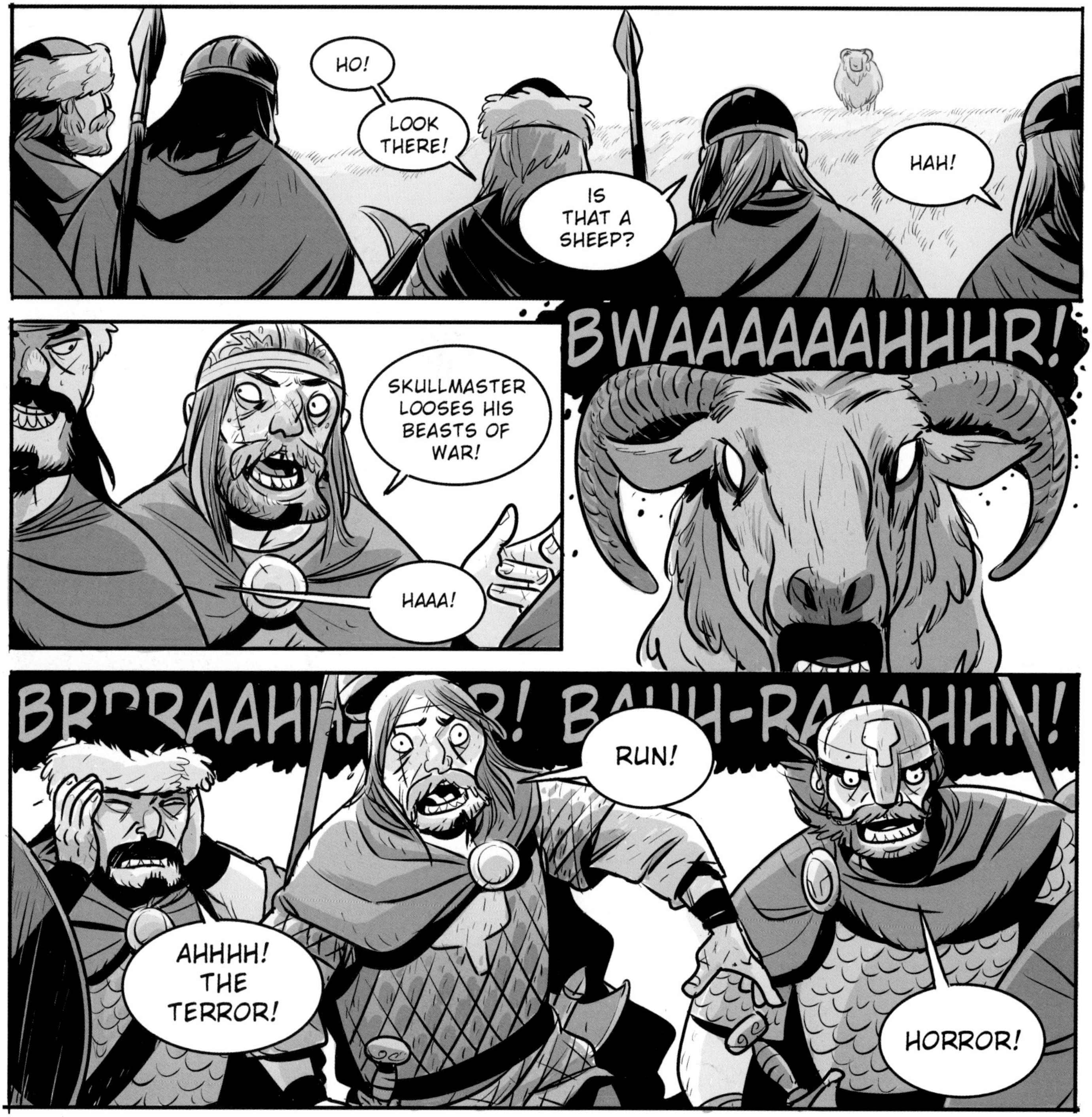
HO!
LOOK THERE!
IS THAT A SHEEP?
HAH!
SKULLMASTER LOOSES HIS BEASTS OF WAR!
HAAA!
BWAAAAAAHHUR!
RUN!
AHHHH! THE TERROR!
HORROR!

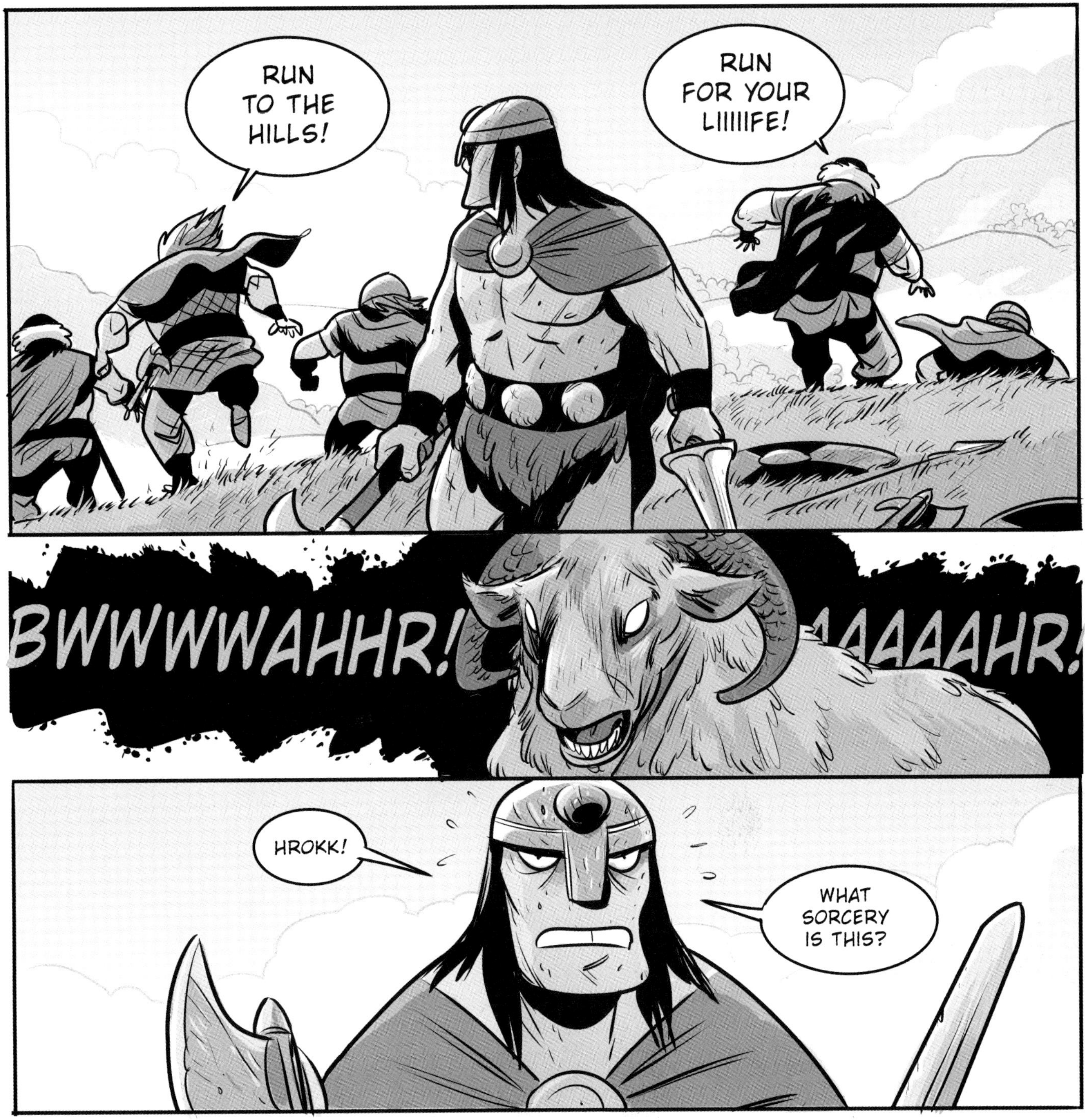
RUN TO THE HILLS!
RUN FOR YOUR LIIIIIFE!
BWWWWAHHR! AAAAAHR!
HROKK!
WHAT SORCERY IS THIS?

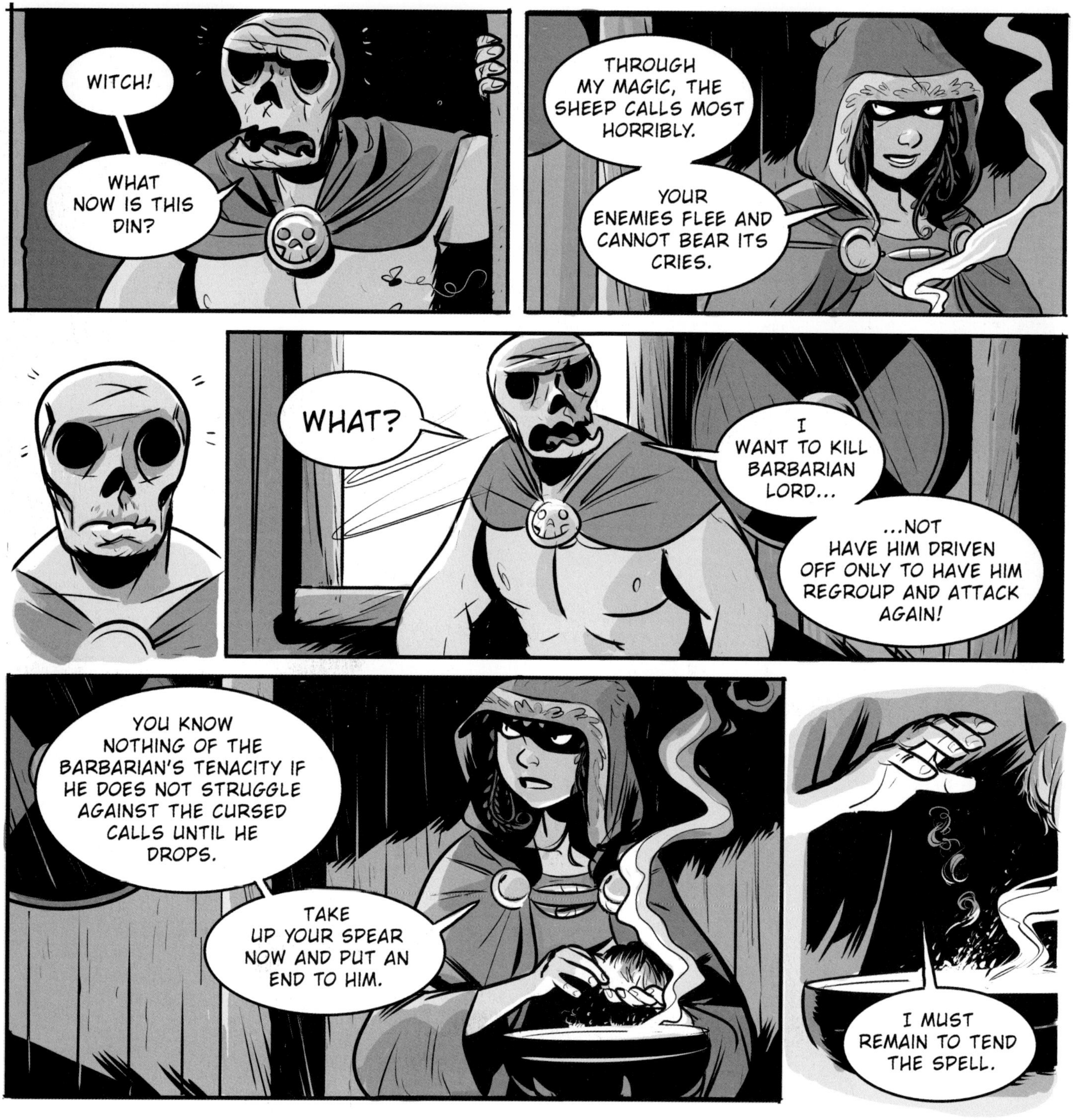
WITCH!
WHAT NOW IS THIS DIN?
THROUGH MY MAGIC, THE SHEEP CALLS MOST HORRIBLY.
YOUR ENEMIES FLEE AND CANNOT BEAR ITS CRIES.
WHAT?
I WANT TO KILL BARBARIAN LORD...
...NOT HAVE HIM DRIVEN OFF ONLY TO HAVE HIM REGROUP AND ATTACK AGAIN!
YOU KNOW NOTHING OF THE BARBARIAN'S TENACITY IF HE DOES NOT STRUGGLE AGAINST THE CURSED CALLS UNTIL HE DROPS.
TAKE UP YOUR SPEAR NOW AND PUT AN END TO HIM.
I MUST REMAIN TO TEND THE SPELL.

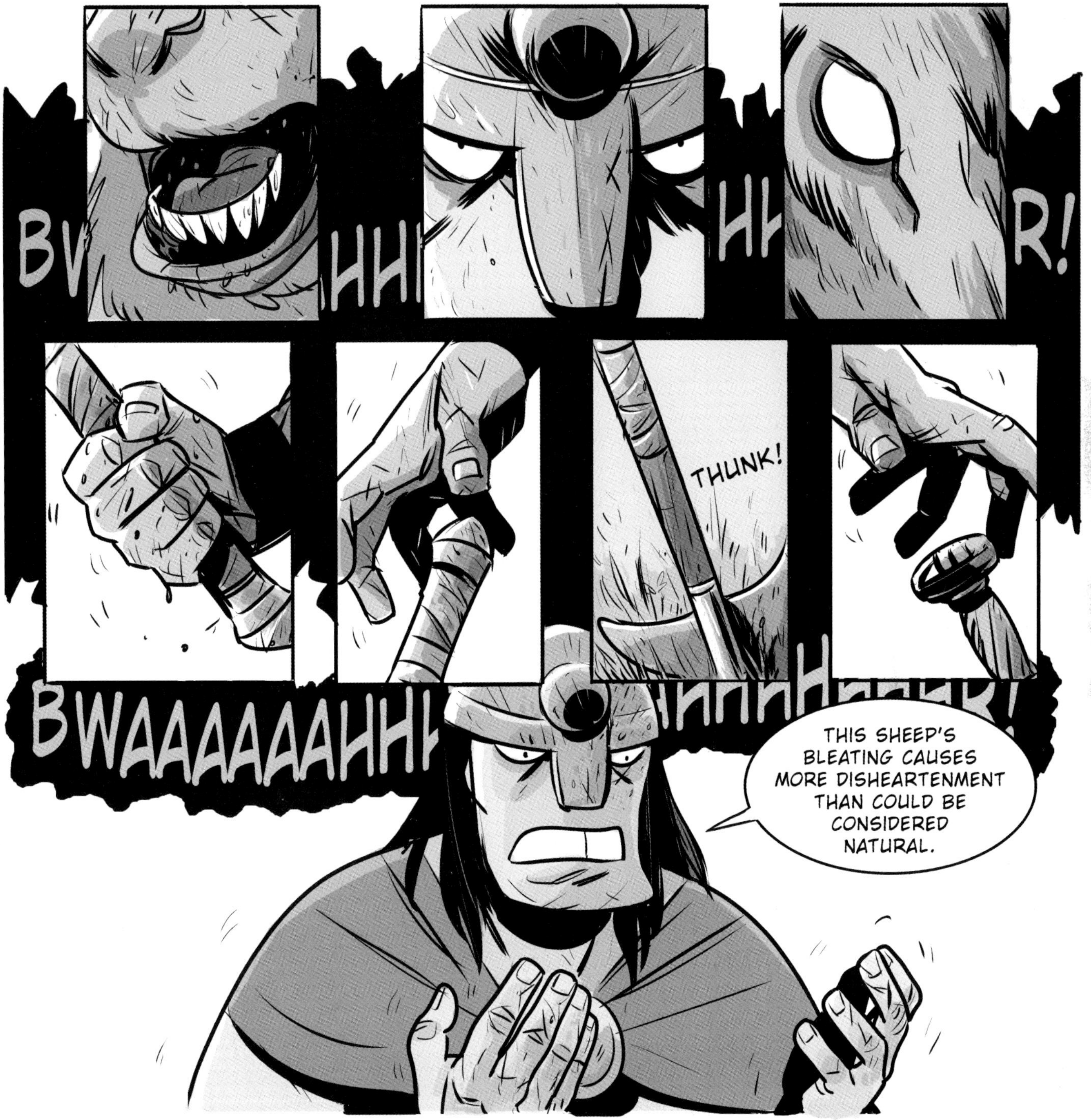
THUNK!
THIS SHEEP'S BLEATING CAUSES MORE DISHEARTENMENT THAN COULD BE CONSIDERED NATURAL.

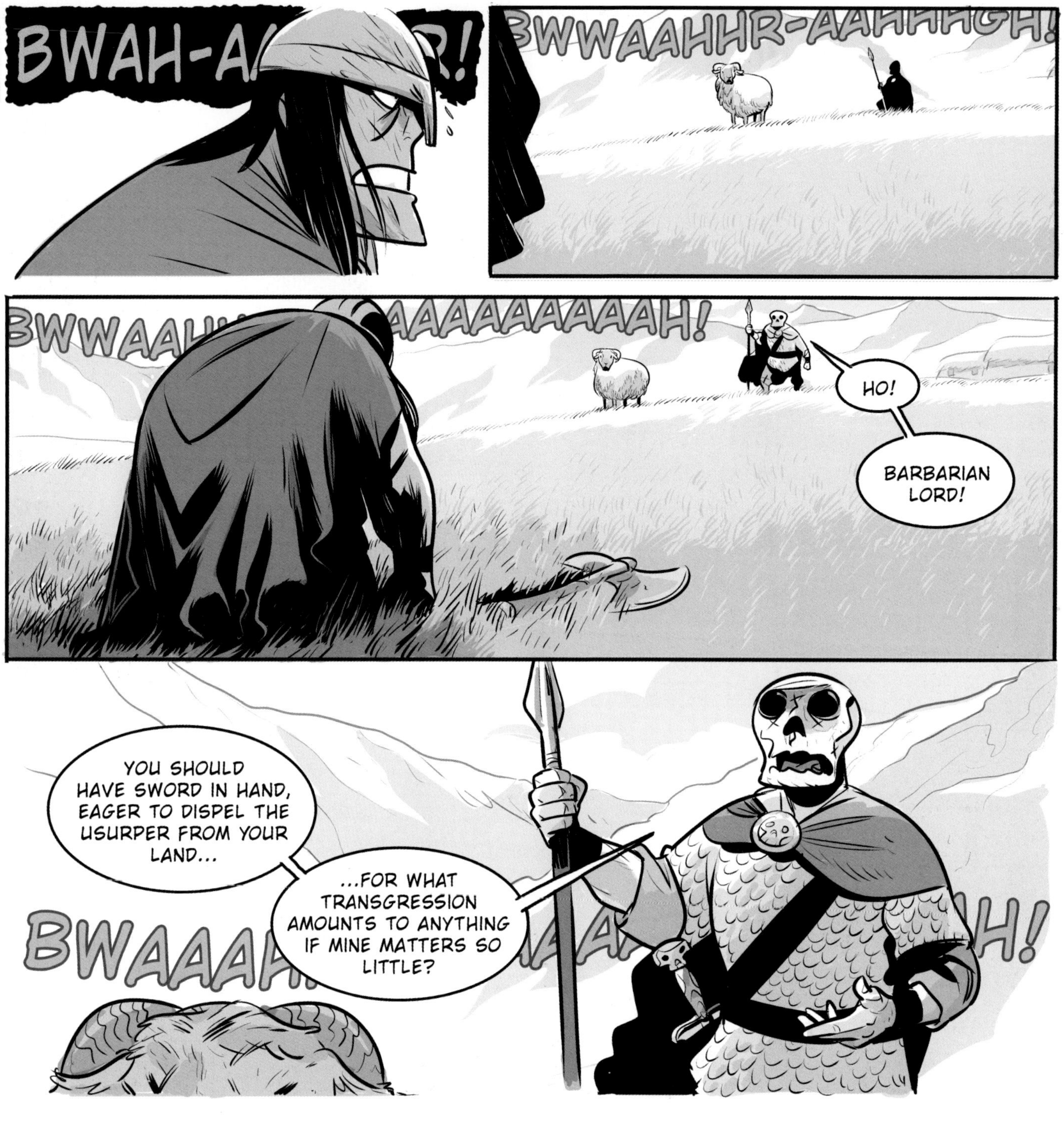
BWWAAHHR-AAHHHGH!
HO!
BARBARIAN LORD!
YOU SHOULD HAVE SWORD IN HAND, EAGER TO DISPEL THE USURPER FROM YOUR LAND...
...FOR WHAT TRANSGRESSION AMOUNTS TO ANYTHING IF MINE MATTERS SO LITTLE?

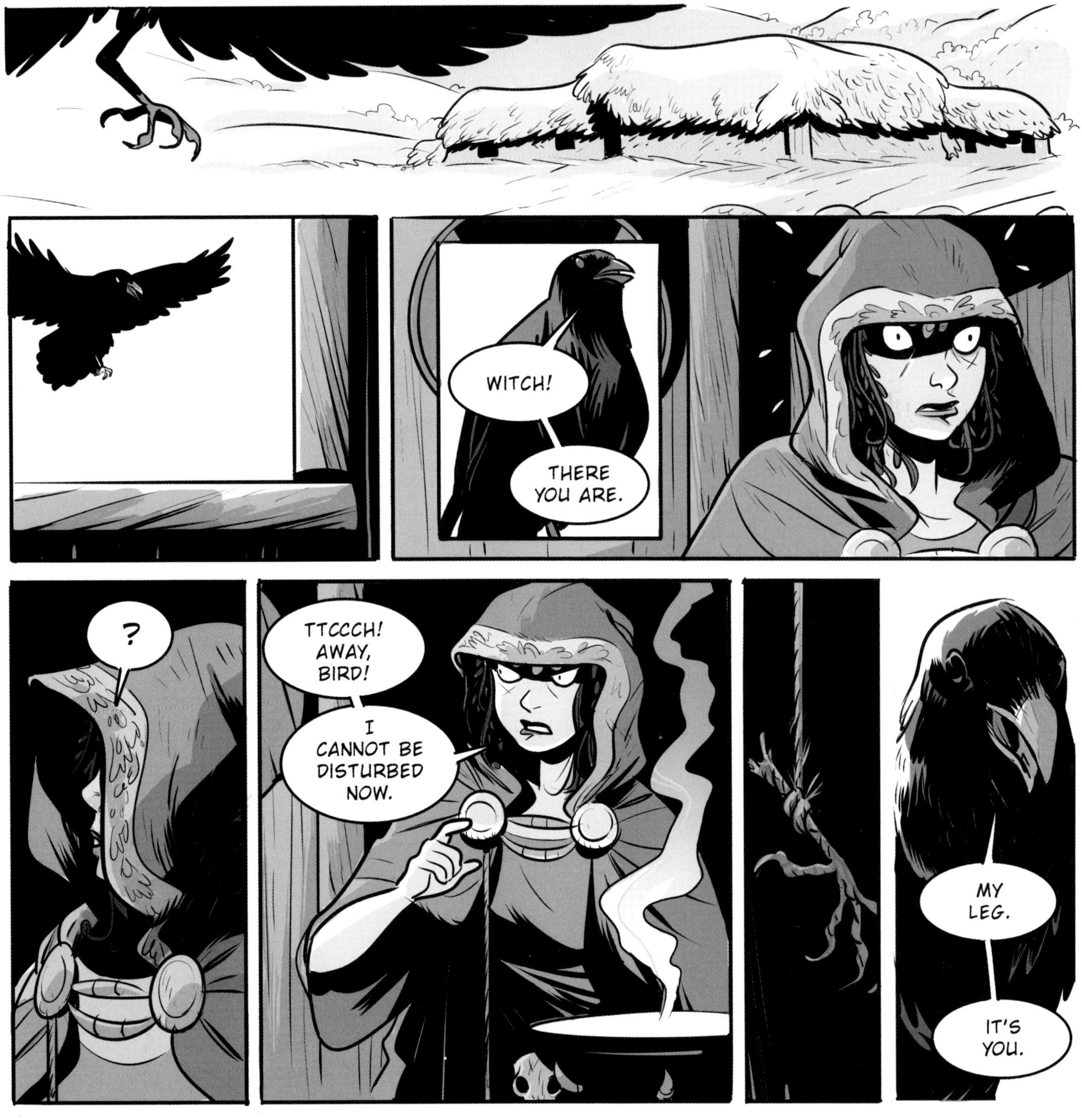
WITCH!
THERE YOU ARE.
?
TTCCCH! AWAY, BIRD!
I CANNOT BE DISTURBED NOW.
MY LEG.
IT'S YOU.

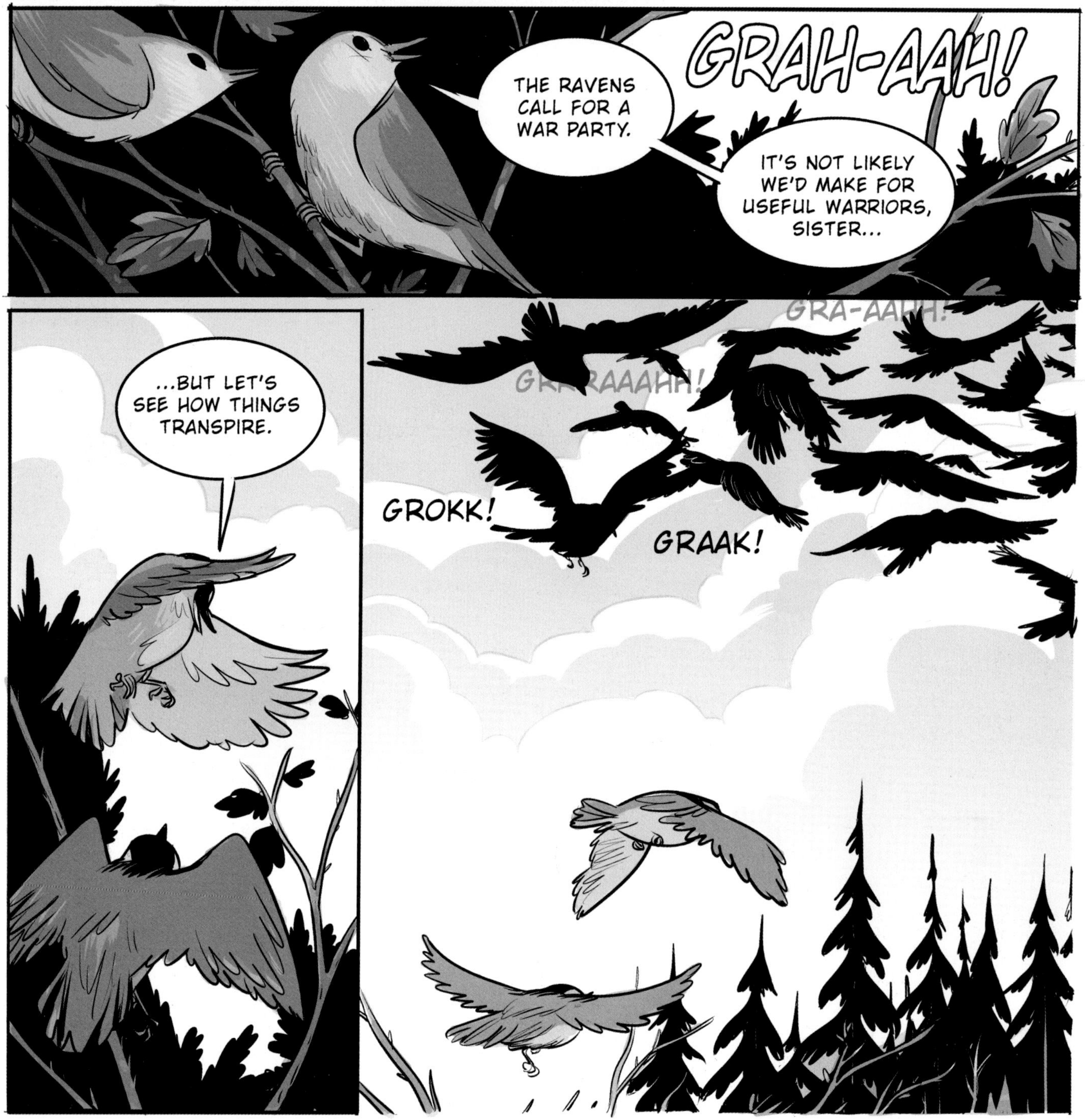
THE RAVENS CALL FOR A WAR PARTY.
GRAH-AAH!
IT'S NOT LIKELY WE'D MAKE FOR USEFUL WARRIORS, SISTER...
...BUT LET'S SEE HOW THINGS TRANSPIRE.
GROKK!
GRAAK!

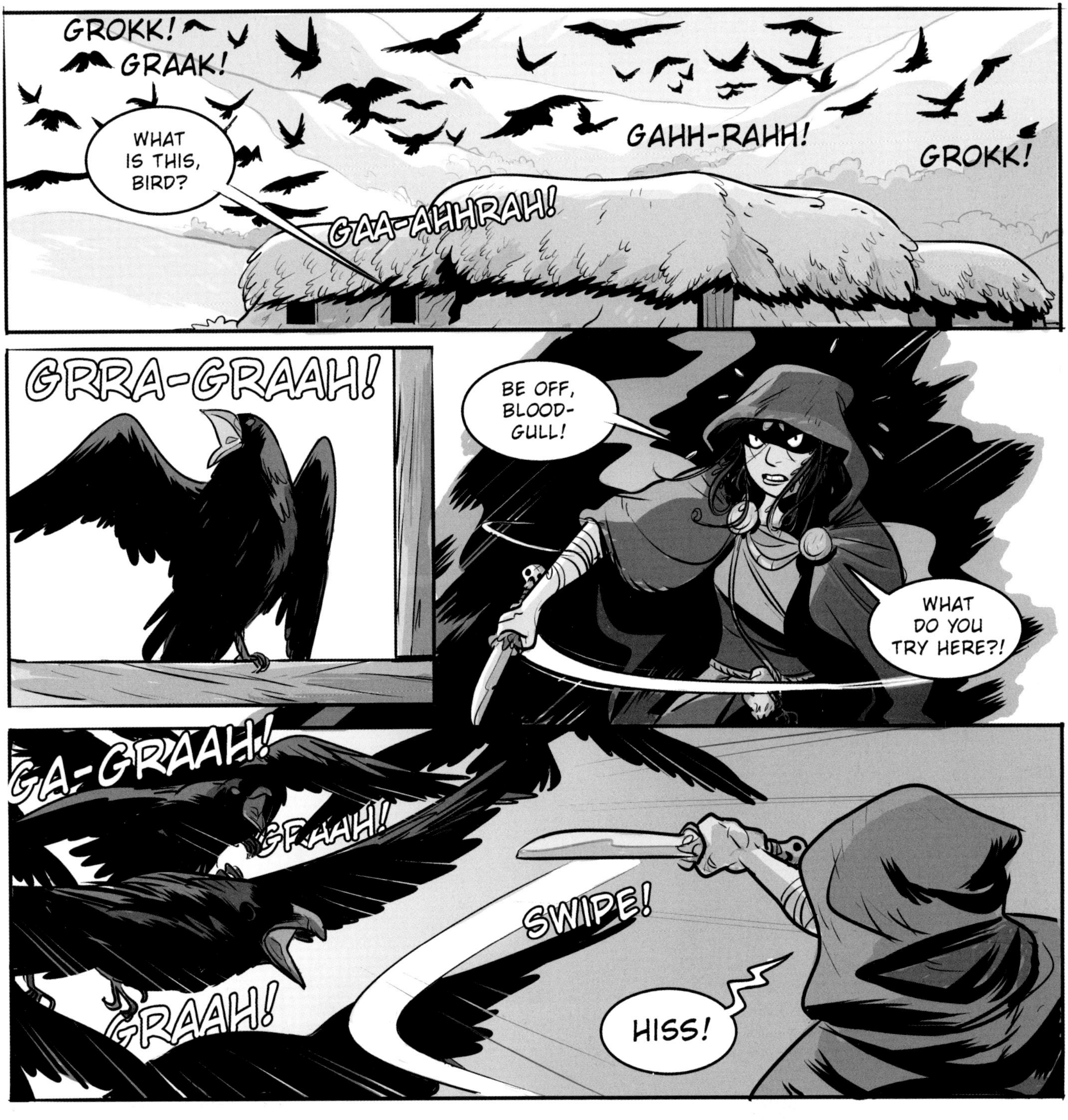
GROKK!
GRAAK!
WHAT IS THIS, BIRD?
GAA-AHHRAH!
GAHH-RAHH!
GROKK!
GRRA-GRAAH!
BE OFF, BLOOD-GULL!
WHAT DO YOU TRY HERE?!
GA-GRAAH!
GRAAH!
SWIPE!
GRAAH!
HISS!

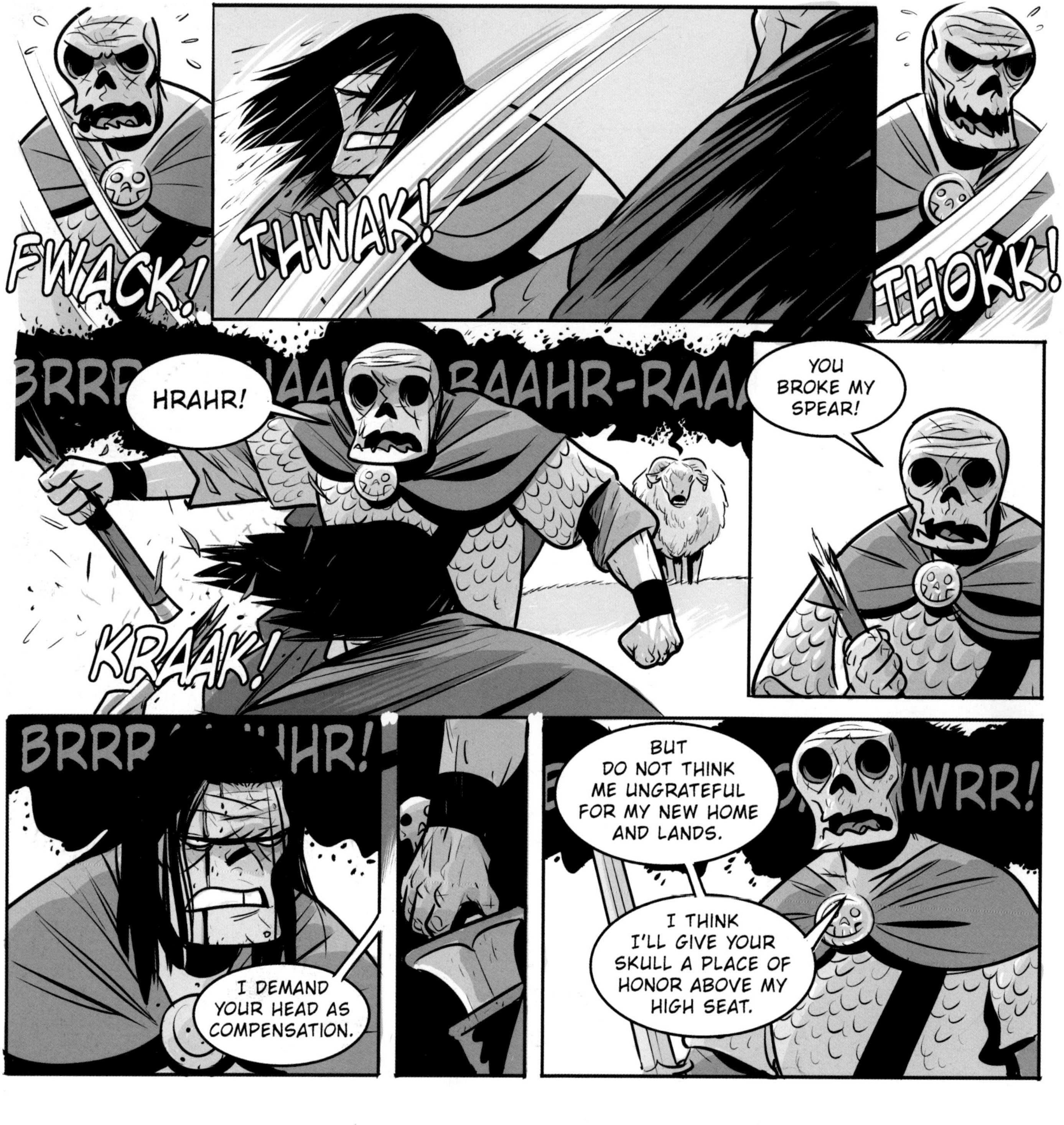
FWACK!
THWAK!
THOKK!
HRAHR!
KRAAK!
YOU BROKE MY SPEAR!
I DEMAND YOUR HEAD AS COMPENSATION.
BUT DO NOT THINK ME UNGRATEFUL FOR MY NEW HOME AND LANDS.
I THINK I'LL GIVE YOUR SKULL A PLACE OF HONOR ABOVE MY HIGH SEAT.

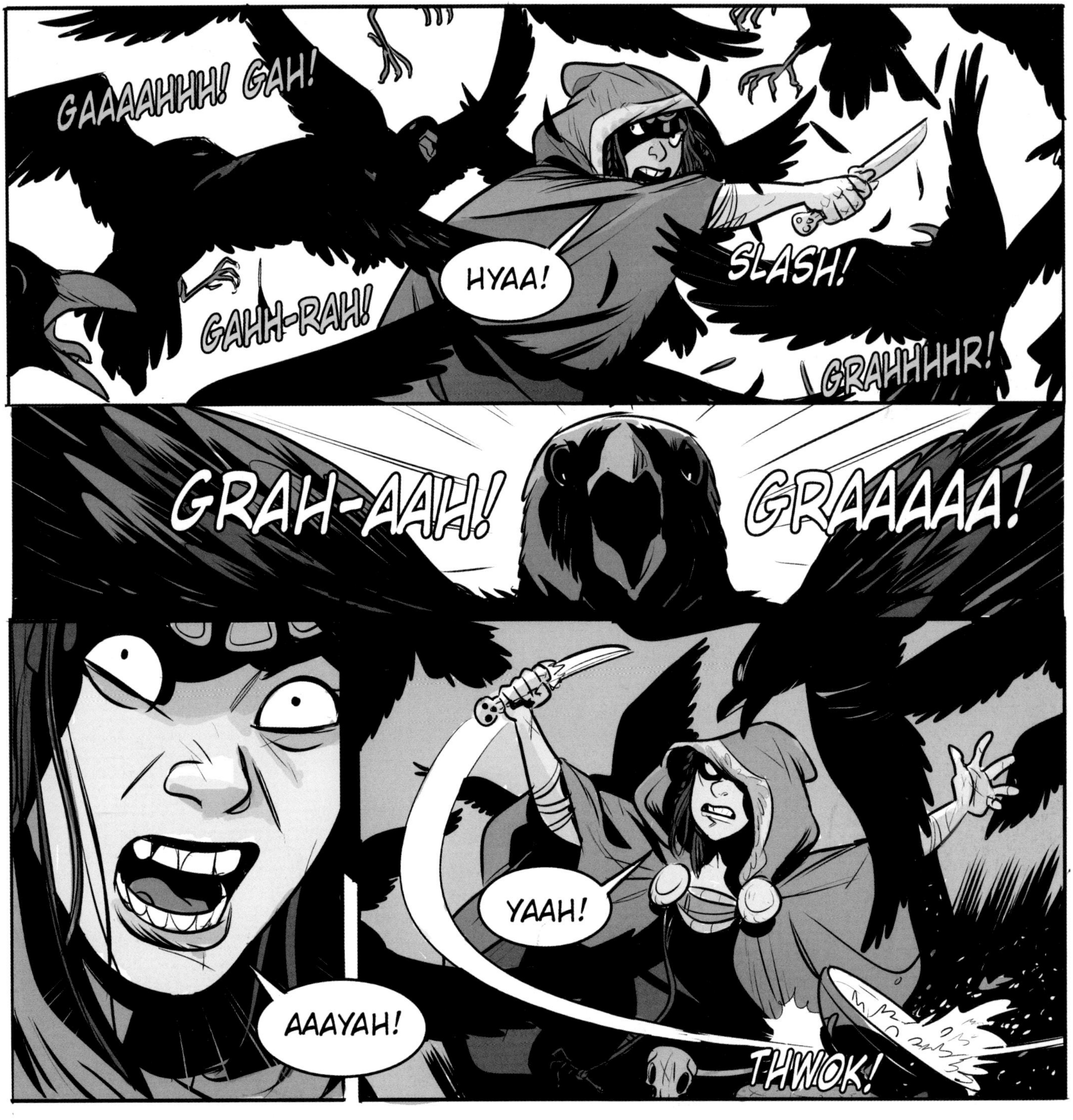
GAAAAHHH! GAH!
HYAA!
SLASH!
GAHH-RAH!
GRAHHHHR!
GRAH-AAH!
GRAAAAA!
YAAH!
AAAYAH!
THWOK!

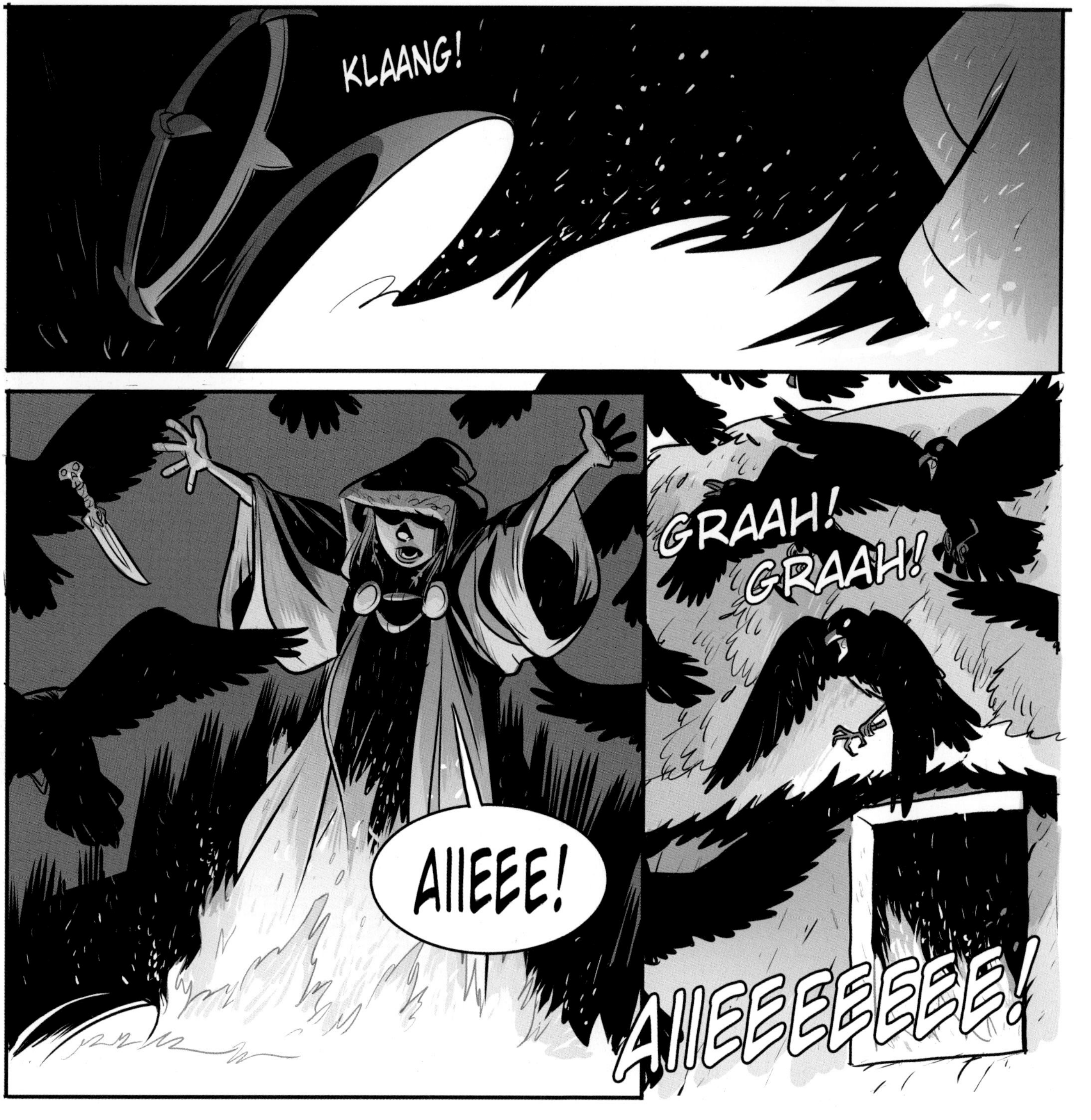
KLAANG!
AIIEEE!
GRAAH!
GRAAH!
AIIEEEEEEEE!

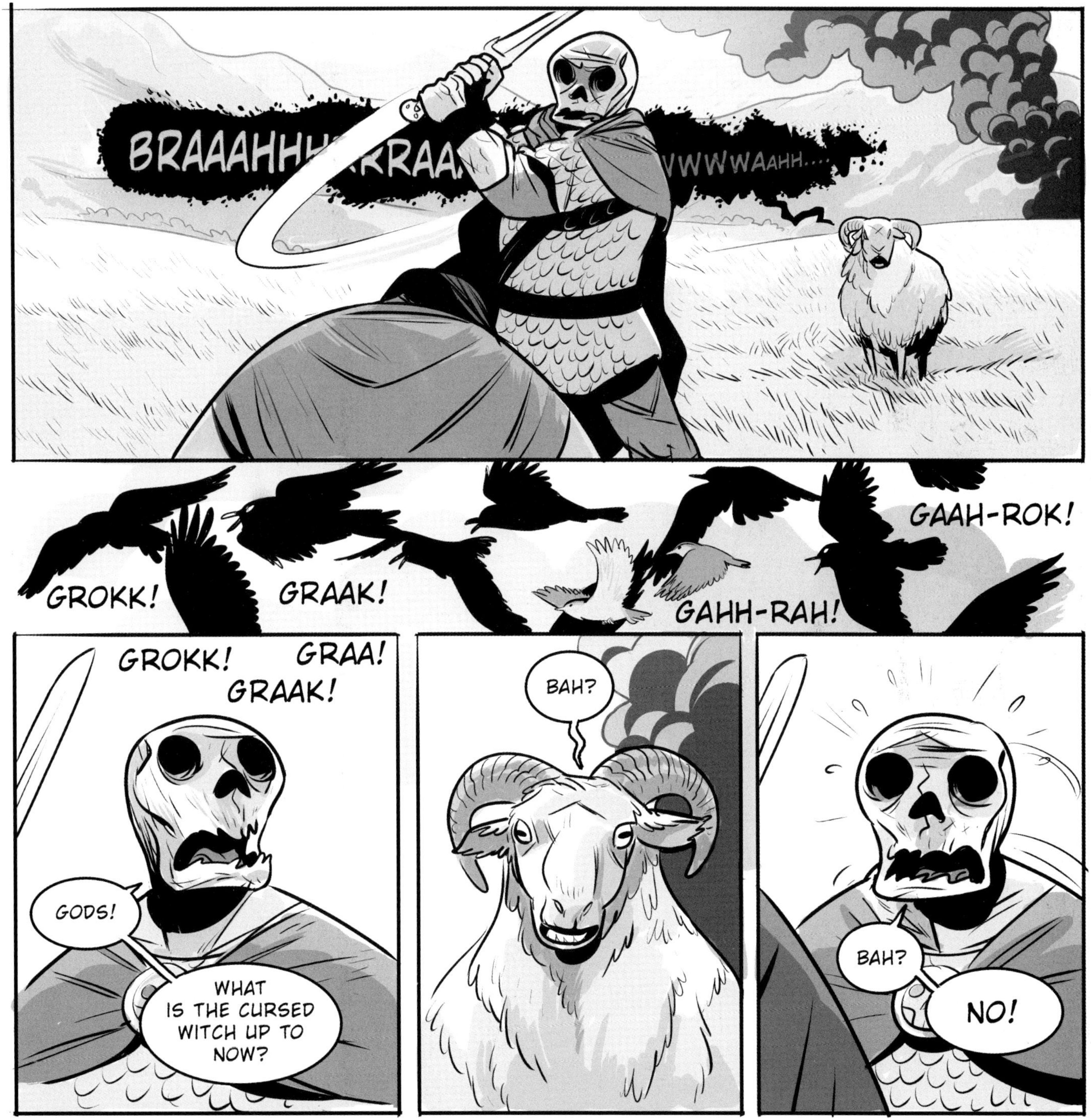
BRAAAHHH
KRRAA
WWWWAAHH....
GROKK!
GRAAK!
GAHH-RAH!
GAAH-ROK!
GROKK!
GRAA!
GRAAK!
GODS!
WHAT IS THE CURSED WITCH UP TO NOW?
BAH?
BAH?
NO!

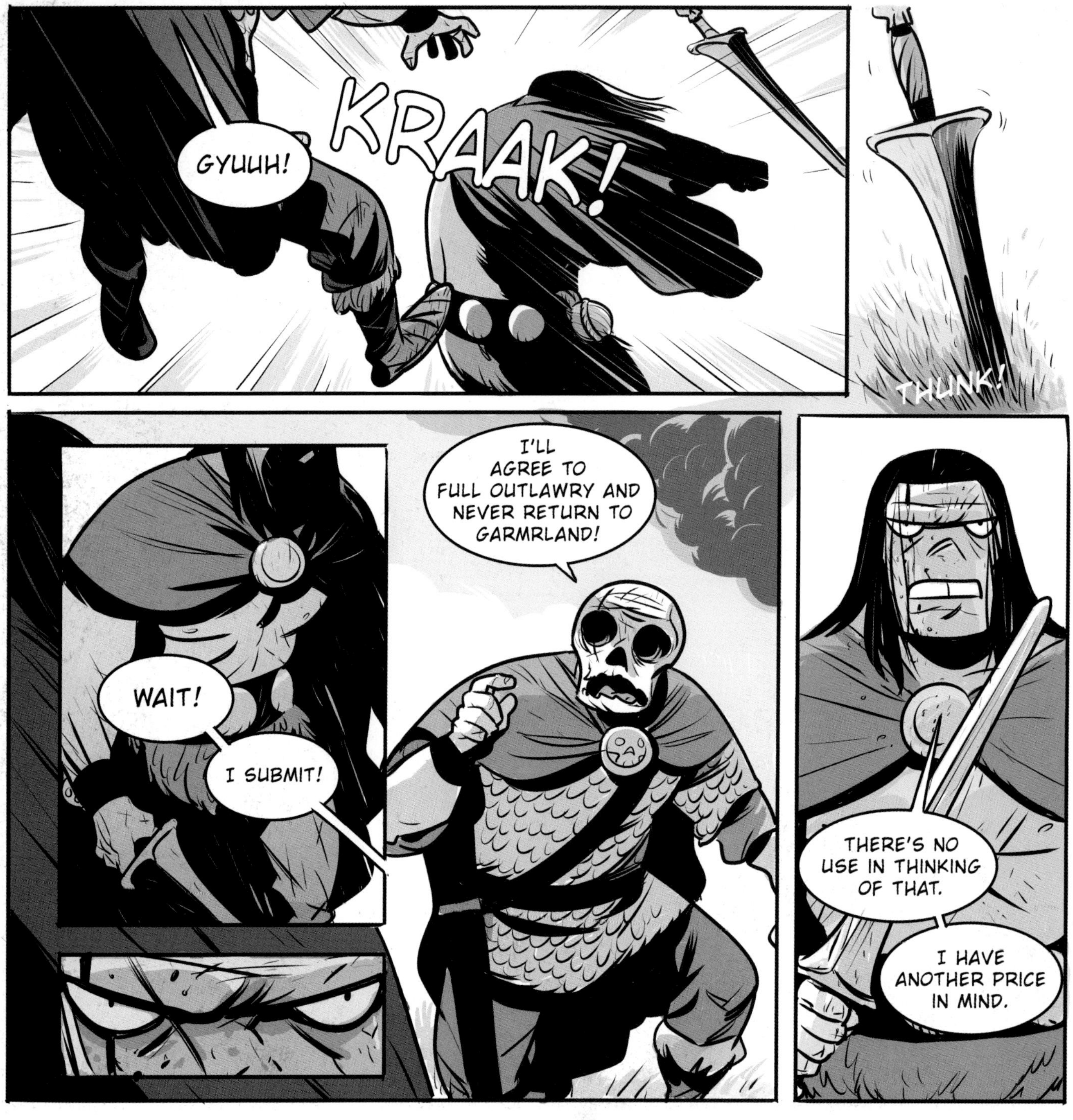
GYUUH!
KRAAK!
THUNK!
WAIT!
I SUBMIT!
I'LL AGREE TO FULL OUTLAWRY AND NEVER RETURN TO GARMRLAND!
THERE'S NO USE IN THINKING OF THAT.
I HAVE ANOTHER PRICE IN MIND.

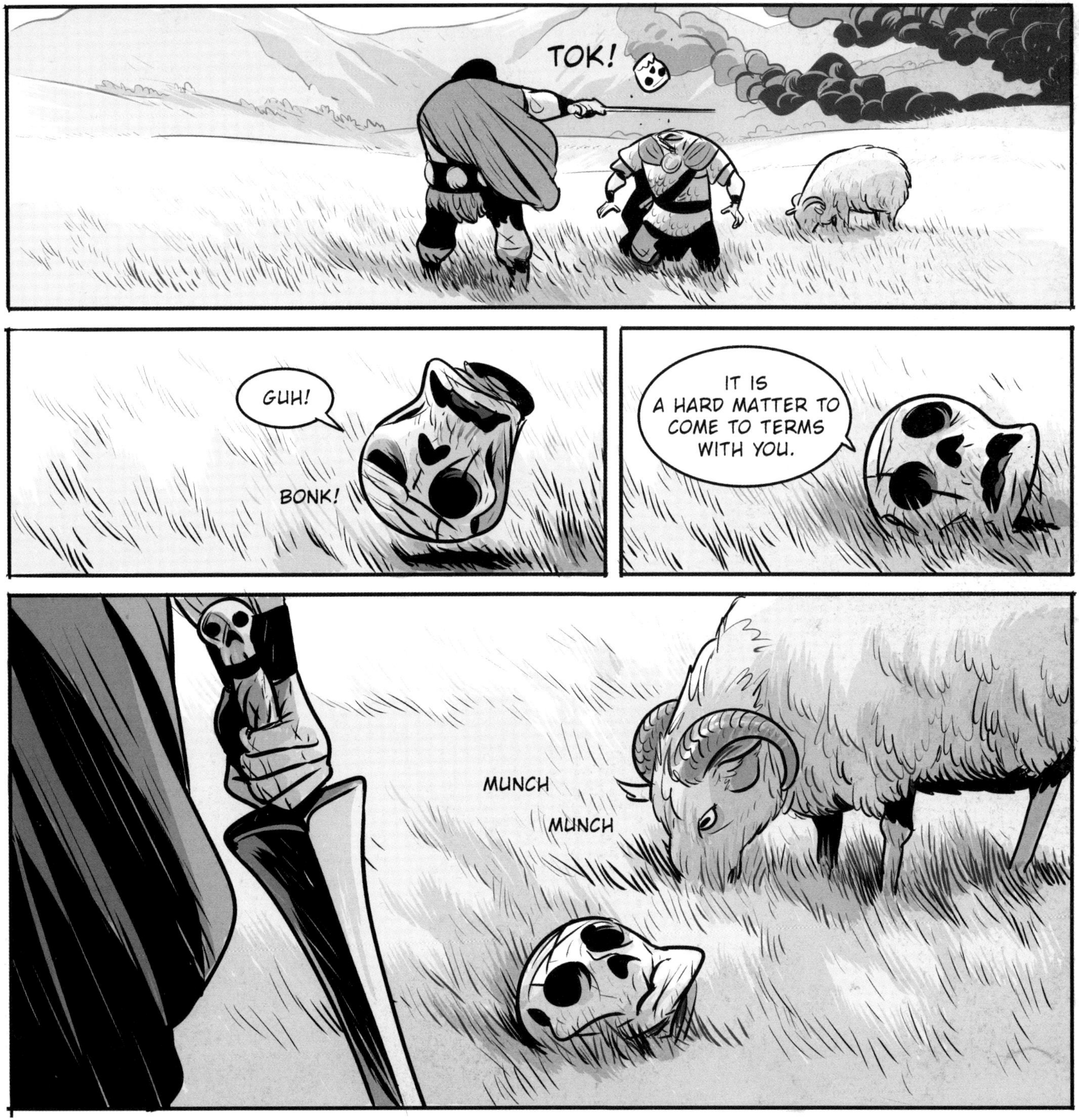
TOK!
GUH!
BONK!
IT IS A HARD MATTER TO COME TO TERMS WITH YOU.
MUNCH
MUNCH

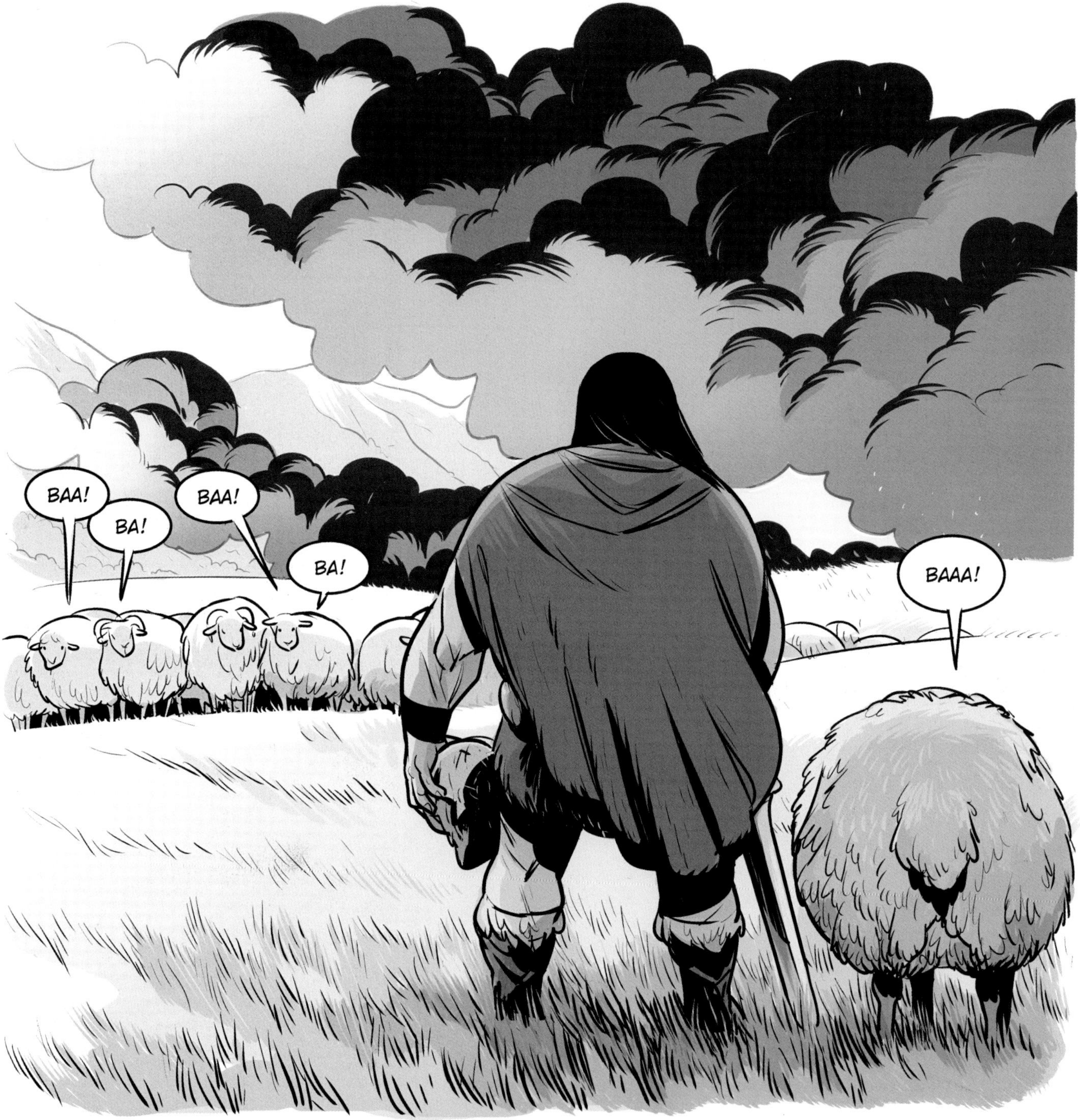
BAA!
BA!
BAA!
BA!
BAAA!

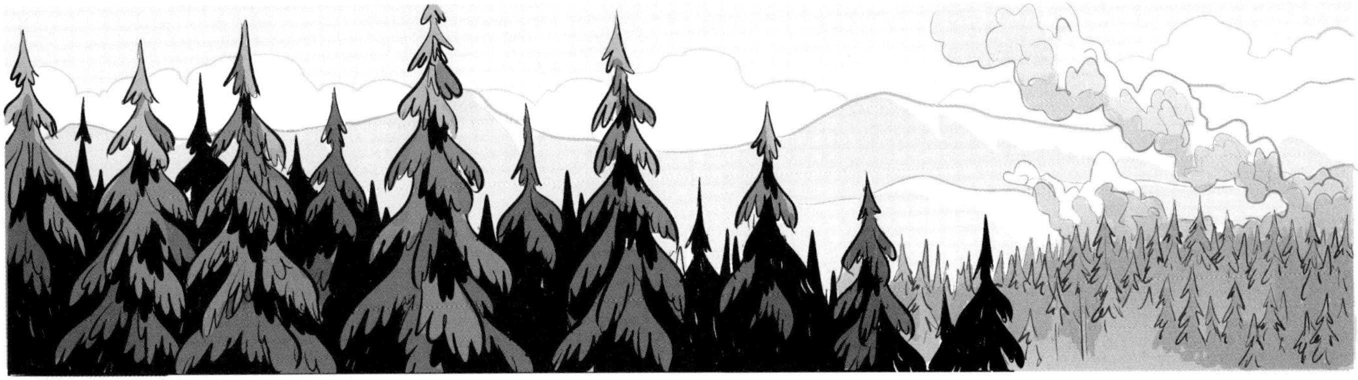

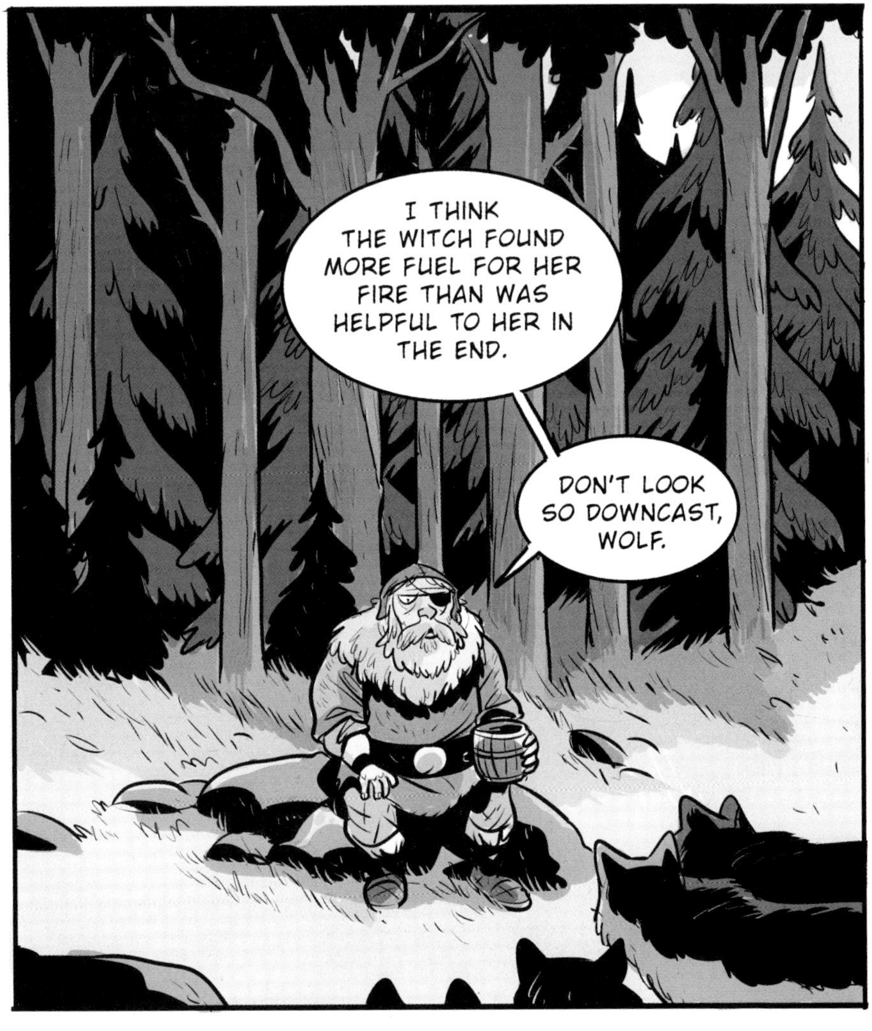
I THINK THE WITCH FOUND MORE FUEL FOR HER FIRE THAN WAS HELPFUL TO HER IN THE END.
DON'T LOOK SO DOWNCAST, WOLF.

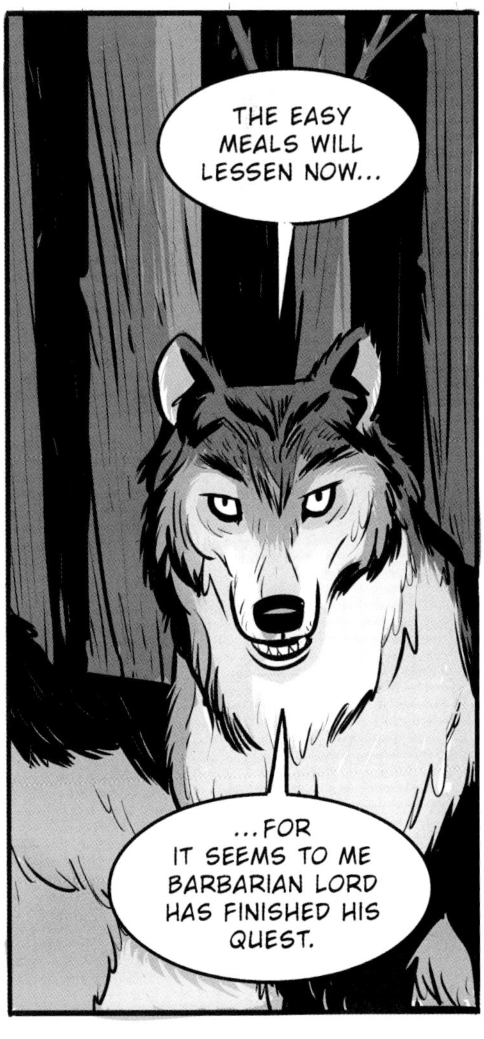
THE EASY MEALS WILL LESSEN NOW...
...FOR IT SEEMS TO ME BARBARIAN LORD HAS FINISHED HIS QUEST.

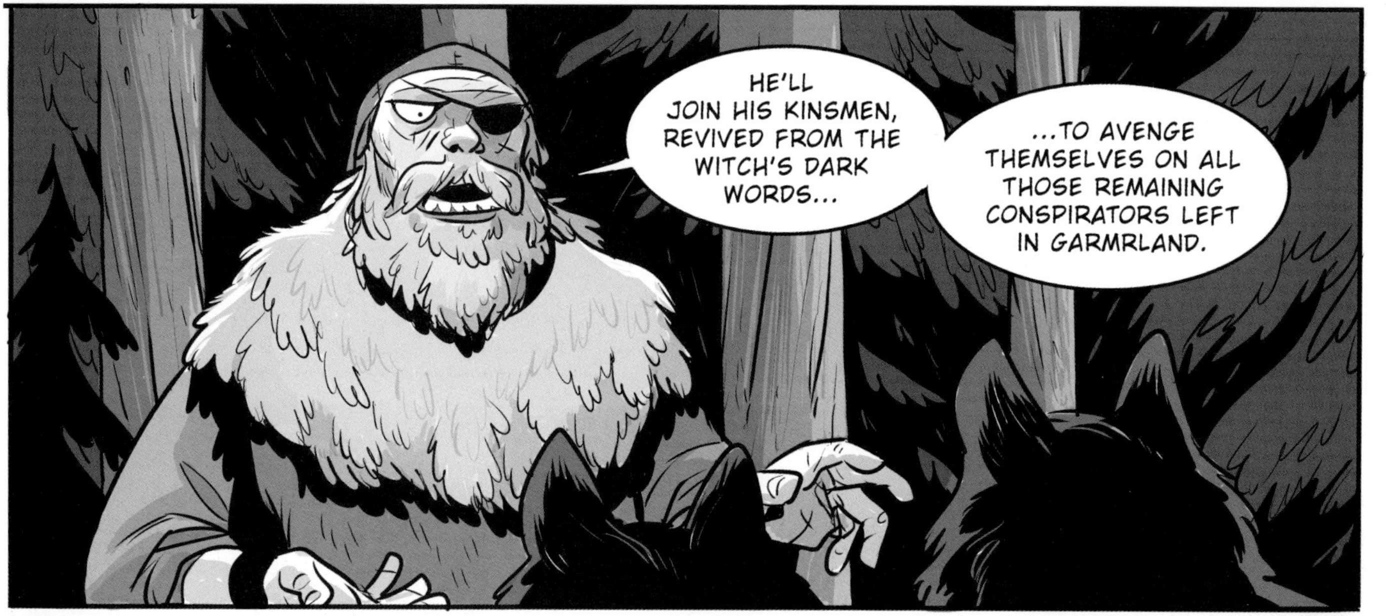
HE'LL JOIN HIS KINSMEN, REVIVED FROM THE WITCH'S DARK WORDS...
...TO AVENGE THEMSELVES ON ALL THOSE REMAINING CONSPIRATORS LEFT IN GARMRLAND.

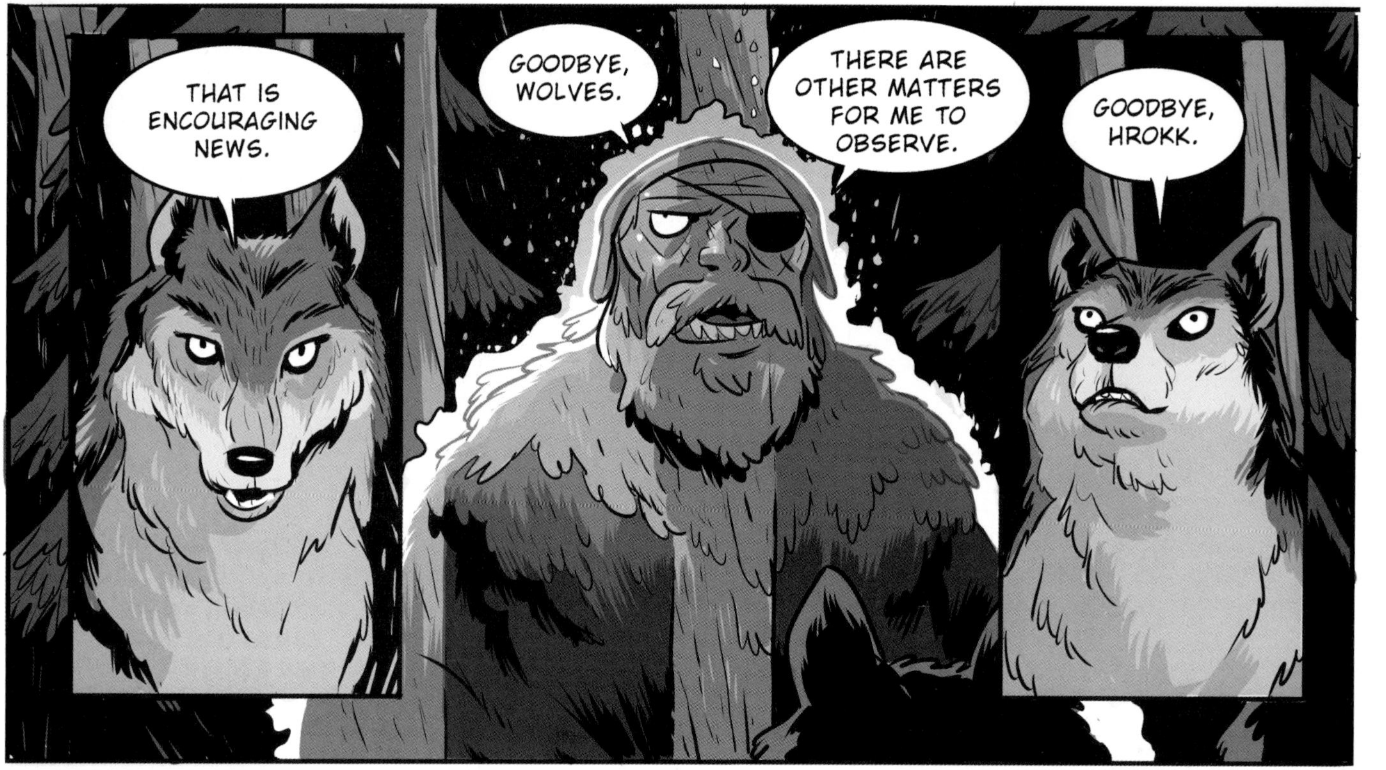
THAT IS ENCOURAGING NEWS.
GOODBYE, WOLVES.
THERE ARE OTHER MATTERS FOR ME TO OBSERVE.
GOODBYE, HROKK.

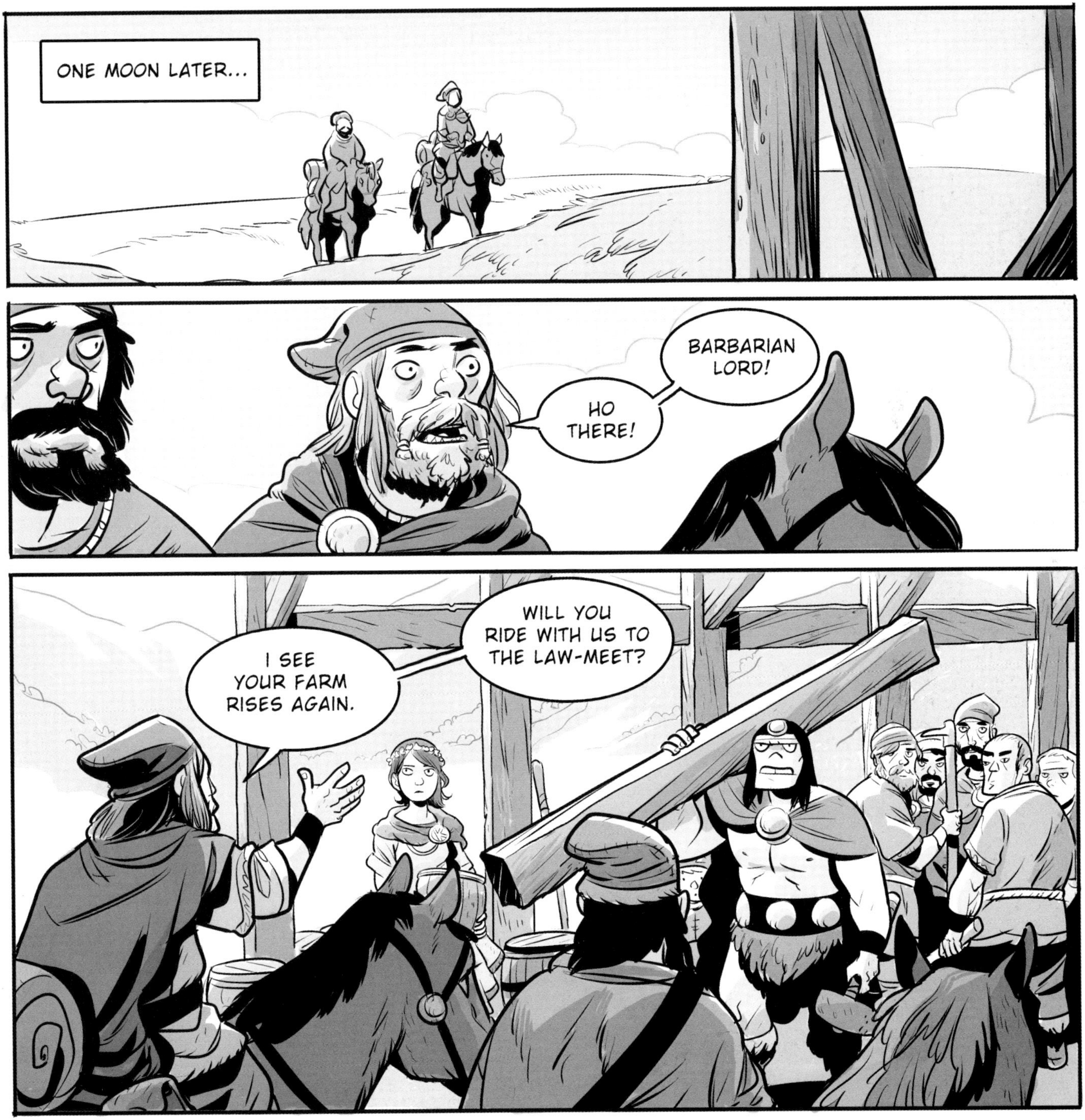
ONE MOON LATER...
HO THERE!
BARBARIAN LORD!
I SEE YOUR FARM RISES AGAIN.
WILL YOU RIDE WITH US TO THE LAW-MEET?

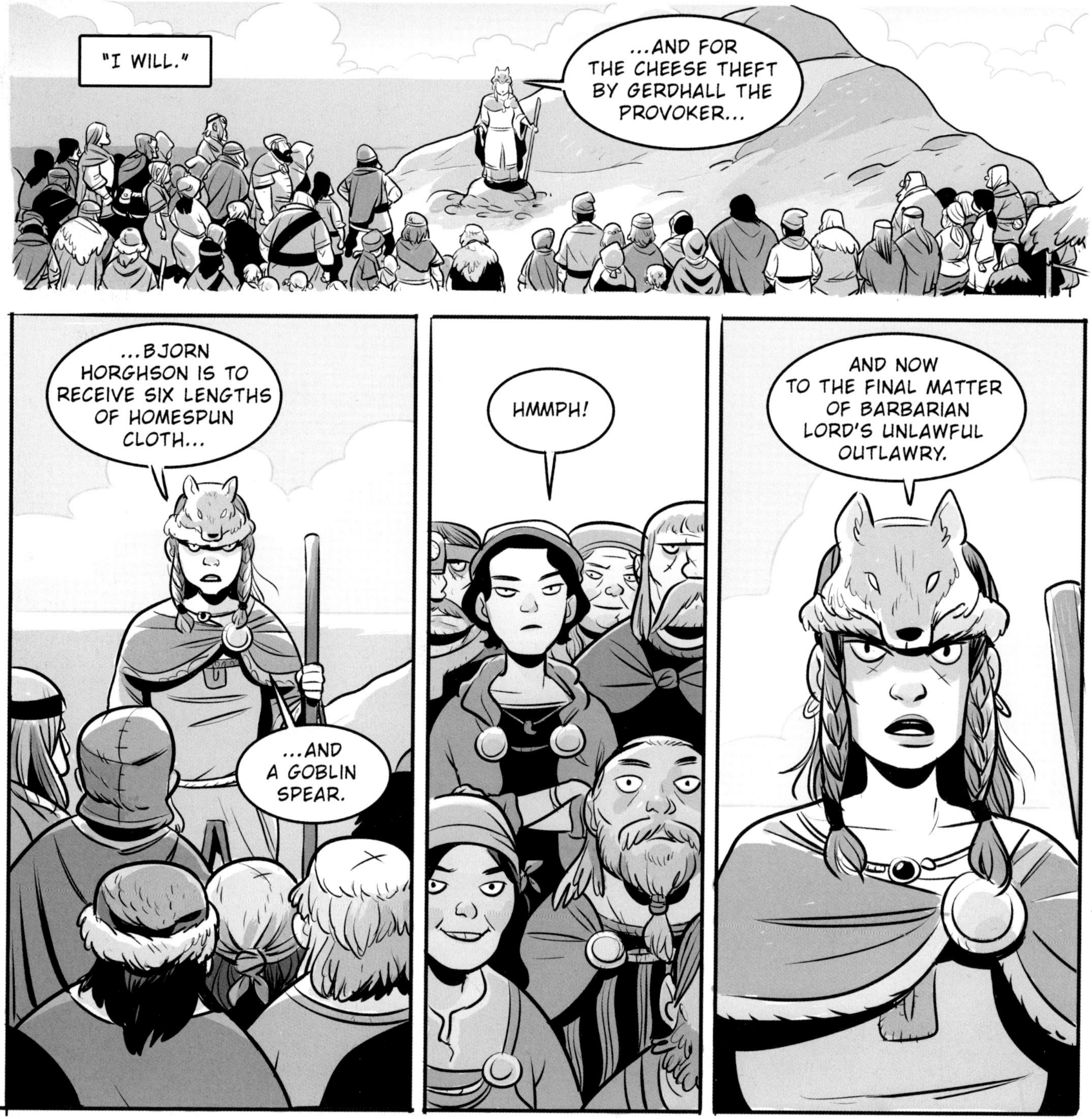
"I WILL."
...AND FOR THE CHEESE THEFT BY GERDHALL THE PROVOKER...
...BJORN HORGHSON IS TO RECEIVE SIX LENGTHS OF HOMESPUN CLOTH...
...AND A GOBLIN SPEAR.
HMMPH!
AND NOW TO THE FINAL MATTER OF BARBARIAN LORD'S UNLAWFUL OUTLAWRY.

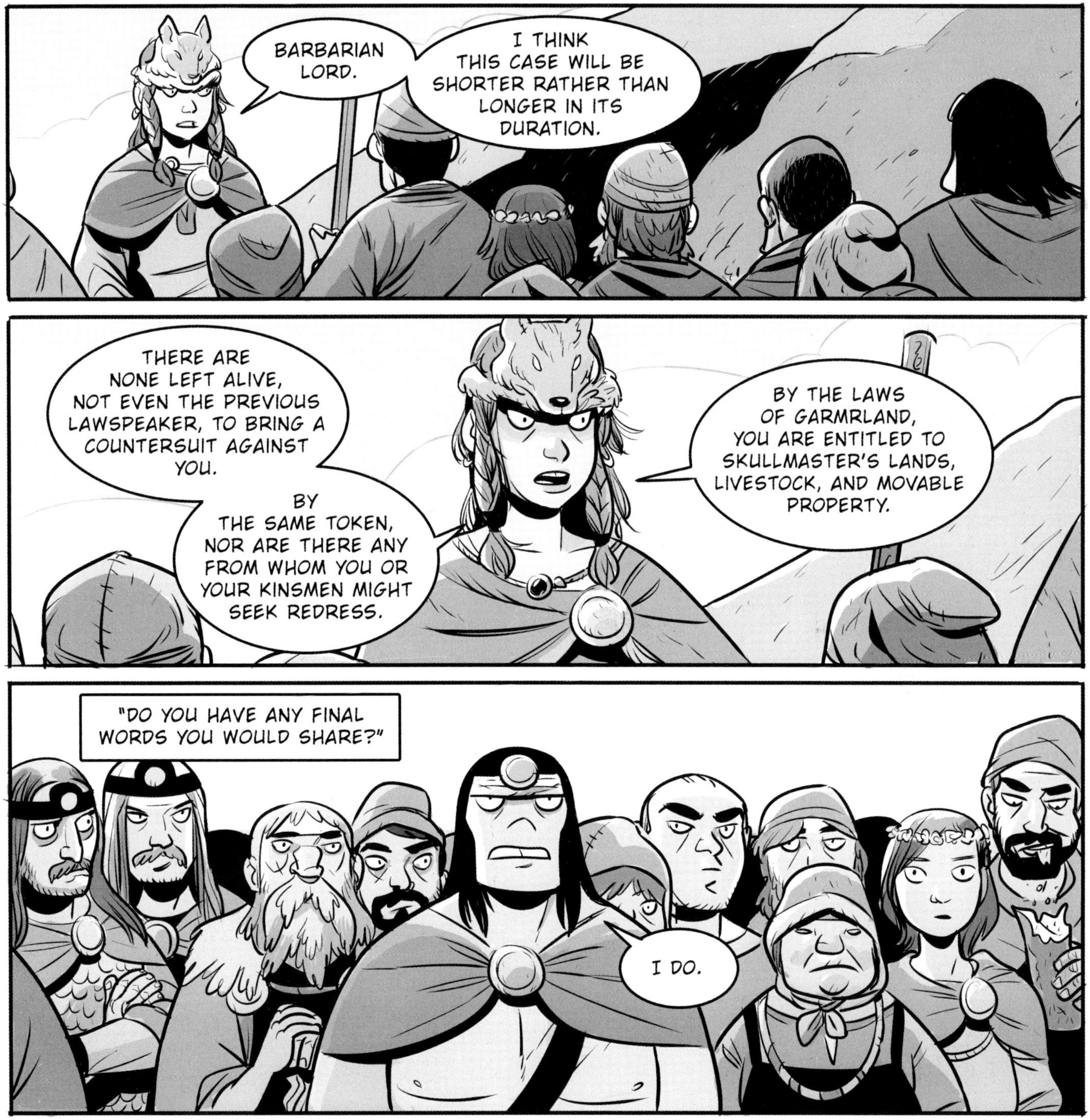
BARBARIAN LORD.
I THINK THIS CASE WILL BE SHORTER RATHER THAN LONGER IN ITS DURATION.
THERE ARE NONE LEFT ALIVE, NOT EVEN THE PREVIOUS LAWSPEAKER, TO BRING A COUNTERSUIT AGAINST YOU.
BY THE SAME TOKEN, NOR ARE THERE ANY FROM WHOM YOU OR YOUR KINSMEN MIGHT SEEK REDRESS.
BY THE LAWS OF GARMRLAND, YOU ARE ENTITLED TO SKULLMASTER'S LANDS, LIVESTOCK, AND MOVABLE PROPERTY.
"DO YOU HAVE ANY FINAL WORDS YOU WOULD SHARE?"
I DO.

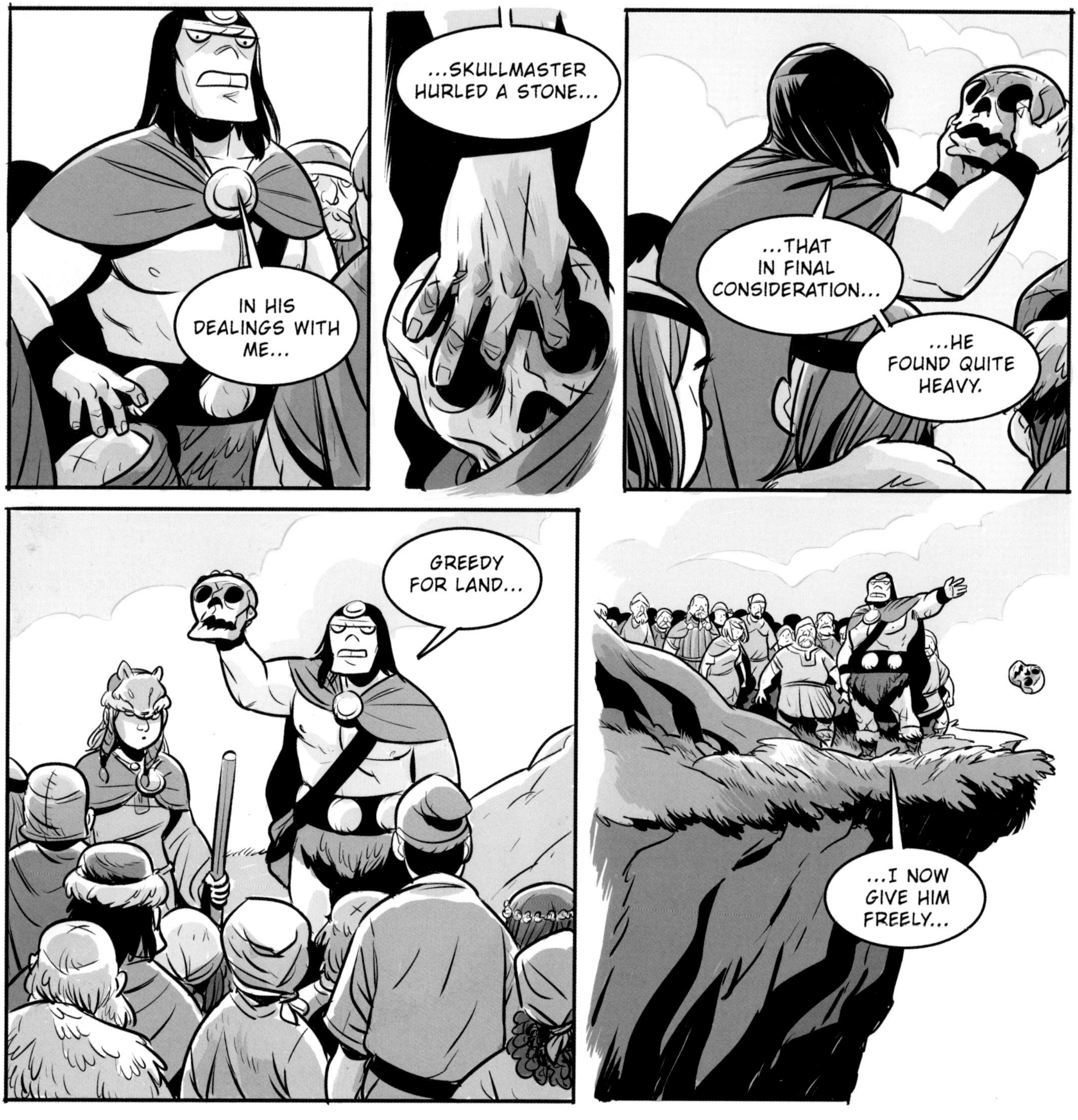
IN HIS DEALINGS WITH ME...
...SKULLMASTER HURLED A STONE...
...THAT IN FINAL CONSIDERATION...
...HE FOUND QUITE HEAVY.
GREEDY FOR LAND...
...I NOW GIVE HIM FREELY...

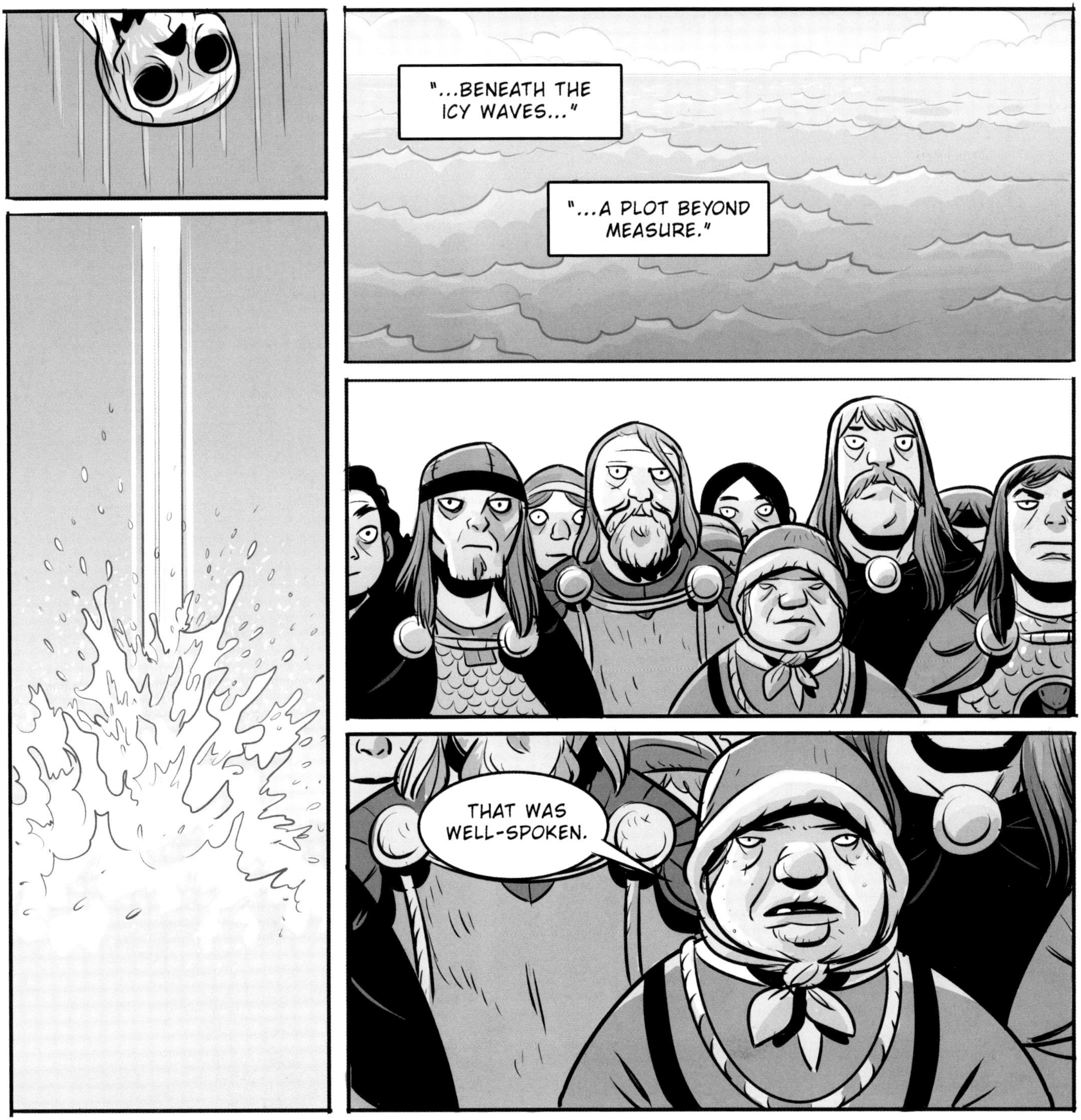
"...BENEATH THE ICY WAVES..."
"...A PLOT BEYOND MEASURE."
THAT WAS WELL-SPOKEN.

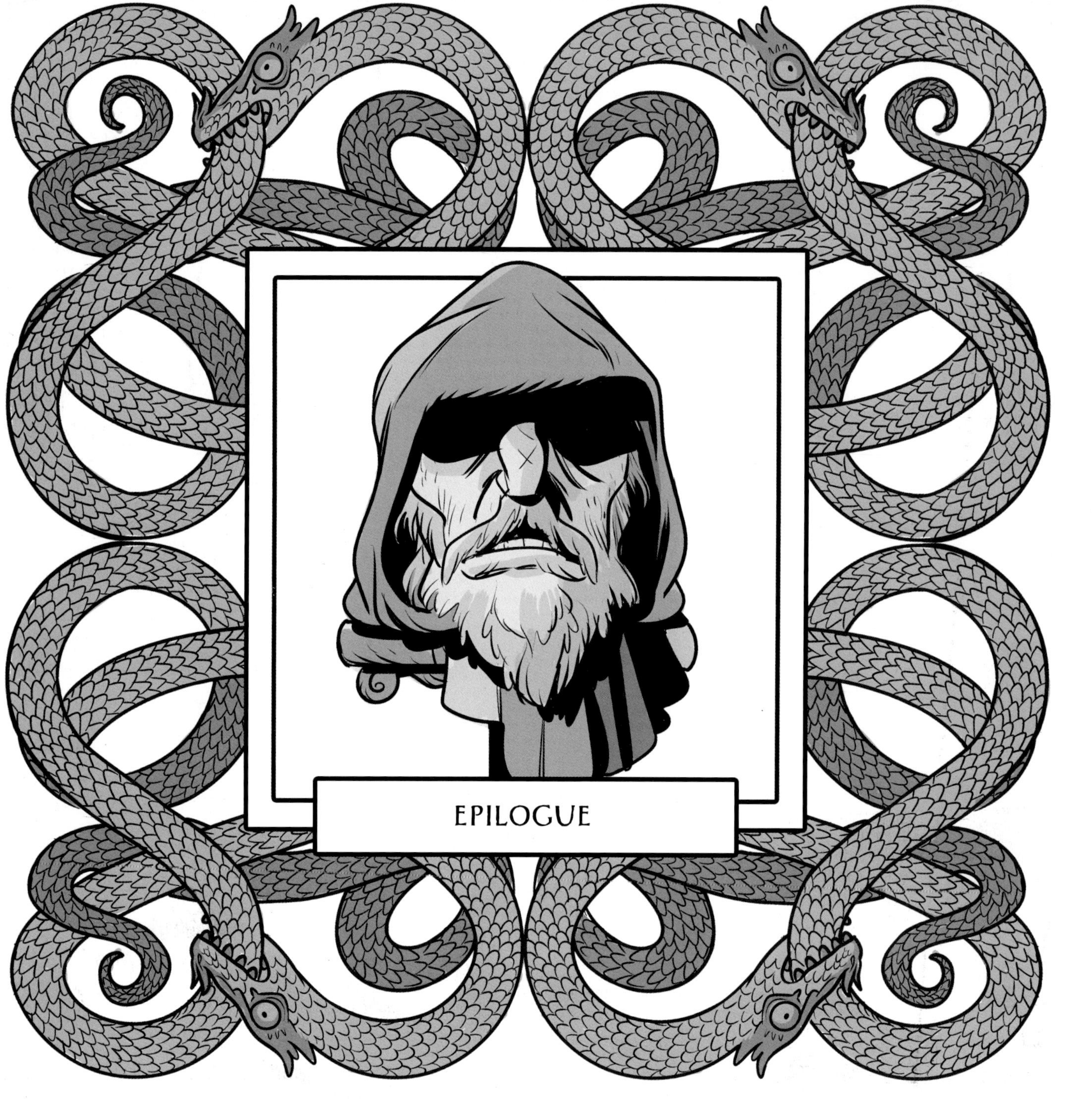

EPILOGUE

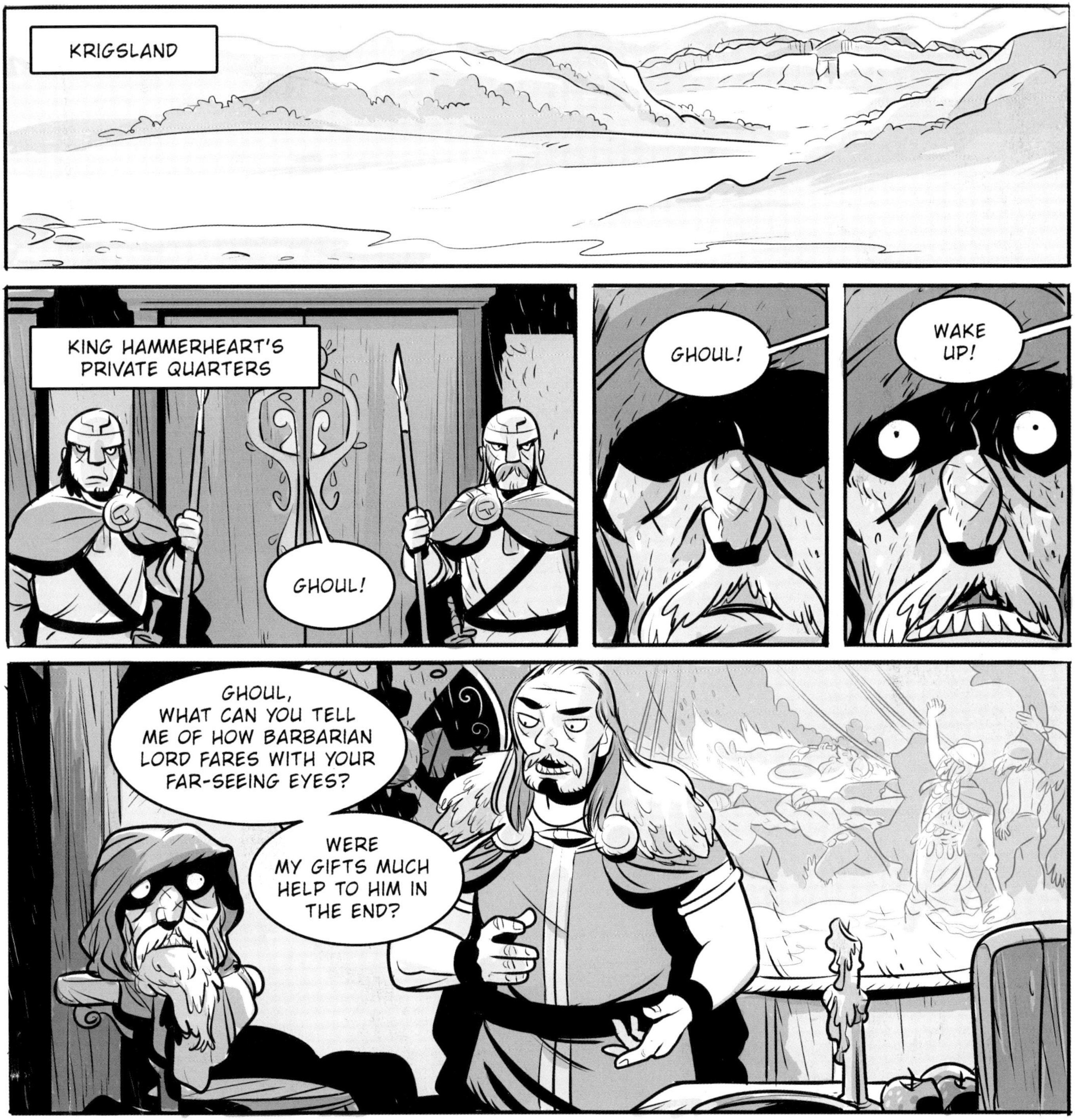
KRIGSLAND
KING HAMMERHEART'S PRIVATE QUARTERS
GHOUL!
GHOUL!
WAKE UP!
GHOUL, WHAT CAN YOU TELL ME OF HOW BARBARIAN LORD FARES WITH YOUR FAR-SEEING EYES?
WERE MY GIFTS MUCH HELP TO HIM IN THE END?

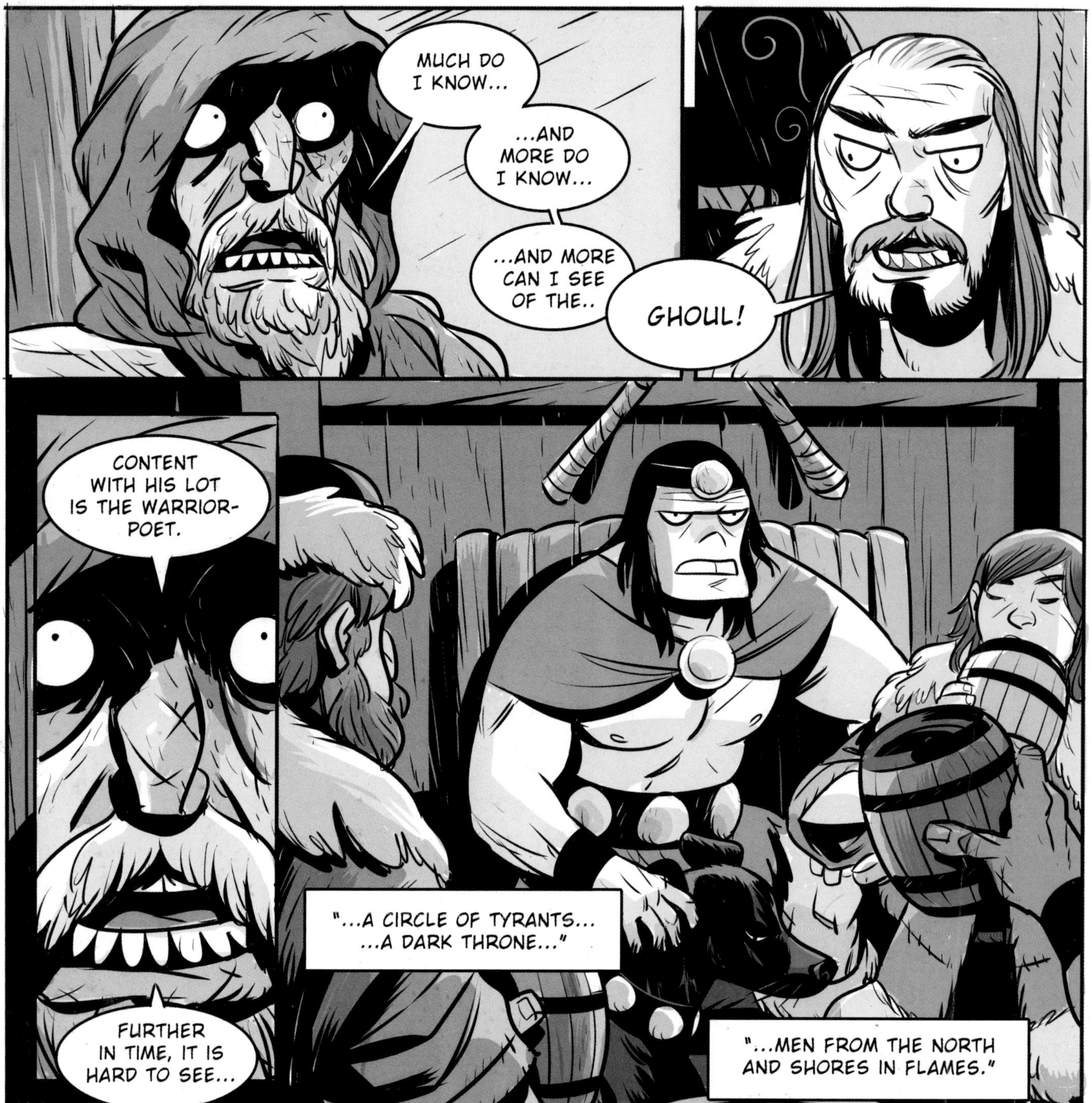
MUCH DO I KNOW...
...AND MORE DO I KNOW...
...AND MORE CAN I SEE OF THE..
GHOUL!
CONTENT WITH HIS LOT IS THE WARRIOR-POET.
FURTHER IN TIME, IT IS HARD TO SEE...
"...A CIRCLE OF TYRANTS... ...A DARK THRONE..."
"...MEN FROM THE NORTH AND SHORES IN FLAMES."

AUTHOR'S NOTE

THE BOOK YOU HOLD IN YOUR HANDS is a mix of favorite books, films, and music, long cooked in an iron kettle, bubbling over a steady flame.

For decades.

Into the kettle went heaps of rough-hewn cuts of inspiration from Robert E. Howard and J.R.R. Tolkien. Into it went fistfuls of Norse mythology harvested in myriad formats. In went seasonings culled from the animated 1980s cartoon warriors He-Man and Thundarr. Although this mixture boiled and swirled, it took a final ingredient—Icelandic sagas—to thicken the idea of Barbarian Lord into form.

The sagas, written in the thirteenth and fourteenth centuries and describing events of hundreds of years prior, engaged me on many points when I first encountered them. Chief among these was their unvarnished, straightforward tone, and also the use of skaldic poetry. I was immediately taken with the poetry's kennings, the semi-standardized metaphors that give brilliant—and often wonderfully grim—descriptions of common places, people, and ideas found within the sagas. Examples of kennings include "whale's road" (for the sea), "battle dew" (for blood), and "feeder of ravens" (for a warrior).

And now, barring a few experimental tastes in the shape of short Barbarian Lord strips and stories, we have the first fully developed serving of this barbaric stew. Formed and flavored by all of its various parts, and hopefully developing some qualities of its very own, the world of Barbarian Lord is expanding and evolving still. Since drawing the last page of this book, I have found new ingredients to cast in, and the kettle continues to boil.

MATT
JUNE 2013

ACKNOWLEDGMENTS

FOREMOST I MUST THANK MY WIFE, Kathleen, for her brilliance, her support, and her double-handed broadsword +50 vs. despair/quitting, -5 vs. Displacer Beasts.

Anne Hoppe and Daniel Nayeri: better editors won't be found this side of the gray mists.

Tom Pappalardo, Scott Magoon, and David Tilton: three good guys without whom this book would not exist.

Snorri Sturluson, Robert E. Howard, Quorthon, J.R.R. Tolkien, Mike Mignola, Jeff Smith, Dan Brereton, Scott Chantler, Hergé, Professor Timothy B. Shutt, Susan Paradis, and Basil Poledouris: in one way or another, each contributed a major influence.

Clarion Books
215 Park Avenue South
New York, New York 10003

Clarion Books is an imprint of Houghton Mifflin Harcourt Publishing Company.

www.hmhco.com

The text was set in CC Wildwords.

Library of Congress Cataloging-in-Publication Data is available.
LCCN: 2013955384

Manufactured in China
SCP 10 9 8 7 6 5 4 3 2 1
4500463713